Praise for *The Two Lives of Louis & Louise*

'Julie Cohen has really created something special with *Louis & Louise* . . . [It is] full of raw emotion – violence that will leave you reeling, small kindnesses and ironies that make for brilliant humour, and a heartfelt message at the centre of the novel which declares that regardless of gender, what really matters to humans most is love'

Stylist

'An engaging, moving novel' *Sunday Times*

'The idea behind *Louis & Louise* is one of the cleverest I've seen . . . This tender, moving, fantastically readable story is expertly handled by Julie Cohen'

Good Housekeeping

'Emotional and seriously powerful'

Fabulous Magazine, Sun on Sunday

'Told over two, initially parallel, narratives . . . this is a nuanced exploration of how the social expectations of gender can push us down certain paths' *Independent*

'Poignant and heartfelt' *Prima*

'Julie Cohen has written a powerful and memorable story of small-town secrets, family dynamics, and the sense that some things are just meant to be'

Sunday Express

'Tender and thought-provoking' *Woman & Home*

'This elegantly written novel examines much that is universal: teen love, parent-child relations, class division and small-town prejudice' *Daily Mail*

'In this fascinating novel, Cohen explores the paths taken by Louis and Louise . . . A poignant look at how our gender can determine the way we are treated and the knock-on effects that can have' *Emerald Street*

'This is a modern take told with heart' *Grazia*

'An intriguing look at gender and destiny' *Sunday Mirror*

'Brilliant. Such a clever, entertaining way to demonstrate how gender predetermines a life. I enjoyed it hugely' Marian Keyes

'Not often does a story remind us of what beautifully complex creatures we are. Julie Cohen has given us that rare gift' Christina Dalcher

'Moving and beautiful, but it will also make you wonder and question' Joanna Cannon

'Julie Cohen at her absolute best' AJ Pearce

'Elegant, thoughtful and powerful' Daisy Buchanan

'Fierce, intricate and intriguing' Fanny Blake

'A beautifully written, heartbreaking and important novel about gender, self, family and, ultimately, love'
Claire Frost

'A timely read that will stay with you long after you put it down' Libby Page

'Hugely originally and heartbreakingly real'
Rosie Walsh

'What a brave, warm and wise book this is. I loved it'
Tamar Cohen

'Beautifully written and thought-provoking'
Kate Eberlen

'A cobweb of a book: beautifully intricate and delicate'
Veronica Henry

'What a beautiful, ballsy and brilliant book'
Sinead Moriarty

Julie Cohen grew up in Maine and studied English at Brown University, Cambridge University and the University of Reading. Her award-winning novels have sold over a million copies worldwide, and she has twice been selected for the Richard and Judy Book Club in the UK. Her bestselling novel *Together* has been translated into eleven languages and optioned for television adaptation.

Julie runs an oversubscribed literary consultancy which has helped many writers go on to be published. She is a Vice President of the Romantic Novelists' Association, founder of the RNA Rainbow Chapter, and a Patron of literacy charity ABC To Read. She lives in Berkshire with her family and a terrier of dubious origin.

You can find Julie on Twitter @julie_cohen or you can visit her website: www.julie-cohen.com

Also by Julie Cohen

Dear Thing
Where Love Lies
Falling
Together

The two lives of Louis & Louise

Julie Cohen

ORION

An Orion paperback

First published in Great Britain as *Louis & Louise* in 2019 by Orion Fiction
This paperback edition published in 2019 by Orion Fiction,
an imprint of The Orion Publishing Group Ltd
Carmelite House, 50 Victoria Embankment,
London EC4Y 0DZ

An Hachette UK company

1 3 5 7 9 10 8 6 4 2

A CIP catalogue record for this book is
available from the British Library.

ISBN (Mass Market Paperback) 978 1 4091 7984 9

Printed and bound in Great Britain by Clays Ltd, Elcograf S.p.A.

MIX
Paper from
responsible sources
FSC
www.fsc.org
FSC® C104740

www.orionbooks.co.uk

For my mother
For my father
For my brother

Orlando had become a woman – there is no denying it. But in every other respect, Orlando remained precisely as he had been. The change of sex, though it altered their future, did nothing whatever to alter their identity. Their faces remained, as their portraits prove, practically the same.

—Virginia Woolf, *Orlando*

Gender is a shell game. What is a man? Whatever a woman isn't. What is a woman? Whatever a man is not. Tap on it and it's hollow. Look under the shells: it's not there.

—Naomi Alderman, *The Power*

Daddy's Girl

1978

Louise Dawn Alder was born on the 8th of September 1978 to Peggy and Irving Alder of Casablanca, Maine.

Peggy was two weeks past her due date and it was hot. August had refused to give way to autumn; the leaves hadn't started to turn yet and the grass was sere and yellow. Peggy lumbered around their house, sweating through her pregnancy smock, drinking glass after glass of lemon iced tea, catching her belly on the corners of furniture and the edges of doorways.

'I want it over with,' she moaned on the telephone to her best friend, Mary Phelps, who had given birth to fraternal twins six months earlier.

'You don't,' Mary said. In the background, there was crying, either from Allie or Benny. 'Keep that baby inside you for as long as you can. At least when they're not born yet you can *sleep*.'

But Peggy couldn't sleep. She was up every hour or so to pee and when she lay in bed, Irving breathing deeply beside her, she was too hot and her tired mind wouldn't stop racing. Did they have the crib set up correctly? What if she was a terrible mother? Had she packed the right things in her overnight bag? What if there was something wrong with the baby?

'I don't even care if it hurts,' she told Mary.

'You will care,' Mary promised her. 'Ask for all the drugs.'

Peggy knew that one of Mary's greatest regrets about the whole childbirth experience was that she'd given birth too quickly to

Benny to be able to have any drugs, and although Allie wasn't born for another hour, the doctor had thought Mary had done so well with the first baby that she didn't need them for the second.

'I'm worried,' she whispered, though Irving was at work and there was no one else around to hear her. She wound the phone cord around her fingers, tight. 'What if it hasn't been born yet because there's something wrong?'

'Is it kicking you?' She interrupted herself, 'Oh, Allie, *enough*, you're sucking me dry, leave some for your brother.'

'Yes.' Though how long since the last kick? It had become so normal, being battered from the inside, that Peggy barely noticed any more unless a small foot hooked behind a rib or something and made her gasp with pain. She put her hand on her swollen belly and felt a thump in return.

'Just did,' she said with relief.

'Well, then, you're fine. I bet you anything it's a girl.'

'I think it's a boy.'

'Nuh-uh. Boys do what they're supposed to. Look at little Benny, good as gold, while his sister's got colic, diaper rash, can't stop eating – it's your brother's turn, you little piggy.'

Peggy listened to this with more than a little comfort. Alongside all those fears she never expressed during the night there was one that didn't even make sense: what if, after she had a baby, she wasn't herself any more? As if giving birth would rid her of her own personality, as if suckling an infant would dry up her thoughts and emotions.

But Mary had always been just like this. Sarcastic, tough, with a well of caring underneath. Having twins had made her even more like herself, not less.

'I keep thinking that Irving should have got the car serviced early, because months ago he made an appointment at the garage tomorrow, thinking that the baby would be born by then, but it hasn't been born, and what if it comes while the car is in the garage? How will I get to the hospital?'

'I'll drive you,' said Mary, so promptly she couldn't have even thought it over.

'But you've got Benny and Allie.'

'They fit in a car. Besides, Donnie needs to learn how to look after them sometime, he's their father and he doesn't do a damn thing. Do you know how many diapers he's changed in the six months of their life? Exactly none. Meanwhile, I'm elbow deep in baby shit every day. I dream about it, when I finally get the chance to sleep. And when I'm not dreaming about baby shit, I'm dreaming about a martini. Beefeater and vermouth, on ice, with a twist. You remember how we used to make those?'

Over the line, Peggy heard a lighter flick and Mary drag deep on her cigarette. She remembered the martinis the summer before last at Mary's bridal shower up at Morocco Pond, the two of them making sophisticated drinks and trying to blow smoke rings. Adults, acting self-consciously as adults, in this place where they'd been children.

And now Mary was a mother and Peggy was about to be. Peggy thought about ice-cold gin and lemon oil, lying on the beach in their bikinis, a glass of condensation resting on her flat stomach, cooling the skin, both of them a little breathless thinking about getting married, having their own houses and husbands. It had all seemed impossibly glamorous then.

She wasn't sure she was ready to be a grown-up, now.

She got up from the kitchen chair with a grunt and walked to the window, tweaking aside the flowered cotton curtains she'd sewn herself soon after they'd bought the house. Or, rather, after Irving's parents had bought it for them. They had a big backyard which Irving kept mown and weed-free. He'd already pointed out the space where he wanted to put up a swing set.

This would be the first grandchild in the family. Irving's parents, Vi and David, had always been distant to Peggy when she was dating Irving – they thought their son was too good for her – but as soon as they were married and she and Irving had announced her pregnancy, they were as attentive as anyone could hope for.

Irving was delighted about being a father. He'd flung himself into the idea wholeheartedly, could barely keep his hands off her belly, seemed to find her more attractive than ever before. 'I love you pregnant,' he kept on whispering. 'I want you to be pregnant all the time.'

But Peggy didn't particularly like being pregnant. For the first three months she'd vomited constantly, and then her skin had erupted into acne, and her boobs hurt, and then she'd gotten so much bigger, and the weather had become so hot. What if she decided she didn't want any more children after this? Would Irving still love her? Would he even be attracted to her any more, after this one was born?

They'd got married because she was pregnant. They'd planned to marry anyway, of course, but her pregnancy had made it so that Irving couldn't change his mind. She hadn't done it deliberately, but… They'd eloped to Portland to get married in the city and had a two-day cold April honeymoon on the coast. Not exactly the huge Catholic wedding that Peggy's mother had expected, or the huge society wedding that Vi Alder had expected.

'Mary,' she began, hesitantly, not even really sure what she was about to ask, only that Mary was the only person she could talk to, the only one who didn't pretend that motherhood was all a perfect walk in the park. 'Do you ever wish—'

She felt something warm gush down her leg, as if she'd wet herself. When Peggy looked down, there was liquid on the linoleum floor.

'Wish what?' asked Mary on the other end.

'I think my waters just broke.'

A small near-silence of cigarette crackle and indrawn breath, as Peggy clutched the phone in both hands, staring down at the growing puddle. For the moment, she had completely forgotten what she was supposed to do, how she was supposed to put down the phone and call Irving at the paper mill so he could come get her and drive her to the hospital.

'I was wrong,' said Mary, at last. 'It's not a girl, it's a boy. Only a male would interrupt a conversation right when it was getting interesting.'

By hour nineteen of labour, Peggy didn't care about whether she was going to be a good mother or not. The obstetrician had refused to give her an epidural because he said it would stop her contractions, and the gas and air only made her feel sick.

She was flat on her back on a table, feet in stirrups, clenching her hands and her teeth, hair soaked with sweat, riding the worst contraction yet. For the first few hours she'd experienced a strange elation despite the pain of the contractions and the boredom of waiting for something to actually happen. She walked the corridors of the maternity ward, hearing the cries of other babies and of other mothers. Irving was allowed to walk with her, holding her hand.

As the contractions got worse, she was removed to a private room and Irving was banished to the waiting room to drink coffee and pace. By then, things had started to really hurt and she was glad he was gone. He'd been hovering, trying to make sure she was all right, and it was exhausting trying to pretend for his sake that she wasn't tired and frightened and in pain. At this point she wanted it to be over with, and then she wanted to curl up in a bed under cool sheets and sleep and sleep and sleep, until someone woke her up and presented her with a clean, beautiful baby wrapped in a pure-white blanket.

Now, though, Peggy wasn't thinking about getting it over with. The future had ceased to exist. She, Peggy Grenier Alder, once Miss Western Maine, had ceased to exist. She was nothing but a body that was splitting apart in a world of pain and stink and pushing. The words of the obstetrician and nurse were no more than buzzing sounds in her ears. She could be in a medieval hut, with her ankles tied to a torture rack, instead of a high-tech hospital with her feet in metal stirrups.

'It's coming, there's the head!' said the nurse in an excited voice, and Peggy thought *Thank Christ*, and then she thought nothing because she was in a white and red space, eyes closed, pushing.

'Nearly finished now,' said the obstetrician, who had only turned up for the exciting part. 'Here's your baby. One more push, that's a good girl.'

'I can't,' groaned Peggy, but she gripped the nurse's hand and she pushed anyway, and felt a slipping-away, something being taken from her, and her eyes flew open.

'It's a girl,' said the obstetrician.

'Could've told you that,' said the nurse. 'Made you wait for two weeks like a princess, didn't she?'

'Always late for everything,' said the obstetrician, 'just like my wife.'

The baby started to cry.

'You'll have to watch out for this one,' said the nurse, taking the baby as Peggy watched with hungry eyes. 'She's going to run rings around you.'

'She'll wrap her daddy round her little finger,' said the doctor, who'd already diverted his attention to delivering the placenta.

Peggy held out her hands for her daughter and the baby was placed into her arms; and despite all the fear and pain and sweat, this was a moment that she would remember for the rest of her life. This tiny curled red creature, with slits for eyes and claws for hands, a comma of humanity. Her daughter.

In that moment she had never loved anything or anyone so much. This was a piece of her, another girl like her, who one day would open her arms, tired and sweaty, to welcome her own child.

She barely noticed as the obstetrician left and the nurse tidied up. She was too busy gazing at this little thing. Ten fingernails, each paper-thin. Eyes complete with eyelashes. They'd decided to call the baby Dawn, if it was a girl, because it was the start of their new life. But at that moment Peggy wasn't thinking of a name at all. She was thinking: *I made this. This little person.*

But then the nurse said, 'I'll go and get Daddy,' and Peggy snapped to attention.

'Not yet,' she said. 'I can't let him see me like this, I'm a wreck.'

'Believe me, he's only going to have eyes for Daddy's girl.'

'Can you give me my make-up bag from my overnight case? And my hairbrush?'

The nurse (frizzy hair in a bun, no make-up, broken veins on her cheeks that Peggy hadn't been able to notice before, but did now) rolled her eyes. She rummaged through the bag, extracted Peggy's flowered make-up case and a pink hairbrush, and held them out to Peggy, who had her hands full with the baby. The nurse, who'd clearly seen it all before, took the baby and put her into the bassinet by the side of the bed while Peggy opened her compact mirror and saw what a sight she looked. *You'll never get a man looking like that,* her mother's voice said in her ear.

Fortunately, nearly a year of waking before Irving did every morning and doing her make-up in a dimly lit bathroom meant that she was skilled in making the best of what she had. There wasn't much that could be done to her hair, but she brushed out the tangles and smoothed it back away from her face, then quickly applied powder and blush to her face and a few careful swipes of mascara. Pink lipstick, and she was a blushing new mommy, like in the pages of *Good Housekeeping* magazine. Or close enough, maybe, to pass.

'OK,' she said. She pulled the sheet up over her lower half. Her stomach was barely any smaller than it had been yesterday, but maybe Irving wouldn't notice that part.

She took the baby back. She'd held Mary's twins before but her own baby felt different. When Irving came into the room, she smiled up at him. A modern Madonna and child.

He didn't even look at her. His eyes were fixed immediately on the baby. He crossed the room quickly and stood gazing down at the child.

Suddenly, Peggy saw the baby as an outsider would. Wrinkles at the wrists, nose a stub, sparse hair slicked to its head, a curled-up pink little thing. It was ugly, her daughter was ugly, and Peggy was ugly, this girl-child had sucked all the prettiness out of her, had sucked out everything, and in that moment Peggy was sure that Irving was going to walk out of the room in disgust and never come back.

'She's beautiful,' Irving said.

And just like that, with a marvellous cool rush of relief, Peggy saw he was right. The baby *was* beautiful. All babies looked like that: squished and red. She hadn't done anything wrong.

'She looks like you,' said Irving.

'Do you think so?' asked Peggy doubtfully. 'I don't think she really looks like me. She looks more like you.'

'Maybe a little.'

Irving reached down to take the baby and Peggy handed her over, feeling as if she was bestowing some great gift. As soon as the baby was in her father's arms, she squirmed, squinted, and wrinkled her soft forehead, and Peggy saw who she looked like.

'The painting,' she said. And it was true: in that moment, their daughter, who was less than an hour old, looked exactly like the portrait of Louis Alder, Irving's illustrious great-great-grandfather – founder of the Casablanca Paper Company – which hung at the top of the stairs in Irving's parents' house.

Irving burst into laughter, which made the baby widen her eyes. 'Louis! Yes, she looks like Louis Alder. Poor thing.' He held his daughter up to his face, nose touching. 'My little Lou.'

The baby made a little squeaking sound.

'She knows her daddy,' said Peggy.

'Daddy's girl,' he said, tucking the baby into the crook of his arm and rocking her. He looked as if he'd been born to this

– unlike Peggy, who'd felt happy but also decidedly awkward with her baby in her arms.

'We could name her Lou,' Peggy said.

'Lou's not a girl's name.'

'Louise is.'

'We were going to call her Dawn if she was a girl.'

'Louise Dawn.'

Irving glanced up at Peggy from the baby and his face was full of wonder. 'It would make Dad happy, I suppose.'

Peggy heard what he wasn't saying, maybe what had never even occurred to him to say. She heard *My parents have never liked you and they're going to be upset that you gave birth to a girl who can't carry on the Alder name*. She heard Vi Alder saying, after they came back from their elopement, practically through gritted teeth, *Welcome to the family*. She heard her own mother saying, *You should get this one to marry you, because you'll never get a chance like Irving Alder again. He may not be rich now, but he will be.*

'Louise Dawn,' Peggy said. 'Definitely.'

Mummy's Boy

1978

'Hey Irv, that baby born yet?'

Irving paused on his way across the lunch room. Donnie Phelps, Mike Beaulieu, Ed Venskis and Brian Theriault were all sitting at the same table, sandwich wrappers and cans of Coke strewn on the surface. For a moment he was back at Casablanca High School, a skinny teenage bookworm confronted by a table full of jocks. Donnie, Mike and Brian had all been in the same class as him; Ed was two years older. There was a time when he would have scuttled by them, head down, hoping that they wouldn't notice him.

Now, of course, things were different. He stopped and smiled. 'Not yet,' he said to Donnie. 'Peggy is just about going crazy.'

'When was it supposed to be born?' asked Ed. Like the other three, he wore a plaid flannel shirt over a T-shirt, even though it had to be eighty degrees outside. The four of them all wore baseball hats: Mike and Donnie had Red Sox hats, Brian wore a Casablanca Paper Company hat with the CPC green pine tree logo on front, and Ed had a novelty hat that said ASK ME IF I GIVE A SHIT.

Offensive logos were against company rules, technically, but no one seemed to follow that rule. Irving looked at Ed's chin instead of his hat and said, 'Two weeks ago. She's really feeling the heat.'

'You've gotta be climbing the walls waiting, eh,' said Brian. 'Nat was a week late having BJ and I almost moved out, she was so grouchy. Had to sleep on the couch.'

'You still sleep on the couch,' said Mike, elbowing him. 'Nat don't like your snoring.'

'*Your* wife don't mind it.'

Irving stood awkwardly by, half a smile on his face. He wasn't these men's boss; he wasn't anyone's boss, not yet anyway, although some people treated him as if he were, and in any case, they worked on the machines and he was in Engineering. But he wasn't their colleague, either. Donnie's wife, Mary, was Peggy's best friend so he saw Donnie outside of work pretty regularly: barbecues, days at Morocco Pond, and once, when they moved into their house, an ill-conceived dinner party where Peggy burned the pot roast and Mary drank too much wine. On all of those occasions, the girls chattered like they always had since age five, and Irving stood awkwardly next to Donnie, each holding a can of Budweiser, and tried to think of something to say. Once they'd exhausted the topic of the Red Sox or the Patriots or the Celtics or the Bruins, they didn't have much else to cover. They'd never talked at school, so they didn't have any reminiscences to fall back on. They didn't even know the same people at work. Usually, Donnie would put on the TV.

How much easier it would be if they didn't have to pretend to like each other for the girls' sake. If Irving could say, 'I know our wives like each other but you once stood by while your friend Duane Roy beat the shit out of me for wearing glasses, and I haven't forgotten that, even if you have.'

But that wouldn't wash with Peggy. Peggy wanted everyone to get along and be friends. So, for Peggy's sake, he read the sports pages before the get-togethers so he'd have something to talk about.

At least Donnie had never actively picked on Irving at school. He'd never cared. If Donnie had felt anything, it was annoyance that he had to wait to go to football practice so that his friend could teach a nerd a lesson.

But now they would have something in common. They'd both be dads. Their kids would play with each other as they grew up. Irving liked Donnie's twins, Allison and Benedict, and although he couldn't think of anything to say to their father, he could spend hours happily chattering nonsense to the babies.

Donnie seemed mostly to ignore his kids, though, so maybe they wouldn't be swapping stories of first words and teething.

The plastic box with the lunch he'd packed this morning was greasy in his fingers. Donnie and co. didn't seem to bring their lunch in plastic boxes; from the detritus on the table it was all paper bags and Saran wrap. Irving's father had always come home at noon for a proper cooked lunch and still did. 'I don't understand why Peggy doesn't cook for you,' Irving's mother said all the time, and Irving always said, 'Oh, I don't mind a sandwich. I usually work through lunch anyway.'

He wished he'd worked through lunch today, too. It was much less awkward eating lunch in between calculations, typing with one hand while he held a sandwich in the other. Standing in front of these guys, he might as well be holding the Howdy Doody lunch pail that he'd carried in fifth grade.

'Anyway,' he said, because it seemed rude to walk away, 'the baby will come sooner or later, no matter what.'

'Sit down,' said Donnie, jerking his head to a spare seat. 'You're making me nervous, standing there.'

Irving sat.

'You know the best way to get those babies out,' said Brian. 'Do what got 'em in there in the first place.'

'Worked with Mary,' said Donnie. He took a bite of ham sandwich on white bread and spoke as he chewed. 'Might be why they came out three weeks early.'

Irving felt himself blushing. 'Well, I . . .'

'With Peggy it's no hardship, huh?' Mike said. 'I remember when she was a beauty queen. You got lucky there, man. Never would've saw that coming.'

He flushed harder, with anger this time, but they were all smiling and it was all done in the spirit of camaraderie, right? They weren't in high school any more, and he wasn't the skinny little nerd with the Howdy Doody lunchbox any more, either. He had a degree in electrical engineering, a wife, and a kid on the way. These guys were just shooting the breeze. They were co-workers, husbands and fathers, and they'd known each other all their lives. If he couldn't take a little teasing…

'Anyway,' Irving said, 'I've waited my whole life to become a dad, I guess I can wait a little longer.'

They all laughed and he almost flinched.

They're not laughing at you, he told himself. Why would they?

But they were. He knew it as surely as he'd known it ten years ago. He'd grown up, he'd been away to college – MIT, no less – he'd married a beautiful girl and now was about to be a parent. He'd changed, but nothing ever changed in Casablanca.

He unwrapped his sandwich: peanut butter and jelly. He'd made it himself; Peggy was far too pregnant to get out of bed to make his breakfast or pack his lunch – and besides, he didn't mind peanut butter and jelly, he wasn't choosy about food. Just as well, as Peggy wasn't the world's best cook. Not a patch on his mother… but he hadn't married Peggy for her cooking.

He thought about her in their bed this morning, wearing only a pair of white pregnancy underwear and one of his white undershirts, stretched tight over her belly. Irving still found the height and width difference between him and his wife fascinating: he could not get used to how small and delicate she was, even when pregnant, how graceful her wrists and ankles were, her long slim neck. He often took her hand in his to marvel at the size difference. He was not a big man, never had been, but next to her he felt large and protective.

This morning, she'd been turned away from him and if he hadn't known she was pregnant, two weeks overdue, he wouldn't have been able to tell. He'd snuggled up to her, knees folded into her knees, arm around her waist, pushing the T-shirt up so his hand could rest on her naked belly. Sometimes when he did this he could feel the baby kicking but not this morning; this morning he felt only the slightly damp warmth of her skin. He buried his face in her hair, felt her breathing, smelled the sweat on her neck and he wanted to trail his hand up the curve of her belly to find her soft, pregnancy-swollen breast, but Peggy had made it clear to him over the past couple of weeks that she felt too much like a whale to feel sexy.

She'd said it with a strange look, as if she thought he was odd to find her so attractive when she was pregnant. Irving thought it probably was odd. He had no idea if other men felt this way about their pregnant wives.

He wished he could ask someone, but who could he ask? He glanced at the men sitting at the table with him, and then looked back down at his sandwich.

Irving had never heard a man ask another man for advice about sex, or whether something was normal. Men joked about sex, like Donnie just did, they joked about it all the time, but he never joined in. He didn't want to talk about his private life over sandwich wrappers, as if it were no more important than baseball.

He got the distinct feeling that women talked about it all the time. Peggy and Mary often stopped talking abruptly when he entered the room.

'Mr Alder!'

It was Melanie from the office, at the door to the lunchroom. Irving looked up for his father, who never came in here. The lunchroom was for the working men, not the mill owner. But Melanie was walking towards him.

'Mr Alder!' she said. 'Your wife called! She needs you to drive her to the hospital to have the baby!'

Cheers and whistles erupted from the eating men.

'All right, Alder!'

'Way to go, Irv!'

Mike Beaulieu punched him on the shoulder.

Irving left his lunch on the table. As he walked across the room, hands patted him on the back. His stomach churned, his skin was cold. But he wasn't scared. He felt tall, strong, like he could do anything.

He felt like a man.

It was so hot that the sulphur scent of the mill reached even here, in the waiting room of the hospital. He couldn't hear Peggy, though. She was separated from him by two doors, a corridor, and several white-clad nurses who didn't allow fathers in the delivery room.

In the cartoons, fathers-to-be paced back and forth, distracted and distressed while their wives gave birth. They had cigars and champagne ready for the big moment, a bouquet of flowers for their wife.

Irving had the *Lewiston Daily Sun*. It was the only newspaper the hospital shop had. He didn't smoke or drink, beyond the odd can of Bud. And he'd never been a pacer. He'd intended to buy Peggy a bunch of flowers, the biggest one he could find, but they didn't sell those in the hospital shop, so he bought a teddy bear instead, and then he waited.

He sat in the plastic chair underneath the window. Every hour or so he went out and used the payphone to call Peggy's parents and his parents to tell them that the baby hadn't been born yet, and no, they shouldn't come down, he'd call them as soon as anything happened. Twice he had to go to the hospital shop again to get more change for the phone. He got plenty, because the shop closed at five. He bought some potato chips and a Snickers bar and a Coke, though he wasn't hungry and besides, his mother had stopped by about six o'clock to drop off some sandwiches. (Chicken salad and devilled ham. She thought peanut butter was common.)

Aside from the smell, this beige room could be anywhere in the world. He could be waiting in New York, or Paris, or Vancouver. He could have a job building bridges in South America or building a dam in California. Waiting was the same anywhere.

He could be living any of the dozens of lives he'd pictured for himself, any of the dreams he'd been so determined to follow before he met Peggy Grenier in her little bikini on Morocco Pond and, instead of ignoring him, she'd looked up at him and smiled – and he'd fallen so deep in love with her that he'd asked her out there and then. It was the bravest thing he'd ever done.

Irving Alder had wanted to leave Casablanca from the age of about seven. He'd wanted to escape the rotten-egg scent of the mill, the thundering pulp trucks, the small-minded baseball-cap-wearing bullies, the snowy winters that made each house a sealed-in island. In another place, he thought, he could be courageous, he could be self-assured and popular, valued instead of derided for being smart. Seen for himself instead of as the son of David Alder and the heir apparent to the Casablanca Paper Company.

At MIT for four years he'd finally found people like him, who wanted to talk about mathematics and physics and computers, who had a curiosity about the world and how it worked, who had ambitions greater than getting a good job at the mill and making enough money to buy a house and a truck and retire to Florida. People who thought that family traditions were less important than intellect.

But then he'd come home for the summer and Peggy Grenier had said she'd go to the movies with him, and from that moment, Irving didn't have a single dream that didn't involve her. He'd been applying for jobs in California, was ready to fly over for an interview, when she got pregnant. And how could he take her halfway across the country, away from all her family and friends, when she was going to have a baby?

Staying in Casablanca, taking the job his dad found for him

at the mill, living less than a mile from his parents, seemed like a small price to pay for Peggy and for this baby that was going to be born.

At about two in the morning Irving dropped off to sleep, stretched across three chairs pushed together. It was a strange half-awake sleep, like the kind he used to have in the library sometimes when he was studying. He dreamed he left the waiting room and walked down the corridor, pushing aside a phalanx of nurses to burst into the delivery suite where Peggy lay, sweating, her face screwed up in pain. 'Let me give birth to the baby,' he said in his dream, lying down next to her and opening his arms. 'I'll do it. You can rest now.' He put his feet up in the stirrups (in his dream he was still wearing his shoes, brown Hush Puppies) and he pushed.

'Mr Alder,' said the nurse, and Irving opened his eyes. He scrambled to sit up.

'What's wrong?'

'Nothing's wrong. You have a son.'

A son. A child. A son.

'Can I see him?'

'Of course.' The nurse led him down the corridor and opened the door for him and there they were: Peggy, cradling their son to her breast. The most natural thing in the world.

Irving wanted to cry. He wanted to scream and laugh and float. He approached the bed with wings on his feet.

'He's perfect,' he said.

Every little finger, every little toe. A crease between his smoky eyes, pouted-up lips.

We've made this, Irving thought in wonder. *This human being*.

'It's a boy,' Peggy said. 'We've got a son.'

He reached out his arms and Peggy put the baby in them. He was solid, real. He squirmed in Irving's arms and scrunched up his face and beside him, Peggy laughed.

'Oh my God,' she said. 'He looks like that painting in your parents' house.'

He laughed. He felt dizzy, as if the world had broken itself up and rearranged itself around a single point, this child in his arms. 'Little Louis Alder,' he said.

'We … we could call him Lou,' said Peggy, sounding almost tentative. 'If you wanted.'

'After my great-great-grandfather, the paper tycoon? It seems like a big name to put on a little baby.'

'Well, at least it's better than Irving.'

He tore his eyes from the baby and looked at his wife. She looked tired but beautiful, and she was smiling at him.

They were a family now, he thought. A real family.

'Wouldn't your parents like it?' she said. 'If we named him after Louis Alder? We could even use Louis David, after your dad.'

Her words wavered at the end, as if she were uncertain, as if she didn't know if he would be pleased that she wanted to carry on the family name.

A wave of love swept through him and Irving realised that no matter what his dreams had once been, nothing in the world could compare to this moment, right now, with his wife and his son. He'd never felt part of Casablanca so much as he did right then, in this present that was linked inexorably with the past, generations and generations of his family going back in this same place.

It was time to put those dreams of leaving aside. Their future, all of theirs, was right here. Together. The proof was this little boy in his arms.

'Louis David,' he said. 'Welcome to Casablanca.'

Louis & Louise

1978–1982

In this moment of birth, Louis and Louise are the same person in two different lives. They are separated only by the gender announced by the doctor, and a final 'e'. Their genitals are different but their faces are the same – and really, in most lights and most expressions they look more like Irving than his great-great-grandfather, although there's some Peggy in there, too, especially when they're asleep. When Peggy and her baby are asleep together, Lou with their head on their mother's naked breast, their peaceful closed eyes and relaxed mouths are identical.

Louis and Louise aren't twins – not like Mary's fraternal twins Allie and Benny, whom we will know much better, in time. Peggy and Irving Alder only ever have one child. Peggy, who fell pregnant so easily the first time, never carries another baby to term. Louis and Louise at conception are one egg and one sperm. Except in this version of life, the sperm carries the X chromosome and, in that version, the sperm carries the Y. Sperm and egg meet and begin to divide and multiply.

As a foetus, Lou's sex is at first indistinguishable. At seven weeks' gestation, their genitals begin to develop. Unseen inside Peggy's body in 1978, with an uncomplicated pregnancy, they could be any sex. They could be any gender. There are so many other things about them, equally unseen, that are also true. Eye colour, hair colour, the curve of their smile, myopia, a mole on their thigh, a propensity to hay fever, their future love for salty food and science fiction, the steady beat of their heart.

But when Lou is born, their biological sex is the first thing that anyone sees. The first question anyone asks. The beginning of every single choice made about this person, even before they have the power to make choices for themselves.

At this moment of birth, even before they've taken their first breath and cried their first cry, Lou Alder is the nexus of all their parents' dreams.

But those dreams are different for son and for daughter.

Louise will go home and be put into pink. (When it comes in, her hair is bright red; it will clash horribly.) Louis will be put into blue, which goes better with red hair. The grandparents will arrive with gifts: dolls or teddies, dresses or a tiny baseball mitt. See them sitting in Peggy and Irving's living room in this new house, drinking tea and trying to make friends with each other for the sake of the baby. David Alder wears a suit and tie despite the heat, which hasn't broken yet. Bob Grenier is in work pants and a plaid shirt so newly out of the package that it still has creases. Vi Alder wears a twin set and pearls and Yvette Grenier has on her best polyester slacks and a sleeveless blouse. They are all from Casablanca, born and raised, but they might as well be from different planets. Bob Grenier's father emigrated from Québec to cut timber for the Casablanca paper mill, and Bob has worked on Machine Two in the mill since he was seventeen years old. David Alder's father inherited the mill from his father George, whose father Louis Alder of the Pennsylvania Alders founded it in 1862. Yvette is the daughter of a lumberman and Vi is the daughter of a man who owned a chain of shoe shops across Western Maine until he sold them to his son and retired to Key West. Yvette notices that Vi lifts her pinkie when drinking tea, like she thinks she's the Queen of England, and Vi has to keep herself from flinching when Bob coughs a big gob of smoker's phlegm into his handkerchief and then picks up the baby without washing his hands. Peggy's parents spend more than they can afford on their gifts and they still look shabby and cheap next to Irving's parents' gifts, which were bought in Portland in Macy's.

Lou is both couples' first grandchild. Maybe this is the child that will give them something to talk about. Maybe this is the child that will give them common ground, erase these differences once and for all between owner and worker, white and blue collar, Protestant and Catholic.

They're doing their best, the grandparents, with their dolls and their mitts, their dresses and bears, and they're handing down stories and histories and limitations. Steadily fencing in those infinite dreams.

But this happens to everyone and it's all done out of love. We want our children to live in the world we know, to fit in, to do what's expected of them, because that is how you are happy. You can't dream *anything*; you have to dream what's possible. Louis Alder will inherit a controlling share in Casablanca Paper Company, which is riches almost unimaginable for his maternal grandparents who still have mortgage payments to make on their compact two-bedroom house; Louise Alder . . . well, that's not so straightforward, but it's the seventies after all, nearly the eighties – feminism isn't a dirty word so why can't a woman run a mill one day? And maybe she'll have a brother, or marry someone and produce another heir, even though he'll have a different surname.

Lou doesn't understand any of this yet. Lou's world is milk and warmth, familiar voices and softness, blurred colours and the pattern of faces, the wet squish of a soiled diaper and the utter comfort of a breast. They're a hungry baby. When Irving picks up Lou they try to suckle from him, too.

Their favourite toy, both Louise and Louis's, is a small stuffed chicken which is neither pink nor blue but yellow and red. Their first word is 'Ick', which means 'chicken'.

Ick, cuddled and sucked, gets steadily more threadbare and dirty despite frequent visits to Peggy's state-of-the-art washing machine. Lou, in pink or blue, learns to walk, but what they really love to do is to run. And climb. They defeat crib rails and Peggy's stairgates; once Peggy leaves Lou outside on the lawn for less than five minutes to answer the phone and when she comes back Lou has climbed to the top of the big rock in the back of their yard and is sitting there, happy as a clam, only a few inches away from tumbling off and breaking their head open.

'He can do anything, that boy,' says Grandma Alder.

'She'll give you trouble when she's a teenager, that girl,' says Mémère Grenier.

Lou learns to whistle at three years old. A real lips-pursed, full-lunged, whistle. Loud blasts of it, like a sailor. They tuck Ick into bed every night. They help Peggy paint the walls of their house, working with a tiny brush beside their mother. Four days later they find a red crayon and draw their family on the newly white wall: three round blobs, Mummy, Daddy and Lou.

Lou wants a baby brother or sister but one doesn't come. Sometimes Lou hears their parents whispering in the kitchen at night, but they don't understand the words.

There are other words they understand, though. Words like 'pretty' or 'strong'. Words like 'sweet' or 'clever'. 'Boy' or 'girl'; 'tomboy' or 'sissy'. They decide they don't like pink or blue and only let their mother dress them in red or yellow or purple, which *really* clashes with their hair. They still climb rocks and trees when they can. But Louis only cuddles Ick at night now, and when Louise whistles, she shapes it into a tune.

Louise

2010

It's 3.10 p.m. and Lou sits behind her desk, looking through her students' final assignments as the sun streams through the barred windows of the Brooklyn middle school where she's taught for the past six years. *My Summer Adventure* was the title, but some of the kids have put their own titles on their stories.

My Battle With The Giant Space Ants

How I Burned Down Brooklyn

Summer School At Hogwarts

She should have marked the assignments and given them back straight away so the kids could take them home, stuffing them into backpacks full of drawings and geography projects, but she wants to have time to actually read them, to hold on to the school year for a little bit longer. She likes this class, 8G, and the kids probably wouldn't want their assignments back anyway. They have bigger things on their minds than English assignments. They're on their way to their real summer adventures, and high school after that.

This summer is going to be the best summer ever. That's because this summre is when Justin Bieber is going to fall in love with me. Let me tell you about how this will happn. First let me tell you what I look like I have long raven black hair with blue and purple streaks and my eyes are large and violet. I always dress in thighigh black leathr boots and lacey dresses with rips in them and evryone says I am beautiful but I don't know it. One day I woke up and my mom said Sydny you have a ltter and when I opened it it said I had won a round trip tickt to las angles and I was so excited because this is where justin lives. OMG will I finally meet him!?!?!?!?

Lou smiles. This year, Akia Hassan has written every single assignment Lou has given her, no matter the presumptive topic, about how Justin Bieber will fall in love with her. The essays aren't usually very coherent, and Lou has tried in vain to get Akia to use spellcheck more and OMG less, but she has to admire the eighth-grader's dedication to Mr Bieber, especially when the title of the essay has been something like 'Small Steps We Can All Take To Reduce Global Warming'.

She leafs to the last page to find out how many children Akia/Sydny and Justin will have in their blissfully happy marriage (it varies between one and six) and instead of the usual heart-embellished THE END that Akia puts on her papers, it says *I no Ill never marry Justin Bieber but thank u 4 letting me pretend all year. I will miss you Ms A!*

Lou blinks back tears.

She hates the last day of school. All of the students are always so happy and even the most nostalgic of her fellow teachers look forward to six weeks of vacation. But for Lou, it's a letting go of the little world she's inhabited for the past ten months. Not an adventure but a loss.

She sighs and takes a pink cardboard folder from her desk drawer. She'll end up keeping these essays under her bed with all the others. Dana will tease her for it and Lou will say 'When you're grown up, you'll understand,' though she hopes, deep inside, that Dana never will understand. That Dana will find it much easier to step forward, to let go. And that Dana will have to do much less of it than Lou has done.

'Lou?'

'Dad?' The response is immediate, spoken before she looks up, even though her father has never been in her classroom before, her school before, and she hasn't seen him since the day after Christmas. Her dad is in the doorway. She knows it as much by the sight of him as the emotion in her chest: something balanced on an edge halfway between happiness and guilt.

'Hi,' she says, standing up. 'What are you doing here?'

He steps into the classroom. He's wearing the same style of short-sleeved button-up white shirt he's worn all her life, but he has new glasses. At least, she thinks they're new glasses. Aren't they?

'I wanted to see you,' he says, and Lou comes out from behind her desk and hugs him. He hugs her back, hard. She's about an inch taller than him, a fact which always takes her by surprise.

'Did you fly down?'

'I drove.'

'You drove seven hours just to see me?'

Irving shrugs his narrow shoulders. 'You're my little girl. And besides, I like driving.' He keeps his hand on her elbow, as if he wants to keep touching her. 'I thought they wouldn't let me in the building and I would have to wait for you outside. There are metal detectors! In a school. It's not like Casablanca.'

'No, it's not.' At the mention of their home town, Lou pulls back from him so they aren't touching. 'But they let you in?'

'I told them I was your dad. I guess I looked harmless.'

You *are* harmless, she thinks, and can't help hugging him again. 'What are you doing here?'

'I need to talk with you about something. In person.'

'What?'

This time, he's the first to let go. He walks to her desk and looks at the stacks of essays. 'Looks like you still have a lot of work to do over the summer.'

'It's only a vacation for the kids, not the teachers.'

'I've always wondered what your school looked like.'

She follows his gaze around the classroom. She's taught in this same room for five years, but there are a lot of things she's never really noticed about it until she sees it through her dad's eyes. How small it is. How the paint is peeling. The grilles over the window. The sound of traffic and music and shouting outside: all the noise of Brooklyn, loud even over the rattle of the ancient air conditioner.

How different that must seem to her dad, who went to elementary school in a white clapboard schoolhouse by the Pennacook river, with a wide fenced-in playground built around a big glacial rock that the kids used to climb so they could eat their packed lunches on top of it. Pettingill Primary. Lou went to that school, too, until third grade when they opened the new Casablanca Elementary in a modern building.

'I don't pay much attention to the room,' she says, in defence, of – what? Her school? Her life? Herself? 'It's the kids that make it interesting.'

'I bet they do.' He runs his finger over the top of a kid's desk next to him: someone's carved I ♡ OMAR and then filled in the heart with red pen.

'It's a different environment,' she tells him, 'but the kids aren't that different than I was, at that age. Probably you, too.'

'Where's Dana?' he asks. 'She's finished with school by now too, isn't she?'

'Her school got out at two thirty.'

'Where is she, then? Does she come here to wait for you?'

'No, she's got soccer practice and then she takes a bus home. She's got a key for the apartment in case I don't get back before her.'

She says it defiantly, because she knows what her mother would say to the idea of a twelve-year-old girl taking the bus by herself through Brooklyn, not to mention being in an apartment alone, but Irving merely blinks behind his glasses and says, 'Well, she'll be there when we get there, will she?'

'Her practice doesn't finish till four thirty, so we'll probably beat her home.' Her dad squidges up his nose as if he's about to sneeze. 'It will be good to see her. I bet she's grown. It's hard to tell in pictures.'

'She grows about half an inch every time I look at her, it seems. She's got a good appetite.'

'Just like you used to.' He takes off his glasses to polish them and she realises: he doesn't look different because of new glasses. His hair has gone grey. All of it. Over Christmas there was still quite a bit of brown, but less than six months later and it's all gone, turned to silver and white.

It's seven hours' drive from central Maine to Brooklyn. More than that with traffic and road construction in Connecticut, and there's always traffic and road construction in Connecticut.

'Are you OK, Dad?' she asks.

'I'm fine.'

'This is a long way for you to come to discuss my students' work.'

'Well, I wanted to see you and Dana, obviously. The student work is a bonus.'

All the chairs are upside down on the desks, legs up like black antennae. She takes one of them down and sits on it. 'Tell me what's up, Dad. Why did you drive down here without telling me you were coming? Why did you come to my school instead of the apartment? I mean, you're welcome, of course, but you never do these things. We're not a family who drops in on each other.'

'I wanted to talk with you on your own, without Dana. And it's not something you can say over the telephone, what I need to tell you.'

Oh God, he's leaving my mother and I'm going to be responsible for her now.

There's no reason for her to think that – either that her parents are splitting up, or that Lou will end up being responsible for her mother in any way. It's unlikely that her mother would even let her, anyway; it's not as if they're close. And Lou doesn't see enough of her parents' relationship to know how stable it is on a daily basis.

Dana's friend Farah's parents are in the process of splitting up and Lou and Dana talked about it a couple of nights ago over Chinese food and *Star Trek Voyager* reruns. 'She's really messed up,' Dana told her. 'She wasn't in school two days last week. She says she doesn't even know who she is any more. It sort of makes me glad.'

'Glad of what?' Lou asked.

'Glad I don't have a dad,' Dana said, snagging noodles with chopsticks. 'Farah thinks her parents hate her and they're splitting up because of her. She keeps on going through everything she's done, trying to figure out what went wrong. At least if my dad doesn't know I exist, he can't possibly hate me. One problem removed.' She shoved the noodles in her mouth and chewed, but though Lou looked at her carefully, she couldn't quite tell if she was kidding or not.

Twelve years old, and Dana is already a great bluffer.

But Lou looks at her dad now, perched with his backside on the edge of her teacher desk, his hair completely grey, his face looking pinched and worried, and thinks: *They're getting divorced.* And her first emotion is dismay and panic. Not only because she thinks she'll have to look after her mom; it's a sort of ripping feeling, as if one of the core facts of her own identity is being torn from her. Suddenly she sees what Dana meant when she said her twelve-year-old friend Farah didn't know who she was any more. Lou is thirty-one years old and stopped needing her parents a very long time ago. They're no longer the unit of three that they used to be when she was a little girl: mommy, daddy, Lou.

But she feels exactly the same way.

'You're not getting a divorce, are you?' she asks.

Irving's forehead wrinkles. 'No. No, your mother and I aren't splitting up.'

'What is it, then, Dad?'

'Well. It's like this.' He pushes up his glasses in the same way he's been doing for her whole life. He's skinnier, too, which is saying something, because her dad is usually pretty thin. His cheeks are hollowed and his wrists are bony. She can't believe she hasn't noticed that. Too worried about the appearance of her classroom, what her mother would think of Dana being alone.

'You're sick, aren't you?'

'Louise—'

Fear makes her explode. 'You can't drive seven hours while you're sick, Dad! Why didn't you call me? I would have come …'

'Would you?' he asks quietly. 'You'd come all the way up to Casablanca if I called you?'

'Of course—' But she stops. Because in the thirteen years since she's left Casablanca for good, she's been back exactly six times, every single one of them at Christmas.

'Of course I would,' she finishes, quietly. 'If you needed me.'

'Well, I need you now. I need you to come back to Casablanca.'

'But what's wrong with you? Why do you need me? Is it cancer?' Her father, so unassuming and gentle and easy. 'Does Mom know?'

'It is cancer,' he says. 'And yes, your mother knows. I don't have cancer, Lou. Peggy does.'

'Mom …?'

'That's why I came down by myself. She's not well enough to make the trip. And she … well, she's not well enough. It's not the sort of thing you can say on the phone.'

'How long has she had it?'

'Not long.'

'Breast cancer, or . . . ?'

'Breast.'

'So they caught it early. That's good, right? They can – there's all sorts of good treatment for breast cancer.' She's thinking pink ribbons, women running in bras for charity.

'No. It's a fast one. She didn't see a doctor for a long time. She was scared, I guess, but I made her. It started in her breast, but it's spread. She's got it in her womb and her pancreas and in her lungs.'

Lou can't breathe. Her father, on the other hand, looks the same as he did when he walked in. He's had longer to get used to this.

'So what treatment is she getting?'

'None. She's done.'

'So she's better now?'

'No.'

Irving straightens from the desk. He lifts the upside-down chair from the desk beside hers, rights it, and sits on it, close beside her. He puts his arm around Lou's shoulder, like he used to when she was a little girl, crying over something that happened at school, a disagreement she'd had with Allie, that one C she got on her report card.

'She's not getting better, Lou-Lou,' Irving says to her gently. 'She's only got a little time left. The summer, if that. And that's why I need you and Dana to come home. That's why *she* needs you to come home. She needs to spend the time she's got left with her daughter and her granddaughter.'

She hears the music blasting from their apartment as they climb the stairs to the third floor.

'I thought young people all listened to music on their phone with headphones these days?' her dad says. He's only got a light overnight bag and he won't let Lou carry it; he's clearly not come for a visit, but to deliver news.

'She shouldn't be home yet from practice.' Lou digs her keys out of her bag and unlocks the door. The minute it's open, the music hits them like a wall. That Alice Cooper song about school being out for summer.

They sang that song every June, her and Allie and usually Benny, too: blaring the CD from Allie's portable player, rocketing around the house pretending to be playing guitar.

Except for that last year when they were eighteen, when school was out forever. The strike, Allen's Coffee Brandy, a crack in the ceiling. *School's out.*

'Dana?' she calls above the music, and it shuts off. Her ears ring.

Her daughter's sitting on the sofa with her phone in her hand, exactly as if she hasn't been risking the police being called for a noise nuisance. 'Grampa?' she says in surprise and jumps off the sofa to give him a hug.

He enfolds her in his arms and closes his eyes. 'My little girl,' he says, and in that hug are all the hugs he ever gave Lou, too. Her dad's a good hugger.

'I didn't know you were coming,' says Dana.

'It was spur of the moment.'

'Did practice finish early?' Lou asks, turning off the speakers so they're not ambushed by the volume the next time they try to play music.

'I didn't feel like it.'

Dana has been known to go to soccer practice with a fever of 102. 'Was it Farah?' Lou asks.

Dana looks down at the floor.

'Dana, I know she's having a hard time right now, but you shouldn't let her—'

'You don't know anything about it.' She throws herself back onto the sofa.

'I could sure use some coffee after that drive,' says Irving. 'I'll make a pot while you girls talk.'

He goes through to the kitchen. The move is familiar. It's exactly what he always does when Lou and her mother argue – make up a pretence to leave the room – and it makes Lou feel the same way as it always has: guilty and helpless and a little angry, too, because when does she ever have the chance to leave the room instead of having the argument?

Dana's glowering at her.

'All I'm saying, is that you love soccer and it's a shame that you're letting friendship issues interfere.'

'Mom, don't talk to me in your teacher voice.'

'This isn't my teacher voice! It's my mom voice.'

'Ugh! Same difference.'

Twelve years old, going on sixteen. 'Anyway, I need to talk with you.' She sits on the sofa next to her daughter. 'It's about why Grandad is here.'

'Yeah, that's weird. He always calls first – since that time he walked in on you and Megan.'

Not for the first time, Lou thinks she should probably share less information with her daughter.

'He needed to tell us something about Nana.'

'What is it? Did Nana die?'

Dana looks frightened and Lou doesn't have time to reflect on why Dana's thoughts have gone instantly to death, whereas Lou's own first went to being responsible for her mother.

'She's got cancer,' she says gently. 'Grandad thinks we should be there to see her.'

'So she's dying? Is she, like, really sick? Can she walk around and stuff?'

'I don't know,' says Lou, realising all the questions she hasn't yet asked, that she hasn't had the courage to ask.

'So we're going to go up and say goodbye?'

'Yes.'

'And then come home.'

'I don't know how long we're going to stay. I think Grandad wants us to be there ... until the end.' She wonders how much of this conversation her father can hear from the kitchen. Probably all of it.

'But how long is that? The whole summer?'

'I don't think it's kind to put an end date on it. Obviously, we'll need to be back here for school, but ... we'll have to wait and see.'

'But ...'

'I know you had soccer camp, and we'll have to cancel that. I'm sorry.'

Dismay dawns on her face. 'But Mom, I have to go to camp.'

'I know it's a disappointment. Maybe we can find you a camp in Maine, or a local team you can play with for the summer.'

'It's not soccer, it's Farah! She was going to go.'

'But if you and Farah aren't getting along ...'

'You don't understand *anything*. You don't even *like* Nana.'

'Dana! That's not true.'

'Everything all right in here?' Her father pokes his head out of the kitchen, looking distinctly nervous.

Dana jumps off the couch and goes to him, wrapping her arms around his waist. 'I'm sorry about Nana,' she says into his neat shirt front.

'I know, sweetheart,' says Irving, patting her back. 'I know.'

'I'll pack tonight,' says Lou, 'and tomorrow we can all drive back to Casablanca.'

Back to Casablanca. Suddenly she wants, very much, to join her father and her daughter in a hug.

But more than that, she wants to run away.

Louis

2010

Lou's in another bland hotel, the last in a series of bland hotels, surrounded by the remainder of a room-service dinner that he hasn't eaten, and trying to write his wife an email that doesn't sound either pathetic or self-important.

He's lost the tone of it, that's the problem. He's only been away for two weeks, but it's been two weeks of such unrelenting unreality that it's hard to catch the way he used to talk with Carrie. It would be hard to catch it anyway, with how things are between them.

He's mostly been keeping it breezy. 'If it's Tuesday, it must be Minneapolis.' Pictures of his mostly lone dinners in restaurants, travelogue-type texts about the few museums he's been able to visit. He tried to make a few jokes about his publicist, who is in her early twenties and a person of such relentless good cheer and sociability that she knows several people in every city she visits and is Whatsapping them the minute their plane lands to plan post-event evening drinks, but Carrie saw through that right away.

Don't be so cynical, she texted him. *Join her for drinks. Flirt with her or with her friends, now that you're a single man. It might make you less miserable for once.*

He can't flirt with Hayley or her friends. It's too much of a cliché, it's unprofessional, and besides, she's practically a child. But otherwise, the advice is both apt and unfollowable, like most of Carrie's advice. She knows him so well – and not at all.

Which is the whole problem, isn't it?

How can I help but be miserable? he types to her, now. *I must be the only man alive whose wife wants to leave him the minute he becomes successful.*

Now that is cynical. He deletes it.

And also untrue. He knows why Carrie wants to leave him now – why she's left him already, really, because all that remains to be done is for him to come home from this summer book tour for a book set in winter, pack up his things, and move to the apartment he's managed to rent with the help of the internet and a real estate agent in Manhattan. Now that his dream has come true, she thinks he needs her less. She's being kind, as always.

The truth is that he never needed her, not in the way she thought he did. But to say that would be very much less than kind.

So he's tried to let her believe she's right. Played up the excitement, played down the disillusion. Joking about his publicist (his publicist!) and marvelling at the sights and sounds of this great country; plenty of photographs of his book jacket – stylish white and grey – in front of historic buildings and landmarks. Tactfully omitting to mention the times when there were only four people in the room, each looking awkward and not wanting to be the first to go. He thought the world would change when *Light in Winter* was published and that the world would shake when it hit the *New York Times* bestseller list (just), but in reality, hardly any normal people care about a love story set in a nineteenth-century logging camp and almost everything is the same. In his emails to Carrie he's built a castle in the air of his dream come true, a slightly more comedic and much less hyperbolic version of what his publisher is putting on social media, which doesn't include the cold half-hamburger and fries on the tray next to his elbow, or the fact that each evening after the events he excuses himself to write the next book and spends the time lying on his bed instead, surfing channels to find as many iterations of the *Star Trek* franchise as he can. Brain candy, where everything always works out fine, there's such a thing as a Prime Directive, and the universe is preserved another day.

His life is these carefully curated lies. No wonder he likes to write fiction, only loosely based on a few known details.

But tonight he should email Carrie, tell her his flight time for tomorrow, arrange whether she wants to be there or not when he comes home to the house that isn't his home any more. He tried calling her earlier, but she was in a meeting. He'd known she would be in a meeting, which was why he called her then. She's not in a meeting any more, she's out with friends tonight, which is why he's choosing to email, because she'd pick up a phone call, but not check her mail. He's perfected these little avoidances in their life together, too.

It's going to be weird seeing you, he types. *It feels like these two weeks have been a break from reality and when I get back to New York it's all going to go back to how it was before. Except it won't be how it was before.*

Are you sad, Carrie? I know we said we'd be friends, no hard feelings, nobody's fault, but we've made promises to each other that we've broken, even though we never meant—

His phone rings before he can finish the sentence, which is just as well because it's descending even further into another untruth, badly written. He reaches for it, expecting to see Carrie's number, but instead, it's his mom.

'Hey, Mom,' he says. 'You don't usually call on a Wednesday. What's up?'

He smells Casablanca before he sees it: rotten cabbage and boiled eggs. It seeps through the closed windows and air conditioning of the car he rented at Portland Airport. The joke is that tourists, driving through the town on the way to Morocco Pond or the

New Hampshire mountains, smell something bad and roll down the windows of their car, thinking that one of their passengers has farted. But that only makes it worse.

In Casablanca, they call it 'the smell of money'. When Lou was little, he thought that meant that the Casablanca Paper Company actually made the paper that money is printed on. When he asked his dad, he said, 'Might as well be.'

He hasn't been back here for years, but when he breathes in this smell he's a child again. It's about a quarter of a mile onwards that he rounds the corner and sees the actual mill. Two tall smokestacks pour grey plumes of smoke upwards. There used to be three, but the mill has seemingly downsized.

You used to tell the weather by the smoke: if it went straight up, there was going to be a change of weather. If it went upstream, it was going to rain, and if it went downstream, it was going to be fine. *Is that even true?* Lou wonders. He never bothered to notice whether the rain came or not, while he was living here. He had more important things to think about, or at least he thought he did.

The mill is a collection of buildings, brick and concrete and metal, and a tangle of silver conveyor belts and tubes. He's always thought it looked a bit like a big gleaming spider, crouching there in the valley near the river. The road passes close to it and he can see a pulp truck being unloaded. A machine picks up the whole truck and tips it over like a child's toy in a sandpit so that the wood chips in the back of it slide out onto the pile.

In Mr McKenna's eighth-grade Social Studies class they learned about how the mill worked, a story they knew as well as a fairy tale. Loggers cut down the big pine trees that grew tall and abundant in the mountains of western Maine. It took knowledge and skill to find the right trees and to cut them in a way that they didn't crush the loggers. The men lopped off the branches to make long straight logs, bleeding sap from either end; they came home smelling of sweat and pine and spruce and bug spray.

A hundred years ago, the logs would have been dragged by teams of oxen or mules on wagons or sleds to the Pennacook river, then floated down the river to Casablanca: lumberjacks leaped from log to log with hooks and poles to control the lethal flow. They broke ice in winter, braved floods in spring. Nowadays the logs were stacked onto logging trucks and driven along twisting roads to Casablanca. Every eighth-grader in the class knew those trucks, had seen them thundering with their load held on by chains, got stuck behind them on the journey to Auburn or Bethel. The trucks rumbled through Casablanca in the early morning before school, feeding the mill which crouched in the valley in the centre of town between tall chimneys belching smoke.

The trees were stripped, chipped, pulped, soaked, pressed, coated, rolled. The mill ate trees and out of the other end came paper: high-quality, glossy paper that was used in magazines. Mr McKenna had a stack of them on his desk. He held them up one by one. '*Vogue. GQ. Good Housekeeping. Newsweek.* All these people, all over the country, read magazines on paper that has been made right here in Casablanca.'

Lou, twelve years old, skinny and red-haired and awkward, gazed at the magazine in his teacher's hands. There was a picture of a woman with a perfect oval face, flawless pale skin, charcoal-ringed eyes and lips the colour of shiny ripe apples. She wore something that looked like it was made out of tinfoil. She didn't look anything like anyone he'd ever seen in Casablanca. He'd never even seen anyone in Casablanca reading one of those magazines. Were there people in the world who dressed like that, who sat around reading magazines about other people who dressed like that? Did they ever think about the people who cut the trees or chipped the wood, or someone like his father, who went into the mill every day to program the computers that ran the machines?

No. That was a whole different world, the people who read those magazines and who were in them. Maybe New York or somewhere. He watched his teacher put the magazine back on his desk and he wondered whether if he asked, he'd be allowed to read it.

'I thought it was toilet paper,' said Buddy White, and everyone laughed except for Mr McKenna.

'That's the livelihood of the whole town,' said Mr McKenna, in that stern way he got when his students weren't taking the vital topic of Social Studies seriously enough. 'Who here has at least one parent who works in CPC mill?'

About three-quarters of the class, including Lou, raised their hand.

'And the rest of you have parents who work in industries that support the millworkers. If your mom's a nurse, she's treating millworkers and their families. If your dad's a mechanic, he's fixing the cars of people who work in the mill.'

'What if your dad don't have a job?'

It was shouted out by Jake Flint from the back of the class. Everyone knew that Jake's dad had a job because he was a garbage collector and Jake was always making jokes about it, maybe so that other people wouldn't get there first.

'Taxes paid by millworkers help to support people who are unemployed,' said Mr McKenna.

'Why should we pay for them? My dad says if you can't get a job, you're lazy.'

'We'll talk about taxes and welfare in another class, Jake. Right now we're talking about the mill.'

Allie raised her hand and waited to be called on, her face serious. 'What happens to the forests, if we keep cutting down the trees to make paper?'

'We plant more trees,' said Mr McKenna. 'For every tree that's cut down, another tree has to be planted. And then those trees are left to grow. Trees are a renewable resource. And people will always need paper. CPC could still be making paper for your great-grandchildren, Louis.'

With that last sentence, the eyes of the entire classroom were suddenly on him and Lou felt himself flushing from the soles of his feet all the way up to the roots of his hair. Hot, perspiring, knowing his face was flaming redder than his hair.

'1862, that's when your ancestor founded the Casablanca Paper Company. None of us would be sitting here in this room if he hadn't. He was called Louis Alder too. Did you know that?'

Lou had been told all of this by his grandparents, though his own parents didn't really talk about it. There was a portrait in his grandparents' house of a stern man with ginger hair and white sideburns. 'My— Yeah, I guess. I mean, I know where I got my name.'

He felt the weight of everyone's stare.

'My great-great grandfather was one of the first to work in the mill,' said Mr McKenna. 'He came from Prince Edward Island with his wife and baby daughter. Does anyone else know if their ancestors worked there in 1862, too?'

No one raised their hand, but at least not everyone was looking at Lou any more.

'That's your homework,' said Mr McKenna. 'Ask your parents, your grandparents if you can, great-grandparents if you've got them – find out how and why your family came to Casablanca. You might not find out the full story, but you'll be able to find out part of it, anyway. Our families, especially the older folk, are great resources. Talk to them and write me a paragraph on what you discover for Monday.'

The bell went and Lou scooped up his books and hurried out of the room. He heard sneakered footsteps behind him in the hall and Benny hit him on the head with a notebook.

'What's that for?' Lou said, rubbing his head.

'For not having to do any homework because Big Mac did it for you.'

'I still have to write the paragraph.'

Benny fell into step beside him. He was compact and muscular, and moved with athletic grace. He beat Lou in every sport except for running, and that was only because Lou had longer legs. 'You should see yourself blush, man. It's like you're glowing.'

'I don't see why it matters who built the mill. I don't even know if I'll ever want to work there or have anything to do with it. I might want to leave Maine and go somewhere else and never make paper or even think about paper unless it's to write on. Except whenever I see my grandpa he talks about tradition and family heritage and all that crap.'

Benny shrugged. 'All my old man is going to leave me is his gun collection. Maybe he'll have a decent truck by the time he croaks.'

'You can go anywhere,' said Lou miserably. 'It doesn't matter where you go. My dad tried to escape and he still came back.'

'Cheer up,' said Benny. 'You might flunk out of school and become a wino.' He leaped up and slammed his palm against one of the lockers, making an impressive booming noise that made the group of girls in front of them turn around. He grinned at them.

'At least I don't have to do the homework,' said Lou, elbowing Benny. Benny elbowed him back.

'I don't either,' said Benny. 'I'll copy Allie's.'

Lou, driving the rental car, shakes his head. He tries not to think about Benny. Tries not to think about the Casablanca he grew up in, except in dreams where he can't wake up in time, but the scent of sulphur is enough to set it off again. The mill doesn't have anything to do with him any more. He steps on the accelerator and breaks the speed limit past the mill into the town proper.

Main Street was built in grand style in the nineteenth century: pillars on the town hall, a clock tower on the fire station, a post office that wouldn't look out of place in ancient Rome. Rick's Diner still has the blinking orange neon OPEN sign; the Community Centre has a poster outside advertising soccer games and

Little League baseball matches. There's a new Dunkin' Donuts on the corner and a Subway shop next to the courthouse, but aside from that, nothing much has changed since Lou was eighteen and used to drive up and down Main Street in his third-hand car.

The town's only traffic light is green, so he heads on up the hill to his mom's house, the house where he grew up. It's a two-storey house built in the '70s with tall windows and white clapboards and a carefully tended garden. The curtains are drawn, though it's only three in the afternoon. Other than that, you wouldn't know from the outside that someone inside was dying.

Louise

Louise has been following her father's car up I-95 as if she didn't know the route perfectly well herself. The air con in her ancient Honda broke last year and she hasn't bothered to get it fixed; she hardly drives in New York anyway, and air con is bad for the environment. So they've had the windows down for the entire journey. She hasn't driven up here during the summer for a very long time, so she's forgotten that there's a moment when you get past Kittery on the Maine Turnpike when the air stops smelling like gasoline fumes and tarmac and starts smelling like pine trees and fresh air. It's like crossing an invisible line: you're no longer in the rest of the world. Or at least, no longer in Brooklyn.

Dana's in the back seat. She's been sulking since they left, which is no mean feat, because they stopped at McDonald's on the way up here and Lou bought her not one but two strawberry milkshakes. On a normal day that's enough to put Dana in a good mood, but a flurry of text messages this morning on her phone, Lou assumes with Farah, has made her sullen and silent. 'What's going on with Farah, anyway?' Lou tried asking, while they were stuck in construction in Connecticut, but Dana said 'Nothing' and put in her earbuds.

Lou wishes she'd never got her that phone. She also wishes they'd gone up together in her dad's car so they could have chatted, but there's no way she's going to Casablanca and not having an escape handy.

Driving is boring, especially when your daughter won't speak to you and you're worried about what you're going to find at the end of the journey, so she plays a game where she flicks through the radio and tries to guess the song playing in five seconds or less. That's another way you can tell you're in Maine: 70 per cent of radio stations, when you land on them, are playing either The Eagles or Bob Seger. It's as if the past twenty-five years have never happened.

Off the turnpike, onto twisting roads snaking through mountains. She knows every turn without having to pay attention, as well as she knows all the lyrics to 'Hotel California.' If Dana weren't in the back seat sulking she could believe she was in high school, driving back from a shopping trip in Auburn.

Welcome to

CASABLANCA, MAINE

Est. 1862, Pop. 2500

'As time goes by'

The sign is pretty new. Growing up here, Lou never knew that Casablanca was named after anywhere else in the world until she saw a map of Africa and noticed Morocco, like the pond. And the capital, Casablanca.

Maine is full of other places. You can travel the world in town names. Sweden, Norway, Denmark, Paris, Cairo, Carthage, Athens, Poland, Lisbon, Bangor, Naples, Moscow, Leeds. There's a famous road sign (well, famous in Maine, and as famous as a road sign can be) pointing to all the different towns in Maine, from China to Mexico.

'Maine people are really unoriginal,' said Lou, aged about ten, when her father stopped the car to show her the sign.

'Or maybe,' her father said, 'it's because they were saying that whatever you wanted, wherever you wanted to go in the rest of the world, you could find everything you needed right here.'

He was making the best of things. She knew it even then.

The town wasn't named after the movie, but Lou's best friend Allie loved old movies. She and Lou watched *Casablanca* one night on a sleepover aged thirteen, lights off, each tucked into their own sleeping bag in Lou's rec room, sharing popcorn and then, tissues.

They watched the ending four times in a row.

'Ilsa should've stayed with Rick,' Lou said. 'She doesn't love her husband like she loves him. And maybe he didn't deserve her before but he does now that he's made the sacrifice of sending her away. She should have turned around and come back.'

'But that sacrifice is the whole reason he deserves her,' Allie said. 'She can't turn back.'

'But it's such a *waste.* Such a waste of true love for them never to see each other again. That *song*.' Lou sighed in yearning. She wasn't much of one for romantic soppy stuff, but something about how Bogart and Bergman looked at each other. Their faces close together on the screen: hers smooth, his craggy, worn-in. That kiss. It made her ache inside.

'But helping lots of people is much more important than two people being together,' said Allie. 'She's helping Lazlo with his work. And now Rick is helping people, too. It's a happier ending than happily ever after.'

Lou stuck a pen in her mouth and imitated Bogart. 'Is this the beginning of a beautiful friendship?'

Allie threw popcorn at her. 'I still think that a film that ends in friendship is better than one that ends with love,' she said. 'Friendship lasts longer than love.'

'How do you know?'

'Because you and I are going to be friends forever. But you and Benny fall out all the time.'

'I'm not *in love* with Benny.'

'But you like him,' Allie said.

'Shut up, I don't.'

But… she did. Allie's twin Benny had a grace to him – he was all tanned limbs and muscles – and he was crude, sometimes, but also funny and sharp and unexpectedly kind. He was good-looking, with dark hair and grey eyes like his sister's. And Benny on the baseball field was something else. Lou went to the games just to watch him. He played shortstop and he could catch anything, even the high ones that should have gone to left field. Leapt with glove in air, snatched the ball and landed on his feet. Sometimes he lifted the glove and the ball seemed to come to it like magic. Then an effortless flick of the wrist sent the ball sailing – first base, second to tag the runner out, and Benny would be still again, watchful, as if he'd never moved. In the bleachers, she watched him while he was waiting for the play and felt a melting stab of something new and exciting. An ache, like she got when she watched Rick and Ilsa.

Allie picked a piece of popcorn out of Lou's hair. 'It's OK if you like him. If you two got married we would be sisters. When you had kids I would be their aunt. We could be like our moms, talking every day.'

'I'm not going to have kids with Benny. Besides, I'm not staying in Casablanca and neither are you. We're moving to New York, remember?' They had decided this after watching *When Harry Met Sally* on another movie night.

'Maybe Benny will move to New York with us. It would be cool to have my brother there. He can play for the Yankees.'

'He'd never play for the Yankees.'

'Maybe he would if you asked him.'

'I don't think he likes me.'

Allie just smiled.

'If he does like me, he doesn't like me the way that Rick liked Ilsa. We don't have a song.'

'Except "Bat Out of Hell".'

'It's not exactly romantic, is it? Anyway, who do you like?'

Allie considered.

'Buddy White?' Lou suggested. Buddy followed Allie around like a shadow.

'Really not my type.'

'R.J. Arsenault?'

'He's cute but he's sort of a jerk. I don't think I like anyone.'

Lou took a handful of popcorn, contemplatively. 'I'd like to know what it's like to kiss someone, though.'

'Me too.'

'Maybe we should find someone and kiss them.'

'You can kiss Benny,' said Allie. 'I won't be jealous.'

'I mean both of us find the same person and kiss them so we can compare notes. He's your brother.'

Allie laughed. Then she leaned forward, her sleeping bag bunching around her waist, and kissed Lou on the lips. Her mouth was soft and salty from the popcorn, and her hair smelled of Apple Pectin shampoo. Lou widened her eyes and then Allie pulled away.

'A kiss is just a kiss,' Allie said, and she reached for the remote. 'Want to watch another movie?'

Now, driving past the sign, Lou's got the song stuck in her head. She's kissed a lot of people since that night, but she's never watched *Casablanca* again. Maybe self-sacrifice for the greater good is one of those ideas that sounds better than it is in real life, like being able to travel the whole world without leaving Maine.

She follows her dad's car past the shell of the old Casablanca Paper Company. Usually she comes here in the winter and it's easier to ignore the hulk of buildings and conveyor belts in the snow. One of the smokestacks is still standing, though the other one has either fallen or been taken down. Derelict, the mill is no more or less attractive than it used to be when it was working – a dead spider isn't any better-looking than a live one – but it smells better, anyway. One small improvement.

Instead of going straight on through the light and up the hill to the house, her father signals right. Lou follows him. Now this is different: she's followed exactly the same route into town since 1991. Off the Turnpike, along route 2, past the mill, straight up to the house. She doesn't exactly cruise around Casablanca reminiscing about old times. She usually drives to the house on Christmas Eve, spends Christmas right there, suffering through overcooked turkey for the sake of her dad and her daughter, then on 26 December she leaves and drives straight back down to Brooklyn.

'Where are we going?' Dana asks from the back. It's the first time she's spoken since Connecticut.

'If I had to guess, we're going to the hospital. Or maybe we're picking up a pizza.'

'I hope it's pizza,' says Dana. 'I hate hospitals.'

'You haven't been in a hospital since the day you were born.'

'I still hate them.'

'You and me both.'

The town does look different without snow on it. Lawns are brown; a couple of the houses have been boarded up. There are FOR SALE signs on several others. Once upon a time she could have told you the name of the families who lived in every one of these houses, but not any more. She sees an old man sitting on a lawn chair in the sun, smoking a cigarette, a balding poodle-type dog beside him.

Dana hangs between the front seats, looking through the windshield. 'Where are all the kids?' she asks. 'This place looks like a ghost town.'

'Maybe everyone's gone up to the Pond for the— *Holy shit*.'

She doesn't quite slam on the brakes, but she does slow right down. Her father has pulled into a parking lot beside a large new concrete and glass building. It's taller and broader than anything else and much shinier: all modern curves and sparkling glass, almost like a spaceship has plonked down here among the vinyl-sided ranch houses.

'That's the hospital?' says Dana. She almost sounds impressed. 'I thought this was a hick town.'

'I've never seen this building before in my life.' The hospital in her memory is a low brick building with a flat roof, built in the fifties or sixties. That's what she's always pictured when her dad talks about his job managing the hospital's IT systems – not *this*.

She pulls into the nearly full lot. Dana's out before she is, stuffing her phone into her pocket and letting her earbuds dangle around her neck. 'Hey, Grandad, can we get pizza?' she calls, skipping up to him.

'Sounds good,' he says, putting his arm around her shoulders. 'We're going to pick up some medicine for your grandmother and then we can go to the House of Pizza. Lou-Lou?'

Lou doesn't hear him, because she's close enough to the new building now to be able to read the words that are on it, in big brushed-aluminium letters.

THE BENEDICT K. PHELPS CENTRE FOR CANCER CARE

She stops.

Benny's name, right in front of her, in letters two feet high.

'Lou-Lou? You coming in?'

'I…'

She averts her eyes from the sign and focuses on her father and her daughter, standing there waiting for her.

'I think I'll wait outside, if that's all right,' she says. 'I could do with stretching my legs a little after that drive.'

'We'll only be a few minutes,' says her dad, and he and Dana go into the new building. The glass doors open and close without making a single sound, swallowing her family.

Lou feels sick. She turns her back on the building, shoves her hands in her pockets, and tries to breathe slowly. It's a name. Just a name. Nothing more.

A name is just a name. *A kiss is just a kiss.*

She retches, covering her mouth with her hand, running to the side of the parking lot so that if she throws up, she'll do it on the grass. Her stomach rolls, full of acid. It was such a bad idea to come here. The worst idea in a history of bad ideas. Maybe they can go to the house, see Mom, and turn around and drive back to Brooklyn. Maybe the cancer isn't as bad as Dad says it is. Maybe she can keep herself, and her daughter, safe.

'Are you OK?'

She's bent over at the waist, swallowing hard to keep her coffee down, but at that voice, she straightens. Back of her hand to her mouth. She turns around.

Allie is there, in a pair of green scrubs. Running shoes on her feet. The same hairstyle she used to have in high school, with the heavy bangs. She recognises Lou right away; Lou can tell by the way her eyebrows shoot up, then come down.

'Oh,' she says.

'Allie,' says Lou. She doesn't want to throw up any more; now she wants to run. 'H-how are you?'

'Your mom's at home,' Allie said. 'I saw her yesterday.'

'I know, we're picking up meds.'

Allie is holding her car keys. She passes them from hand to hand, and they make a jangling sound. She looks tired and rumpled. Obviously at the end of her shift. 'Didn't think you'd come back.'

'My mother's sick, so I don't really have much choice.'

'That's what it takes, I suppose.'

She's not really sure what to say to that.

'Welcome back to Casablanca,' says Allie. 'It's changed a bit since you've lived here.'

'Do you work . . .' She gestures to the giant spaceship building behind Allie, that bears her brother's name.

'I'm an oncologist. That's why I know about your mom. Though nothing's secret in a town like this, so I'd know anyway. My mom died five years ago, by the way. Thanks for the card.'

'I'm – I'm sorry. I didn't know.'

She knew. Irving told her. She bought a card and it sat on her dining-room table, reproaching her, until she drank a couple of glasses of wine one night while Dana was asleep and threw it away instead of writing in it.

'Cancer. Ironic.' She jerks her head back to the building. 'Benny was already building this when she got the diagnosis and I'd already chosen oncology. Sometimes life is funny.'

'I'm sorry,' she says again.

Allie shakes her head. 'No you're not. You don't give a shit. Maybe you never did. It doesn't matter any more. We've all moved on. See you around.' She turns and walks to her car, a black SUV that has mud splashes up its side, like it's been used on rough roads.

Lou watches her get in, start the engine with a roar, and drive off. Allie hardly slows down at the exit to the parking lot and swerves into the road, squealing tyres.

Allie is angry. Much angrier than you'd expect someone to be seeing their former best friend after thirteen years, and a cold possibility drops onto Lou's shoulders, settling and seeping in like a ghost.

Maybe she knows. Maybe she blames me.

Louis

He parks in the driveway and takes a long, deep breath in and out. It's his mom. Just his mom, OK? No matter how sick she is, no matter how weak she sounded on the phone, she's his mother. She's going to be the same person inside.

Why didn't you tell me, he said down the phone to her, shocked, when she called yesterday. And she answered: *Please come*.

Out of the car, to the back door, his hand on the doorknob – and he hesitates, unsure of whether or not he should knock. This used to be his home, but it isn't any more.

In the end, he twists the knob and steps into the house.

The back door opens straight onto the kitchen, which is sparkling clean. It's been painted since the last time he was here; it's a light butter-yellow and there's a bowl of fruit on the centre of the table, lemons and nectarines and oranges, far too perfect to eat.

He opens his mouth to call for his mother, but before he can, a woman walks into the kitchen from the living room.

She's wearing a set of light-green scrubs and she's got her hair scraped back into a neat ponytail and he hasn't seen her since the night of their high school graduation, but her oval face, with its grey eyes and freckles and its heavy straight fringe of brown hair, is exactly the same. Exactly the same, even though it's not the same, because they're both older.

'Allie?' he says, at the same time that she says, 'Louis?'

He stays by the back door, and she stays by the door from the living room, and they look at each other. The last time they saw each other they were frozen, like this. Allie at the bottom of the stairs and Lou in the centre of the basement, with blood on his hands and face.

Allie speaks first. 'I didn't know you were coming,' she says.

'Mom called me to tell me she was sick, so I got the first flight. I was in Minneapolis,' he adds, though he doesn't suppose she'd care. 'On a book tour.'

'Oh yeah, the book,' she says. She doesn't say the normal thing, which is to congratulate him or ask him how well it's doing or when he's going to write another. She stands there, looking at him as if he's some sort of space alien or ghost.

'Are you . . .' he starts, and trails off, because there are too many ways to finish that sentence. Are you happy? Are you all right? Are you married? Are you a mother? Are you the same person who told me to leave and never look back, or have you changed?

'I'm a nurse,' she says, though of course he knows that. Once upon a time, she wanted to be a doctor, but things don't always work out. 'I'm a hospice nurse,' she adds. 'I've been talking with your mom about her medication.'

'Hospice?' he says stupidly.

'Yeah. I decided to specialise in end-of-life care, after my mom died.'

'I'm sorry.' It's automatic. 'And – and your dad, too.'

Allie acknowledges this awkward, years-too-late commiseration with a nod. 'My mom was ready to go. Your mother isn't there yet.'

'How is she?'

'I think she'll be comfortable.'

'That's not what I meant.'

'I know. But that's what my job is. I can't really comment on anything else. I don't really know your mom.'

You used to. You used to spend as much time at our house as you did at yours. You and Benny.

'Well, it's kind of you to look after her,' he says.

'It isn't kind, it's my job. Anyway. I have to get going.'

He realises he's blocking the door. 'Oh! Yeah, of course. Sorry.' He pulls his suitcase out of the way and opens the door for her, and she goes past him, and he catches a breath of her scent: laundry detergent and shampoo.

'Nice to see you,' he says lamely, though it's not nice. It's complex and frightening and very sad, and something that there's not a word for yet, the feeling of the weight of everything that might have been.

Allie nods and goes out the door.

He shuts it behind her and looks stupidly at the bowl of fruit before he takes a deep breath.

More than a large part of him was hoping that when he got up here to Casablanca, it would turn out not to be as serious as his mother has said, that she'll admit that maybe she exaggerated a little bit, because she was lonely. Because she wanted him to come up and see her. But his mother isn't manipulative like that, and she's not demanding – she's never once asked him to come home, in all these years he's been away.

And the fact that Allie has been here makes it all true.

He's feeling sick to his stomach. He calls, 'Mom?'

'Louis?'

Her voice is thready and it's coming from upstairs. He goes through the house – polished furniture, dustless mirrors, drapes and rugs perfectly coordinated, a house that looks as if it could be in one of those glossy magazines that the mill used to make the paper for – and up the stairs to the bedroom that used to be both his parents' and now is just his mom's. She's lying, fully dressed, on the bed on top of the bedspread, and if seeing Allie was like seeing a memory made flesh, seeing his mother is like seeing flesh made memory.

She's so thin. So much less of her than the last time he saw her.

She turns her head on the pillow to look at him and she smiles; he goes to sit beside her on the bed and takes her thin hand.

'Hey, Mom,' he says. He bends to kiss her on her cheek. She still wears Chanel N°5 , a perfume so associated with her in Lou's mind that once he had to stop dating a woman who wore it because it was too weird.

'Louis.' She squeezes his hand, and he's relieved that her grip is strong. 'I'm so glad you came.'

'Couldn't have kept me away.'

'How do I look? Do I look all right?'

'You look beautiful.' He sits up so he can look at her, and he's not lying: she does look beautiful. She always looks beautiful, his mother. She's wearing make-up and her hair is smooth and neat. 'How do you feel?'

'I'm fine, now that you're home,' she says.

But Lou, the liar, knows a lie when he hears it, and this is two. She's not fine, and he's not home.

Louise

The dining room has been made into a downstairs bedroom for Lou's mom. The big glossy table where they've always eaten at Christmas, Thanksgiving and other meals too important for the kitchen, has been cleared away and only two of the chairs remain, one in a corner and one next to the incongruous hospital bed set in the middle of the room. Her dad's La-Z-Boy recliner has been brought in to stand next to it. The rug is the same, though, and the curtains, and there's still a mahogany sideboard near the window. Instead of the candlesticks that normally sit on it, there's a television.

Lou doesn't even see her mother when she first walks into the room; she sees the television first, and wonders if the sideboard is still full of cutlery and china, tablecloths and candlesticks, or if it's been emptied and filled with her mom's clothes and drugs. Then there's a small noise from the bed and Lou looks closer and there her mother is, almost as pale as the sheets, and so very much smaller than she has ever been. The head of the bed has been raised so she's sitting up, sort of, supported by pillows.

'Hi, Mom,' she says awkwardly from near the door.

'Louise.' Her voice sounds different too: breathy, as if there's not enough of it.

'How are you doing, Mom?'

'I've been better.'

Lou hovers. Should she kiss her mother? In the kitchen, she

hears Irving and Dana chatting, getting out plates to eat the pizza. She wishes she were in there with them. In the end, she approaches the bed and touches her mother's hand. It's cold.

'It's good of you to come,' says Peggy Alder, as if Lou were a guest she's invited over for coffee or something.

'Well … it's important.' Is she supposed to mention that her mom is dying? Is this the sort of thing you even say? It seems impolite. Peggy's hair is perfectly styled, combed back from her face and falling in soft curls around her head on the pillow. She's got lipstick on and her nails have been manicured. All of this is totally normal for her mom, but it seems out of place for a woman lying in a hospital bed in her former dining room. A grotesque contrast with waxy skin and dull eyes. She wonders how much pain medication her mother is on.

'Allie tells me I've only got a month or two left,' Peggy says. 'You won't have to stay for long.'

Lou winces. 'We'll stay for as long as you need us. It's summer vacation, so …'

'It's good that you don't have to take time off work.'

'I didn't mean that.'

Mom sighs, and it's as if she gets even smaller. 'I'd like to see Dana.'

'I'll get her.' She turns with relief to the door, but Dana is already coming through it.

'Nana,' she says, and goes to the diminished, pale figure on the bed and embraces her without any hesitation, despite how sick she looks. Peggy's hands come up to hold her granddaughter. Dana's relationship with Peggy has always been much easier than Lou's.

'I'll help Dad,' says Lou, though no one is listening to her, and she beats a hasty retreat to the kitchen.

He's laid out three plates and sets of cutlery and is folding paper napkins. The pizza boxes are unopened in the centre of the table. 'Classy,' says Lou, opening a cupboard to get glasses. 'When

Dana and I have pizza it's straight out of the box in front of the television.'

'Well, it's an occasion.' Irving puts a napkin under a fork. He visibly hesitates, then says: 'She's glad to see you.'

'Anyway, it's good for Dana to see her grandmother.'

'I wish the two of you could get along.'

She doesn't say anything to that. Just goes to the sink to fill glasses with water.

'I... don't know what happened between you,' Irving says. 'And maybe I don't want to know. She's never told me about whatever happened to make you go away and never want to come back.'

Her heartbeat has speeded up, and the pizza, which smelled delicious before, is now too strong and spicy. She looks at the glass in her hand. Cold water. Clear and refreshing. Droplets down the side of the glass.

'I need you to get over it,' Irving says. 'Please. Put it aside, Louise. For her sake, because we won't have her for long.'

'Have you said this to *her*?'

'No. Because she's dying, Lou-Lou. So we're the ones who have to try hard.'

She glances at her father and he's blushing furiously. In the thirteen years since she left Casablanca, thinking then that it would be for good, he's never asked the reason why. He's accepted her decision and not questioned it. He's come down to Brooklyn for visits on his own; greeted her on her flying visits at Christmas. She's never been able to tell him why she left and he's never been able or willing to ask.

And as much as she loves her father, that hurts too: that he never asked. That he's not asking now.

She swallows. 'I'll try.'

After dinner Irving brings another chair into the dining room that is now Mom's deathbed room, and he turns on the television. They sit in a row to watch *Deadliest Catch*, Irving in his recliner, then Mom in her bed that's been arranged in a sitting position, then Dana, then Lou. Mom dozes off within five minutes, head lolling to the side. Her breathing is loud – louder than her voice was.

Lou lasts five minutes more and then stands. 'I'm going to take a walk,' she says and leaves the house.

It's not dark yet. She sets off in a random direction. Escape is more important than a destination. She walks past houses without seeing them. Mostly what she's seeing is her mother. Waxy face, sunken cheeks, the lipstick like a mockery of life. How did this happen so quickly?

The truth is, it could have happened slowly; she wouldn't know. She hasn't seen her mother for six months and even then it was for as little time as she could decently spend. The cancer must have been growing then, without being detected. Filling up the body where Lou once grew, a nightmare mockery of an embryo, cells dividing, seeping the life from its host.

Lou remembers when she was pregnant with Dana. In the first months when Lou had a flat belly and the baby was nothing more than an idea, sometimes she pictured it as a sort of a cancer. Something that was going to grow and grow whether she wanted it to or not, something that would change everything about her life and herself. She had morning sickness all day and all night, had to keep taking bathroom breaks at work to throw up and then put more make-up on, refresh her lipstick, and go back to smiling. She lay awake at night, hand on stomach, afraid. Wondering, despite herself, if she should have got the abortion. Wondering if she should give the baby up. Wanting to call her mother, wanting to call Allie. Knowing that calling either of them would be the worst thing she could do.

It got better. She stopped being sick in her second trimester, and started feeling good, maybe the healthiest she's ever felt. The last three months, when her belly was swollen and Dana wouldn't stop kicking long enough to let her sleep, that was great, then, because she was a baby. A real baby with legs and fists, a soccer player even then. Lou knew as soon as the baby started kicking that she could never give her up. She talked to Dana and planned their future. She was going to have a baby who would belong only to her. They would be a team. Buddies. Two against the world.

Except it was never just the two of them. Nothing could ever be that simple.

She's walked right out of her neighbourhood now and is on Main Street. The pillars of the town hall have been spray-painted with graffiti at some point and though someone's tried to remove it, the ghost of letters remains. She makes out TUN but the rest is too blurry. Rick's Diner is still open; she sees a few people sitting in the booths. It used to serve the best breakfast in town: eggs, bacon, home fries, home-made bread and butter. She's never found better onion rings anywhere. Next to it is the old Woolworth's, closed now with its wide windows boarded up. The *Casablanca Herald* office ditto closed and boarded. There's a Subway franchise shop which looks like it's still in business, but it's closed now.

There's a light on upstairs in the community centre. Lou remembers coming here for dances once a month in junior high school. Grape soda and power rock ballads. She always hoped that Benny would ask her to dance and he never did.

She speeds up her steps.

Why do people even live in Casablanca any more? There's no mill now, no industry. There's Morocco Pond, but that's always been more for locals than tourists. It's too far from the turnpike, not big enough to compete with places like Rangeley or Sebago, which have summer camps and resorts. She understands why her parents have stayed – they grew up here, this is all they've ever known, aside from her father's years at college – but why would young people come here? *Do* they even come here? Why would you raise a family somewhere with no jobs, one stop light and one diner and ghosts of spray paint on the town hall?

Why did she keep quiet when her mother asked her to? Who did she save? What good did it do, in the end?

She powers up the hill, more because she needs to feel the ache in her legs than because she particularly wants to see anything up there. Some of these houses have blue flickering lights of televisions in them; lots are dark. No cars in the driveway. FOR SALE signs on the unmowed lawns. Her grandparents' house stood up here, once, behind a tall black gate. Right at the top of the hill looking down on the mill and all the rest of the town. It was a big Victorian house, built for the first Louis Alder, with two turrets and a weathervane shaped like a lightning bolt.

It's been torn down. There's a LOT FOR SALE sign on the fence.

She keeps walking, downhill now. She's at the hospital before she knows it, in front of the brand-new spaceship, and here everything's different. The parking lot is full; a lot of the cars have New Hampshire or Massachusetts plates. Every window gleams with light. She can see the shadows of people moving back and forwards inside.

This, she thinks, is what keeps the town going. All of Casablanca has fallen away, become dirty and abandoned, except for this. The Benedict K. Phelps Centre for Cancer Care, built by her former best friend's brother. Here, business is booming. People are busy. They've come from all over.

The only industry in Casablanca these days is cancer.

Louis & Louise

1983–1992

Casablanca, established 1862, is a river town nestled between mountains. The mill squats in the centre. When Lou was growing up there was a change of shift every eight hours: seven to three, three to eleven, eleven to seven, marked with a whistle that echoed on the mountainside and signalled time for fresh workers. Casablanca Paper Company had rattled and boomed, whistled and muttered, belched smoke and trucks and never stopped – and if you were born in the town this monster was so normal you never noticed it at all. An invisible dragon, a fact of life.

The houses spread outwards and upwards from the mill either side of the river. Some of these were old and grand, built in the 1800s for mill management and entrepreneurs, with turrets and gables and bow windows, white wooden clapboards and servants' entrances and intricate gingerbread-inspired woodwork under the eaves. Some were new – capes and ranches for those who'd worked their way up to comfortable middle class. There were three-storey apartment blocks with outside stairs, and starter homes with neat lawns enclosed by picket fences. Corner shops that sold penny candy, and neighbourhood parks with swings and slides, neighbourhood schools and no fewer than seven churches: two Catholic (one French, one Irish – the Lithuanians and Italians went to the Irish one), a Methodist, a Baptist, an Episcopalian, an Evangelical, and a small static mobile home where the Jehovah's Witnesses met. In 1870, with his mill thriving, Louis Alder built affordable housing for his workers: brick duplexes that looked like houses in Philadelphia where Louis Alder and the nation were both born. Brick isn't a good building material in Maine – it lacks the flexibility of native wood, and heaves and cracks in the frost and thaw – but these houses made Casablanca look different from other Maine towns and when Lou was growing up the 'Brick Park' was a reminder of the essential benevolence of the Casablanca Paper Company. Lou was a kid – there were plenty of kids – and never noticed the cracks. You could walk anywhere in Casablanca and be safe. Everyone knew you. Everyone knew what to expect of you.

Benny and Allie were twins, and although they weren't identical they were special because of it. They looked alike, both with dark hair and grey eyes, male and female, a matched pair. Benny was loud and Allie was polite; Allie was clever and Benny was quick. They watched out for each other, shared toys (though not without squabbling), traded sandwiches, could sometimes tell what the other one was thinking. When Allie was sad, Benny got restless, and when Benny was sad, Allie would cry. Next to them Lou was a cuckoo, red-haired and taller than both of them. Lou wished sometimes to have a sibling, someone to argue with and take care of, but in the absence of a blood relative, Lou took Allie and Benny.

The three of them went to Casablanca Elementary, a single-storey sixties-built school where every surface was shiny. Lou wasn't top of the class – that was Allie's place – and although Lou was always a keen reader, for the first two years they struggled in class until their teacher, Miss Gallant, worked out that they couldn't see the blackboard. Lou got glasses after that and the world became clearer, sharper. (When Louise was fourteen her mother encouraged her to get contact lenses. 'Your eyes are too pretty to hide,' Peggy said, and Louise heard the words that weren't said: *They're the only pretty part of you.* Louis wore glasses until he went to college.)

Louise sat in the front of the class next to Allie. Louis sat in the back of the class next to Benny. They both got As and Bs, though Louise's report said, 'Can do better, is always chattering' and Louis's report said, 'Does well despite frequent distractions.'

Lou's house was on a hill – not quite as high as Grandpa Alder's house with its turrets – and Allie and Benny lived in the valley, closer to the mill and the river. Geography or town planning or maybe even the existence of several very large immovable rocks meant that there was a strip of undeveloped forest behind Lou's backyard. It stretched along the ridge, past Allie and Benny's backyard, and right down to the river near Casablanca Falls. Lou could walk to Allie and Benny's house without ever once going on a road. Go further, and you got to the white-foamed falls, swirling dangerous water that roared in spring and crackled in winter.

This was their playground. This was their Narnia, their Tatooine, their Middle Earth. The largest of the rocks was a castle, a Death Star, the trees their enemies or their shelter. In the distance the mill whistled and boomed and in their strip of wildness Lou and Allie and Benny fought monsters and always won. They knew every dip in the ground, every glacial erratic dropped thousands of years before by slow-travelling ice. They made trails in snow in winter and leaf piles in autumn, picked flowers in spring, left birch bark messages in summer. They left offerings in trees for a Boo Radley they knew would never come. They were Princess Leia and Darth Vader and Luke Skywalker (Lou, male or female, was always Darth Vader because the others were actual twins). Sometimes they could hear their mothers calling for them and sometimes they couldn't and got in trouble for being late. But it didn't matter, they played here the next day anyway and had names for all the places. The Castle Rock. The Face Rock. The Dinosaur Rock. The Dead Tree. The Hollow. The Big Water Rock. They saw raccoons and foxes and squirrels and sometimes a deer. Benny swore he saw a bear's footprints once but Allie said it was only Mr Thompson's big Rottweiler who'd got loose. But they looked for a bear, half-excited, half-frightened, after that, for a long time.

Later, when they were teenagers, their games tailed off. But they used the woods as a shortcut between houses and they played other games here, too. When they were thirteen Benny stole a pack of Camels from his father. Allie refused to touch it, but Benny and Lou (this is both Louis and Louise – some rituals transcend gender) huddled behind Face Rock and struck half a dozen matches before they managed to light one of them.

'You first,' said Benny, and Lou shook their head and said, 'No, you.' So Benny took the dare and inhaled. He held the smoke in his lungs then let it out in a plume and passed the cigarette to Lou.

Lou inhaled and coughed, doubled over. Benny laughed and thumped Lou on the back. The second drag was easier, and the third almost tasted all right. They passed the cigarette between them until it was gone. It was a strange new intimacy between them, as mysterious as sex.

By unspoken accord they didn't light another. This moment was too sacred to extend. Co-conspirators, they buried the butt, hid the pack and matches in a tree, and went back into the house more grown up than when they had left.

This landscape – not quite wild, not quite tame, not quite private, not quite real – is what has inhabited Lou's mind ever since, when they allow themselves to think about Casablanca. When they allow themselves to miss it. The vast spaces of their childhood, bound by treacherous waterfalls and home.

Louis

His mother has terminal cancer. She was asymptomatic but she was feeling a little run down and she was losing weight, so she went to Dr Jacobson and asked if she might be anaemic. Dr Jacobson, about six months from retirement, gave her some iron tablets. They didn't help at all. She kept losing weight, couldn't get out of bed in the morning, cancelled her book club and lunch dates, thought she must have the flu. Peggy never likes to bother anyone, but she made another appointment, and since Dr Jacobson was sick, she saw his partner, Dr Allardyce, who took one look at Peggy and sent her to the hospital for tests.

It had started in her breast, they thought, though Peggy never even felt a lump. But why would she feel her own breasts? she asks her son, who shakes his head because he has no answer. He knows he fed from her breasts as a baby, he knows he fell asleep on them as a child. His mother's breasts are a long-ago comfort to him and it's wrong, somehow, to think of her death arriving that way.

'Mary had breast cancer too,' Peggy tells Lou, as she lies in bed not eating the Campbell's Chicken & Stars soup that he's heated up for her. 'Funny to think that best friends both ended up with the same thing. But she had all of that treatment. The surgery, the radiation, chemotherapy. It was awful. I'm glad I don't have to go through that.'

Because when the tests were done and she sat in the room

in Central Maine Medical Centre in Auburn, forty-five minutes' drive away and the closest specialist unit to Casablanca, the oncologist showed her the scans and she could see for herself that the cancer had spread. He pointed it out to her, the masses in the pancreas and lungs. They looked like grey blobs. She couldn't see it, but it was in her blood too.

'So there's no point in treatment,' she said. She came to the appointment alone, because she doesn't like to bother anyone.

'I'm afraid not.' The doctor was gentle, but he didn't know her. 'I'm going to refer you to palliative care at Casablanca Hospital. The idea will be to keep you pain-free.'

'I want to be at home,' Peggy said firmly. 'I don't like hospitals.'

'With support, that can be done. Do you have anyone who can help you, Mrs Alder?'

'My son,' she said. 'My son will come home and help me.'

Now, her son is looking at the chicken and stars soup in the flowered bowl, on the tray across Mom's lap. This is the soup she used to heat up for him when he was sick as a child. He liked it better than regular chicken noodle soup, because of the star-shaped pasta, even though it probably tastes the same.

'I want to help,' he says, 'and I can stay for as long as—' *As long as you need me. As long as you're alive.* He leaves the sentence unfinished. 'But I don't know what to do. I'm hopeless at medical stuff. I can just about heat up soup.'

'Allie knows. And I have all these leaflets from the hospital, with people for you to call.' She sighs and twists her hands together. 'I don't have any appetite, anyway. I haven't for ages.'

'Why didn't you call me months ago?'

'Because I didn't know months ago. I only found out last week, and you were on your book tour.' She lifts a hand now and strokes his cheek. 'I'm so proud of my son, the writer.'

'Mom, the book tour wasn't as important as this. Nothing is as important as this. You shouldn't be alone.'

'Well, I called you, and you're here now. I'm not alone any

more. You can take care of things. I've been taking care of things myself for so long.'

Guilt. He ducks his head and changes the subject.

'Did you … does Dad know?'

She shakes her head.

'You didn't call him? Mom, why not?'

'I didn't want to bother him.'

'It isn't bothering him to tell him that you've got cancer.' He can't say 'dying' yet.

'It's OK. Maybe I'll write to him.'

'Mom—'

She shakes her head again, and she looks so frail that he doesn't press it. 'Would you like a cup of tea instead? Maybe a cold drink?'

'I'm fine. The medication is making me sleepy. Just sit with me.'

He wants to do something. Lou is not a practical person, not someone who fixes things with his hands – Carrie always says that his special talent is calling someone else to do a job for him – but in this situation, he wants to do anything but sit. He wants to make more soup, repaint the room, change the oil in Mom's car, mow the lawn, call the doctors and talk to them now, right this minute, and see if they might have made a mistake.

But he sits.

His mother looks dreamy now; he supposes maybe that's the drugs that she's taken, which he doesn't know the names and dosages of yet. That's something he can do: learn her drugs, the effects of them, the side-effects. He can study the facts of his mother's death so that when she can't help herself, he can help her.

'Cancer,' she says, and her voice is a little slurred. 'Everyone in Casablanca gets cancer. Pollution from the mill. That's what happened to Mary and my mother. I couldn't be with my mother when she died. We weren't talking. She wouldn't let me see her.' She sighs, and her eyes close. 'Now it's happening to me.'

Once his mother is asleep Lou wanders the house. He hasn't

been here for a few years and some things have changed. Peggy's got a new carpet on the stairs and she's redecorated the living room in shades of blue and green. Lou stands in the middle of it and looks at the place where his father's recliner used to be. There's a forest green wing chair in its place. It's exactly the sort of chair that Lou always wanted to have for himself, to curl up and read in, maybe smoking an old-fashioned pipe or something (he's never smoked, not since that first cigarette with Benny, but something about Victorian detective novels makes him want to). It's strange to see it in the place where his dad always used to sit in his La-Z-Boy to read and watch TV.

As far as he knows, the recliner's been gone for just over six years. Not long after his grandfather's funeral. That's when Irving called him so early on a Thursday morning that he was still in bed and he had to find his glasses and pull on a pair of pyjama bottoms and go downstairs so that he didn't wake Carrie.

'I didn't wake you, did I?' asked Irving on the other end of the phone.

'Uh, no, it's fine, I have to be at work anyway in . . .' Lou glanced at the clock. Seventeen minutes past six. '. . . a couple of hours.' More like four hours, but never mind. His father was an early riser but he usually stayed away from the phone until at least eight. 'Is something wrong?'

'No. Your mother and I are fine. Well . . . we're healthy. No accidents or anything.'

'OK, well good. I sort of worry when the phone rings before sunrise.'

'I thought you should know that I'm selling my share in CPC.'

Lou had automatically started pouring water into the coffee pot, but at this turned off the tap. 'OK. I . . . OK. Really?'

'I had an offer soon after your grandfather died, from Global – they're based in Oregon. I knew my father wouldn't have wanted me to. It's the family heritage. But I'm not cut out to run a paper mill.'

'Family heritage,' repeated Lou. 'Yeah, Dad, this is a little weird. I thought …'

He thought that everything would go on the same way it always had in Casablanca.

'The family have a 51 per cent share, as you know. And that doesn't split neatly into thirds, but what I plan to do is this. One third for me, one for your mother, one for you. Your mother and I both want to sell our shares. But you don't have to. It's your inheritance. And I know this way you won't have a controlling share, but you could still be involved if you want to.'

'I don't want to be involved in CPC. You know that. I'm just surprised you want to make such a big change.'

A long silence, long enough so that Lou thought maybe the call had disconnected.

'Dad?'

'So you want me to sell your share too?'

'Sure. Yes. If that's what you want to do.'

'Global will appreciate it. They want to put a tissue machine in, you know. People always need toilet paper. And then you can have the money now instead of when I die.'

'You're not going to *die,* Dad.'

'Not for a while, no, I hope not. But I'd rather you had the money now anyway. It can help you and Carrie start a family.'

'Uh, well, we um. We don't have any plans for that.'

'In the future, maybe, you're both still young. Or you can take time off work and write that book you've always been talking about.'

'That … would be good.' He sat down at the kitchen table. 'How much money are we talking about?'

Irving told him. It wasn't a huge amount; not a jackpot lottery amount. But … yes. He could quit teaching and write for a couple of years if he wanted to. Finally write that book about Gill Lafayette, the Maine logging camp in winter, the one that had been haunting him for so long.

Or find out once and for all that he wasn't cut out for writing books. That could happen, too.

'Wow,' said Lou. 'That's quite some news for a Thursday morning.'

'Yes. And I, um. Actually, Louis, I, um ...'

At his kitchen table 800 miles away, Lou could perfectly picture his father taking off his glasses, wiping them on his leg, putting them back on. Same gesture he'd done for all of Lou's life. Lou did it sometimes.

'What is it, Dad?'

'Well, there's no easy way to say this, which is why I gave you the good news first. And it's all going to work out, it's all going to be OK; your mother and I have talked a lot about this. I mean, she knows that I never wanted to stay in Casablanca, or even Maine. I always wanted to travel, see things, work on something other than making paper. But then you came along – and it wasn't your fault because we made a good life in Casablanca, the family, the mill, everything, we were happy.'

'You're moving away from Casablanca? That's fantastic, Dad. Are you going to retire early and travel? Where does Mom want to go?'

Carrie came downstairs to the kitchen in her bathrobe, yawning. She looked enquiringly at Lou on the phone. He gave her a thumbs up and she turned to finish putting on the coffee.

'Well, that's the thing, son. Your mother's staying in Casablanca. She doesn't want to leave; it's her home. And her friends, you know... Mary needs her now she's sick.'

Lou sat up straight, daydream broken. 'You're going to travel without her?'

'Well, see, so that's the tricky news. Your mother and I are splitting up.'

Now, Lou sits in the forest-green wing chair which has replaced the one in which his father used to sit. He puts on the

TV, quietly so as not to disturb his mother, and flicks through until he finds a nature documentary, something about penguins.

He hated his father for months for leaving his mother, not least because it was exactly what he himself, Louis, had done. It made him think that maybe he'd been selfish, after all, even though he'd told himself over and over that it was the best thing to do for everyone's sake.

If his father had stayed, he would have detected Peggy's cancer sooner. He would've made her go to a doctor. Maybe something could have been done.

But what if Louis had stayed? Would his mom be on the road to recovery instead of lying on her bed, waiting to die?

Nothing is black and white. They're both guilty, and Irving doesn't even know he's guilty. He's down in Florida and he hasn't got a clue that anything is wrong.

Louis leaves the documentary on, but he looks around the room. Everything's in its place, as always. His mother wasn't a great housekeeper when he was young – the house always looked tidy but she was the type to shove messes into closets and under the bed, and his father was the one who did most of the vacuuming – but once Lou left she seemed to embrace neatness. Even more so since Dad left. Every time he's come back to the house over the years it's been more and more perfect. Even the closets and kitchen drawers, organised. Whenever he's visited – rarely – he's felt as if Mom's thorough tidying and sorting is an attempt to control the world and keep it understandable.

This house is Mom's domain. When she comes down to New York or when they meet somewhere halfway, as they do for Thanksgiving in their favourite restaurant in Boston's North End, she seems ill at ease. She's more brittle, constantly checking her nails, smoothing her hair. Her accent tightens up; she pronounces her 'r's harder and enunciates her 'th's as if to prove she's not another Maine Québequois. Peggy says she loves New York City and Boston, but when she's out of Maine it's easy to see she's a Casablanca girl, a small-town sweetheart.

There's a polished side table next to the wing chair, and on it there's a coaster, the TV remote, and a scrapbook. His mother has been a tireless recorder of the family's achievements for as long as he's remembered. Lou's always been faintly embarrassed by it, while at the same time knowing, deep down, that he'd be devastated if his mother didn't make the effort. His parents' pride in him is both necessary and shameful. He hasn't looked at this scrapbook so much as been aware of its existence as something to live up to.

On the screen, penguins shoot down icy slopes and plummet into the Antarctic water, and Lou picks up the scrapbook and opens it.

When he was a kid he always felt gangly and awkward, taller than both of his best friends. In these photos cut from the *Casablanca Herald* though, stuck carefully on the scrapbook's thick pages, he's cute. Gap-toothed and grinning at a local track meet, in shorts that show knobbly knees. Suitably solemn receiving a perfect attendance certificate from Principal George. Lined up next to Benny on baseball teams and basketball teams, a different photograph for every year with time measured by the kids' height. The three of them, Lou and Allie and Benny, dressed up for Halloween as cowboys and cowgirl. YEE-HAW, HAPPY HALLOWEEN says the headline.

He turns the pages. Irving is in here too, wearing a safety helmet and giving a talk on safety at work for CPC. Being elected vice-president of a local businessmen's association. His mother appears more often, not because she did more but because, Lou suspects, she has always been so very photogenic. Mom with a bunch of flowers for a Mayday celebration. Mom with a book at the local library re-opening. Mom shaking the Mayor's hand at a fundraising lunch. A folded-up, cherished picture of Peggy in an evening gown, tiara and sash: CASABLANCA GIRL IS MISS

WESTERN MAINE 1976. There are several photographs of Lou's grandfather, David Alder, always wearing a suit and looking stern, which is pretty much exactly how Lou remembers him too.

Lou has been living with lies for thirteen years now – knows the texture of them, the way they appear as insistent red shadows in the middle of the night. These black-and-white photographs show a happily married couple and their well-adjusted son. Well off, cheerful, civic-minded and contented with their place in the world. They don't show the cracks that must have been in his parents' marriage, or the cells that maybe even then were mutating into something that would kill. They don't show Lou's own uncertainty about who he was and what he wanted and whether there was something wrong with him.

The last page has a clipping of the Casablanca High School Honour Roll list, with his name underlined (by his mother in blue ballpoint pen) and Allie's senior photo on top. *Allison Phelps will be valedictorian*, says the caption. She's serious, eyes bright under her straight brown bangs, a touch of make-up. At eighteen she doesn't look any different than she did in Mom's kitchen earlier.

He turns the page, expecting to see high school graduation photos maybe, and instead there's a single article pasted in the centre of the page. Benny's senior photograph. Unlike his twin, he's grinning and although the photo isn't coloured, Lou can picture the exact shade of his eyes. It's the sort of face Benny used to make when he picked up a baseball glove. 'Let's play,' he'd say, reaching for a baseball with a sort of fierce confident joy, a smile that said *I am going to blow you away because I am good at this*.

Benny looks so vital. So handsome and young and cocky and alive, a total denial of the words of the headline underneath.

CASABLANCA MOURNS TEEN BASEBALL STAR.

Louise

When Lou was little, there were three supermarkets: the IGA where you shopped if you didn't have a lot of money, the Safeway where you shopped if you did, and Food Town where nobody shopped because it smelled funny but still somehow stayed in business. Now, Casablanca has one supermarket where the IGA used to be and everyone in town shops there.

Lou has been back in town for four days and this is her first time at the supermarket. She's standing in the checkout line. She checks the items on her shopping list again, not because she really thinks she forgot anything, but because it stops her from looking around. She's a mess in jeans, her favourite Sufjan Stevens T-shirt with the hole in the shoulder, her hair uncombed, wearing glasses instead of contacts, and she's already seen seven people she knows, including her old sixth-grade teacher Mrs Deannis, and been forced to make small talk with them. *Oh, you're a teacher, oh, you live in Brooklyn, what's that like, is it full of crime, yes, it's so sad about your mother, I hope she's comfortable at least. I haven't seen you in so long, but you look exactly like you used to, that red hair, I'd recognise you anywhere!*

In Brooklyn people know her, but it's not the same. It's not almost everyone. You can go several days without seeing your neighbours, or ex-students, or people who you used to date. There are enough people that it's diluted. But not here.

Mrs Deannis cornered her by the canned vegetables. 'I see your father sometimes,' she said, 'and he is proud as punch of you!'

That made her stop in the middle of putting stewed tomatoes in her cart. 'He is?' The single mom, the struggling teacher?

'Oh, we all are around here! I always knew you'd make something special of your life. You used to write those stories that were so good. Such an imagination.'

'I'm just a teacher,' she protested, and then remembered who she was talking to and blushed.

'There's nothing more important than a teacher. Now I'm retired, I miss those kids so much. Bet you love them all, even the troublemakers, right?'

She was right. 'Especially the troublemakers.'

Mrs Deannis chuckled. 'And what about that book you were going to write? That nearly done yet? I'd love a signed copy.'

'Uh.' Less guilty now, edging towards the spaghetti sauce. 'I'm working on it.'

Still – at least it proves that she's visible. Her mother isn't talking to her; Lou brought her a cup of tea this morning and she gave Lou the barest of nods. As if this is all Lou's fault, as if Mom never did anything wrong in her life. As if Lou were the one who'd betrayed her, instead of the other way around.

Shopping is penance for her anger. She shouldn't be angry at a dying woman. It's wrong . . . and this all happened so long ago. Why can't she find it in herself to forgive? Like her father asked her to.

'Twenty-three fifty-two,' says the checkout lady, and Lou slides her card into the machine, glancing over at the other checkout aisle. The person with their back to her is Allie. She's wearing jeans and a yellow T-shirt, hair up in a bun on top of her head, and Lou would recognise her anywhere.

'Pin?' says the checkout lady.

'Oh. Oh, yes. Sorry.' She punches in her number and while the cashier is printing out her receipt, while the assistant is finishing packing her bags, Allie takes her single bag and leaves the shop without once glancing behind her.

'You're Louise Alder, right?' says the cashier.

'Yes.'

'Carry your bags, miss?' says the male assistant. 'Got some heavy cans in there.'

'What? Oh – no, thank you. Sorry, I have to go.' She hurries for the door.

This is probably a bad idea. But she needs to know if Allie knows what happened. If that's what she's angry with Lou about. Because having Allie angry at Lou for *that* would even be a bit of relief. It would mean that someone else knows, that she wouldn't have to carry the burden of a secret any more.

And they used to be such good friends. They were each other's everything, once. They knew each other from birth. Hours on the phone, notes slipped to each other in school, every weekend sleeping over each other's house. Gossip and laughter, linked hands and shared ice creams. Until the night of their high school graduation, Allie and Lou knew absolutely everything about each other. Allie is the best friend that Lou has ever had.

Handles of the bags cutting into her hands, she hurries out of the shop after Allie. Lou recognises her car from the hospital. 'Allie!' she calls, and Allie pauses and turns around. As soon as she does, Lou knows she's made a mistake.

'If you want to talk with me about your mother, call the office for an appointment,' she says, her voice ice.

'I don't want to talk with you about Mom. Or that is – I do, but that's not the reason I followed you.'

'What do you want to talk about, then?' She's tapping her foot, hand tight on her shopping bag.

A hot parking lot is not the place to do this, but this is what she's got, so Lou launches into it. 'I'm sorry I haven't been in touch. I'm sorry I left town without saying goodbye. I'm sorry I never explained anything, but I didn't have a choice. You're my best friend and I should have treated you better and trusted you, but I was eighteen and I didn't know how.'

'That's such bullshit.'

'Allie—'

'We talked every day. We were going to go to college together. We were going to do everything together and then you were fucking gone. Not even a note. Do you know how many nights I couldn't sleep wondering what I'd done to make you hate me?'

'You didn't do anything.'

'No, I did not. I did nothing to be treated that way. I know now that you're a selfish, bitter person and you just didn't give a shit about me.'

'That's not true. I did. I do.'

'If you give a shit about someone, you don't abandon them. I stayed here, I went to med school and I came back to help when my mother was dying. Benny did everything he could. Where were you?'

'Oh, *Benny's* the hero.' It bursts out of her. She meant to be apologetic, to make things better, but this is too much.

'Yes. Benny, my brother. He's done more for the people in this town than anything you've ever done. Do you know how many people that hospital wing has helped? Not only the people who are treated there but the people who work there, too. Including your dad, by the way, in case you've forgotten. Meanwhile, you left us all behind like so much filth on your shoe and you expect to come back here and everything will be all right?'

'I wasn't walking away from you.'

'It sure felt like it.' Allie turns and unlocks her car. 'You know what? Forget it. We're not friends any more. It doesn't matter. You really hurt me once, but I'm over it. If you want to talk about your mother, make an appointment.'

She climbs into the high seat of her vehicle and slams the door with such force that Lou has to step backwards. When she does, she sees the other people in the parking lot, with their shopping carts and their bags, watching. Including Mrs Deannis.

Lou wants to shout, 'Mind your own business!' But she can't yell at kind Mrs Deannis, who also loves the troublemakers best. She ducks her head and hurries to her own car.

When she gets back, she hears quiet voices in the dining room. Irving works these days at the hospital, looking after their computer systems, but since Peggy's diagnosis he's gone part-time. 'Just for the summer,' he's told Lou. 'I'm using up my vacation days. They've got a college kid in for the days I'm here at home. Good to know I can be replaced so easily.'

But her dad can't be replaced. He sits by Peggy's bedside and he holds her hand and talks with her. They watch box sets together. At night he sleeps in his La-Z-Boy. He labels her medication, makes sure she has a drink nearby even though she rarely touches it, and helps her get out of bed to make her slow and excruciating way to the bathroom. He heats up soup and makes Jell-O and tries to tempt her to eat. On his days at work, Lou does some of these things, including helping her mom to the bathroom and providing drinks and Jell-O, but she can't sit still in that dining room-cum-sickroom. She's up doing laundry, or cleaning, or finding out what Dana is up to, or checking her email (she doesn't have much email), or searching for natural remedies, or running little errands around the house. She's not very good at any of these things; she tried to fix a window blind yesterday and managed to break it further. But it's too hard to stay still. The silence is far too loud.

But her dad and her mom are never silent when they're together. They talk all the time. She has no idea what they find to talk about, after over thirty years together. What would she find to talk about with someone she'd seen every day for that long? Lou thinks she'd run out of ideas, especially in a small town like this. She hasn't dated anyone for longer than twelve months. She has colleagues, friends, but as a single mom she doesn't have much time to spend with them. Dana is the only person she knows well enough to be quiet with, to feel comfortable letting a conversation trail off, only to be picked up later at a different angle. And lately, it's been hard to do that with Dana, too. She used to do that with Allie, but . . . well.

Now, putting the groceries away, she listens for what her parents are saying to each other. This conversation between them that started before she was born and that's going to end this summer.

Her dad is singing. He hasn't got much of a voice – Lou always pretended to groan and stick her fingers in her ears when he used to sing along to the radio – but Lou can recognise this tune. She stops, in the middle of stacking cans of tuna on a shelf, and listens. It's Buddy Holly's 'Peggy Sue'.

And she should be touched by this, the soft sung love between them, and she *is* touched, but Lou looks at the cans of tuna and she listens to her dad singing and she thinks maybe about a world where this would be different. Where she would still be friends with Allie and she could be in that bedroom, singing to her dying mother.

Louis

Lou was told that the palliative care nurse who was coming to speak with them on Tuesday morning was called Fiona DiConzo, so he's surprised when he answers the knock on the door and the person standing there is Allie.

'Oh,' he says. 'Hi. I ... was expecting Fiona.'

'Fiona's kid has been puking for the past twelve hours. So you've got me.' Allie's expression is more than a little wary. Lou thinks he's probably got much the same expression on his own face.

'OK, no problem,' he says anyway, trying to put on a welcoming smile. 'Mom's upstairs. She wanted to come down. She wanted to be a hostess and she told me which cookies to get and everything. But when I tried to get her out of bed, she was too dizzy. So she had to stay up there.'

'We'll go up,' Allie says. 'I'm used to bedsides. But this is something for you both to think about: whether you want your mom to stay upstairs in her room, or maybe relocate downstairs. Upstairs has the en-suite bathroom so that's more convenient while she can still get up to use it, but if she's downstairs it's going to be easier for you to keep an eye on her during the day. There are pros and cons. In both cases we can arrange for a hospital bed for her, so she can sit up easily and you can get her in and out.'

'This is ... weird,' he says to her as they walk up the stairs to his mother's bedroom. He's thinking that if he'd known he was going to see Allie, he might have worn something better than his old Sufjan Stevens T-shirt with the hole in the shoulder.

'It's my job,' she says briskly, but when she walks into Peggy's room she's all smiles and kindness. Lou gets a chair for her and she sits, her hand over Peggy's, and talks.

She talks to them about what will happen in the long or slow process of Peggy's dying. She talks about the benefits of a PCA, or patient-controlled analgesia device, which she can teach Peggy to use. She talks about commodes and bed pans and intravenous fluids and feeding, but all of it in such a matter-of fact way that it hardly seems as if she's talking about anything unpleasant at all. She says how she or another nurse will be there, or at the end of a phone line, whenever they need her.

Peggy nods. Lou is quite frankly, terrified. He tries to remember it, but hardly any of it goes in. Allie says goodbye to his mother and he walks down the stairs with her to the kitchen.

'I'll write it all down for you,' she says, and he feels like an idiot.

'Would you like some coffee?'

'No, I'm fine, thanks.'

Lou pours himself a cup. His hands aren't quite steady, so he turns his back so Allie won't see.

'It's tough,' she says. 'The practicalities help, because you know how to deal with things as they come up, but the truth underneath it is really hard. Talking about it means you have to face it.'

'It came from out of the blue,' Lou says. He sips his coffee and turns around. Allie is leaning against the wall near the table, not sitting down, but not making any move to leave, either.

'Death always comes out of the blue,' she says. 'Even when you expect it.'

He can't look at her after that because they both know how true it is. He leans against the counter, in a copy of her pose. 'Anyway – thanks. I think it helps Mom to have someone who knows what she's really like. Not someone who sees the weakness.'

'Maybe. She's a brave lady.' Allie pauses and he thinks she's about to say goodbye when she says, quickly as if she's been rehearsing, 'There's a good chance that I'm going to be here a lot and I would sort of like to swap with Fiona and be the named nurse for your mother's care, because of the family connection, but if that happens then you and I have to agree that we can't talk about things.'

He looks at her then. He knows exactly what she means by 'things'.

'I can't,' she tells him. 'I just – it's overwhelming. And though I work in a sad job, I'm not a sad person. I've had to stay positive. I was depressed for a long time, all through university and afterwards, and I've come through that now, and I can't go back to that place. I have to keep busy and happy. So if I'm your mom's named nurse, you and I can only talk about your mom. Nothing else.'

There's a strain to her voice that wasn't there when she was explaining all the mechanics of dying. Although she couldn't have told him what she was going through, he feels like he should have known anyway. But he was too busy running away.

'OK,' he says. 'We'll talk about my mom, and that's all.'

She lets out a deep breath and relaxes, as if she's defused some ticking bomb. 'I mean, it shouldn't be that hard, right? We haven't talked at all since high school.'

But I missed you. I wanted to talk with you every day.

He doesn't say it. He nods and says, 'I'm glad you're here to help my mom.'

'I'm here to help you too. Give me a call whenever you need me.' She checks her watch. 'I've got to go, but I'll see you soon.'

He stands up straight, an automatic reaction when a woman enters or leaves a room. His dad taught him to do it, not overtly, but by example. 'Thanks,' he says again, and then she's gone. He goes to the window and sees her getting into her car, a drab green

Subaru. For a minute he thinks she's looking back at him, but then she starts up the car and drives away.

When he goes back upstairs he half expects his mother to be asleep, but she's not. She's curled so small underneath the blankets that you could miss her. She's holding a tissue, but she doesn't look like she's been crying.

'What are you wearing?' she says to him. 'You look like a tramp. Doesn't your wife buy you clothes?'

'It's my favourite T-shirt.' He sits next to her. 'I didn't expect to see Allie.'

'She's a good girl,' Peggy says. 'Mary wasn't proud enough of her.'

'Do you think?' says Lou in surprise. 'She was top of her class, she always succeeded at everything.'

'Benny was the star of that family. He was the one who was going to make them all proud. Allie, they expected her to do well. She came back to nurse Mary when she was dying, and I don't think Mary ever even thanked her.' Peggy glances at him. 'If I had a daughter instead of a son, I hope I'd encourage her as much as a boy.'

'I'm sure you'd be the same.'

'Then again, maybe it was that pressure that did it for Benny. Maybe he thought that he wouldn't live up to it.' She sighs. 'That haunted Mary till she died. She thought, somehow, that what happened to Benny was all her fault. I kept telling her that it wasn't. But she felt responsible anyway.'

'She wasn't responsible.' He thinks of the bargain he's just made with Allie downstairs. The pact they made thirteen years ago in a blood-soaked basement. He says again, more firmly, 'It was not her fault.'

He doesn't say the words that should come next. 'Because it was mine.'

Louis

1986–1992

Louis Alder married Allie Phelps for the first time in front of the swing set on the school playground. He made her a ring out of the ring-pull of a can of Dole pineapple juice, which was too big for her, so he wrapped tinfoil around it to make it fit. Roy Pelletier's uncle was a priest and Roy said he had been to lots of weddings because of his uncle and also his mom sang in the church choir so Roy had to go to church twice every Sunday, morning and evening. So he married them, even though only Allie was Catholic and Lou was Presbyterian.

Roy said a lot of words that could have been Latin or made-up, and then said, 'Do you, Louis Alder, take Allison Phelps for your lawful wedded wife?' and Lou said, 'Yes.'

'You're supposed to say "I do",' said Roy.

'I do,' said Lou.

'But you don't say it yet. First I have to say "to have and to hold in sickness and healthy until you are both dead".'

'Also I think you're supposed to ask me if I take him first,' said Allie. 'Because I'm the girl.'

'Why would a girl have to be asked first?' asked Lou.

'Manners,' said Allie.

'So she can't run away,' said Benny, who was being best man, which basically consisted of sitting on the swing dragging his sneaker toes through the dirt and trying to flick it at Lou.

'I won't run away,' said Allie.

'You have to promise to obey him,' said Roy.

'Obey?' said Allie.

'It means you have to do what he says,' said Benny.

'I know what it means. I'm not going to do that.'

'Why not?' asked Lou.

'Because my father—' Allie stopped, as Benny swung forward and kicked her on the leg. 'Ow. Benny, cut it *out*.'

'Sorry,' said Benny.

'You don't have to say that,' said Lou. 'Ask her without that stuff, Roy.'

'Do you, Allison Phelps, take Louis Alder as your lawful wedded husband in sickness and health in life and death forever?'

'I do.'

'You're married now. *Spiritus sancti domine.* You can go ahead and kiss.'

Allie and Lou both leaned forward and touched their lips together.

'ALLIE AND LOUIS, SITTING IN A TREE, K-I-S-S-I-N-G!' yelled Benny. 'FIRST COMES LOVE THEN COMES MARRIAGE THEN COMES LULU IN A BABY CARRIAGE!'

Lou pulled Benny off the swing and gave him a noogie on the head. Benny grabbed his arm and gave him an Indian burn. The two of them happily rolled around in the dust wrestling until Allie yanked on Lou's foot and said, 'You forgot to give me the ring.'

'Oh yeah,' said Lou, and fished in his pocket for the pineapple juice ring. He slipped it onto Allie's finger, where she wore it for the rest of the day.

She was still wearing it the next morning, a Saturday, when Lou walked through the woods to play in the twins' backyard. Mrs Phelps was in the yard, hanging sheets up on the line (Lou's mother didn't do this, she had a drier, but Lou loved the way the sheets fluttered in the wind like sails; sometimes he sat underneath them and pretended to be on a ship). Mr Phelps came outside, cigarette in his mouth, about to light it, and said, 'What's that you've got on your hand, Allison?'

Allie held up her hand proudly. 'Me and Lou got married.'

'Seven years old and you're already trying to do better than your mother, eh?'

'Donnie,' said Mrs Phelps quietly.

'What? If she's going to get married, she might as well marry money, right? That's what you told Peggy, isn't it?'

'Not in front of the children,' Mrs Phelps said.

'You're pissed because your own daughter is smarter than you.' Mr Phelps lit his cigarette with the Zippo he always carried in his pocket and which he sometimes showed off to Benny and Lou, flipping the lid and striking a light with the same movement of his thumb. 'She didn't even have to get knocked up first.'

Mrs Phelps put down her basket and walked into the house. Mr Phelps followed her, shoving his lighter into his pocket, slamming the screen door after him.

'I thought he wasn't supposed to smoke in the house,' said Lou.

Allie was watching the door, chewing on her lip.

'Let's play baseball,' said Benny. 'Come on, Allie. You can be catcher. I won't throw it too hard.'

'My dad isn't rich,' said Lou. His grandfather was rich, he knew that. But not his dad. They were . . . normal.

But he was thinking about their house with the two spare bedrooms and the new car his dad had bought this spring, and Mr Phelps's old rattly truck and how all of Mrs Phelps's sewing stuff was kept in Allie's bedroom and how Benny's bedroom was so small that he had to keep his baseball card collection in the garage in a plastic box, and whenever Lou slept over he ended up halfway under Benny's bed because there was no room for him on the floor with his sleeping bag.

He'd never thought about this before. It was just the way that things were.

'Yeah,' Allie said. 'Let's play baseball.' Usually Benny and Lou had to spend ages persuading her to play. 'Let's play it at your house, OK, Lou?'

Lou didn't much feel like playing ball, but he said 'OK' anyway. And he didn't say anything when he noticed that Allie had taken her pineapple juice ring off her finger.

They were sprawled on the Phelps's living room sofa, all three of them aged ten. Lou's birthday had been the week before. Benny's baseball card collection was spread out on the coffee table, arranged by team and then by position, with the doubles stacked on top of each other. Lou's own collection was small in comparison; Benny spent all his pocket money on baseball cards. Allie was rereading *The Little House on the Prairie*, and Lou was watching Benny arrange and rearrange his cards.

'You got this one?' asked Benny, holding up Roger Clemens.

'No, I've been trying for ages.'

'I've got last year's and this year's. You can have last year's if you want.'

Lou was putting the treasure safely in his back pocket when Mr Phelps appeared in the door. 'Boys? C'mon out back for a minute.' He turned around and went outside.

All three of them got up and went into the backyard. Mr Phelps was standing by the woodpile holding a gun.

This wasn't too unusual. Mr Phelps was often holding a gun. He had lots of them, a whole safe full. He hunted, and sometimes in the evenings when Lou was staying over he sat in front of the television and cleaned his guns with WD-40 and a collection of little brushes. Lou had never seen him clean anything else – he didn't help with dishes or the housework like Lou's father did, and for years it had been Benny's job to wash the cars. Sometimes Lou helped Benny wash the car and the truck.

'You can go on back inside and help your mother,' Mr Phelps said to Allie. She shrugged and went back inside and he turned to Benny and Lou. 'This is a man thing. You two are going to be men someday and it's time you learned.'

'Learned to shoot stuff?' said Lou, with a mixture of fascination and horror.

'You've got to learn how to load the gun first. Here.' He gave the rifle to Benny. 'Don't point it at anyone!'

Benny pointed the barrel at the ground.

'Do you know what to do?'

'Pull back the bolt,' said Benny immediately.

'Well, go ahead, what are you waiting for?'

Benny lifted a sort of lever on the top of the gun and pulled it back, so a compartment slid open. He did it confidently, as if he'd done it before, and though Lou had never really been interested in guns, he was jealous of how Benny seemed completely at home with this one.

'You get the ammo,' Mr Phelps said to Lou.

'The what?'

'In the box.' He nodded at a red cardboard box that was sitting on the woodpile. Lou picked it up. It was ridiculously heavy, and when he opened it, it was full of neat bronze cartridges, each one exactly the same, each one pointed upwards. It reminded him of nothing so much as the time when he'd opened a new box of his mother's Tampax to see what it was and seen the rows of identically-wrapped cylinders, packed close together, mysterious in purpose.

He drew one out with his thumb and forefinger. It was a bit bigger than his own finger, shaped like a mini missile. He put it on his palm and rolled it back and forth. It was cold and heavy. 'Is this a bullet?'

'It's a round. The bullet is inside it, along with gunpowder.'

Mr Phelps had never explained anything to Lou before. He'd barely even spoken to Lou before. He'd always seemed big, broad-shouldered, loud. He smelled of tobacco and flannel and sometimes beer, and his face was unshaven. He wasn't like Lou's father or Grandpa Alder – they were completely different species of men, it seemed, who wore white shirts and ties and glasses and sat at desks all day – but Grampy Grenier worked the machines at the mill and went hunting sometimes too, and he wasn't like Mr Phelps: he was wiry and balding, a bit like a bird next to round Mémère Grenier, the sort of man who spent a lot of time digging vegetable beds and humming under his breath. Lou had never seen him touch a gun.

Lou looked up at Mr Phelps with some awe. There was something special in being the focus of attention of a man like this, who didn't seem to like children very much. He felt the weight of the round in his hand and he wanted to ask, 'Would this kill a person?' but that seemed a little wrong so instead he asked, 'Would this kill a deer?'

'If you got the deer in the right place, yeah. Go ahead, put the round in the magazine.'

Again, the word made no sense to Lou. Mr Phelps seemed to be speaking a different language, where sharp bullets were round and they went into the fashion glossies whose paper was made by CPC. But the disconnect only lasted half a second and Lou slid the round into the empty cylinder in the gun. It slotted into place, smooth and satisfying, the gun a perfectly made tool.

'Can we shoot it?' Benny asked, watching as Lou slid another round into the magazine.

'Not in the backyard, your mother'd kill me. We can go up McFarlane's and use their field.'

'Can I?' Lou started to ask, though he wasn't sure if he wanted to, but before he got the second word out, Mrs Phelps opened the screen door.

'Lou, your mom wants you home for supper,' she said, and then, 'Donnie? What are you doing with those boys and that gun?'

Lou let the third round fall back into the box. He'd heard this tone in Mrs Phelps's voice before. 'See you later,' he said quickly, and took off through the woods to head home.

'What did you do this afternoon?' his mother asked him when he came in, and he said, 'Played with Benny's baseball cards. He gave me a Roger Clemens.'

Louis kissed Allie for the first time when they were both thirteen years old.

Every third Friday night there was a junior high dance at the community centre on Main Street. They turned off most of the lights in the hall upstairs, pushed the pool tables to the side, and set up two big speakers to blast power ballads. It cost a dollar to get in, getting your hand stamped by the bored high school student at the door so that the next day everyone could tell that you'd been to the dance. Lou brought extra quarters to go in the soda machine and the foosball table.

It lasted from seven till nine and hardly anyone danced for the first hour. Usually either Benny or Lou got there early and nabbed the foosball table so they could play, but if they didn't get there first, they watched the other boys play. Some girls would get up and dance to 'Rock Lobster' or songs from *Grease* but when the slow music came on again they'd sit back down. Most of the boys sat on the side of the hall with the foosball table and most of the girls sat on the side with the vending machines, so if you wanted a Coke you had to walk past all the girls and they looked up, hopeful that you were going to ask them to dance. One side of the room was Red Sox caps and sneakers; the other was curled hair and bubblegum scented lip gloss. These two worlds stayed almost totally apart until about eight thirty, when there was a sudden exodus to the dance floor as everyone realised that time was running out.

Lou only ever danced with Allie. He didn't even have to ask her; they always danced to their favourite songs, 'November Rain' by Guns N' Roses and the final song, which was always Lynyrd Skynyrd's 'Freebird', so as soon as those songs came on, he found her or she found him and they walked together to the middle of the room. He put his arms around her waist and she put her arms around his shoulders and they swayed together. There weren't any awkward negotiations of how close to get; they fitted comfortably together, not pressed up against each other like some of the other couples, but casual. It felt good. The music was loud but this close together they could hear each other and they talked about stuff, regular stuff like what they'd watched on TV and what books they'd read, in a way that they didn't do as much as they used to when they were little kids, before Lou started hanging out mostly with Benny and Allie found girlfriends.

Except sometimes, when Allie's hip brushed against his, or when they ran out of stuff to talk about for a few minutes and all he could feel was her warm arm against his neck, her breath near his cheek, he didn't think of her as his best friend's sister, or the person he'd known all his life. He felt like this was a *girl* in his arms, strange and exciting. Sometimes he thought about what it would be like to kiss her: not the little-kid smacks that they'd exchanged when they'd pretended to get married when they were in elementary school, but a real kiss. Lips soft, mouths open.

He wondered what she'd do if he tried, maybe in the slow part of 'Freebird', right at the end of the night. If she'd kiss him back, or if she'd laugh.

And what would Benny say? He'd tease them. Scoff and nudge. Especially if Lou tried to kiss Allie and Allie didn't want to kiss him back. Teasing from Benny would be just as bad as rejection from Allie. Maybe worse.

He was thinking about this all the way to this week's dance, not really taking in anything else as he walked down the hill, pushed open the community centre's heavy doors, paid his dollar and got his hand stamped. This was the last dance of eighth grade. Then there would be the summer, and then they would be in high school, and they wouldn't have dances like this any more. They'd have Homecoming and Winter Carnival that freshmen didn't really go to. He climbed the stairs and saw that Roy Pelletier and Buddy White already had control of the foosball table, so he stood by, watching them play, but really keeping an eye out for Allie. His heart leapt when he saw Benny's baseball cap and Red Sox T-shirt.

'Shit,' Benny said when he came up to Lou. 'They got the table.'

'What happened to your mouth?'

'Foul ball.' With his fist he mimed a ball hitting him in the lip. This was nothing new. Benny was a great player, but he got beaned with the ball a lot.

'Where's Allie?' Lou tried to sound casual.

'Some period thing. Ugh.' Benny dug a hand in his pocket. 'Got an extra quarter? I want a Sprite.'

Lou handed over three quarters. 'Get me a grape soda.' He grabbed a couple of chairs for both of them and tried to work out whether he felt more relieved or disappointed that Allie wasn't here.

'You look like you're on the rag, too,' said Benny, returning with the cans. 'You that sad that you don't have a dance partner?'

'I'll have to dance with you,' said Lou, and was surprised to see anger flash across Benny's face. 'Kidding,' he said quickly. 'You'd step on my feet.'

'Fuck you,' said Benny, and walked to the other side of the table, striking up a conversation with Buddy about the Red Sox.

Confused, Lou popped open his grape soda and tried to work out what he'd done wrong. Was Benny bothered that he'd been more excited to see Allie than him? Or did he really think Lou was actually asking him to dance?

Girls danced with other girls to fast songs – and sometimes even to slow songs – looping their arms around each other and singing at the top of their lungs. And sometimes Lou and Benny played air guitar and sang along when they played 'Bat Out of Hell', which was their favourite song. But boys didn't dance with boys. People would think you were gay.

He glanced over to Benny, who was acting like he always did, always moving, tapping his foot, drumming his hand on the foosball table and on the back of the plastic chair that he was standing near, holding his cold can of Sprite up to his fat lip. Sometimes it seemed like Benny had coiled-up energy in all his muscles, joints that never stopped flexing. Even in his sleep, when Lou was staying over, sleeping on the floor downstairs in the Phelps's newly finished basement, Benny tossed and turned and muttered.

He watched as Benny leaned over to hear what another boy was saying and then wrinkled up his nose. Lou couldn't hear what they were saying, but he could read Benny's lips: 'No way.' Both the boys glanced over to the girls' side of the room and started laughing some more. The other boy stuck his tongue into his cheek and moved it back and forth.

The DJ was playing Shakespears Sister. No one was dancing. Lou had had enough. Benny was mad at him and Allie wasn't here. He crumpled up his empty can, tossed it into the bin for returnables, and headed for the door.

He was halfway down the stairs when the glass doors at the bottom leading out to the street opened and Allie walked in. She was wearing jeans and a T-shirt with a rainbow on it. She was alone. Allie looked up the stairs.

'Hey,' she said, smiling. 'You leaving?'

He didn't even really think about it. He skipped down the rest of the stairs, put his hand under her chin, tilted it up, and kissed her. Her mouth was as soft and warm as he'd imagined it was going to be, but he could also feel her breath on his skin and the soft brush of her hair against his hand. She felt perfect.

'Hey,' said the high school kid minding the door and the stamp, 'save it for the dance floor.'

Lou pulled back a little but Allie was smiling at him. He smiled down at her.

'Wanna dance?' she asked him, and he nodded.

No one was on the dance floor yet upstairs but they went to the centre of the room and started dancing. Just the two of them, to whatever music they played. They danced the whole dance, sometimes alone, sometimes with other people on the floor, and when the slow part of 'Freebird' came on, Lou kissed her again and she kissed him back.

That was the end of junior high school. He thought it was the beginning of everything.

Louis & Louise

Lou isn't prepared for the casseroles.

The first one turns up the second day Lou is there. They're in the kitchen reading the *Lewiston Daily Sun* when footsteps sound on the path outside but there's no knock on the back door. A little shuffling and then the footsteps walk away. Lou hears a car start up.

When Lou opens the back door there's a tinfoil-covered dish on the step. It's got a yellow Post-it stuck to the top of it: *Best wishes to Peggy. Joyce and Bill.* Under the tinfoil there's a lasagne.

They keep coming after that, on average one every other day, but sometimes two come at once. Chicken salad, baked ziti, macaroni and cheese, beef stew, chilli, baked beans. Sometimes it's not a casserole but a cake or a tin of cookies. It's always rib-sticking food, high in starch or gravy or sugar. It's always delicious. Sometimes it's left by the door with a note from people who want to help but not disturb, but sometimes people knock and Lou invites them in for a cup of coffee and a little visit with Peggy if she's awake. Lou stays in the kitchen during these visits. It's not what a dutiful child would do, but Lou finds it hard enough to keep secrets and deal with Peggy dying to be able to make small talk at the same time.

Lou sees people they haven't seen in years. Most of them are from their parents' generation or older: their neighbours the Rouleaus, whose daughter used to babysit Lou, Mrs Kozaks, who owned the corner shop, Grandma Alder's oldest friend Esther Ames, who still drives around town in her big Pontiac despite having the thickest glasses in the world, like the bottom of fish-bowls. But there are a few close to their age, including Georgia Bigelow, who used to be an object of fascination to most of the boys (and girls) at Casablanca High because of her breasts. She runs the funeral home on Aroostook Street now.

'You should leave your card,' Lou jokes, and then winces, because that is too close to home.

But Georgia says, seriously, 'You know where I am. It'll be a privilege to help Peggy.'

Lou has never been very good at cooking. It's too easy to get distracted or impatient, and meals are often burnt or raw in the middle. This unbidden bounty is close to a miracle. The less of Peggy there is, the more food seems to arrive. Lou portions it into plastic containers and puts it in the freezer, which fills up day by day with the goodwill of the people of Casablanca.

Peggy has been on a diet almost constantly since 1971, when she was fourteen. That's when she started the beauty pageants, though she could only do the local ones because there wasn't enough money to travel out of state. Miss Junior Oxford County 1973. Casablanca High Homecoming Queen 1974. Casablanca High Prom Queen 1975. Miss Western Maine 1976. Second runner-up Miss Maine 1976. When she was sixteen she got a job in the IGA bagging groceries to save up enough money to get a portfolio done. They went to a photographer in Norway. Her mother drove her in their old Ford. Catalogue shot, fashion shot, swimsuit shot.

'You're not going to make it,' her mother told her on the way home. 'You're pretty, but those models are tall and skinny.'

She sent out her portfolio to agencies in Portland Maine, Manchester New Hampshire, and Boston Massachusetts. Meanwhile, she couldn't control her height – her mother was barely five feet three so Peggy came by it naturally – but she could control her weight.

She did the cabbage diet and the egg diet. She lived on celery sticks and radishes. She spent her IGA money on SlimFast shakes. When her friends went out to Rick's for French fries and vanilla Cokes, she had a coffee and a water. She never got a modelling contract, but by the time she was married to Irving, deprivation was such a habit that she had to retrain herself not to ignore her hunger when she was pregnant, give herself permission every day to eat peanut butter sandwiches, fried eggs, pork chops, baked potatoes with sour cream, apple pie, as many grapes as she liked. How strange to feel a need and satisfy it immediately. She gained forty pounds in her pregnancy, kept twenty of it throughout breastfeeding, and as soon as Lou was weaned, she went back to celery and low-fat cottage cheese, toast without butter and chicken with the skin cut off.

Now, lying in this bed, dying, she thinks about that time when she was carrying Lou. With her present body melting away to feed the cancer inside her, she thinks about what it was like to be so big she couldn't get behind the wheel of the car. How her breasts swelled like balloons filling with water, how her stomach was round and tight. How Irving wanted to touch her all the time. She runs her hands over her hipbones and her ribs, stark even under her nightgown, and she thinks about how crazy she was not to appreciate it. How stupid she was all her life not to eat the French fries and drink the vanilla Cokes. As if her slimness and beauty were the most valuable things she could ever own.

People bring food – they always bring food for sickness or death – and someone gives them an apple pie, still warm, homemade. She can smell it from her bed. She asks Lou to bring her a slice as soon as it's cut. Ice cream melts over the crust, pools in the cinnamon-flecked juice from the apples, and Peggy manages one bite. One perfect, sweet, crispy, creamy bite, and that's enough.

Louise

Dana thinks Casablanca is a dump. An utter dump. Brooklyn is dirty and noisy and there are some weirdos wandering the streets and sometimes the stairs leading up to their apartment smell like piss, but Casablanca is ... nothing. She's been here a week and it's the most boring place on earth. Closed shops, shitty phone signal, everybody looks the same and there is nothing to do. No wonder her mother left as soon as humanly possible. And now they have to spend probably the whole summer here, and her grandmother is dying, and her grandfather is trying not to act sad, and her mom is literally on edge all of the time.

Dana finds her mom's old bike in the garage – her grandparents never throw anything away – and she greases the chain and fixes the brakes and pumps up the tyres and rides it around crappy Casablanca. There's one good thing about being here: there isn't much traffic so her mom doesn't fuss about her being safe out on her bike on her own. She rides to McDonald's and she rides to the lake, though she's pretty sure her mom would pitch a fit if she knew she'd gone that far. The town's in a hollow with the closed-down mill at the bottom, so she has to ride up a hill to get more than two bars on her phone.

Farah has only texted her like once. Her Facebook page is all about everything she's doing with Hunter. Dana should stop looking, but she can't.

She would understand it if she'd done anything wrong, but she hasn't. One day Farah was her best friend, confiding in her, crying about her parents, and the next day, she's all Hunter this and Hunter that and they're going off by themselves and not telling Dana what they're doing or where they're going. She only sees it on Facebook. She hoped that soccer camp would mean she and Farah would be friends again, because Hunter wasn't going, but coming here has ruined that.

Why don't you like me any more? she texts to Farah, but then she deletes it before sending. She's trying to keep some dignity.

There are some kids around but they don't say hi to her. They watch her as she rides by. She pretends not to care. They're all wearing baseball caps and they look like rednecks. There is not a single person who isn't white.

She's going to go crazy if she has to stay here all summer. Literally insane. She wants to go back to Brooklyn so bad she can taste it in the back of her mouth.

There's a sports field next to the high school, and when Dana cycles by, she sees some kids playing soccer. Five against four. So she stops to watch. A couple of them aren't bad, so when they stop for a break she walks over.

'Can I play?' she asks.

'You're a girl,' says one boy. He's red-faced, dressed head to toe in Adidas.

'So? You need another player for five-a-side.'

'Have you even played before?'

'Try me.'

Another boy, with freckles, shrugs. 'Ask Piss-Pants.'

'Who's Piss-Pants and why should I ask him?'

'He's the coach.' He nods to a guy who's standing on the side of the field, talking on his phone. He's a grown-up wearing shorts and a Red Sox T-shirt.

'I assume I shouldn't call him Piss-Pants,' says Dana.

'Mr Phelps,' says a short boy who was in goal. 'He used to play for the Red Sox and now he coaches the high school teams. They call him Piss-Pants because he had a fit or something once.'

'Was he drunk?' Dana asks, interested.

Short boy shrugs. 'Dunno. Didn't see it. He's a pretty good coach.'

'How about I don't ask him and just start playing?'

Short boy shrugs again. He must be one of the leaders because the other boys don't disagree, not even Adidas Kid.

They've played for ten minutes and Dana has scored two goals when the coach seems to notice what's happening. He jogs across the field and calls, 'Hey!'

Dana pauses, wondering if she's going to get in trouble.

The coach stops in front of her. He's not out of breath after running, and despite his nickname, he seems like a normal enough type of person.

'I'm Benny Phelps, the coach. What's your name?' he asks her.

'Dana.'

'Where have you played before, Dana?'

'I'm on my school team. And a summer intramural.'

'You here for the summer?'

'Uh-huh.'

'OK. Let's see what you've got.'

'She's a girl,' says Adidas Kid.

'I did notice that, Shaun. Jim, you take goal, she'll kick some penalties.' He kicks the ball to her and jogs back to the sidelines to watch.

'Supposed to be a boys' team,' mutters Shaun.

'Is there a girls' team?' asks Dana.

'Dunno.'

'The American women's team is number one in the world,' says the short boy, Jim, and he stations himself in goal.

He isn't a bad goalie. Better than Farah. She gets six out of ten past him, the last four in a row, and then she looks expectantly over at the coach, who still isn't having a fit.

'Can I play?' she calls.

'You're striker today,' he calls back. 'Don't hog the ball.'

'I never hog the ball,' she mutters, but as she takes position, she feels better than she's felt since she got to this godforsaken town.

'Where're you from?' Jim asks her, after practice is over. Coach has told her to come back tomorrow, and she can play their match on Tuesday if she gets parental permission. That shouldn't be a problem; Mom will be happy she's doing something with her time other than moping.

'Brooklyn,' she tells him. He's got a bike too, which looks nearly as old as hers and too big for him; he gets on and they cycle together.

'Cool. I've only been as far as Massachusetts. Why are you here? Are you up the Pond?'

'I wish. My mom and I are here staying with my grandparents.' She doesn't mention the cancer, or the fact that Nana is dying in her dining room. It's not exactly the sort of thing you tell someone when you first meet them.

'What about your dad?'

'I don't have a dad. My mom says he was a truck driver she met when she was working as a waitress. He got her pregnant and drove off and she never saw him again.' This is maybe more personal than Nana's cancer, but it's an explanation she's offered many times, family legend, and it flips off her tongue easily.

'Wow. You're not curious?'

'No, I figure he's sort of a dick. What about you?'

'I don't really have a dad either, but that's because he lives in New Hampshire. My mom runs the funeral home on Aroostook Street. We live above it.'

'What, straight up?'

'Straight up.'

'You have corpses in your house?'

'Sometimes, but not like in the place where we live. They're in the funeral home part.'

'Cool,' she says with honest appreciation. He shrugs.

'Most people think it's weird.'

'I don't mind weird. How long have you been playing soccer?'

'Since fifth grade. You?'

'Forever. It's the only thing I'm good at.'

'I'm good at gaming too. How do you like Casablanca?'

'I hate it.'

Jim laughs. 'At least you're only here for the summer. Anyway, I turn off here. See you tomorrow?'

'Yeah,' she says, and he pedals off in another direction, while she rides home, wondering if she might have actually made a sort of friend.

Lou and her mother are alone in the house. Dana is out on her bicycle. Irving is at work. Mom is lying in the dining room watching soap operas. She used to watch them in secret when Lou was at school – it was her guilty pleasure – and Lou only knew about it because once she came home sick from school and caught her mom with a box of tissues in front of *The Young and the Restless*. 'Oh,' she said, getting up quickly when Lou walked in the door, 'I just turned this on.' She switched off the television as if she'd been caught watching pornography.

Lou wasn't quite sure, then, why her mother was so ashamed of liking soaps; plenty of people did. Now, she thinks it's probably because her Mémère Grenier was an unashamed fan, who got up especially early in the morning so she could clear all her chores and make herself a pot of coffee before *General Hospital* came on, and then she watched one soap after another until it was time to turn off the TV and make Grampy Grenier's dinner. Mémère Grenier always had a stack of *TV Guides* next to her recliner, and *Soap Opera Digest* magazine. She used to let Lou cut up her old ones to make collages.

Lou thought for a long time that her mother pretended not to like soaps because they were too working class, too full of blatantly aspirational characters and storylines, because the magazines were sold next to tabloid newspapers at the grocery store checkout aisle. This didn't fit with the carefully fashioned life that her mother had made as a member of the Alder family, the most important family in town.

But then, this morning, Lou was looking through a box of her old stuff that her parents had stored in the attic, and she came across a battered copy of *A Wizard of Earthsea* by Ursula K. Le Guin. She brought it to Dana's room. 'You're going to love this book,' she said to her daughter, who was scrolling through her phone, as usual.

Dana glanced at it and shrugged.

'It's wonderful. It's Harry Potter before Harry Potter, but more mythical and lyrical.'

Dana took it. Lou hovered, waiting for her to start. Dana loved science fiction and fantasy. Lou raised her on *Star Trek* and *The X-Files* and *Lord of the Rings*. But Dana put it on the bed next to her and resumed scrolling through her phone, and Lou had gone back to the attic, strangely deflated.

Now, making a cup of tea in the kitchen with the sounds of *General Hospital* in the background, Lou thinks that maybe her mother outwardly rejected soap operas for the same reason that Dana is so deliberately indifferent to Ursula Le Guin. It's the nature of daughters to turn away from their mothers, to try to define themselves as someone other, in any way that they can. Isn't this why Lou cut her hair short when she was thirteen, why she played sports and liked to wear jeans instead of dresses, why she never played with dolls until she had a baby of her own?

So she makes two cups of tea and brings them into the dining room. As always, she's shocked to see how thin her mother has become; no matter how many times she sees her, several times every day, Lou can't get used to it. It's only been a week since Lou came home and Peggy's noticeably lost weight. It's like she's melting.

Her mom used to have a bombshell figure. There are photographs of her as a young woman in a bikini on Morocco Pond. So beautiful. Even if she'd wanted to, Lou could never compare: she was tall, awkward, bespectacled, red-haired, straight up and down instead of curvy. Just by existing, her mother gave her lessons on how to be female which Lou could never follow.

Her mother glances away from the telly at Lou. It's not a good day. Although her mother doesn't complain about her pain, Lou can see it in her eyes, in the hollow of her cheeks, in the way her beauty has been washed away to leave this suffering. She puts a cup of tea beside her mom and settles beside her in the chair. She's not going to argue; it would be cruel. 'What's happening in Port Charles today?'

'Ugh,' says her mother. 'I don't know why I watch this trash. They're all having sex with each other.'

'At least someone is.'

When was the last time she tried to joke with her mother? Mom's lips don't quite smile, but there's a little twitch.

'I'm more interested in the clothes than the sex,' she says.

'I know what we should do,' Lou says. 'I can wash your hair, maybe do your nails and make-up. Would you like that?'

Her mother regards her. They both know what this offer really means: a truce.

'That would be nice,' her mother says at last. 'Your father, bless him, doesn't really understand how to apply nail polish.'

There's an inflatable basin specially designed for hair washing; it's one of the things that Irving showed her when she first arrived, along with the commode chair, the bedpans, the kidney dishes – all of the accoutrements for keeping dignity. Lou hasn't used any of them yet. Irving has managed without her. She has been dreading the day when she will have to. But a shampooing basin seems tolerable. It's a similar shape to the sinks in a hairdresser's, with high sides and a space for a person's neck, and a rubber tube to drain the water afterwards. Lou blows it up and shows it to her mother.

'Have you used this before?' she asks.

'No. Your father's been helping me to have baths.'

It's testament to how much her mother's ability has declined even in the week since she got here, because Lou can't imagine getting her mother in and out of the bath, let alone up the stairs to the bathroom in the first place.

'Well,' she says, putting a brisk cheerfulness into her voice, 'I think I should cover up the bed in case it leaks, or I make a mess. Right back.'

She returns with piles of towels and a couple of garbage bags, to be safe. Another trip, this time to get shampoo and a basin of warm water. 'OK, Mom, can you sit up so I can get this all in place?'

She has to help her to sit by putting an arm around her mother's shoulders. Peggy's spine is a row of hard beads under thin skin. She feels more like a bird than a human being. Peggy gasps in pain and Lou says, 'Sorry, so sorry.'

'You didn't cause it,' says Peggy. 'Only . . . be quick, all right?'

Lou lines the bed, positions the basin, helps her mother to lie down into it. 'Pretend that I'm Sally,' says Lou. 'Is Sally even doing hair any more?'

'She moved to South Carolina.' In gasps. Peggy settles into the basin and closes her eyes. 'I've never been able to find anyone half as good.'

'I still have a grudge against her for that bowl cut she gave me in third grade.'

'Pageboy. You looked cute. It was in style.'

'It has never been in style, Mom.' Gently, using a plastic jug, she ladles water over her mother's hair. There's silver among the auburn, but not much. She's only fifty-two. Mom was always the grown-up, always the one who knew best, but now that Lou is a grown-up herself, a mother, fifty-two seems hideously young.

'I used to wash your hair, I remember,' Peggy says as Lou squeezes shampoo into her palm. 'You never liked brushing it and you'd get it all in rat's nests. And then there was that time when you and Allie—'

'—had a bubble blowing competition with bubblegum and mine burst all over my head.'

'I had to use peanut butter to get it out,' says Peggy. 'What a mess.'

Lou remembers when this happened. She'd been upset, partly because Allie's bubble had been bigger than hers, but mostly because her hair was a clot of pink gum and she was afraid that her mother would yell at her.

But Peggy didn't yell. She sat Lou down in the kitchen and reached for the peanut butter and a comb. It took hours, it seemed, to get all of the gum out. But Peggy never tugged or pulled. She teased the gum out, strand by strand, until Lou was gum-free and smelling of peanuts, and then she said, 'Next time you blow bubbles with Allie, wear a swimming cap.'

Now, Lou tries to be as gentle as her mother was that day, when she'd done something stupid and expected to get in trouble for it. She remembers when she used to wash Dana's hair in the bath in their tiny first apartment. Dana's head was so small that it fitted into the palm of Lou's hand and she looked up at Lou with her baby eyes, calm in the warm water.

Peggy's hair is not as fine as that, but nearly. It spreads like silk in the basin and Lou slowly pours water, cup by cup, to rinse out the lather. Peggy's eyes are closed, her face relaxed. She could be asleep, and for a moment, when Lou finishes, she thinks that she is, but then Peggy opens her eyes and looks up at Lou.

'That feels lovely,' she says.

'You've still got quite a head of hair.'

'One benefit of not getting any chemo.'

Lou helps her sit up again and wraps a towel around her wet hair while she removes the basin and drains the water. Towels on the pillows, towel off the hair, slow, gentle strokes with a comb. She lays her mother down and she wonders: when was the last time she, Lou, was so tender with anyone? Dana hasn't needed her to be for some time now – or wouldn't allow her to be. And lovers are few enough and far between.

Her mother seems exhausted even by this. Lou doesn't speak as she clears everything away, goes to drain the water. Dana's in the kitchen wearing shorts and a T-shirt, carrying her soccer boots, filling a water bottle.

'Soccer practice,' Dana tells her. 'I played with some kids yesterday and they asked me to join their team. Coach says I can play in their match on Tuesday.'

'That's good,' says Lou, both pleased at Dana's initiative and a little alarmed that her pre-teen daughter has arranged all of this for herself without Lou's input. 'Who's the coach?'

'They call him Piss-Pants.'

'Piss-Pants?'

Dana shrugs. 'Some nickname. He seems OK. He coaches the high school team too. Grandad said he'd pick me up on his way home from work.'

'Can you get over there by yourself? Nana shouldn't be left home alone.'

'I'll ride my bike.' Meaning Lou's old bike, the one that she used to pedal all over town, sneak up to Morocco Pond on. Dana heads for the door and Lou taps her shoulder on the way by. She points to her cheek, waiting for a kiss. Dana gives it to her and rushes out the door.

Lou goes upstairs to her parents' bedroom to find emery boards and nail polish. The bottles are in rows on her mother's dressing table next to her rose-patterned make-up bag. She remembers the day she was discovered playing with Peggy's make-up bag, tempted by all the little compacts and bottles and brushes, and how Peggy sat Lou down and taught her how to feather blush onto her cheekbones, how to apply mascara with a delicate flick, how to spray perfume in the air and walk into the cool cloud of it. It felt like an obscure art, a clue to a mysterious realm of adulthood and womanhood, somewhere that Lou didn't quite belong.

She peruses the bottles and chooses a cheerful shade of bright peony pink.

When she comes back to the dining room, her mother is fast asleep. Her damp hair is in soft curls, the same way Dana's hair used to curl after a bath. Sometimes Lou would sit watching Dana sleep, even when she had laundry to do, bills to pay, housework to be done. Sometimes she felt as if watching her sleeping daughter and keeping her safe was the most important job she could do.

Lou puts the nail polish aside. She sits beside her sleeping mother, takes a sip of her cooled tea. She'll watch over her for a while in this truce, even if it's a temporary one. On the television behind her, with the sound turned down, the soap operas keep on playing.

Louise

1985–1992

She had to wear a dress to visit her Grandmother Alder, and when she stayed overnight in the big house with the two turrets she had to pack a nightgown and not the T-shirt and leggings that she liked to sleep in. Her father's parents' house was good manners and quiet voices, but it was also expensive chocolates in boxes and a bed that was much bigger than her own bed at home, where she could sprawl out and pretend to be a princess with servants at her beck and call.

Grandpa Alder was at work in his closed-door study at the top of the house, the room with the portrait of old Louis Alder outside it. At age six, Lou found both her grandfather and the portrait a little bit scary. They both knew important things. Grandma Alder was teaching Lou how to cut the crusts off sandwiches because she was having her ladies over to play bridge that afternoon. The sandwiches that Grandma Alder cut were straight and perfect, lines of triangles all in a row on the flowered china plate. Lou's were crooked and the bread was all squished where she put her hand on the sandwich by mistake when she was cutting.

'Well,' said Grandma Alder, 'you didn't inherit your mother's looks but you inherited her cooking skills. Are you going to get married one day, Louise?'

'I guess?' said Lou, scratching the waistband of her dress where it was itchy and smearing mayonnaise on it. 'I could marry Benny.'

'You won't marry Benny Phelps,' said her grandmother, pursing her coral-colour lips. 'You're an Alder. Never forget that.'

'OK,' said Lou, though she wasn't sure why her grandmother thought she would forget her own last name.

'You might be plain, but as an Alder you'll be able to marry anyone you like. And you'll have a big white dress and a huge cake and lots of flowers, like I did. What do you think about that?'

'I like cake,' said Lou, cautiously.

'Your mother didn't have a white dress,' said Grandma Alder, pursing her lips again. 'She didn't have the cheek.'

Her kitchen was big, but old-fashioned, with a huge deep white sink and an actual dumb waiter that still worked if you pulled on a rope. She said that the dining room used to be on the floor above and servants used to cook the meals and put them in the dumb waiter. Lou begged for a ride in it every time she visited but Grandma always said no. Her other grandparents' house wasn't as fancy or as big as this one, so it wasn't as much of an adventure to visit, but they played the radio and sometimes Pépère Grenier gave her rides on his shoulders and she never had to worry about making a mess.

Lou rearranged her sandwiches, trying to make them as neat as her grandmother's. Some of the filling leaked out and got on her fingers. She went to lick it off and then she remembered that Grandma Alder didn't like it when she licked her fingers so she wiped it on the skirt of her dress.

'And then once you get married, you can have children.'

'Oh, I don't want children,' said Lou before she could stop herself. 'I'm going to travel the world and have adventures, and then I'm going to be an author and write books.'

'Hmm,' said Grandma Alder. 'Louise Dawn Alder, what is that all over your dress?'

'Egg salad?'

Her grandmother clucked and went to get a dish cloth. 'Sometimes I despair of making you into a young lady.'

Young lady. It didn't sound as interesting as *princess* or *Darth Vader* or *author*.

'Did you like being a young lady?' she asked her grandmother as she wiped her dress.

'Yes. I used to go to all the dances and all the young men would line up to dance with me.'

That didn't sound bad. 'And did you like getting married and having children?'

'Just the one child. Your father. Yes, I did. He's the apple of my eye. I hope you don't make the same mistake he made.'

'Daddy made a mistake?'

'He got your mother in trouble.' Grandma Alder busied herself with rinsing out the dish cloth.

'How was Mommy in trouble?' asked Lou, worried now.

'She had a baby in her belly.'

'Babies are trouble?'

'They are sometimes.' Grandma took the cookie jar from the counter and put it on the table. 'If you help me by arranging these on a plate, you can have one. Nice and pretty, in a circle. Like this.'

Lou concentrated on putting the cookies down evenly on the plate, with exactly the same space between them. 'How did Mommy get a baby in her belly?' she asked, mostly looking at the cookies and wondering if she could have two instead of one.

A spoon clattered on a plate and Lou jumped. Her grandmother was glaring at her. 'Don't be rude. That's not something young ladies need to know about until they're married.' The doorbell rang. Grandma Alder smoothed back her grey hair. 'Oh dear, they're early. Don't take any of those cookies until I say.'

She left the kitchen and Lou immediately slipped a cookie into the pocket of her dress.

During Health class at the beginning of seventh grade they sent all the boys to the gym and all the girls stayed behind in the classroom and Miss Doughty showed them an animated video about periods. This video was famous at Casablanca Junior High because it was, implausibly, about a superhero called Ms Menstruation who saved women from cramps, mood swings and bloodstained clothing by throwing sanitary pads at them.

Lou and Allie already knew everything about periods. They'd read *Are You There, God? It's Me, Margaret* years ago, and besides, Allie had got her first period the summer before, right after her twelfth birthday. She shared every detail with Lou, from the huge zit on her chin that appeared like clockwork three days into her cycle, to her mother's advice that you had to use cold water, not hot, to wash out your underwear because hot water cooked the blood into the fabric. Lou listened, both horrified and desperately envious, especially when Mrs Phelps took Allie bra shopping and Allie came back with two, one white and one with pink daisies on it.

Lou didn't want a pink daisy bra, even though she thought it looked cute on Allie when she modelled it for her the next day. When she got a bra, *if* she got a bra, she wanted something as plain as possible. But after Allie left she closed the door to her bedroom and took off her clothes and looked at herself in the mirror, naked. Her chest was freckled and flat. She could see her ribs through the skin. She was skinny and her hips were narrow, like a child's. You could only tell she was a girl and not a boy because of the cleft between her legs. Lou lifted her arms and looked for armpit hair, but she didn't have any. She sat on the bed and looked for pubic hair, but she didn't have any of that, either. Just reddish-blonde down on her arms and her legs.

As the months went by, the other girls changed and Lou didn't. They curled their hair and started carrying handbags with them instead of backpacks – handbags with lip gloss and scented gel pens and hair brushes and sanitary pads and tampons. They wore their shirts shorter and they giggled at the boys (including Benny) and in the changing rooms before and after Phys. Ed. Lou could see that they all wore bras. Some of them even had lacy bras with matching underpants. She glanced at them as she changed, trying not to be obvious, hiding her own flat braless chest with her towel and shirt, caught between desire and envy, wondering how they could all be so effortless.

Peggy kept all her pads and tampons in the cupboard under the bathroom sink and she showed Lou where they were, even though Lou already knew. Once she asked Lou if she'd started yet and Lou said 'No,' so vehemently that Peggy didn't ask again, though she kept topping up the bathroom supplies. Every time Lou opened the cupboard for a spare roll of toilet paper there they were, the boxes of Tampax and Always, showing her what she'd failed to do, all the awkwardness and mess that women lived with.

'You're lucky you haven't started yet,' Allie said on the telephone. The two girls talked to each other on the phone almost every night while their parents were watching TV. Sometimes, having coordinated this beforehand, they crept downstairs after their parents were asleep and called each other, picking up quickly before the ringing phone woke anyone else up. Sometimes they fell asleep with the phones snuggled to their ears. 'It *hurts*,' Allie told her. 'Anyway, you'll start soon. You're younger than almost everyone in the class because you were born in September.'

'I don't care,' said Lou. But she did care. She wasn't sure if she cared because she wanted it to happen, or because she didn't.

In the end, it happened when she least expected it, near the end of Science class in the spring of their eighth-grade year. Allie was home from school with a stomach bug so Lou didn't have a lab partner, and when she stood up at the bench at the front of the room to put some slides under the microscope she heard sniggering behind her. When she looked over her shoulder it was R.J. Arsenault and Tom Ellis, elbowing each other behind their own bench.

'What?' she said. They shrugged, so she went back to her slides. Dust mites. Gross.

Whispering. A high-pitched giggle from the side of the room. When she looked, Denise Mullins had her hand over her mouth and she was looking at her. Denise's partner Jodi was looking at her too. In fact, everyone was looking at her.

It was at that point that she stepped backwards and she felt the warmth between her legs and she knew. Lou froze, not knowing whether she should run out of the room or raise her hand and ask to be excused and the bell was about to ring so everyone in the hallway would see her anyway and before school ended it would be the whole grade, the whole school, who knew. Her lower belly cramped with sharp pain. She turned around, backing up against the bench so no one could see the back of her shorts, and then Benny was there beside her.

'Here,' he said, shoving his sweatshirt at her. 'Wear this.'

The bell rang and the other students crowded out of the room while Lou averted her eyes and shoved her arms into Benny's sweatshirt. Although he wasn't much taller than her, his sweatshirt was big and it hung down over her backside, hiding the stain. In her confusion, she realised she'd forgotten to thank Benny but when she looked up, he was gone and the room was empty except for Mr O'Leary who was grading papers at his desk.

Knowing that everyone would be talking about her, wishing desperately that Allie was here to help, she grabbed her stuff and ran to the bathroom where she stuffed her underwear with a huge wad of toilet paper. The thought of asking anyone to borrow a pad was too embarrassing, especially when she heard two of the other girls talking about her as they washed their hands.

She was late to English, which was the last class of the day. She huddled inside the big sweatshirt, feeling like she was wearing a diaper, afraid she was going to leak through the toilet paper. She felt everyone looking at her. Benny wasn't in this class but with his sweatshirt zipped up to her neck, she could smell him, which was weird because she hadn't noticed that he had his own scent before. There was a trace of sweat, mint from gum, a piney scent of deodorant or something. It was strange but a bit comforting, even though it was way too hot to wear a sweatshirt in May, and she buried her nose in the collar as she tried to concentrate on *Death of a Salesman.*

When class ended, she lingered behind, pretending to take a long time packing her stuff. She didn't want to have to see anyone outside. When it was pretty much quiet, she went to the bathroom again and changed the wad of toilet paper for a fresh one. By now the cramps had settled in and they were less a sharp pain than a constant digging at her insides.

To her surprise, Benny was waiting for her outside the school. He was leaning against the wall, arms crossed on his chest, but he straightened when she emerged.

'Oh,' Lou said, confused. He never waited for her. She and Allie always walked home together, but Benny hadn't walked with them since they were in elementary school. He usually had practice, or he walked with some of the boys. 'Do you want your sweatshirt back?'

'Nah,' he said. He walked over to her, arms still crossed almost like he was angry, but his face didn't look angry. 'You can keep it till tomorrow.'

'Oh, OK. Thanks.'

Outside it was hotter, but she kept the sweatshirt zipped up as they started in the direction of home. There wasn't anyone else around. After a few minutes of walking in silence, Lou said again, 'Thanks.'

Benny shrugged. 'No problem. Not a big deal.'

'It was a big deal to me.'

'Everyone will have forgotten about it tomorrow.'

'Yeah, maybe.' But people still talked about Georgia Bigelow's bikini top falling off in the Pond last summer, so Lou wasn't so sure.

As they walked, she glanced at him. It was sort of a revelation to know that Benny had his own scent and to be wearing his sweatshirt. He was broader than her; the sweatshirt hung off her shoulders and dangled from the ends of her hands. Benny wasn't exactly the person she'd expect to be her knight in shining armour – he treated her like he did his sister, which was to say he teased her, stole her stuff, copied her homework, drew rude cartoons in her notebook, occasionally gave her a noogie. And he had no problem making fun of other people. He was the one who'd told her and Allie about Georgia's bikini top. But he'd seen what she needed today and given it to her right away, when she hadn't even known what to do.

She didn't often look at Benny, because she'd known him pretty much since the day that she was born, but she looked at him now as they walked in silence together. He was growing up, too. Turning into a man. The signs were maybe not as visible on him as the red stain on the back of her shorts, but they were there inside him. His dark hair was thick and stood up; his jaw was angular and he had long dark lashes on his eyes. Allie sometimes said it was unfair that he had better eyelashes than she did. He had definite muscles in his arms.

He was wearing a short-sleeved T-shirt and she could see, now that his arms were by his side, the marks on his upper left arm above the elbow. They were black and red, fresh bruises. 'What happened to your arm?' she asked.

He crossed his arms immediately again, hiding the bruises. 'Nothing.'

He'd said it too quickly. And he'd been wearing this long-sleeved sweatshirt on a hot day. She stopped walking. 'Did you get in a fight or something? I won't tell.'

'Nah just horsing around.'

He was lying. For all his goofing off, Benny was a proud person. He was a sports star and he liked it. If he'd been beaten in a fight, he wouldn't want anyone to know. She was tempted to ask him more, to find out if he was in some kind of trouble. But when he'd helped her today he hadn't asked her any questions, and she'd been relieved about that.

'OK,' she said, and he shot her a look of gratitude which made her think she'd done the right thing. It wasn't until much later that she found out how wrong she'd been.

Louise

When she opens the door Allie is standing there. She's wearing slacks and a blouse and an expression that Lou can't quite read.

'I thought I'd pop in and see how your mom is doing,' she says.

Lou refrains from saying anything about having not made an appointment. She steps back to let Allie in. She's wearing a lemony perfume. 'Go on through.'

Allie goes into the dining room and Lou hovers in the doorway. Her mom's asleep. 'The nurse was in this morning,' she says, since Allie seems disinclined to shout at her.

Allie gently takes her mother's wrist and checks her pulse. 'How is the nurse working out? Who's with you?'

'It's Fiona. She's very kind. She helps a lot with the harder stuff like washing and getting the bed changed. And even with the PCA thing, the idea of morphine is a little scary to me, so I'm glad she's helping. I wish my dad would let her stay overnight. I don't think he's sleeping much.'

Allie glances at the recliner and its blankets. 'I'm sure he isn't. You should advise him to see his doctor for a check-up, too. These end-of-life situations can take their toll on the carers' health.' She touches Peggy's face with feather touches, gently lifts the bottom of the blanket to look at and touch her feet. 'How are *you* feeling?'

'Me? I'm fine.'

'As if you'd tell me if you weren't.'

'Mrs Deannis was ready to give us both a detention in that supermarket parking lot.'

At that, Allie smiles. Only a little, but it's there. She smooths the blankets down over Peggy. 'Can we talk?'

'I'll make coffee.'

Lou's nervous as she fills the coffee maker, spoons grounds into the filter. She's not in the mood for another confrontation. Being here in Casablanca makes her feel raw and on edge. Things have been less tense between her and Mom since Lou did her hair, but they're far from reconciled. Let alone the fact that her mother is clearly dying, worse every day. She eats nothing.

Lou gets down cups and pours milk into one of her mom's nice jugs. When they were little she and Allie used to beg Peggy for permission to have tea parties with the good tea set. It all looks so seventies now with its orange and brown flowers.

'I'm going to keep your mom's medication where it is right now,' Allie says, 'but if there's any change at all, or if you feel they're not working for her, please call me right away. It's a delicate balance, to allow her to be alert and yet not in any pain.'

Lou nods. 'Do you pay house calls on all your patients?'

'I'd like to, but the truth is that most of my time has to be taken up with treating patients who might recover. Palliative care is really important, which is why we have specialist nurses. And the families have to do a lot of work. Families and friends.' She sits at the table. 'I remember my own mother's death. Your mom spent a lot of time with her. It made it easier.'

'They were best friends, ever since they were kids.'

'Yeah.'

What to say after that? Lou pours two cups of coffee and puts the sugar bowl on the table next to Allie's elbow.

'I gave up sugar in med school.' Allie wraps her hand around the mug. 'Listen, Lou, I was a bitch. You tried to apologise and I yelled at you. Don't get me wrong – it felt good to yell at you.

But then I got in my car and they were playing "You Can't Hurry Love".'

Allie's CD player in their basement, jumping up and down on the sagging plaid sofa bed, singing into hairbrushes.

'The Supremes or Phil Collins?' asks Lou.

'Phil Collins.'

'Ah.'

'I was still mad, but it hit me. You were my best friend. You knew me better than anyone. I had friends in college, in med school, but they weren't like that.'

'No,' agrees Lou, not because she knows what Allie's friends are like but because she knows what hers have been like, and none of them have ever come close.

'My mom's gone, and my dad, and there's no one alive who knows me like you do, except Benny. But I've never been close to Benny in the same way that I was to you. And Benny's ... well, he's not the same as he was. The older I get ...'

'... The more I realise how special that friendship was,' Lou finishes for her, thinking of all the things she's done without Allie. Pregnancy, childbirth, life with a toddler. First dates, her degree, decorating her apartment. Every single milestone in her life, she's wished Allie was there. 'I ruined it. I know. That's what I was trying to say the other day. I'm sorry. I should've written to you or something. But I couldn't.'

She still doesn't think she can explain her reasons. Not right this very minute. Maybe after this coffee. Maybe after another thirteen years or so. She could do with a shot of whiskey, but that's not a good idea when she's the sole adult in charge of a dying woman. So instead of liquid courage, she says, 'So has the power of Phil Collins saved our friendship?'

Allie laughs. She has a lovely laugh, deep-voiced, and it's just as Lou remembers it.

'Maybe not exactly. But he'd want us to talk.'

'Good thing it wasn't The Supremes' version.'

'I'm pretty sure Diana Ross would want us to talk, too.'

It's Lou's turn to laugh. It feels good.

'So.'

'So.'

'What have you been doing for the past thirteen years?'

Allie runs her thumb over the handle of her mug. 'Med school, mostly. Then residency. I was lucky to get to do some of it up here in Portland, so I could see Mom.'

'Are you married? Do you have kids?'

'Honey, I haven't had time to do much more than occasionally screw another med student. It's slim pickings up here in Casablanca. And … my job is important. I didn't want any distractions. I graduated debt-free, thanks to Benny. I didn't want to let him down.'

'He paid for your med school?' The coffee leaves a bad taste in her mouth. Benny the saint.

'When Dad had the heart attack, Benny sort of … took over looking after me and Mom. He was still playing baseball then, so he had money to burn, but he didn't have to spend it on us. He chose to, and I won't forget that. So – what about you?'

'One kid. Dana. She's great.'

'Her dad?'

'Isn't in the picture.' She gets up to pour more coffee, even though her cup is still nearly full.

'So are you married? Boyfriend?'

'I'm single. My last partner was a woman called Megan, but we split up. She had to go back to Ireland and it fizzled out.'

'Oh – I'm sorry. I thought … when I knew you, you always liked boys.'

'I like men *and* women.' More coffee in her cup, in Allie's. In Brooklyn, she's unafraid to talk about her sexuality, but Casablanca is a whole different place. This is her childhood friend, her childhood home. Her mother could wake up and hear. She sneaks a glance at Allie's face; her cheeks are a little pink, but she's not avoiding Lou's eyes. 'It's the person who counts, not their gender.'

'Neither one of us has met the right person yet,' Allie says. 'Isn't that funny? Both of us were sure we'd be married by thirty.'

'You wanted twins.'

'At least you made it to New York.'

'Yeah. I teach junior-high English.'

'You wanted to write books.'

Lou sits back down and shrugs. 'Hard to write books when you're getting a teaching qualification and then working full-time while being a single mom.'

'You don't write at all?'

'I can hardly call it a book. It's a collection of notebooks I keep under the bed.'

'What's it about?'

She takes a deep breath. 'It's based on a true story. Did you ever hear of Gill Lafayette?'

'No.'

'Gill was born in New Brunswick in the 1850s as a girl. Her whole family died and she needed money. Her dad had been a mule driver so Gill dressed in men's clothes and went down to Maine and worked the logging camps as a teamster. Around here, up the Pennacook.'

'No way.'

'It's fascinating. I've wanted to write about Gill for ages. It was such dangerous work, with horses and massive logs, outside all the time. People got sick, they got crushed, they lost limbs. They lived out in the woods, far from civilisation, for months and months.'

'What happened to her?'

'Her … him … they. No one knows how Gill thought of themselves, so they might have been a trans man, though that concept didn't really exist then. Or a woman wearing a man's clothes to work in a man's world. They drove logs. And then they became a stagecoach driver later. And when they died, at age sixty-four, it was discovered that Gill had been born a woman and had given birth at some point.'

'Did Gill ever get married?'

'No.'

'So that's what your book is about?'

'Sort of. I'm not sure … Gill is a fascinating person but nothing really happens. I keep writing bits but I can't find my way into it.' Lou hasn't told anyone this. It's her turn to have flushed cheeks. 'Anyway. I might finish it one day. Maybe when Dana's in high school.'

'It sounds amazing. You were such a good writer.'

'Key word being "were".'

Allie rubs at a bit of coffee on the tablecloth. 'It's funny, isn't it, how we all got our dreams, but in a different way than we thought. I'm a doctor, but I'm still here. You moved to New York and wrote a book, but it's still under your bed. And Benny played for the Red Sox, but then he got injured and now he's … well …'

'Now he's what?' she asks despite herself.

'Didn't you see it?'

'I don't watch baseball.' Understatement. For a while she left the room when it was on TV, couldn't go into a bar with it playing. It's better now. 'My dad said he had an accident and had to retire,' she adds.

'Got hit by a line drive. We thought he'd been killed. He was in a coma for nearly a month.' Allie takes a long drink of coffee. 'Anyway, he's got his place up at Morocco Pond now. That's one reason why I took the job here at the hospital, so I could be near him.'

'He's *here*?' She could run into him, in the supermarket, on the street, in Rick's Diner? Lou catches herself. 'I mean – I didn't know that.'

'I didn't really expect him to come back after our mother died, to be honest. But I think he felt safer here.'

Safer.

When she first saw Allie again, she thought that maybe Allie knew what had happened between her and Benny and that Allie blamed her. But now, hearing the way she talks about her twin, Lou is certain that Allie doesn't know anything. Allie doesn't know what kind of person Benny is. The things that Benny has done.

Lou gets up. She isn't quite sure what to do with her hands.

'Are you OK?'

'I thought I heard Mom stirring. I'll be right back.'

Mom's room is quiet. A fan blows cool air. A bar of sunlight shines across Peggy's chest and it'll be on her face soon. Lou lowers the blinds. Her mom's sleeping with her mouth open, something Lou never remembers her doing before she was sick. There's a plastic cup of water with a straw in it beside the bed; her mother was having trouble sitting up enough to drink last night. Soon, she won't be able to drink at all, or use the bedpan, and unless they want thirst to claim her before the cancer does, they'll have to pump more saline into her along with the drugs and run a catheter line into her body. Invading her to keep her alive so she can die.

A soft hand on her shoulder makes her jump.

'Hey,' says Allie quietly, beside her. 'Lou, I'm sorry. I shouldn't have been talking about comas and almost dying. It's a hard subject for you.'

Lou nods.

'I'm glad we talked, though,' says Allie. 'I've missed you.'

'I've missed you too. A lot.'

'Are we friends again?'

Lou nods again. She puts her hand over Allie's on her shoulder and squeezes it.

She's going to have to tell her what happened.

That night when everyone is asleep she opens her laptop and Googles it. *Benny Phelps Red Sox accident*. There are a bunch of links and a YouTube clip. She turns off the sound and clicks on the video.

It's the TV broadcast of the game, but the picture has been cropped so that the screen only shows Benny. He's in his white Red Sox uniform with the blue cap and even though the quality is blurry because it's been edited, Lou would know him anywhere. That cock of the hip as he stands, the same as when he was a kid on the field. She can't see any other players but he's looking forward, presumably at the batter, and then his attention is suddenly distracted by something. He's playing shortstop, so maybe a player is stealing second, but Benny turns his head to the left and then the ball comes into shot. It's only a white blur.

The clip goes to slow motion, and the ball's still a blur, but Benny isn't. Mid-air, glove dangling, legs almost balletic. His hat hangs for an instant in the place where his head was. Then he lands on his side on the green grass, limbs splayed. He looks dead, his hat a good ten feet in front of him, the ball rolling, harmless now, red on one side with blood.

The clip ends. She clicks it again.

Louis

Carrie drives all the way up from New York in her Audi, even though she's only planning to stay one night. She beeps her horn several times as she pulls into the driveway and Lou, sitting upstairs watching the news with his mom, pulls aside the curtain to look.

He goes out to greet her, but when she gets out of the car she doesn't even say hello. She opens the back door and a bundle of fox-coloured fluff comes leaping out and tries its best to jump high enough to reach Lou's face and lick it.

'Hello, Mulder,' he laughs, kneeling so the dog can greet him properly by climbing onto his lap and licking his face all over. He sinks his fingers into the dog's thick fur and breathes in his familiar dog scent. He hasn't seen Mulder in six weeks. 'I missed you too, buddy.'

'He's been pining,' says Carrie. 'Fortunately I'm not the sensitive type, or I'd be bothered that you've greeted him first.'

'He hijacked me,' he says, but he stands up and wipes his face. She's wearing sunglasses and lipstick, looking great as always, and he's not quite sure how to greet her. He left her six weeks ago with a kiss on the lips, almost automatic, but their separation has become so much more separate since then. She settles it by kissing him on the cheek and then wiping away the lipstick mark.

'It's all your stuff in the trunk of the car,' she tells him. 'I've got everything I need in my purse. Where's your mom?'

'Upstairs in her room.'

'Do you have any booze?'

'Red or white.'

'Pour me a glass of red – I forgot how bad this town smells.' She goes inside the house.

Mulder frisks around his legs as Lou takes a couple of suitcases out of the trunk of the car. They're heavy, and Lou wonders if Carrie has taken this chance to get rid of some of his stuff. Then he thinks, *Stop it, she's driven all the way up here to see Mom and bring the dog. This has nothing to do with our breakup.*

Mulder barks. 'OK, hold on, boy, I'll pay you some more attention when I've got these inside,' Lou says, glancing down at him, and he sees the pink rhinestone-studded collar. He crouches to peer at the name tag. *Fifi.*

'Carrie,' he mutters, not without a smile, and carries the suitcases inside the house. Mulder sticks close to his heels. He's a rescue, a mysterious mix of breeds and a year old when Lou adopted him. He dislikes being left alone. Which is fine for a writer's dog, but while Lou's been on the road and up here, Mulder has had to spend his days in the apartment while Carrie's at work. Lou predicts a few days of having a furry ginger shadow.

Up in his room he opens one of the suitcases. As he suspected from its weight, it's full of well-read paperbacks. Carrie's chosen his favourites, though, which makes him think her motivation was more kindness than getting some clear shelf space. (She probably wanted some clear shelf space, too.) Mulder's regular collar is on the top and Lou replaces the pink rhinestone one. Not that a dog's masculinity is going to be threatened by a pink collar, but his own … well, he doesn't really want to think about the nuances of that one. Sometimes it's easier just to blend in with what people expect.

By the time he's gone downstairs and poured a large glass of Malbec, and then taken it back upstairs, his mother and his wife (ex-wife? Is she, already, if all they've done is agree?) are chatting. He can hear their voices as he comes up the stairs.

Carrie has pushed her sunglasses to the top of her head and is holding up a pink lipstick so his mother can examine the colour. 'Try it, here let me,' she says, and leans forward to smooth it over Peggy's lips. 'Look, it suits you.' She puts her ever-present phone on selfie mode and gives it to Peggy so she can use it as a mirror.

'It's pretty,' says Peggy, pursing lips, and Lou has a sudden childhood memory of a time in this very room when Peggy caught him playing with her make-up, and she took a pink lipstick out of his hands and shooed him away.

'I'll send you some,' says Carrie to Peggy.

'There's probably no point.'

'Oh don't be silly. I get so many samples for work, and just because you're dying it doesn't mean that you can't look good doing it. What do they say – "Live fast and leave a good-looking corpse"? I've got some tinted moisturiser and blusher for you too.'

Mulder jumps on the bed and scampers up, intent on licking Peggy's face. Glass of wine still in hand, Lou swoops in. 'Mulder, no! Off!'

Carrie grabs the glass of wine before he can spill it. Mulder pauses, alarmed, paws on Peggy's chest.

'Sorry, Mom,' says Lou, scooping him up. 'I'll keep him off the furniture.'

'You didn't bring a glass for your mother?' asks Carrie, taking a sip as if she hasn't just saved it from splattering all over the bed.

'Mom's on a lot of meds.'

'Do you want one, Peggy?'

Peggy considers. 'Do you know... I think I do?'

'You do? Is that OK? Maybe we should call Allie.'

'For goodness' sake she's dying, Louis; it's not going to make very much difference is it?'

'I... suppose not.' Dog tucked under one arm, he trots downstairs to get two more glasses of wine. Small ones.

Carrie and his mother have always got along. Although they are radically different in many ways, they seem to speak a common feminine language. Sometimes he wonders if he married Carrie partly because she's so different from anyone he knew in Casablanca – someone who not only reads those glossy alien magazines that CPC used to make the paper for, but who *works* for them – and yet she's still the kind of woman his mother likes. Of course that's ridiculous: he married Carrie because he liked her – loved her – and he was attracted to her, and they both thought it was a good idea at the time. He still likes her. His mother never came into it. And yet, aren't the foundations for these preferences and choices laid down from the moment we're born?

His mother only drinks a single sip of wine before she puts the glass down on her bedside table. Carrie is telling a story about some of her work colleagues and Peggy is listening, but Lou can tell that she's tired already. He checks his watch: it's time for today's nurse visit, and as if summoned by his thought, he hears a knock on the door downstairs before it opens and Allie calls out, 'Hi, anybody home?'

'Up here,' he calls, though of course the question, like the knock on the door, are both formalities. Allie knows where the spare key is hidden and has full authority to enter the house at any time. He's been asleep on the sofa downstairs and she's walked past him on quiet rubber soles without waking him. The only way he knows she's been there sometimes are the signs that his mother has been quietly tended.

'Hi,' says Allie, popping her head in before entering the room. Her scrubs are clean and pressed, as usual, her hair pulled back in a no-nonsense ponytail. 'Wow – wine and a dog. Have I walked in on a party?'

'This is Carrie,' says Peggy. 'Lou's wife.'

Allie casts a swift glance from Carrie to Lou, and then back to Carrie. 'Nice to meet you,' she says, holding out her hand to shake, but Lou's seen her moment of surprise, and he's sure Carrie didn't miss it either. But all Carrie says is, 'You too.'

'And this is Mulder,' says Lou.

'I'll shake his hand later,' says Allie. 'How are you feeling, Peggy?'

'Tired,' says Peggy. 'I can't socialise as much as I used to.'

'I'll be staying for a little while, so if you want to have dinner, go ahead and get something to eat,' says Allie to Lou and Carrie. 'It's chicken pot pie night at Rick's. Best in town.'

Lou takes the hint and ushers both Carrie and Mulder out of the bedroom to let Allie do her work.

'You haven't told your mother that we're splitting up?'

They're ensconced in a back booth in Rick's Diner, which is nearly full. Chicken pot pie night is popular, apparently. Lou's ordered it ('100 per cent clear meat chicken, home-made'), along with a side of onion rings, but Carrie has ordered the soup, no roll. Rick's doesn't serve alcohol so they've both got coffee. Lou hasn't been in Rick's for over a decade. It's had a bit of a makeover – the vinyl in the booths is brand new and vibrant orange – but he could still recognise it in his sleep. And the onion rings are still the best he's ever tasted.

'I think she's got enough on her mind,' says Lou.

'Is that the reason? Or are you having second thoughts?'

'I . . . have second thoughts about everything. Parents dying tends to do that to you.'

'But not about getting back together.'

He shakes his head.

'If I suggested it, though,' Carrie says, 'you'd go along with it to keep the peace.'

Carrie is probably right, as usual. Mom dying is enough change for his world at the moment. But he says, 'No. We're better as friends.'

'We won't *be* friends if we stay married. There's only so much indifference I can take.'

'I'm not indifferent to you.'

'You're distant. You always have been.'

'I don't mean to be.'

'You have such a hard time letting go that it's easier for you never to attach in the first place.' She spoons up soup. 'Small-town boy, trying to shake off the small-town boots. You always keep a part of yourself back. You've never talked about this diner, for example, even though it's clear you've been here a million times. You never talk about your childhood at all. The books you read, yeah. The films you saw, the music you listened to. But where you grew up – never.'

'It's . . . easier. It's not because of you.'

'I don't take it personally.' Carrie shrugs. 'Or, at least I try not to.'

He looks at her and wonders if there was a moment where their marriage went wrong, or whether the seeds of their split were always there. Maybe she's right; maybe he can't attach. 'It's really not your fault, Carrie. You understand me better than just about anyone.'

'Yeah. But it would be nice not to have to do all the work myself, you know? Imagine how I felt when I read your book. Here I am married to this quiet guy, normal guy, and BOOM. He's written this huge epic tragic love story set in the Maine woods, the most emotional thing I've ever read, and I had to learn with the rest of the world that my husband was a romantic.'

'I'm sorry.'

'It is what it is.'

One of Carrie's favourite expressions, and one that he's never quite been able to see eye to eye with, because so often, in his experience, things rarely simply *are*. Truth is mutable depending on what point of view you use. They've had arguments about this and it's not worth going into now. Instead he says, 'Are you… have you found someone else?'

'Not worth mentioning.' He knows this means that she has. 'How's the chicken pot pie?'

'The onion rings are better.'

'I would never knowingly eat an onion ring. Let me taste the pie.'

He offers her his plate, and she digs in with her spoon. 'I thought splitting up with you meant I'm not obliged to share half my meal when you under-order in restaurants.'

'You will always have to share half your meal with me. Marriage can end, but food-sharing is a lifelong commitment.' She chews. 'Not bad. Not bad at all.'

'You'll have to order it next time you're here on Chicken Pot Pie Night.'

'Aside from your mother's funeral, I never intend to come back to this smelly town in my life.'

'I honestly don't notice the smell,' he says, and it's true. He noticed it for the first day or two, and then the Casablanca paper mill smell receded into the background, less noticeable than the green lawns or pine trees or the wide river reflecting the sky. It was simply there, like it was there every day of his life until the summer he was eighteen, when he exchanged it for New York traffic fumes and hot dog stands and drains and hot concrete.

Carrie smiles in pity. She spoons up some more of his pot pie. 'So this Allie – she's an old girlfriend, isn't she?'

He nearly coughs up his own bite of pie. 'Um… a long time ago.'

This time her smile isn't pitying at all. 'Still like her?'

'I… it was a long time ago, Carrie. Like I said.'

'I'm glad you still like her. I was beginning to wonder if the reason why you never opened up to me was because really you were gay.'

Old habits die hard; he glances around Rick's Diner to make

sure no one is listening in before he replies, in a quieter tone. 'Carrie, you and I only met because I'd hooked up with your housemate the night before.'

'Yeah, I know, but I thought that was just you experimenting.'

'It was me enjoying myself. I don't really care about gender, it's the person. I've told you this before.'

'Now that we're split up, are you going to date a man next, or a woman?'

'I don't know. I don't want to date anyone right now. Would it matter?'

'Maybe I hoped that I'd changed you a bit.' She drops her spoon on the plate and sits back in the banquette.

'You've changed me in lots of ways.' She doesn't look convinced, and so he says, 'Look. When I first got to New York, there were lots of things I could do that I couldn't do here. This is a small town and back then, people were narrow-minded. That doesn't mean I was experimenting; it means I was being myself.'

'When you were sleeping with men, you didn't have to deal with any messy emotion, you mean. Hook up and fuck. Don't forget the condom.'

'That's a stereotype.'

'But it was true for the men you chose.'

'I . . .' He owes it to her to be truthful. Because those first years in college in New York – the clubs, the bars – were liberating, exciting, a straightforward transaction of pleasure which was unlike anything he'd ever known, a raw shameless truth about what he wanted. But it was human contact without human consequences, and he was tired of it by that morning when, hungover and dressed in his clothes from the night before, he met Carrie in her own kitchen.

'Yes,' he admits. 'Whenever I started liking anyone, I broke it off. I had fun for a while, but I wasn't happy. You made me happier, Carrie. I liked being with you. That's all there is to it, nothing about gay or straight or whatever.'

'And I wanted more than that. So here we are.' There are tears in her eyes now. She flips down her sunglasses. 'God, is there a bar in this town? Let's go get drunk.'

'I don't think I can be drunk in charge of my mother. I'll take you to a bar, though.'

'Forget it. I'll drink the rest of the wine in your mom's house and pass out in the guest room.'

He reaches across the table and touches her hand. 'I really am sorry, Carrie. I wish I could be someone else for you.'

'It is what it is.' But she lets her hand linger for a moment under his. Neither one of them is wearing their wedding ring.

'Thank you for coming up here and seeing Mom and bringing Mulder and talking with me. I'm glad you're here.'

She nods and stands up. 'Wine, Louis, now. Before we end up staying here until Meatloaf Night.'

He stands too. 'By the way… Fifi?'

Carrie just smiles.

That night in his childhood bedroom, with his wife (still his wife), asleep two doors down, Lou dreams about Benny. Sometimes when he dreams about Benny it's a nightmare: ghosts and shadows, an explosion and an endless scream. This dream is different. It's a memory that's been rehearsed again and again until it has the texture of a much-laundered T-shirt.

He's fifteen and he's sleeping over at Benny's house. He's been going out with Allie for over a year but when he sleeps over at the Phelps's, he's always Benny's guest and not allowed in Allie's room unless they keep the door open. Benny and Lou sleep in the finished basement, because Benny's bedroom is too small for both of them to fit. The basement has been turned into a rec room with a stereo and a TV and a PlayStation in the middle, but the plaid-upholstered sofa pulls out into a bed so the family use it as a guest room when relatives like Benny and Allie's cousins from Connecticut come to stay from out of town. The concrete walls have been covered up in pine panelling that Mr Phelps nailed in place and varnished himself, and the concrete floor has brown carpet tiles on it. There are two pictures on the walls: a framed collage of photos of Benny and Allie when they were babies, and an inspirational quote about Jesus' footprints on a picture of a beach. Connect Four, Life, Monopoly, Trivial Pursuit are stacked on a shelf. Most of the boxes are held together with tape. A couple of small windows sit high up in the walls. There aren't any curtains on them, so in the morning the sun shines right in. Benny can sleep through anything, but Lou is always woken up at six o'clock with the sun in his face. He doesn't mind, though. He likes lying here in a quiet house that isn't his own, listening to Benny breathe, thinking about Allie sleeping upstairs in her own bed.

Other than the stuff in the middle of the basement that everyone uses, the rec room is split strictly into gender lines: on the far side, away from the stairs, is a little sewing area for Mrs Phelps, with her sewing machine and her boxes of fabric and thread and stuff. She's got a dressmaker's dummy on a pole and sometimes, when they're watching TV on the couch together and Lou and Allie are cuddling, Benny will get the dummy and pretend that it's his date. He'll offer it popcorn – though it doesn't have a head – or pretend to cop a feel of its unyielding breast. Sometimes Allie dresses it up in silly costumes made of her mother's sewing supplies: loops of lace, a plethora of zippers. For a reason Lou doesn't quite fathom, she calls it 'Mo'.

On the other side, closer to the stairs, is Mr Phelps's gun cabinet. It's made of green metal and it has a combination lock. You're supposed to keep a gun cabinet locked, but Mr Phelps doesn't always bother to shut it and spin the combination dials. He's got a dozen guns in there: rifles for hunting, pistols for shooting practice, a handgun for self-defence. There's the rifle he taught Lou and Benny to load, though Lou can't tell it apart from the other ones; his memory of that day is mostly of astonishment and unease. It was an experience that was never repeated. Mr Phelps has got a couple of antique rifles too, one dating back all the way to 1900, which has been handed down from father to son for generations. One day it'll be Benny's.

Mr Phelps takes Benny hunting with him. Lou's glad that his dad says he can't go too. They hunt ducks, deer, moose when Mr Phelps can get a licence for one. They nearly always shoot something and there's a guy who lives out on Route 27 who'll butcher your game for you, wrap it in neat waxed paper and plastic packages that nestle in the chest freezer which is also in the basement, underneath the stairs. The packages are labelled: Deer steaks. Duck breast. Mooseburger. Rabbit. Lou's never eaten game at his own house – they stick with chicken and hamburger, normal food – and when he eats dinner here, he doesn't really ask what he's eating.

With the TV off and everyone upstairs already in bed, the only sound in the basement (and in Lou's dream) is the hum of the chest freezer full of dead animals. He and Benny have pushed the coffee table aside – it's still covered in half-empty bags of Doritos and cans of Coke – and laid their sleeping bags out side by side in the middle of the room. Lou lies in his sleeping bag, drowsing off, thinking about the movie they've just watched for the fifth time and what a shame it is that there aren't many opportunities to say 'Yippee-ki-yay, motherfucker' in real life.

A stealthy noise from the sleeping bag next to him. Small and rhythmic. A hitch of breath. Lou, half-asleep until now, is awake. He opens his eyes; Benny is a shadow next to him, a few inches away. Lou can't see a thing but he knows what that sound means.

Lou's hot, suddenly, too hot in his sleeping bag. He doesn't breathe. He closes his eyes in case Benny sees he's awake, and he listens.

Benny's holding his breath now too, and the movements are a little freer, a little louder. Shifting of material, a furtive rubbing.

Lou pictures him. Right hand snuck under the elastic waistband of his boxers, curled around himself. He's never seen Benny do this before, never seen anyone do this before, but he knows what he does himself in his own bed, in the shower, a few times in the school toilets, and he knows the grip and shift and friction, the tight O of finger and thumb, sweaty heat of palm.

Lou's hard. Slowly, so as not to make a noise, he slides his own hand downwards, inside his own waistband. He holds himself. Doesn't dare to move. Breathes soft and even, as if he's asleep. He wonders what Benny's cock looks like erect. They've been naked together plenty of times – their whole life, changing rooms and showers, swimming and sleepovers – and he's taken furtive looks. He knows the dark hair, the curve of his soft dick, but how does it fill Benny's hand? Is he bigger or smaller than Lou? How does the skin feel under his fingers, stretched tight over a hard core, a swell at the tip? What's his colour, his smell?

He squeezes and breathes and the movements beside him stop. Lou also stops, eyes wide.

'I hope you're not thinking about my sister,' says Benny.

'No.' He whispers it. 'I'm not.'

'Don't.'

'OK.'

Benny starts again first. He's not furtive now; Lou can hear him moving quickly, almost as if he wants to get this over with. Lou doesn't want to get this over with. He listens and closes his eyes so Benny doesn't know in the darkness that Lou wants to watch him, and he matches Benny's rhythm. Short and fast, urgent.

Benny takes a sharp breath and that's it, that's all the noise he makes, but Lou knows what it means. Lou releases a moan like a cough, and he rolls so he's on his side and his face is pressed into Benny's bare shoulder, mouth against his neck. He moans once more, squeezes everything tight and comes into his hand.

His heart races. He can smell Benny's sweat. Lou doesn't open his eyes and Benny doesn't move. Just lets him lie there while his breathing slows down, the hum of the freezer going on like normal.

Lou wakes up in the present with a gasp. His pyjama bottoms are sticky and wet. He sits up, strips them off, rolls them into a ball. Can't take a shower, he'll wake up Carrie.

The next day he and Benny didn't talk about it. Lou woke up first and threw away the two balled-up tissues that were on the floor. He kept thinking about Allie, how she'd be upset, even though he hadn't cheated on her, even though he and Benny had never touched. Except for those few minutes at the end, when Lou touched Benny's naked skin with his face and breath, when Benny let him feel close to him. Lou never talked to Benny about it, and he never talked to Allie about it, either.

He's dreamed about it now because of his conversation with Carrie in the diner. Because of what she said: *When you were sleeping with men, you didn't have to deal with any messy emotion*. Because maybe that was true about the men he slept with in college. But it was never true about Benny, even though they never did anything more than that, even though Benny said all those things before he died. Maybe Lou was trying to erase that moment in his own mind in the months before he met Carrie. Maybe he's been trying to erase it ever since Benny died in that same basement, right in the same spot where he and Lou almost loved each other.

He puts on a new set of pyjamas and falls asleep again, and when he wakes up in the proper morning, Mulder isn't on the blanket Lou put down for him on the floor. Carrie's door is shut tight. He goes into his mother's room to check on her, and Mulder is curled up in a tight, foxy ball at the end of her hospital bed, nose tucked under tail. Peggy is awake with the TV on low. The morning news.

'Oh God, Mom, I'm sorry. Mulder knows he's not supposed

to sleep on beds.' He snaps his fingers and Mulder's ear twitches, but he doesn't move.

'It's all right. He's been keeping me company.' She makes a kissing sound and Mulder lifts his head to look at her. His fluffy tail thumps on the bedspread. 'Animals know when someone's sick. It's an instinct they have. I've often thought I should have got a cat when your father left.'

'He's good company to me. When I'm writing, I mean.'

Peggy nods. 'Will we see Carrie before noon?'

'I'm guessing eleven thirty.'

'And she's going back today?'

'Yeah. She can't get the time off work.' This is a lie, of course.

'Why didn't you tell me you'd split up?' His mom asks the question kindly. 'You've been here two weeks and you haven't mentioned it.'

'I was going to tell you after my book came out, but then ... We didn't want to worry you. How'd you know?'

'Neither one of you is wearing your wedding ring.'

'Sharp eyes, Mom.'

'It's the only sharp thing I've got left, and even that's gone when the drugs kick in.'

Lou sits on the bottom of her bed. Mulder, sleepy, puts his head on Lou's thigh and he scratches behind the dog's ears.

Peggy says, 'I like Carrie. She's not right for you, though. She never put you first. Not like your father and I put each other first.'

He frowns. 'Dad left you to travel. He doesn't even know you're sick. That's not putting you first.'

'Is that what he told you?'

'What else would he tell me?'

Peggy sighs. 'Irving blamed himself for everything. For you leaving Casablanca, for Benny's death. I argued with Mary – didn't speak with her for years, until she got sick. And then he blamed himself for her sickness, too. He thought it was pollution and her grief that did it.'

'Why would Dad blame himself for Benny's death?'

'Because of the mill and the way it split up the town.'

'But Dad didn't own the mill then. As soon as he did, he sold it.'

'He still felt responsible. It was his family who owned it. He felt it was poisoned. He had to get away. Your father's a good man. I knew I couldn't keep him. I knew it as soon as I met him.' She closes her eyes, speaks on another sigh. 'Do you still love Carrie?'

After what his mother's said, Carrie is the last thing on his mind. Which should tell him the answer, really. Instead he says, 'I don't know. Do you still love Dad?'

'I never loved anyone else.' Her thin hand reaches to stroke the dog's head, on Lou's knee. 'I should have got a cat.'

Louise

'Who's *Rick*?' Dana asks as they walk into the diner that time forgot. And not in a good way. The walls are fake wood panelling, the light fixtures orange plastic. The tables are of the same fake wood as the walls and the upholstery on the booths and on the stools at the lunch counter is faded enough that it's hard to tell whether once it matched the orange light fixtures, or if it was always this sort of pukey yellow. 'Is it that guy?' She points to a man with a big gut barely constrained by a white T-shirt, who's working the grill. The whole place smells like the ghost of every French fry that's been fried here, since the fifties at least.

'I don't think there *is* a Rick,' says her mom. Lou is dressed up, or at least more dressed up than she usually is when she's not working: she's wearing a sleeveless blouse with her jeans, she's got her contacts in, and she's put on some make-up and a pair of earrings. All of this seems like way too much effort for this place which is almost empty. Dana is wearing shorts and a T-shirt for soccer practice and she has her boots in her backpack.

'What, no Rick?' asks Dana. 'There isn't even a dead Rick?' Probably rotting somewhere out back.

'I'm pretty sure it means Humphrey Bogart. He was called Rick in the film *Casablanca*.' Mom spots her friend sitting at the back of the room in a booth, and she waves. 'There's Allie, come on.'

When Lou told Dana that they were going to meet her friend Allie for breakfast, she realised she had no idea what gender they were, never mind how they looked or fitted into her mother's life. The Allie who's waiting for them is wearing a yellow summer dress and she's got brown hair tied back in a ponytail and she doesn't really look like a doctor, but who knows what doctors look like on their days off anyway? Like normal people. The person looks up and smiles when they approach her.

'Hi, you must be Dana,' she says, and holds out her hand for Dana to shake, which most people don't do with kids. Dana shakes it and sits down across from her. Her mom sits on the seat next to Allie.

'Is this place hygienic?' she asks Allie because presumably a doctor would know.

'Some dirt is good for you,' says the Allie person. 'As long as you don't eat your food off the floor, I think you'll be fine. Here, I got us some menus.'

Her mom is looking around like this is some sort of museum. 'Holy crap, this place hasn't changed at all.'

'They still have onion rings,' says Allie. 'I eat way too many of them after a night on call. Sometimes for breakfast.'

'Can I have them for breakfast? That's wrong.'

'Nothing's illegal for breakfast.'

'Most important meal of the day, right?'

'Can I have coffee?' asks Dana, partly because she wants to remind her mom she's here, and partly because her mom seems in such a good mood that she might actually say yes.

'No,' says Lou. 'You can have one of my onion rings if you want.'

'Ew.' Dana picks up one of the laminated menus and looks at it. It's so old that the prices have been crossed out and other higher prices written in. 'What's edible here?'

'The blueberry pancakes are recommended,' Allie tells her. 'And the onion rings. As recommended by your mom. Remember that time—'

'—after the all-night yearbook meetings, oh my God. And that time you—'

'—the whole bottle of ketchup—'

'—and the Barbie doll—'

Both of them, two grown women, collapse into giggles. Dana rolls her eyes and puts down the menu. 'Two eggs, sunny side up, and bacon,' she says to the waitress who has approached without the other two noticing. 'And a chocolate milk.'

'Got it, hon,' says the waitress, and then says, 'Good to see you two together again.' She pours coffee into two cups and walks off.

'Hey,' says Dana. 'She didn't take your order.'

'She doesn't need to,' says Allie. 'So, Dana, tell me about yourself.'

Dana shrugs. What's she going to say, when a grown-up asks her that question? 'I like sports.'

'You take after your mom that way. Lou was good at track.'

'And you weren't,' said Lou.

'I only joined because you did. I still can't run half a mile without fainting. Or throwing up.'

'Oh my God remember that time—'

'*Yes.*'

They keep on like this, finishing each other's sentences, talking about shit that happened years and years ago, while the waitress brings them their food (an omelette for Allie, and basically a plate full of onion rings for her mom), and while they eat, and Dana eats her own food – and because her phone isn't working – the only option is to watch them across the table. Her mother never behaves like this. Even when she's teaching a class she's excited about, even when she's dating someone new, which Dana's not supposed to notice because she's too young, but she totally does, she's never seen her mother act like this. She's nervous and yet comfortable, talking fast and laughing a lot, her face constantly moving. Eyes lit up.

Her mother looks *happy*. And Dana realises that this Allie

person knows her mom really, really well. Better than anyone Dana's ever met. She knows all this stuff about Lou from when she was a kid; they have lots of stories. And then there's the things that they're not saying, but that run under everything like a current. This Allie person knows Lou maybe nearly as well as Dana does. In some ways, maybe even better, because even though she's seen the photographs, Dana can't imagine her mom as a teenager or as a skinny kid. This person has seen Lou when she wasn't even really Lou, back in the mysterious days before Dana existed.

The eggs and bacon aren't bad. Pretty good. She steals one of her mom's onion rings, though, and they're nothing special. She answers some questions from Allie about school and the music she likes, but the two adults keep on being drawn back into conversation with each other instead of her, which gives Dana plenty of time to look around the diner. The lunch counter takes up most of one side of the room, although no one's sitting on the stools. The cook is standing behind it scraping down the grill, a bit sadly, as if cooking gives his life meaning and now that there are no more customers he doesn't know what to do with himself. The only other customers are a couple of old ladies, two booths away from them, who are sitting absolutely silent. They look like they've been sitting there since this place opened this morning. Maybe they've been sitting there since this place first opened eighty years ago or whenever. Their coffee cups have lipstick marks.

In Brooklyn, you can't even get a seat at their favourite diner at breakfast time. There are hipsters lined up on the sidewalk waiting to go in. How on earth does this place make enough money to stay open?

Most of the framed photographs on the walls are black and white and of high school sports teams. A big colour photograph hangs near the cash register at the front; she recognises Piss-Pants Phelps in a Boston Red Sox uniform – town hero. Three collection boxes for various causes crowd in front of the cash register: they all look dusty.

Her mom's phone rings and she gets up and goes outside to answer it. As soon as she's gone, Allie pushes her recently refilled coffee cup over to Dana. 'Don't tell your mom.'

'You're trying to curry favour,' says Dana, but she takes a big gulp anyway. 'Mom says it will stunt my growth.'

'As a doctor, I can tell you that's not true. I can tell you that it might give you a bad stomach, heart palpitations, insomnia and coffee breath, but you're not my kid, so none of those are my problem.'

Dana takes another big drink and passes the cup back to Allie before her mother comes back into the restaurant.

'Dad,' she explains, sliding into the booth. 'He needs me to pick up a few things from the supermarket pretty urgently. Do you mind making your way to practice yourself, Dana, and I'll come watch you when I've dropped them off?'

'Ugh, Mom, it's like a mile away, and I don't have my bike.'

'Then I can take you after I've done the shopping for Grandad. You might be a little late but that's OK.'

'I'll take her to practice,' says Allie. 'Then you can join us, Lou.'

'But don't you have stuff to do?'

Allie shrugs. 'Weeding the garden. I haven't done it for two months; it can wait until my next day off.'

'No, there's no need, it's fine, we can—'

'Thanks,' says Dana, before her mother can object any further.

Allie's car is cooler than their car. Though it's not hard to be cooler than their car, to be honest. It's a big four-wheel-drive sports vehicle, and it still smells of new leather. Dana slings her bag into the back, climbs into the high passenger seat and says, 'My mom doesn't like taking help from anyone.'

'I can see that.' Allie buckles her seatbelt and waits for Dana to do the same before she starts the car. 'I don't remember that from when we were younger.'

'You were really good friends?'

'Hardly ever apart. Have you got a friend like that?'

'I... thought I did.'

'But something happened?'

'She got another friend who she likes better than me. I don't even think she misses me.'

'Well, I'm not an expert.' Allie puts the car in gear and pulls out onto Main Street. 'But up till last week, I would've said that any friend who abandons you isn't a good friend in the first place.'

'And now?'

'Well, the verdict's still out. But your mom and I are still friends, so yeah. I guess forgiveness is pretty important.'

Dana grunts. She looks out of the window. Allie's got the car radio tuned to an oldies station, and Dana's listening to the music, not really aware she's going to say anything, until suddenly she does. 'Do you know who my dad is?'

Allie is silent for a minute. Then she says, 'You don't know?'

'I know he was a truck driver. But I've never met him. I just thought you might know.'

'I don't. I'm sorry. I guess I would have been in college when you were born. Your mom didn't tell me anything.'

'OK. Worth asking.'

'Do you want to know him?'

Any other time she's asked this question, she says an immediate No. Why would she want to know someone who never gave a shit about her? But something about Allie and her mom has got her thinking about history. They know exactly where they came from, even though that place is currently a dump. But Dana... she's got a nameless truck driver and grandparents she only sees a couple times a year.

'It might be nice to know something about him,' she admits.

'Have you asked your mom?'

Has she? It seems like this has been a way of life forever. 'I decided when I was a kid that I didn't want to know.'

'Why not?'

Good question. 'Safer, I guess. In case she wouldn't tell me if I asked. But also, we're OK just the two of us.'

'I can see that. Tell me something – does your mom still whistle?'

'Whistle? I don't think so. I don't remember hearing her.'

'Ask her sometime,' says Allie.

It's hardly any distance from the diner to the playing field if you're driving. Allie parks the car and Dana says, 'Well, thanks for the lift.'

'I'll come watch you for a while. I know the coach.'

Jim is already there and they start practising some passes. They've been doing this for ten minutes maybe, fifteen, when Dana glances over her shoulder and sees that her mother's arrived and has parked her car. *Good*, she thinks, because although she doesn't really like to admit it because it makes her sound like a little kid, she likes it when her mom watches her. She likes making her mom proud.

Which is why it's such a surprise when Lou grabs Dana's shoulder out of nowhere, right there on the field, and says, 'We have to leave now.'

Dana stares at her, eyes wide. Lou's face is dead pale. 'What's the matter?'

'You can't be here. You can't do this. Let's go now.'

'But Mom—'

'*Now*, Dana.'

'I've got to tell Coach.'

'*No you do not.*' Lou takes hold of Dana's wrist and begins pulling her off the field.

Frightened, Dana mutters goodbye to the rest of the team, who are all staring at her. Across the field she can see Allie standing with Coach Phelps and they're staring at her, too. Lou is walking rapidly, tugging Dana along.

'What's going on?' she asks her mother, who says nothing, just pulls her to the car.

'We're going home.'

'I've left my bag on the field.'

'We can get it later. Come on.' She opens the driver's door and waits for Dana to get in. Then she gets in, starts the car, and drives off before Dana can even buckle her seatbelt.

Her mother is a different person than the one who was in the diner with them. There's no trace of humour or happiness on her face at all; she's stiff, white, mouth pressed together into a very thin line. She's either so pissed off that she can't talk straight, or she's scared.

'What the *hell*, Mom,' Dana says. 'I was having a practice.'

Lou doesn't say anything.

'Mom, you're scaring me. Is it Nana? Did she …'

For the first time it really hits Dana that Nana is dying, she could be dead, and she feels cold all over.

'Nana's the same,' says Lou, through tense lips. 'It's not Nana.'

'Then Grandad?'

'No. You just – you can't play soccer any more. That's all.'

'*What*?'

'Please, Dana. It's important. It's for your own good. You can still play, but not on that team.'

'What? Why?'

'I can't tell you. Listen, we'll find another team for you to play on, OK.'

Hot anger rushes in to replace the cold fear. 'Mom, there is no other team. This isn't Brooklyn, this is a shit town in Maine. This is it, this is all there is.'

'Then you can't play. I'm sorry, honey.'

'This is the only thing that I like here! It's the only thing that's stopping me from going crazy!'

'It's just – I can't explain. I'm sorry.'

Dana clenches her fists, kicks the footwell with her boots. 'You drag me up here in the middle of nowhere, away from all my friends, pull me out of soccer camp, and then when I make a friend and find something I like, you say I can't do it any more? What are you trying to do, ruin my life?'

'I'm trying to protect you.' Lou's eyes are trained on the road ahead, not looking at Dana.

'Protect me from what? Being happy?'

'I'm sorry.'

'That's all I get? No explanation, just a "you can't do what you like for no reason at all, I'm sorry"?'

'I wish I could explain, but I can't. You're going to have to do what I say. It's not for long.'

'You are such a *fucking bitch*.'

The words seem to echo in the small car. Dana bites her lip. She has never said words like that to her mother before. Half of her expects her mother to fly into a fury, for the sky to fall down, for the car to explode, something. The other half of her is glad she said it.

Lou flinches. She says nothing. She drives the car to Nana and Grandad's house, parks it in the driveway, and turns off the ignition before she speaks quietly.

'I need you to go to your room until you have calmed down enough to apologise for calling me that name.'

'I'm not going to calm down! You don't care what I want. You've hardly spoken to me since we got here. All you care about is that I do what you tell me to.'

'That's not true.'

'You know what? Sometimes I wish I did have a dad. Because then I could get away from you.'

Like the swearing, saying that feels good, in a horrible way. Like squeezing a pimple and making it explode. Dana opens the car door and runs into the house, slamming the door behind her.

*

When Lou comes into the house, Irving is standing in the doorway between the dining room and the kitchen. He's rumpled from dozing in the chair and he has his glasses in his hand. 'What's up?' he asks her. 'Dana just slammed through here like a hurricane.'

'We had a minor disagreement,' she tells him.

'I thought she had soccer practice?'

'She's not playing on that team any more.'

'Oh.' She sees him wanting to ask more and then deciding not to. 'Well, your mother is sleeping now, so I'm going to try to get forty winks.'

'Go ahead upstairs, Dad. I'll sit with her.' Although sitting with her mother is the absolute last thing that Lou wants to do right now. Well, the second-to-last thing. The last thing was seeing Benny Phelps coaching her daughter's soccer team.

'No no, I'm fine here. I think that chair is more comfortable than my bed anyway.' He takes a step into the kitchen, kisses Lou on the forehead, and then shuffles back into the dining room. She hears him grunt softly as he settles into the recliner.

Lou goes upstairs, past what used to be her parents' bedroom to her own bedroom. The door on the end of the corridor, the one to Dana's room, is closed. She imagines it's been slammed with some velocity. What was she thinking, forbidding Dana from doing the one thing that she loved and then demanding an apology from her?

She wasn't thinking at all. Because she can't think, not properly. Lou's heart is hammering, her stomach is acid and she feels like she might throw up or pass out or both. So she goes into her own bedroom and lies down on the bed, fully dressed, shoes still on.

This is the bedroom she slept in growing up. It's been redecorated since she was in high school – the *X-Files* and Jeff Buckley posters are gone, and the walls have been repapered with a tasteful, understated leaf pattern – but this is the same bed, the same walls and ceiling that saw her for her entire life up till eighteen.

This is the room where she came after it happened, leaving

her mother downstairs in her bathrobe with a half-finished cup of chamomile tea and her illusions of everything turning out for the best.

And this is how it's turned out instead.

Lou stifles a sob. What she really wants is to go find Dana and curl up on her bed with her, hold her and apologise and tell her that everything is going to magically work out. That she will sort it out, because she's her mother, and she should be able to protect her from everything bad that might ever happen. Because that's the vow she made to herself, wasn't it, when Dana was born?

That she would protect her, no matter what. Always keep her safe, and always put her first.

Her phone buzzes in her pocket and she pulls it out, glad of the distraction. It's a text from Allie. *Meet me on Big Water Rock?*

The town is full of big rocks, but she knows which one Allie means. She also knows why Allie is texting her.

It would be so much easier right now to pack up Dana and drive back to Brooklyn. So much safer and better for both of them.

Fifteen minutes, she texts back.

In their private childhood geography, Big Water Rock is by the falls.

In high school they learned all about this valley, as if it was important. They learned that these mountains of western Maine, the start of the Appalachians, had been carved by glaciers into smooth rounded shapes. That the glaciers as they retreated further north dug lakes, made valleys, dropped boulders, wore the granite landscape down into something scraped and rocky.

They learned about Casablanca Falls, too, which is the longest single drop of water east of Niagara. How the Anasagunticook tribe used the falls for salmon fishing, how loggers floated cut trees downstream from the camps, how people dammed the water, used the falls to make electricity for the town. It all seemed logical back then: glacier, Native Americans, white people, progress.

Now the falls have no meaning. The Anasagunticook are long gone. The falls don't make electricity; it's cheaper to buy it in. Roads replaced rivers, the mill dumped chemicals into the water and air, the salmon are gone. The water tumbles over boulders, roars and thunders, a noise signifying nothing.

Big Water Rock is a slab of grey and white granite that has veins of quartz and mica running through it so that it sparkles in the sun. It sits next to the water, partly over it, so you can sit on it and dangle your feet above the river. Allie is already there when Lou gets there. Walking here, using the road instead of their childhood trail, Lou realised that Allie might have Benny with her, and she almost turned around. But then she remembered that soccer practice was still probably going on. Still, she's relieved to see that Allie is alone. She's left space beside her to sit.

'Hi,' Lou says. She hesitates to take off her sandals, because what if she wants to leave quickly? But she also doesn't want them falling off her feet into the water, so she slips them off and sits beside Allie.

Allie is watching the water as it falls and foams over the rocks. It's loud here, which is one of the reasons why she and Lou used to come here to talk; no one else can hear what you're saying, even if they're quite close to you. Some days, when the water is high, you get soaked with a fine spray misting up from the falls. In winter, the trees are coated with ice from the spray. But today the water is low.

'Erratics,' Lou says. 'Boulders dropped by glaciers are called erratics.'

'I remember.' Allie keeps looking out at the water.

'I always thought it meant they were mistakes, like errors. But it's from the Latin for "to wander". They're wandering rocks.'

This rock is the same as it always was. All the rocks are the same. She's the one who's wandered. Is still wandering.

'Is my brother Dana's father?' Allie asks her.

She doesn't expect this question so bluntly, but it doesn't surprise her either. It does, however, make her throat thick with dread. 'Did you ask him?'

'Of course I didn't ask him. You might not want him to know. I'm asking *you*.'

'What... what makes you think that he might be?'

'Because Dana told me in the car that she doesn't know who her dad was. Because she's about the right age, and you always had a thing for Benny. Because she's good at sports and has got my Aunt Francine's hair.'

'I don't remember your Aunt Francine.'

Allie shakes her head sharply. 'It doesn't matter. I'm not asking about my Aunt Francine. Did you tell Benny?'

'No.'

Allie hasn't taken her eyes off the waterfall, tumbling and falling. 'Did you tell anyone?'

'No.'

'Don't you think my brother has a right to know? I mean, let alone me, your best friend, who's got a niece. Don't you think Benny would want to know that he has a daughter?'

Lou doesn't answer. Now that it's time to say it, it's too hard. All the words stick in her throat. Allie won't believe her.

But she has to tell her anyway.

Louis & Louise

1997

Maybe if there had never been a strike at the mill that spring and summer, none of this would have ever happened. Maybe Lou's dreams would have come true like they thought they would: the apartment in New York with Allie, the book, the children. Irving would stay in Casablanca with Peggy; the mill wouldn't shut down; Benny would go on to a long and successful career with the Red Sox and retire a rich and happy man with his face on lots of very valuable baseball cards. Maybe Dana wouldn't exist.

But this is useless speculation, anyway: we can't decide that one thing happening controls everything else in our life. Every choice is the result of other choices, which are a result of choices before that. We can't control what bodies we're born with or how people treat us because of them. Maybe the world is similarly out of our control: small forces, large ones, one choice leading to another, a machine of causation beyond understanding.

So, this happened. In April 1997, when Lou was eighteen years old, the workers of the Casablanca Paper Company went on strike. CPC wanted to eliminate overtime to save money. The workers, many of whom depended on the extra income, wanted guaranteed double time on Sundays and holidays, as it had always been. Management said they couldn't afford it. Orders were down and they'd had to make significant investment to reduce the mill's environmental impact. The union's demands grew with their anger, and the company met them all with a flat refusal.

For Lou – for Louis and for Louise – this was all distant noise. Talk about the strike was forbidden at school. Lou was running track meets, studying for finals, thinking about prom, watching movies with Allie, playing sport with Benny. Lou had enough money and always had; Lou lived in a new house on the hill; Lou's great-great-great-grandfather had founded the CPC and his portrait would always hang on the wall of Grandpa Alder's house. Lou had been accepted to college and just had to decide which one to go to: the one in New York City, or the one in Orono, Maine, where Allie was going and where Benny had been given a full baseball scholarship. Irving went to work every day like normal, though he spent more time on the phone with Lou's grandfather, and he seemed to leave most of his dinner on the plate.

Every day the twins' father Donnie Phelps put on his Local 45 T-shirt and his Local 45 baseball hat, doused himself with Avon Skin So Soft to keep away the black flies, and went to stand in front of the gate on a picket line, drinking coffee and passing around boxes of doughnuts and glaring at the members of management in their white shirts and ties, hard hats and pocket protectors, who crossed the line to work every day.

Lou didn't talk about this with Allie or Benny. Instinctively, they all knew that to broach the topic would be to acknowledge a gap between them, a gap which they had successfully ignored for their entire lives and yet was as familiar to them as that rocky landscape that connected their houses. Besides, it would all be over soon.

Everyone said the strike would last for a week. Then two weeks.

On Peggy's birthday, Irving set up the barbecue in the backyard. Mary and Donnie were supposed to come over with the kids to have hamburgers and hot dogs and a cake from the supermarket. But just as Irving was opening the first package of Oscar Mayer Franks, the phone rang. Peggy answered it and came outside ten minutes later, with pink around her eyes.

'They can't come,' she said to Irving. 'Something came up.'

'Something?' said Irving.

'Mary says she's not feeling well. She said maybe we can get together in a couple of weeks.'

Is it still a lie if everyone knows it is? Peggy put the hamburgers in the freezer, where they stayed.

After six weeks of running a skeleton operation, the heads of the mill – Lou's grandfather – hired temporary workers from out of state. The fashion and lifestyle magazines needed paper for their glossy visions of how the world should be, and the mill had to keep producing it or shut for good. The workers came on yellow school buses and wore flannel shirts and baseball caps, just like the striking workers in Maine. Some of them were dark-skinned, some of them were desperate. Police came to stand in front of the striking workers as the temps crossed the picket line, battered by outraged yells. *Scabs. Niggers. Scum.*

Someone threw a bottle. No one, afterwards, said who.

Overnight, chain-link fence went up between the road and the entrance to the mill.

Mémère Yvette Grenier came to the house on Sunday after church. Lou was sent upstairs to do homework, but actually read a book. Escape was that easy, if you were a teenager. Peggy made tea and put out Oreos and Yvette touched neither of them but got to the point. 'You've got to tell your husband to stop this. People are suffering.'

'Irving can't do anything, Ma. He's an engineer.'

'He's the son of the boss.'

'But he's kept himself away from all this. He's not interested in the mill. All he wants to do is his job.'

'That's all your father wants to do, too. And all the other working men in this town.'

'I don't know what to say to you, Ma.'

'Say you're going to fix it! What good is you marrying an Alder if you can't fix it?'

'I married an Alder because I loved him. He's talked to his father, but his father doesn't listen.'

'Call your mother-in-law. That Vi. Tell her to talk to her husband. Say that people are suffering. It's been nearly two months. Some people have savings but lots don't. They don't have enough to put food on the table.'

Peggy's forehead creased. She twisted her fingers together. 'Maybe – maybe there's some way to help people. There's a food bank in town, isn't there? Maybe we can—'

'We don't want charity, we want to work. Is this what marrying him has made you? One of them?'

'Ma, I can't call up my mother-in-law and tell her to tell her husband to end the strike.'

'Why not?'

'Because – because she barely tolerates me as it is.'

'You're afraid of her. So you won't help the people in this town? Your father put clothes on your back your whole life!'

'It wouldn't do any good, Ma. She wouldn't listen to me.'

'Then tell your husband to tell her. She'll listen to her son, he'll listen to his wife.'

'Ma, you don't understand. This isn't something they *want* to do. They don't want to bring the outside workers in. They don't want to keep everyone on strike without pay. They can't afford to do what the union asks for. Orders are down. No one's reading magazines any more. If they give in, pretty soon there won't be a mill at all.'

Yvette's face hardened. She looked like her daughter, but battered and wrinkled, skin leathery from a childhood outdoors. She dyed her grey roots auburn every six weeks with Clairol Nice'n Easy. Peggy had made her an appointment at Sally's once for a professional hair colouring but she refused to go. She only went to Mass on Christmas and Easter but she carried her Québec heritage in her hard pronunciation of 'th' and her habit of drinking hot black coffee with meals.

'You're talking like one of them,' Yvette said.

'I'm – maybe I can see both sides more clearly, because—'

Yvette stood up.

'There aren't two sides. There's only one side. People are hurting. This has to end. And you won't do a single thing.'

'Ma, there's nothing I can do.'

'You're not the daughter I raised. This fancy house and those clothes on your back – what are they? More important than your family?'

'Irving and Lou are my family.' Peggy's eyes filled with tears.

'I thought when you married him it would be a good thing for our family. I thought you were going to make something of yourself. I was wrong. You just made yourself a stranger.'

Yvette headed for the door, and Peggy jumped out of her chair. 'Ma—'

'Don't talk to me any more. I won't ask you for anything else.'

She shut the door hard behind her – so hard that Lou, upstairs on another planet, rereading Le Guin's *The Left Hand of Darkness*, jumped.

After Avery Wilson died in 1985 in a drunk-driving accident, every year after graduation the Casablanca chapter of Mothers Against Drunk Driving held a drug- and alcohol-free party at Norway Racquetball Club, about twenty miles away from the school. The graduates could play racquetball, swim in the pool, bounce on the trampoline, crowd into the hot tub. All the graduates knew, but the chaperones seemed not to, that there was a broken fire door on the side of the building which meant you could sneak out and have sex or a cigarette, or both, in the unlit parking lot, surrounded by trees. There was a barbecue and fireworks at midnight and everyone was put on a bus home at 2 a.m., high on unlimited Coca-Cola and newly-minted nostalgia for their high school days.

On graduation day in 1997 the paper mill strike had lasted for nearly three months. The ceremony, though it went forward in the sports hall of the high school, was muted and smaller than usual. Many students didn't attend. Of thc oncs who did, thc audience of their family was split neatly into two: the larger side, family of millworkers; the smaller side, family of management. Both sides wore their best clothes and expressions of anger. Families who didn't work in the mill had to choose carefully where to sit. Some, who didn't want to offend anyone, sat in the neutral zone of the very back row of bleachers against the wall. Neither set of Lou's grandparents was there.

Allie Phelps was valedictorian. Her speech had been vetted by the principal. 'No politics,' he told her so instead of what was on everyone's mind, she talked about following dreams. For every single graduate in the sports hall that afternoon, following dreams meant getting the hell out of Casablanca, preferably sooner rather than later.

The party was cancelled. Ninety-six high school graduates left Casablanca High School for the last time to get on with the rest of their lives. Some of them even thought that maybe their lives would make a difference.

Louise

1997

'No,' said Peggy. 'You can't go over to Allie's tonight.'

'What?' Lou paused in the middle of stuffing a pair of pyjamas into her backpack. 'Why?'

'I just don't think it's a good idea.'

Lou had changed out of her graduation dress into cut-off shorts and a T-shirt, but Peggy still wore the two-piece she'd worn to the ceremony and then out for lunch afterwards. It was pink, retro, a sheath dress and jacket that looked a bit like something Jackie Kennedy would have worn.

'Mom, the party's been cancelled. It's my graduation day and Allie and I want to celebrate.'

'I think you should stay home with your family.'

'I've spent all day with my family. I want to spend time with my friends. If you're worried that we're going to be drinking, that's not what we're planning to do. Allie and I are going to watch movies.'

'You could watch movies here. I could make popcorn. A girly night in, you and me.'

Her mother hadn't proposed a girly night since she was about seven years old. 'Let's do that tomorrow night,' said Lou. 'Tonight, I really want to see Allie and Benny.'

'You don't have to see them tonight. You've got the whole summer. You've got plenty of time.'

There was pleading in her mother's voice and Lou looked at

her more carefully. Her make-up was perfect as always, but her eyes were red and watery. Then again, she'd been crying at the graduation ceremony, like lots of other parents.

'I always go over to Allie and Benny's. Why don't you want me to tonight?'

'I just don't, that's all.'

Lou sighed. 'Is it the stupid strike? That has nothing to do with me or my friends.'

'It's ... I'd prefer if you didn't go over.'

She put down her backpack and made for the door. 'I'll ask Dad.'

'No!' Peggy put her arm across the door. 'No, Louise. You can't get around me by asking your father, like you always do. I'm your mother, and I say you can't go to your friend's house, and that's final.'

'I'm an adult. I graduated high school today. I can do what I want.'

'Not while you're living in this house, you can't.'

'Then I can't wait to leave this stupid house and this stupid town! My own grandparents didn't even come to my high school graduation because of the strike. Do you know how that makes me feel?'

'It's not all about you, Louise.'

'Leave me alone.' She threw herself down on her bed and didn't look at her mother until she left. Then she got up and slammed the bedroom door.

Her father came up half an hour later. She'd heard them talking downstairs, but she couldn't hear the actual words. It was about her, she knew. How moody she was, how difficult she was being, wanting to spend time with her friends on this day that was supposed to be hers. She didn't care; she'd already made the sneaky phone call to Allie from the extension in her parents' bedroom.

'We're having sandwiches and cake,' Irving said through the

door. 'I thought you'd like to come downstairs and have some with us.'

'Still full from lunch.'

'Your mother ... she wants us to spend time together as a family. We're all proud of you.'

'I'm tired.'

Irving didn't answer and she pictured him there, hovering outside her door, taking his glasses off and polishing them on his shirt.

'We love you, Lou-Lou,' he said at last. 'Your mother and I only want what's best for you.'

Then let me see my friends. She turned over on her bed and looked at the ceiling, and after a little while, he said, 'Well, there's cake downstairs when you're hungry.'

She waited until she heard them going to bed, then she took the screen off her bedroom window, climbed onto the roof of the porch, and let herself down by dangling from the edge by her hands and then letting herself drop. She'd done it plenty of times before.

It was still light out as she negotiated the wilderness to Allie's house. Past Castle Rock, through The Hollow where she used to tell her friends stories about the headless horseman. The air was close and still and the scent of the mill lay heavy. On humid nights you could almost taste it: yellow, like boiled eggs. Finally she emerged in Allie's backyard. She tapped on the back door, hoping that Allie was waiting to open it and not her mother who would tell Lou's mother.

Allie opened it right away. She'd changed out of her dress too and combed out her hairdo. Music was playing in the background.

'Where's your mom?' whispered Lou, creeping inside.

'It's OK,' said Allie at normal volume. 'She's not here. Mom and Dad got into a fight so she's gone to Gramma's. Dad's at the Eagles and he'll probably sleep at one of his buddies'.' She held up a glass of brown milk. 'Want one?'

Lou took the glass and tasted. Milk mixed with Allen's Coffee Brandy, which everyone called the champagne of Maine.

'I put in a squirt of Hershey's syrup,' Allie told her. Mascara was smeared around her eyes. This obviously wasn't her first drink.

'I'll have one without the syrup,' Lou said. 'Make it strong. Where's Benny?'

Allie turned to the counter where the milk and brandy were already out. 'He went out. He fought with Dad.' She held up the plastic litre bottle of Allen's. 'Here's to families, huh?' She took a swig from the bottle, and grimaced.

Lou had a swig and handed the bottle back to her. 'Here's to families. Graduation day, supposed to be the happiest day of our lives . . .'

'Only in *Grease*,' said Allie. She poured a huge shot of brandy into a plastic glass and filled it up with milk.

'What did your parents fight about?'

'Money. It's always money. These days.' She poured more brandy into her own glass and a dollop of syrup. 'I can't wait to get out of here.'

'Same. I don't know what was with my mom today.'

'She fought with my mom.'

Lou swallowed her gulp of drink and stared at Allie. 'Really?'

'Uh-huh. Your mom called after my mom left and I answered it because I thought it was you. She said to tell my mom she was sorry. I don't even know what happened.'

Lou digested this. Their mothers never argued with each other. 'What did your dad and Benny fight about?'

Allie shrugged. 'Same thing *they* always fight about. Dad telling Benny to man up and stop being a pussy.'

'Was he . . . was he drunk?'

'Of course he was drunk. He started drinking before the graduation ceremony. That's why we don't have any money, because of Dad's beer and cigarettes. Ugh.' She made a face like she had a bad taste in her mouth and took another long drink. 'He punched Benny.'

'He hit Benny?'

'It's not the first time. Especially when he's drunk.' A tear fell and she wiped it away, leaving black marks on her fingers.

'Oh my God, Allie. Why didn't you ever tell me?'

'I don't know. Maybe because it felt like if I didn't tell you, it wasn't real. Benny doesn't want anyone to know. He made me promise not to say anything to anyone. But I can't deal with keeping secrets any more.' She took a paper towel from the roll and wiped her face.

Lou looked at her unhappily. 'I'm sorry, Allie.'

'It's OK. It'll be OK. We're all leaving soon. Following our dreams, just like my fucking awful speech.' Allie stepped forward and wrapped her arms around Lou's shoulders. She talked into Lou's neck. 'Don't you fight with me, all right?'

'I'm not going to fight with you.' She hugged Allie hard. 'And your speech was good.'

'It wasn't. But thanks for saying so.' She leaned her head on Lou's shoulder. 'Let's get drunk and watch *Pretty Woman*.'

They got drunk. Allie was already drunk, to be honest, but Lou tried her best to catch up. Lou sat on the couch in the living room in front of the TV with Allie's head on her lap. Allie was covered with the crocheted blanket that her grandmother had made. Dorito and microwave popcorn bags scattered the floor, like the discarded shells of insects.

On the screen, Julia Roberts and Richard Gere were kissing. Allie yawned. 'It's really a shame,' she murmured.

'What?' Lou asked, absently braiding Allie's long hair.

'That Benny went to prom with Debbie Nye not you.'

'Debbie Nye's a cheerleader.'

'She's a bitch. I'd like it much better if you were his girlfriend. You still like him, don't you?'

Lou's face flushed. 'Shut up.'

'He's an idiot. He keeps on choosing girls because they're pretty, when he should be choosing someone like you.'

'You mean someone who's not pretty.'

'Shut up. You're pretty.'

'Nope. You're pretty, I'm not.'

'You are. You're ... striking, which is better than pretty. Look at Julia Roberts. Her legs are too skinny and her mouth is too big. She's not pretty. She's striking.'

'I think she's pretty as well, Allie,' said Lou, a little sadly, because her own mouth was too small and her legs were too muscular. She knew the imperfections of her own body: every flaw catalogued and ranked in her mind. 'The film's called *Pretty Woman*. So that's sort of a clue.'

'Anyway that's not what I meant. What I meant was Benny needs someone he can talk to, someone intelligent and caring. He's not going to talk to Debbie, or any of the boys on the baseball team. Not about anything that matters. And I've tried, but he won't talk to me. I worry about him. I have you to talk with. But he has no one.'

'Maybe he talks to his friends and we don't know it.'

Allie shook her head without lifting it from Lou's lap and one of the braids slipped out of her hand and started coming undone. 'Guys don't talk. They just grunt at each other occasionally.'

'My dad's not like that.'

'Your dad's not like anyone. Especially not my dad.'

Allie sounded so sad. Lou bit her lip and watched the screen without really seeing what was going on. Because she wanted to ask something, a simple and complicated question, and she wasn't sure how to ask it even though the words were obvious enough.

'Does ...' She started, then swallowed and started again. 'Does your dad ever hit you?'

Allie didn't answer. Lou curled herself around so she could see Allie's face. Her eyes were closed and her face was relaxed. 'Allie?' Lou whispered, but she was asleep with her cheek resting on

Lou's thigh. Lou sighed and leaned back on the couch to watch the rest of the movie.

She woke up with the credits rolling on the screen. For a minute she wasn't sure what had woken her up, but then she heard it again: someone shuffling and stumbling in the kitchen. Was it Allie's dad? Alarm and fear froze her but then she heard the distinct bump of a body against furniture and a familiar voice saying, 'Shit.'

Benny. Home, drunk probably, after drinking beer with his baseball buddies in some parking lot. She heard him swear again and then she heard a door open and heavy footsteps thudding down. He'd gone down to the basement rec room where they always hung out when the twins' parents were home.

Lou thought about what Allie had said: how Benny had no one to talk to. She thought about that time, ages ago, when he'd had those bruises on his arm that he'd tried to hide from her. She should have guessed something then, but she'd been too worried about being embarrassed at school. Maybe he'd wanted to talk to her, but she was never listening?

Lou carefully lifted Allie's head and put it on a cushion so she could stand up. Allie groaned a little and curled up, hand fisted near her mouth.

When Lou stood up she felt how drunk she was. She had to grab the back of the couch to steady herself. But then it passed and she went into the kitchen and carefully down the stairs to the basement.

The light was on down there but not the TV. She didn't see Benny while she was coming down the stairs, because he was sitting in an old armchair that was right up against the far wall. But then she stepped off the last stair and she saw him and she stopped. He was holding a gun.

She knew the gun; she'd seen it before. It was a hand gun, and it usually lived in the gun safe in the corner of the basement. Lou glanced at the safe; it was open.

'Benny?' she said, and her voice sounded small. Suddenly she was very aware that there were no adults in the house. Only them. 'Why have you got your dad's gun out?'

He looked up as if he'd only just noticed she was there, though he must have heard her walking down the stairs. 'Why the fuck are you here?' he asked her, and she gripped the banister.

'Watching movies with Allie. Is ... is that loaded?'

'Maybe.'

She knew nothing about guns. Everyone around here owned them but her father didn't and she'd never touched one. The pistol in Benny's hand was sleek and dark, with a wooden handle, or at least one that looked wooden, anyway. She remembered that she'd been told that Donnie Phelps's gun collection was the most valuable thing he owned. Some of them were antiques. They'd been passed down the generations like the portrait of Louis Alder in her grandparents' house.

There was a box of ammunition on the coffee table in front of Benny.

'Could ... could you put it down?' she asked him.

For a minute, he didn't do anything. He held the gun in his hand, running his thumb up and down its wooden grip. Then he pointed it at her. She took a step back, bumping against the railing, hands flying to her chest.

'Bang,' he said. He turned the gun on himself, touched it to the side of his head. 'Bang. All done.'

Then he laughed, a strange laugh that sounded nothing like Benny, and he put the gun down on the low coffee table between the armchair and the sofa.

'Happy?' he said.

'Jesus, Benny, don't scare me like that.' She could hear her pulse thundering.

'Sorry, Lou. Lou Alder. Lou-*ise*.'

She took a step closer. Benny was drunk, that was clear, but he was drunk in a way that she'd never seen anyone be drunk before.

His movements weren't sloppy, and he wasn't talking too much or laughing or slurring his words. Instead, everything seemed very deliberate. Like it meant something that she couldn't quite understand, even though she'd known Benny all her life.

'Are you OK?' she asked.

'OK? Me?' He laughed that strange way again.

'Allie said that you fought with your dad earlier.'

'Yeah, well, that's nothing new.'

He sounded angry rather than sad, but she thought about what Allie had said and came to the couch to sit down near him. Her bare knees were near his, almost touching as she leaned towards him. His eye was bruised and nearly swollen shut. 'Do you want to talk about it?' she asked.

'Talk about it? Sure, I'll talk about it.'

'He hit you?' It was a bit easier to ask Benny this question than it had been to ask Allie, because she knew the answer.

Benny leaned forward, still with that weird calm he'd had when he'd pointed the gun at her and then at himself. 'No, that's not what we've gotta talk about. Let's talk about *why* he hit me. Do you know why?'

The confirmation that Donnie had hit him brought tears to her eyes. Poor Benny. 'There's no reason for him to hit you. He should *never* hit you.'

Benny snorted. 'Your dad doesn't hit you, huh?'

'No!'

'Because your dad never does anything wrong. He's so much better than my dad.'

'That's not what I'm saying.' Though she believed that. Donnie Phelps scared her. Her father was ironed shirts and chess games, photographs and tucking in at night; Mr Phelps was cigarettes and clenched jaw, baseball caps and rough hands.

'Except that my dad hit me because your dad tried to give him money.'

She frowned at that. 'What?'

'After graduation. He took my dad aside and tried to slip him some cash. He said some bullshit about it being a present for me and Allie but my dad knew what it was, and my mom, too. Your family is the one keeping my family from working, and he wanted to offer *charity*.'

Benny spat out the words deliberately, with venom, and Lou tried to figure out what they meant. 'Why would your dad hit you because my dad was trying to be nice?'

Benny stood up and for a terrifying second Lou thought he was going to reach for the gun.

'Fuck you, Lou Alder. Fuck you and your fucking family and fuck you. You think you're so much better than us.'

'I don't think I'm better than you,' she said quickly. 'I don't think anyone is better than anybody. I'm trying to understand.'

'Why would *you* want to understand me?'

His voice broke. Tears welled up in his eyes and he wiped them away with his fists.

She'd never seen Benny cry before. It was worse than the black eye or the drunkenness or even the gun.

'Because I love you,' she said.

'*Shut up*!'

He screamed it, towering over her, and she flinched.

Benny launched himself onto her, pushing her down backwards onto the couch. She braced herself for a punch but he didn't punch her; instead he pushed his hand up under her T-shirt and grabbed her boob through her bra and Lou's first thought, through the shock and fear, was *Oh my God he does think I'm pretty.*

He squeezed, both hands now on her chest, kneading and holding her down with his arms and his body.

'Stop it,' she said. 'Ow! Stop it, Benny, that hurts.'

'Shut up.' He pulled up her shirt and pulled down her bra and Lou twisted underneath him, pushing him, trying to escape, all thoughts of prettiness gone.

'Benny! Stop.'

'Shut up.' He lay on top of her and kissed her, stuck his tongue in her mouth and she thought, *I should bite it*, but it was Benny. Benny, who she'd known all her life, who she loved, who five minutes ago she was worried about being hurt, who she'd thought about kissing and wanted to kiss for years and years, and he tasted like beer and his teeth clashed with hers and his hand was fumbling at her shorts.

She could yell. She could wake Allie up; but this was Allie's brother. He was so much bigger than her, bigger than he looked because he was heavy; and she was strong but he was stronger and he knew what he wanted and she only knew what she didn't want. She didn't want to hurt him, she didn't want Allie to have to see this, she didn't want Benny to be drunk or angry or his father to have hit him, she didn't want him to do this to her here and this way. He was stronger than her. His want was stronger than her didn't want.

There was a crack in the ceiling, a water stain at one end. She looked at it until Benny was finished.

Then he stood and zipped up his jeans. She lay there, looking at the water stain. That stain was there ten minutes ago and it was there now and it hadn't changed and maybe it was proof that this hadn't happened.

Benny didn't speak. She heard him climbing the stairs. Then she heard his footsteps crossing the kitchen floor above her. Then she didn't hear anything.

Gingerly, painfully, she sat up. She couldn't breathe for a minute; she felt like she was still being held down by the chest, so she leaned her elbows on her knees and wondered if she was going to breathe again or if she was going to pass out. Then her throat opened and a bit of breath came through and she sat there until she was breathing almost normally.

She pulled up her bra. She pulled down her top. She pulled up her underwear and her shorts.

She saw the gun lying on its side on the coffee table and she thought *I could have used that*. But she couldn't. Not on Benny. He could have used it on her. He'd pretended to use it on her.

Maybe she'd been very lucky. If his finger had slipped or if he'd got even angrier or drunker. Maybe she could have been dead.

Lou reached out her hand and touched the gun. She didn't know she was going to wrap her fingers around the handle until she'd done it.

She could have done this a few minutes ago. Picked up the gun. She didn't have to let him do it to her. She could have stopped him. Why didn't she stop him?

What was wrong with her?

She thought about pointing the gun at her own head, as Benny had. *Bang. All done.* For a moment it seemed so easy, so much easier than walking out of this basement.

She dropped the gun and stood up quickly, her bare arms and legs covered in gooseflesh. Lou walked up the basement stairs and into the empty kitchen. Her legs felt like they'd been running, running too fast, that shaky feeling after a hard 400 metre race. The almost-empty bottle of Allen's Coffee Brandy still sat on the counter.

It was dark outside now. Lou let herself out of the house and walked home through the woods. The kitchen light in her house was on and she didn't climb up the side of the porch like she'd planned to do but walked straight in through the back door.

Her mother was sitting at the kitchen table in her bathrobe, a mug in front of her. She looked up when Lou walked in. 'What are you— Oh my God, are you all right?'

Did it show? Lou rubbed her eyes, to check if she was crying. She wasn't. She was dressed. There shouldn't be any visible marks on her, although she felt them. How did her mother know?

'Mom,' she said, and her voice sounded strange to her. As careful and dead as Benny's voice had been when he'd been holding the gun.

Her mother jumped up from her chair and went to her. She

pulled Lou into her arms and although Lou was taller than her mother, she sagged into her, head on her shoulder. Her bathrobe was soft and she smelled of Chanel N°5 and chamomile tea.

'What happened?' her mother asked, holding her tightly, stroking her back.

Lou pressed her face into her mother's neck. She shut her eyes as hard as she could and saw the crack and the water stain.

'I didn't want to,' she said into her mother's skin. 'I tried to push him off me but he was bigger than me.'

She did push him, yes? She did try to push. Then she stopped trying and let it happen. Why did she let it happen?

'Oh my God,' said her mother. She drew away from Lou enough to look her in the face. 'Oh my God, Lou honey. Did he – are you OK? Did he hurt you?'

'He held me down, he didn't hurt me, I just . . . I didn't want to.' For the first time she felt that her underwear was wet and sticky, that he'd left her with that inside her, and she began to cry. 'I told him I didn't want to.'

'Oh my God. Oh my God, my baby. My baby girl.' Peggy's hands fluttered around Lou, stroking and petting, pulling her close. 'My poor baby girl. We need to tell your father. We need to go to the police.'

Lou nodded against her mother's shoulder. Police. Yes, that's what they should do, because she'd been . . . she'd been raped. He held her down and raped her. The word in her head, contaminating everything else, made a huge sob rise from her stomach and she couldn't do anything for a minute but cling to her mother. This wasn't supposed to happen. She went downstairs to talk to him. To make him feel better. Allie was asleep upstairs the whole time.

'Who was it?' her mother asked in a whisper, stroking her back. 'Was it someone on the street? All those strange people in town. Did you recognise him?'

She nodded again. 'It was Benny.'

Her mother went very still. No more stroking, no more soothing. Only the scent of Chanel N°5.

She said, carefully, 'Benny?'

'I was at their house, watching movies with Allie. And he came home and I went into the basement to talk with him, and he…' Deep breath. Because saying it made it real. But she could still feel him there, between her legs. 'He raped me.'

Her mother was shaking her head. 'No. Benny couldn't do that.'

'He did, Mom.'

'He's your friend. He's my friend's son.'

'That didn't stop him.'

'Are you sure you… you didn't encourage him? I know you like him. He's a good-looking boy.'

'I said no.'

'You couldn't have.'

That feeling of not being able to breathe was coming back. Like she was being held down. 'I said no, Mom. I pushed him. I tried to get him off of me. I did everything I could to stop him.'

Had she? She didn't yell. She didn't hurt him. She didn't reach for the gun.

Her mom walked away, reached for a chair and sat down, twisting her hands in her lap. She didn't say anything.

'Mom. Mom? It wasn't my fault.'

I think it was my fault.

'We can't tell anyone.' Her mother whispered it.

'*What?*'

'We can't – your father. Your grandfather. It would rip everything apart.'

Tears were still falling from Lou's eyes, but she couldn't feel them. She walked to the table. Put her hands on the tabletop. Bitten nails. They looked real, familiar, unlike what her mother was saying.

'I don't understand,' Lou said.

Her mother took a deep breath. Her own hands in her lap were shaking.

'With what's going on in this town,' her mother said, 'the strike, families turning against each other – everything. If – if we told the police what happened, if it got out that a striking worker's son attacked the granddaughter of the owner of the mill...' She raised her eyes to Lou's and they were full of tears, too. 'It would ruin everything. There would be... There's already the fence, and the guards, and broken bottles. Families are hungry. It would... I don't know what would happen. But it would be terrible.'

'But Mom. He—'

'He shouldn't have done that. He shouldn't have done that to you and I'm so sorry that it happened. But there's more at stake than just you. We need this strike to end.'

Lou swallowed. She'd fallen one time during a race and broken a tooth and cut her lip and it had tasted like this. Like blood, and something broken.

'Are you sure you didn't lead him on at all?' asked her mother. 'You've been drinking, I can smell it. Are you sure he didn't just make a mistake?'

Blood and broken. She couldn't be sure, no. She needed her mother to help her to be sure. She didn't answer.

Her mother rubbed her forehead as if it were aching. 'Why don't you go upstairs and have a shower. You'll feel better after.'

She touched Lou's wrist, and Lou pulled it away.

Louise

She tells Allie all of this, sitting beside her on the rock that looks over the waterfalls, the rock that used to be the far boundary of their world. She says everything: how she loved Benny, how she said no to Benny, how she didn't reach for the gun or call for help, how for weeks and months and years she thought that maybe she could have done something different. She tells Allie about what Peggy said that night, about how the next day, while Irving was at work and Peggy thought she was going to the library, Lou put a suitcase into her battered second-hand Civic, withdrew as much of her college money as the Casablanca Savings Bank would let her and drove south, down the Maine Turnpike and I-95 to 287, across the Tappan Zee Bridge and down into Hoboken, New Jersey, because New York City was too frightening to face by herself. She tells Allie about the tiny studio apartment she found and the two jobs, days filing in an office and nights waitressing in a diner, how she worked as much as she could not only because she needed the money (Irving sent her money as soon as he knew where she was), but because she didn't want to think. She tells her how when hot summer turned to autumn, still too hot, she woke up one day and knew there was something different about her, something she hadn't noticed because everything about her, inside and out, had changed. So she did the test and she knew, when she held the stick with a blue cross in her hand, that even though she was too young to be a mother she could never do what her mother had done to her. She could never put anything else, even her family, even a whole town, above her child.

'I wanted to call you,' she tells Allie now, because now is a flow of words after silence, like the river after a long drought. 'I didn't have anyone to talk to and I wanted to talk to you. But I couldn't. I didn't think you would believe me. I thought you would be angry. He's your twin brother. And now that you know, you can't tell him that he's her father, Allie. You can't tell Benny and you can't tell Dana, either.'

She's spoken most of these words to the river. But now she turns to Allie, who has been watching her this whole time.

'Please,' Lou says. 'I don't care if you believe me or not. It's for Dana's sake. I love her more than anything, and I need to protect her from knowing.'

Allie doesn't look away. She reaches over and takes Lou's hand, which has been resting on the rock, on a vein of mica that looks like fool's gold. She says, 'I believe you.'

Louis

It's the third of July, the day before the fireworks. He has Allie's number in his phone, and though he's promised not to talk about their shared past, he hasn't promised not to talk about anything else, so he texts her: *Happy birthday! Lou x*

Then he deletes the kiss and sends the text.

Mom's sleeping, Mulder at her feet, so he's sitting in the living room in the green wing-back chair with his laptop, fiddling around with some scene ideas for this next novel he's supposed to be writing when the text comes back: *Thanks. Some people are meeting at Meany's tonight for a few drinks. 8.30. Come if you feel like it. A*

He doesn't feel like it, but the idea of it builds in his mind as the morning goes on, so at lunch, while his mom is staring at a soap opera and not eating her chicken and stars soup, he says, 'Would you mind if I got someone from the agency to sit with you for a couple of hours tonight? It's Allie's birthday.'

'Go,' she says, not taking her eyes off the screen where a woman with big hair is crying. 'Elaine from next door will come. You two made such a cute couple.'

'What?' he says, but she keeps watching her soap. The medications whack her out, he knows, but sometimes he suspects she plays it up.

He's never been to Meany's before – when he lived here, he wasn't legal drinking age – so he takes a little while to consider what to wear. He doesn't want to look like a city boy, like someone who's moved away and thinks he's too good for Casablanca, but he also doesn't want to look like he's trying too hard to blend in. (What, is he kidding? He never blended in.) So he showers and shaves and puts on a plain blue button-down shirt and a pair of jeans, and then he looks in the mirror and thinks he looks way too much like Irving, so he puts on a plain black T-shirt instead, and then he thinks he looks too gay (Carrie's words still in his head – she's changed him all right). So he puts on a checked shirt and rolls up the sleeves. It's only as he's doing this that he realises that he doesn't give a shit what anyone else in the bar thinks he looks like: he's only nervous about what to wear because he's meeting Allie socially for the first time since he was a teenager.

Cute couple.

They were a cute couple. Cupid's Couple in the yearbook, a photograph of Allie sitting on his knee giving him a cut-out paper heart. They were never popular enough (and Lou was never good-looking enough) to be Prom King and Queen, and no one would have voted for the grandson of the owner of CPC anyway, not with the strike going on, but they were the couple everyone knew. Allie 'n' Lou. He loved her, loved everything about her, and he was a little afraid of her, too: afraid that she'd see too deeply inside of him and see things that would hurt her, even though none of those things meant that he loved her less. Maybe that's what love is supposed to be, the sort of love that lasts, the sort of love he's never had. Being afraid and still not leaving.

Meany's is downtown, around the corner from the police station, which has always been the occasion for jokes. Irving never used to drink in there but Donnie Phelps did, when he wasn't drinking at the Eagles Club. In Lou's teenage imagination, it was hazy with smoke and reeking of beer fumes, lit only by a blinking Miller Lite neon sign, red and blue. In Lou's imagination there were *Playboy* centrefolds tacked up on the unfinished wooden walls, sawdust on the floor, tall bar stools and a table out back for illicit poker games to which the cops, drinking after work, turned a blind eye. Maybe there was a spittoon. He'd heard there was a stuffed bear head on the wall and he pictured it snarling, its glass eyes reflecting the flicker of the neon sign, gazing down at half-naked women who looked nothing like any of the girls he saw in Casablanca, Maine.

When Lou pushes open the door he's hit by a Bob Seger tune and the scent of beer. But otherwise it's nothing like he imagined. There's no smoke and no Miller Lite sign. Instead, most of the walls are taken up with a painted mural of Casablanca: rolling mountains, the river valley, the falls, town hall and CPC. He can't make out the details because the room's full of people, but it looks like the same scene reproduced four times, each with a different season. Orange autumn, white winter, green spring. The pool table is in front of snowy mountains. Summer, he presumes, is mostly hidden by the bar.

It takes him a minute before he spots Allie leaning against autumn with a bottle of beer in her hand. He makes his way through people who all look vaguely familiar, attention focused on Allie. She's wearing a yellow dress that bares her shoulders and her hair is loose. She's put on lipstick, or lip gloss, and when she spots him, she smiles and he feels something in his stomach flip over.

'You came,' she says.

'Yeah. Our neighbour's sitting with her.'

'Lou Alder?' says the guy standing next to Allie, who Lou didn't even notice. 'Hey, man, it's been years. Nice to see you, buddy. You even know who I am?'

The guy is balding and has a thick beard but Lou shakes his hand and imagines him thirteen years younger, slimmer, without the beard. 'Buddy White?' he guesses.

'You got it! How you been, buddy?'

'Pretty good, Buddy.'

Buddy laughs as if this joke hasn't been done about a million times before and slaps Lou's back. 'Yeah, you wrote a book or something, right? I'm not a big reader but someone told me about it.'

'I told you about it,' says Allie quietly, and Lou turns to her in surprise. 'It's called *Light in Winter*.'

'So is it a good book?' continues Buddy, who seems more than a little drunk. 'Should I read it?'

'If you want to,' says Lou.

'Makes you a lot of money, huh? Books.'

'I wish.'

'You know what you should write? You should write that Jack Reacher shit. That makes a shit ton of money. Tom Cruise. All that shit. Am I right?'

'You're not wrong.'

'Or Stephen King! He makes loads of money. And you're from Maine, you're halfway there, right?'

'Never thought of it that way.' He glances at Buddy's half-full glass of beer and turns to Allie. 'I'm going to get a drink. Another beer?'

'I'll come with you,' she says. They walk to the bar together and Lou can see earrings in her ears, a thin silver chain around her neck.

'I thought this place had a bear head on the wall,' he says.

'It's behind the bar.' And yes, there it is, looming over the bottles of Jägermeister and Jack Daniel's: a big brown head mounted on a wooden plaque. It isn't snarling; it has tiny eyes and a dog-like nose. It looks a little sad.

'I always built up Meany's – in my mind – as some sort of Wild West saloon or something,' says Lou.

'Everything's disappointing when you grow up, I guess,' says Allie. She tips back her head to drink the last of her beer and her neck is smooth and pale.

You're not disappointing me, Lou thinks. He says, 'Buddy White didn't disappoint me. He's exactly like he was in school. He used to follow you around then, too.'

'They say your character's fixed by the time you're seven years old.'

'Do you think that's true?'

'No. I think your character's fixed before the time you're even born.' She holds up the bottle. 'I'll have one of these, please.'

He orders two – it's a craft beer brewed in Maine that he's never tried before – and when they come, he clinks his bottle with hers. He hands her the gift he's brought. 'Happy birthday,' he says. 'This is for you.'

She takes the tissue-paper wrapped present with surprise. 'You didn't have to.'

'I didn't. It's something I had anyway, that I thought you might like.'

'It's a book. Is it yours?'

'Fortunately not. Apparently, you've already got a copy.'

Allie actually blushes a little at that. 'Maybe a late-night Amazon purchase. I know the author, I had an excuse.'

'It's not as good as Stephen King.'

'I liked it.'

Lou smiles, looks down. 'Thanks. Open your present.'

Allie tears off the tissue paper to reveal a battered paperback. '*A Wizard of Earthsea*. I haven't read this since I was a kid.'

'Look at the bookmark in the middle.'

She takes it out: a slip of lined paper, folded slender. Unfolded, there's a message written in purple ink, lower-case i's dotted with circles:

I loved this book! Thank you for lending it to me. I don't want to give it back. Allie. xxx

'Wow,' she says. 'I don't even remember that you lent it to me.'

'Now you don't have to give it back,' says Lou.

'Thank you.' She smiles, and she's the girl he's known all his life, the girl who borrowed his favourite book and took care not to break the spine or crease the pages.

'Allie,' he begins, not sure what he's going to say, wanting to feel the texture of her name in his mouth again, when she's greeted by several other people and the moment's gone.

The beer is good. He has a few of them while he talks to people – some of them he knows, some of them he doesn't know. It's not as hard as he thought it might be. When he arrived in Casablanca three weeks ago, he thought that nothing had changed at all from when he was a kid, but the people haven't stayed still. They've grown up, got jobs, had kids. They all know he's written a book but he steers the conversation off in other directions. Allie knows everyone; maybe that's why it's easier. Because Allie is here beside him, drinking her beer, challenging him to a game of pool, and for one split second when she's just potted the eight ball and beaten him, she punches the air and looks like a kid again, and he thinks that this is how it could have been, if things had been different on that June night thirteen years ago. This could have been the two of them, still together, enjoying a night out on her birthday. Cupid's Couple.

Then someone clinks the side of a bottle with a knife and they all stop and turn towards the noise. Buddy White is standing on a chair, clinking the bottle for attention.

'Ladies and gentlemen,' he says, and he's drunker than he was before, though for the moment at least he doesn't seem in imminent danger of falling off the chair. 'I wanna say something. It's Allie Phelps's birthday! Happy birthday, Allie Phelps!'

Cheers. Applause. Lou looks at Allie beside him and she's smiling, blushing. He toasts her along with everyone else.

'But!' yells Buddy, talking over the general buzz, 'let's not forget who else's birthday it is too. Benny Phelps was a great guy, a great athlete. The best baseball player that Casablanca's ever had, by a million miles. He told me one time, "Buddy, I'm gonna play for the Sox." And I believe he would've done it.'

A murmur of assent. Lou, beside Allie, cannot look at her. He can't look at anything except for Buddy White, who he's not really seeing, because he's seeing Benny instead.

'What Benny did brought this town together. All of you remember it. We were falling apart – fighting, arguing, some of us were going hungry. Families were turned against families. Casablanca was eating itself. But when Benny died, we smartened up. We realised that nothing else matters except for this town, and that we're all in it together. Maybe Benny didn't mean for that to happen, but that's what he did. That's what he gave to Casablanca.'

Buddy's voice, though still loud, is choked with tears.

'He stopped the strike and that saved this town. None of us would be here right now if not for Benny, and he had to die to make that happen. So let's say: Happy birthday, Benny Phelps.'

Buddy holds his beer up again and the people around him hold up their drinks too, and Lou reflexively reaches out for Allie, but she's gone.

While they're toasting his dead best friend, Lou turns and quickly makes his way to the door of the bar. The night outside is cooler and it seems very dark and quiet after the colour and noise inside. Allie is standing half a block away on the bridge over the river, with her hands shoved into the pockets of her dress.

She doesn't look up as Lou approaches, but keeps staring at the flat water far beneath the bridge. He stands beside her, leaning on the railing too.

'I hate birthdays,' she says fiercely, to the water. 'I hate our birthday. That's why I never do this. I thought maybe…'

'Maybe it could be about you, instead of about him?'

She bows her head. 'I love him. He was my brother. I miss him every day.'

'So do I.'

'At least you got away. You're not reminded of him all the time.

Everything about this town reminds me of him. Every single thing. The mill, the baseball diamond, our old house.'

'I still think about him.'

She turns to Lou. 'We did the right thing, didn't we? The strike ended. His death was used for a good thing. It had some meaning to it.'

'Yes. It had meaning. It helped people.'

'It doesn't have any meaning to me. It's stupid and pointless and it hurts.' She swipes away tears. He wants to put his arm around her, but he's not sure that's a good idea.

'It was... I still don't understand it, Allie. I still... I know it was my fault.'

'You didn't kill him.'

'I didn't stop him.'

'You tried.'

'If I'd asked him. If we'd been able to talk more. But we didn't talk like that. He wasn't interested in talking about how he felt. I didn't know. But I should have.'

'I should have known. I knew how my father treated him, I knew he kept everything inside. On the morning before it happened, he sat on my bed and listened to my speech three times. I was so worried about being valedictorian, and I wasn't worried about him at all.'

He chews his lip. Allie sniffs, and digs the heels of her hands into her eyes. Below them the river flows past them towards the mill. Water, air, landscape, people. Who dies and when. It all comes back to the mill. All back to paper. Just paper.

'My dad blames himself,' he says to Allie. 'He says that Benny died because of the strike and that the strike happened because of our family. My mom says that's why he sold the mill and left Casablanca.'

'It wasn't your dad's fault.'

'No. I've been angry with him for leaving, and then it turns out that he left because of something that I did.' He takes a deep breath and says something that surprises him. 'I think I need to go and tell him that.'

She's quiet for a moment. 'Because you want him to come back to Casablanca to see your mom.'

'She says he's the only man she's ever loved. She still loves him. They should be together, Allie.'

'Life doesn't work like that.'

'But she's only got a little while left. I don't think that she needs to know the truth. But I think my dad does. He needs to have a clear conscience, so he can come back and see Mom.'

'So you're going to tell him the truth.'

'It can't do any harm now, can it? For him to know?'

Allie is quiet and he risks looking over at her. She's stopped staring at the water and now she's staring at him. He thinks about the two of them, either side of that basement, staring at each other in shock and horror. Making the choice that will change everything, for everyone.

He thinks about how in that moment, they were the closest they'd ever been.

'If you go,' she says, 'I'll go with you.'

Louise

I believe you.

The words keep going through Lou's head. Three words, maybe more profound than *I love you.*

Two days after she told Allie her truth, it's Allie's birthday. Lou buys a cake and brings it to Allie's office in the hospital. It's Benny's birthday too and she doesn't want to risk running into him. Between patients, Lou lights a candle on the top of the cake and Allie blows it out and then they cut the cake into pieces and share it with all the other doctors and nurses. Neither Lou nor Allie talk about the past, but Lou feels Allie's belief in her lying between every word that they say to each other.

The next day is the Fourth of July. When she was a kid they used to spend every Fourth at her grandparents' camp at Morocco Pond, swimming and watching the fireworks over the lake. It was called a camp because all summer places in Maine, from shacks to mansions, are called camps, but really it was a large house on a private beach. It was sold long ago and the public beach will be too crowded, so Irving plans to barbecue some hot dogs in the backyard, even though Peggy won't eat any. Dana's friend Jim has invited her to go to the town fireworks display with his family after. A relief for Lou, who doesn't feel like the argument with her daughter that is hanging over their heads like a storm cloud.

On the morning of Independence Day Lou goes down to the river – not at the falls, but farther down, downstream from the mill, where there's a path that leads along the river near the sports field. To get to it, you have to walk past apartment buildings that, when Lou was a child, had lawns full of children's toys and dogs on ropes. The people who lived there used to work in the mill, but now, when she walks past, some of the houses are boarded up and one looks as if it's been gutted by fire. There's an abandoned car on blocks. A man in a stained undershirt sits on a porch, smoking. He raises a hand in greeting to Lou as she passes.

Lou slips between the scoreboard and the fence and goes down a slope through scrubby trees to the river. She walked this path as a teenager sometimes, mostly when she wanted to be by herself. It wasn't used much then. Unlike at the falls, the water here was brown, slow-moving, flecked with yellow foam. The foam scummed the water and built up behind the rocks. It caught in weeds along the banks and coated their stems and leaves. It looked like the smoke that came out of the smokestacks and it had the same chemical smell, overlaid with shades of rotten fish.

You could swim in Morocco Pond and you could swim in the shallows up above the falls, but you couldn't swim here. People said that if you dropped a Coke can in the river it would dissolve instantly, that if you ate a fish from this part of the river you'd get sick. It was the price of the clean-bleached glossy paper that rolled out of Casablanca on trucks.

Casablanca, when Lou was a child, was white-painted fences and a bustling main street, ball games and Christmas lights and snow that fell white and gradually turned grey. It was the skating rink on the football field with the little shack that sold hot chocolate. It was junior high dances at the community centre and trips on summer days to the beach and big rocks to climb on and feel like you were on top of the world. It was autumns when the mountains were painted in vivid splashes and the wilderness at the back of her house was the map of her childhood imagination.

But it was also the brown, dead, soggy ground when the snow melted and revealed what it had hidden. It was the days when the smoke lay hazy on the town and caught in your lungs. It was this part of the river down below the town that no one wanted to talk about.

Lou has only ever told two other people besides her mother and now Allie that she was raped. The first time she told someone, Dana was four and Lou was working part-time in an insurance office while her daughter was in nursery. In the evenings Lou took courses at the community college, and that's where she met Raul.

Raul was covered in tattoos. Tropical flowers and plants in every colour twined up and down his arms. Like her, he was studying to become a teacher. He had eyes the colour of chocolate and four piercings in each ear. By day he drove a truck for a bakery. He told her this on their first date, which was a before-class coffee date because her neighbour couldn't stay late to babysit Dana. Lou had laughed, then immediately apologised and said something lame about how, if that were her job, she'd eat all the croissants. He looked at her oddly, but let it pass. On their third date, when she'd booked a babysitter to stay overnight, he filled her glass with cheap red wine as they sat on his sofa and asked her why she'd laughed. 'Do you think it's because I look stupid?' he said.

'No,' she said, surprised that someone so outwardly confident, who decorated himself so boldly, would ask such a thing. 'You don't look stupid. You look great.'

'Then why is my job funny to you?'

'Your job isn't funny. It's just that I tell everyone that Dana's dad was a truck driver, even though I'd never met one before. So I thought it was funny that I was attracted to someone who drives a truck.'

Raul touched her knee. He wanted to be a primary school special ed teacher. His older brother had Down's syndrome and lived at home with their parents. He'd told her on their second date that his tattoos were all based on Enrique's favourite plants, and he'd told her all the scientific names, which Enrique also knew.

'Can you tell me why you lie about Dana's father?' he asked.

'Because I don't want her to know where she really came from.'

He didn't ask anything else, though she told him a little more a few weeks later. That first night he just nodded and kissed her and let her take the lead. He let her know she could trust him. And although it didn't work out with Raul in the end, she was grateful to him for that acceptance and gentleness, and for being the first person she was fully intimate with as an adult.

Raul made her feel safe by accepting her story. A few years later, on a date with Megan, walking along Brighton Beach on a cold April afternoon, Lou told her what happened and Megan said, 'It happened to me too. Different, but the same.' And she told Lou her story of working in a bar and a co-worker in the alley and how she was the one who lost her job when she reported it. And then the two of them clasped hands and ran together as fast as they could, kicking up fountains of sand behind them until they were out of breath and felt ... not free, but better.

Raul and Megan, in their different ways, silence or words, made Lou feel like she wasn't crazy, that this experience that had changed her entire life was valid and true. It meant she could put all that unspoken stuff behind her and move on.

But when Allie said *I believe you*, it was different. Because unlike Raul or Megan, Allie had reason to doubt her. This was her brother, and Lou had kept quiet about it for thirteen years. Allie could have said she was going to ask Benny for his side of the story, or she could have said that maybe Lou was blaming Benny for something that she'd really wanted to happen. But she didn't.

When Allie said *I believe you* it was as if a weight had been taken off Lou that had been on her since the night of their high school graduation. And now Lou walks lighter along this path.

The river is still brown as it meanders through the rock, but there's no foam any more. That's gone with the mill and the chemicals and the paper. She takes a deep breath and smells earth and rotting. Brackish water. Time passing.

A movement catches her eye and Lou stops. A little bit ahead of her, feet in the river, stands a heron. Slender and prehistoric, it sees her and freezes. For a long moment, neither move. A mosquito buzzes near Lou's ear; she ignores it. The bird could be a stick or a shadow, but then it tilts its long beak and focuses its eye on the water instead of on Lou. She breathes, watches, conscious of the privilege of being ignored.

A quick duck of grey head into water and the heron lifts its neck again. A silver fish flops in its beak. Jerk, swallow: Lou can see the fish travel as a lump down the heron's throat. And then, unhurried, the bird stretches its wings and flies away. Long legs dangling, a shadow flying downstream into the green woods, the brown, living river.

Louis

On the flight out of Portland after the holiday weekend, Allie reads *A Wizard of Earthsea*. Lou has a book, too, but he can't concentrate enough to read it. Instead, he doodles in a notebook.

'Shouldn't you be *writing* in that?' asks Allie, once they've caught their connecting flight in Philadelphia and they've ordered a drink and Lou has got the notebook out again. He's no good at drawing; it's all curlicues and mazes, a visual representation of his mental state, which keeps doubling back on itself.

'Not in the mood.'

'Are you allowed to wait until you're in the mood? That seems self-indulgent.'

'Compared to being a nurse it is self-indulgent.' He doodles. 'No, I don't wait till I'm in the mood to write. But I don't think I have the head space right now.'

'Are you working on a second book?'

'In theory, yes.'

'It was weird when I read *Light In Winter*. I hadn't seen or spoken to you in so long. And it took me ages to open it. I bought it and it sat there looking at me until I got a little drunk one night. But when I did read it, it was like you were in the room with me, talking.'

'Thanks,' he says. Usually when someone says they liked his book, he thinks they're probably being polite. But this is a compliment from someone who knows him well. Knew him well.

'I was surprised by the yearning in it. Well, maybe not surprised but more – I don't know, touched by the way that Gill had to keep their secret from everyone, even while falling in love with Pierre. And all the snow and the coldness out there, miles from anywhere. I could feel it. And then how Gill tells Pierre and they have to keep their love a secret for two reasons, because they're two men and because Gill was born female. And then what happens to Pierre. It's so sad. You really did it well.'

'To be honest, Allie, I don't know if I can do it again.'

'You will. Maybe you have to concentrate on real life first for a while. But you'll write another one. You've always written. It's what you've always wanted to do.'

'You always wanted to be a doctor,' he says, gently.

'Well, becoming a doctor is expensive and it takes a long time. My mom needed me after Benny died.'

'You would've made a great doctor.'

'I still get to help people this way. I probably have more meaningful contact with patients as a nurse than I ever would have as a doctor, and I'm proud of what I do.'

'You should be proud. You're really good at it. And thanks for coming with me. I know this isn't something you want to revisit.'

'It's OK,' she says, and picks up her book again.

In the six years since he's left Casablanca, Irving has been to China and Australia. He's been to India and Venezuela and Kenya and Iceland. He flew around the world once, and then again, stopping where he liked, and Lou was glad his father was travelling because it meant he didn't have to speak to him more than for a few minutes or by email, and he never had to tell his father that he was sad, angry, disappointed.

Irving has been in Florida for about six months – before that he was in California, both of them about as distant and as different as you can get to Maine and still be in the continental US. Lou hasn't been down here, though Irving always passes on his phone number and address for every place he goes, and answers emails within two hours at most. He sends albums of photographs via Flickr and he sends interesting gifts in the mail: packs of incense, a drawing done by a street artist, a second-hand book in Spanish from a stall. Every time Lou opens a package from his father he looks at the content, turns it over in his hands, and puts it on a shelf in his office, never to look at it again.

In return, Lou has sent his dad a copy of his book in the original English and every time he receives a translation too, and he always gets thank-you notes. Irving is polite. Scrupulous. Apologetic, without ever quite saying 'I'm sorry.'

Lou and Allie rent a car at Orlando airport and drive to Cape Canaveral, about an hour away. Allie uses her phone to direct them to Irving's address. It's a big block of condominiums near the ocean front, a characterless white building with balconies and a swimming pool and palm trees in front. He rings the buzzer and immediately hears his dad's voice through the speaker: 'Lou?'

It's eager, as if Irving has been waiting by the door for him to arrive. He exchanges a glance with Allie and replies, 'Hi, Dad,' and the door buzzes open right away.

They pass through an interior as bland as the exterior, take the stairs to the third floor. He's waiting for them, apartment door open behind him, stocking feet on the white tiles. He looks the same as he always has, except there's a tiny bit of grey at his temples. 'Lou,' he says, and shakes his hand. Then he hugs Allie. He touches both of them as they walk to his apartment, one hand on Lou's shoulder, the other on Allie's elbow, as if he can't quite believe they're here.

'I'm so glad to see you two!' he says. 'This is such a treat. Such a surprise. It's been so long. Did you have a good Fourth of July?'

The apartment is small and incredibly neat, with cream-coloured furniture that Lou thinks probably came with it. No recliner. There's a clock on the wall and a pastel-coloured painting of a beach with palm trees which probably also came with the apartment. The only signs of his father he can see in this place are a stack of *Scientific American* magazines on the glass coffee table and, on the shelf near the television, the copies of Lou's book that he has sent him. There's no ocean view; the windows look out over the parking lot.

'Nice place,' Lou lies. This isn't what he pictured at all. This place isn't a travel dream come true; this place is a penance.

'What made you choose Cape Canaveral, Mr Alder?' asks Allie.

'Irving please. You're not a child any more. I have a friend here who's an engineer, I've kept in touch with him since we were at college together, so that was part of it, I guess. I always wanted to see the rocket launches.'

'Have you seen many of them?'

'No, not many at all. Isn't that funny? How about some coffee? Have a seat, have a seat.'

Allie sits in a chair and Lou sits on the cream-coloured sofa. Irving bustles about, putting on coffee in the tiny white kitchen, putting cookies on a plate, and in this featureless space and the special cookies from the supermarket bakery Lou can see how very lonely his father is. Lou can see, for the first time, his own part in what's happened. What he made happen by leaving Casablanca, by hiding the truth, by not visiting, by being angry.

His father genuinely thought he was doing the right thing by leaving. Irving thought he was helping Peggy by releasing her from the family. His apologies weren't for selling the mill, following his childhood dreams away from his family: they were for being heir to the mill in the first place. He was trying to go back to a time that should have been, a time when families weren't split apart and a young man wasn't dead.

Irving comes in with a tray of mugs and plates, cream and sugar, and Lou stands up and takes it from him. He puts it on the glass table next to the stack of magazines and says, 'Dad. We've got some things to tell you.'

Louis

1997

On the night of his high school graduation, Lou didn't bother arguing with his parents when they said he couldn't go out. He said he was tired, went to bed early, and then, once Irving and Peggy were asleep, he climbed out of his bedroom window and let himself dangle and drop from the porch roof onto the lawn. He took the wilderness path to the falls.

The nearby parking lot was full. Music blasted out of speakers and people leaned against cars. They drank beer from cans and bottles and the girls passed around bottles of Allen's Coffee Brandy or litre bottles of Coke, already mixed with vodka at home while their parents weren't looking. They poured dark liquid into red plastic cups and toasted each other. 'Fucking out of here,' they said. 'Finally.' Alice Cooper sang about school being out forever.

Lou scanned the crowd of his classmates, but he didn't see Benny or Allie. He knew everyone here, but nobody was his particular friend. Most of these people spent a lot of time hanging out in their cars, getting drunk; they came into school with stories about avoiding the cops, lies about who screwed who in the back seat of their car. They were the popular kids who weren't good at sports or school, the people who were cool because they were reckless and didn't give a fuck. In other words, the people who made Lou feel anxious and looked at. They were almost all from millworkers' families and he felt their eyes on him as he walked across the parking lot and down to Big Water Rock. He hunched up his shoulders, ready for them to say something. But they didn't say anything. Just went back to their beer.

It was probably a mistake to come here. The parking lot had streetlights but the rocks didn't, they were shadowed by tall pine trees, and the evening light was fading. The bugs were thicker near the water and they buzzed in his ears and settled on his skin to bite. He'd wait, he decided, for fifteen minutes, and if Benny didn't turn up, he'd go back home. Meanwhile, he had his own plastic bottle, half Coke, half rum. He took it out of his sweatshirt pocket and took a medicinal-tasting drink. Watched the water go over the falls. He'd decided to go to college at the University of Maine in Orono so they could all be together. But would it be the same? Maybe Allie would meet someone she liked more, who was better-looking, less selfish. Someone who deserved her more. Maybe Benny would like his baseball buddies better than he liked Lou. Maybe they'd drift apart and only see each other when they came back to Casablanca for the school breaks.

He'd been waiting twenty minutes by his watch when Benny turned up. He wore his letter jacket in the school colours, yellow and blue. He carried a bottle of Southern Comfort and the first thing Lou saw was the bruise on his face: red and purple on his cheekbone, swelling his left eye partly shut. It hadn't been there at the graduation ceremony this afternoon.

'What happened to you?' he asked.

Benny sat beside him on the rock, twisting open the cap of the SoCo. 'Not asking where your fucking girlfriend is?'

Lou had been expecting a joke, like usual. The anger took him by surprise. 'Um. Where's my girlfriend?'

'She decided to stay home and watch movies instead of drinking in a parking lot with the losers.' Benny gulped the liquor from the bottle. A long drink and a shudder. His words were a little slurry, as if he'd been drinking for a while.

'What happened to your face?' Lou asked cautiously.

'My dad fucking decked me.'

Lou stared. 'He hit you?'

'He hits me all the time, asshole. You never noticed?'

The cloy of rum and Coke. 'I— You always said it was a baseball.' Or a door. Or a tree branch.

But Lou knew. He'd always known, hadn't he, and accepted what Benny said because that's what Benny wanted him to think and because it was the less scary option?

'You're an idiot,' said Benny. 'And your dad's a son of a bitch.'

'*My* dad?'

'He went up to my dad after graduation. Didn't you see him?'

'No, Mom wanted to go to lunch, she was all worried about the reservation.' But Irving had been late joining them at the car. Flustered. Lou thought he'd forgotten something. 'What did he do?'

'He tried to give my dad money.'

Lou felt sick. That was why Benny was acting like this. 'Why?'

'You know why. Said our kids are friends, he wanted to help out. My dad threw the money in his face, then he came home and got in a fight with me.' Benny drank more, swiped furiously at a mosquito. 'I can't wait to get out of this shithole.'

'We'll be gone soon,' said Lou, because this was the only thing he could think of to make it better.

'*You'll* be gone.'

'What do you mean? You're going too. Full baseball scholarship. All three of us together.'

'Allie got in because she's smart. You got in because you can pay. I can't do anything except baseball. That's it. If I'm not good enough, or if I get injured or something, I'm right back here. Living at home. If the strike ever ends, I'll be working in the mill next to my old man for the rest of my life.'

'That's not going to happen.'

'What, now you can tell the fucking future as well as being rich?'

He flinched. 'I'm sorry, Benny.'

'You're sorry? This should be your black eye, not mine. I should beat the shit out of you. That's what I was planning to do when I came down here.'

'Why aren't you?'

'Because you're my only fucking friend.'

Benny drank. Lou watched him. Saw the bruise, all the bruises there had ever been. Donnie Phelps was an angry man. He walked around the house with jaw clenched, fists tight, sucking at cigarettes as if they owed him blood. Lou didn't speak with him if he could help it. He'd known Mr Phelps hit Benny. He'd known, and he'd never said anything, never done anything.

He was Benny's only friend.

'I'm sorry,' he said again, and he put his hand on Benny's shoulder, half expecting Benny to swing the bottle at his face. Half expecting Benny to round on him and beat the shit out of him like he said he was planning to because it wasn't fair. None of this was fair. But Benny didn't move. He didn't pull away. He bowed his head onto his chest, curled into a ball of self-hatred. Lou felt it too: burning in his stomach like cancer.

A whistle in the dark.

'Hey girls, you gonna put on a show for us?'

'You fucking the enemy, Phelps?'

Lou twisted his head around. Shadows behind them; maybe four or five people. It was hard to tell who, with the light behind them, though he recognised Jake Flint's voice and one was a girl. They had bottles in their hands.

He took his hand off Benny's shoulder. Sweetness rose in his throat.

'Let's go,' he said to Benny. Benny sat there.

'Fucking homos,' said someone. He heard them hawk and spit.

'I've got a girlfriend,' said Lou, trying to keep his voice steady. He glanced to the side. They could go through the wilderness and not have to walk through the parking lot, but were there other people in the shadows?

'*I've got a girlfriend*,' said someone in a falsetto.

'Just one, Alder, or are you fucking all the scabs too?'

'Scabs.' More spitting. Something wet-sounding landed beside them.

'Benny, let's go,' Lou said. 'Let's get out of here.'

'This why you couldn't get it up for Debbie, *Benedict*? You like your scab-loving boyfriend Louise better?'

'*Benny*.' He reached for Benny to pull him up but then he thought twice of it. He clutched his plastic Coke bottle instead, as if that could help. 'Let's go.'

'I'm not afraid of you,' muttered Benny, under his breath.

'Let's go. Don't fight them. C'mon, Benny. Let's go back to your house, have a drink, meet up with Allie. Come *on*.' He wanted to run, get the hell out of here, get home. He knew who these people were and they were assholes. Druggies who got into fights, who drunk-drove their trucks around the backwoods. But he couldn't leave Benny behind. Not with what these guys were saying, not with Benny's black eye from his dad, not with the money that his own dad had tried to give to Mr Phelps. Lou stood, ready to run, wanting to haul Benny to his feet but afraid of what the others would say if he touched him.

Benny took a long drink out of his bottle. Then he stood up and turned around to face the shadows behind them. In the fading light he was a compact coil of strength, eyes slitted, chin out. Lou involuntarily stepped back.

'I am not. A fucking. Faggot,' said Benny. 'And I'm not. Afraid. Of you.'

'Let's go,' Lou whispered. Benny, like this, could take on anyone. Could throttle the world and win. Lou couldn't. Lou was weak-kneed, shaking, afraid. 'Please Benny, let's go.'

'Pussy,' said someone, it might have been Jake, and Benny the baseball star, the best arm that Casablanca High School had ever seen, maybe even that Maine had ever seen, reared back his right hand and threw the bottle of Southern Comfort as hard as he could. Lou saw the bottle fly, saw someone fling their hand up, heard a thud and a shatter and a cry of pain, and then Benny was running past him onto the path, through the trees, and Lou ran right after him.

The path was uneven and their sneakers thumped on the ground. Lou's own heart and breath were so loud in his ears that he couldn't tell if they were being followed until he looked back and saw nothing. Empty woods. He thought he heard laughter in the distance along with the music.

Lou was fast, but he couldn't catch Benny, not tonight. He ran behind him around rocks and trees to the Phelps's backyard. The house was dark with only the flicker of the TV coming from the living room windows. Benny pushed inside and when Lou reached the screen door, he half expected it to be locked against him, but it gave when he leant against it.

The kitchen was empty. There was a bottle of Allen's Coffee Brandy on the counter and an empty container of milk. The TV in the other room was playing music, 'Must Have Been Love' by Roxette, and the door to the basement was open and the light had been turned on. Breathing hard, Lou stood, his hand on the screen door, and hesitated. Into the living room with Allie? Into the basement with Benny? Or should he go home, do what his mom wanted him to do, stay out of trouble and away from conflict and wait until all of this blew over, until the three of them were at Orono together and they could be normal again?

He went to the basement door. Because this was all his fault. He was the one whose family owned the mill and got the scab workers in. He was the one who looked at Benny sometimes and wanted to kiss him, who lay awake sometimes at night, knowing he loved Allie and wanted her, but had dreams about that time in the basement and the scent of Benny's skin. He was the one who they were calling a homo, because they could see his secret thoughts and how afraid of them he was.

'Benny?' he called softly and started down the stairs.

Benny was sitting in the plaid armchair by the couch, holding a gun in his hand.

Lou stopped at the bottom of the stairs, hand on the banister. 'What are you doing?'

'What does it look like I'm doing?'

'Why have you got that gun out?' He glanced at Mr Phelps's open gun cabinet.

Benny clicked something and the round cylinder on the side of the gun swung out. He had a box of ammunition on his lap; as Lou watched, he took out a round and slid it into one of the chambers of the cylinder.

'Benny, stop it.'

'You're scared.' Benny's voice was flat. 'You were scared at the falls, too. What's scarier, then or now?'

'Right now because you're not acting like you. Stop it, Benny. Put the gun down.'

Benny laughed. His laughter was flat, too. His head was bowed over the gun so Lou couldn't see his face. 'You didn't want to fight. They were saying those things and you wanted to run away.' He clicked the cylinder back in place and spun it with his thumb.

'Those guys were assholes. Come on, let's forget it, let's have another drink and watch a movie or something.'

'I hate you.'

Lou inhaled sharply, the words a punch in the gut. Almost worse than the gun in Benny's hand.

'I'm your friend,' Lou said.

'That's OK. Don't take it personally. I hate myself too.'

Benny raised his head. He pointed the gun at the side of his own forehead. His face was shiny wet with tears, leaking past his bruised and swollen eye.

Lou had never seen Benny crying before.

In the years to come, he would think about his choice in this moment. How he should have run away, gone upstairs. How he should have called someone: his dad, the police. How he should've wrestled the gun away from Benny somehow or found the right thing to say, the magic thing that would make everything all right.

He didn't do any of that. He strode over to the chair where Benny was sitting and he squatted in front of him so they were face to face. 'Benny, stop it.'

'You think you're better than me. OK, prove it. Prove you're a man. There's one bullet in this gun. One chance in six. Point it at my head and pull the trigger.'

'No. I can't do that.'

'Then I'll do it to you instead.'

'Please, Benny. We don't have to do this.' He swallowed hard, heart thudding fast. 'I love you.'

Benny grabbed Lou by the back of his head. He forced the barrel of the gun into Lou's mouth, between Lou's teeth. Lou could taste it: metal and oil. He tried to pull back but Benny was too strong.

'Do this,' Benny said, 'or I swear to God I will pull the trigger and pull the trigger until I shoot your fucking head off.'

Lou made a choking noise and nodded, as much as he could with Benny holding the back of his head. Benny pulled the gun out of his mouth and Lou spat into his hand and rubbed it on his shorts.

'OK,' Lou said. 'Once.' He was shaking. His eyes leaked helpless tears.

This was the first night of their adult lives. The first night they were men. He couldn't run to someone else. This was all on him, now. All on him and what happened in this room.

'You first,' said Benny. He pointed the gun at Lou's temple, between his left eye and his ear. The barrel didn't touch him, but Lou could feel it anyway: a cold circle where the bullet would enter his brain.

He closed his eyes. Listened to the blood rushing through him. Tasted the gun, still, between his teeth. The empty click, when it came, was so loud that Lou's head jerked back as if it had taken a bullet.

It took a second or two to realise that nothing had happened. He opened his eyes to see the gun still pointing at him and he thought, *Is he going to shoot me again since it didn't work the first time?*

'My turn,' said Benny, and he turned the gun around and offered the hand grip to Lou.

'I don't want to,' said Lou. 'No.'

'My turn,' said Benny again, more vehemently, and he leaned forward, pushing the gun into Lou's hands. 'Take it, don't be a pussy, you promised.'

He hadn't promised but he took it anyway. This couldn't be real. Benny must have only pretended to put a bullet in there. He was trying to freak Lou out, trying to prove Lou was a coward. Why was he doing this? Lou's hands were shaking but he tried to hold the gun steady with both of them. It was warm from Benny's hands, heavier than it looked, and it smelled of WD-40 and the way it had tasted. 'What – what do I do?'

'You pull the fucking trigger.' Benny grabbed the barrel of the gun, which was pointing at the ceiling by now, and put it right up against his temple. Poking into the skin, pushing it up a little into wrinkles like the ones Benny wouldn't get until he was old. 'Just pull it, do it now.'

The trigger was harder to pull than Lou would have thought from movies and TV, especially because his hands were wet with sweat. He had to really pull on it with his finger, watching Benny who didn't even close his eyes, Benny who pressed right up against the gun like he wanted this to happen, and he had time to think *If you were dead I wouldn't have to feel so guilty about how I feel about you.*

Click. Nothing. No bullet.

Relief flooded through Lou so hard it stole his breath. 'Thank fuck,' he said, and relaxed back onto his haunches, lowering the gun. It was over. They could stop this, put away the gun, lock the cabinet, have a drink. He needed a drink. Benny did too, and they could stop acting crazy, put this behind them, get back to nor—

Benny lurched forward. Wrenched the gun out of Lou's hands. Turned it back on himself, barrel to his head, and Lou tried to grab his wrist, pull it away, tell him *Stop it the game's over*, and then an explosion and recoil so Lou fell back onto the floor and when he looked up all he saw was blood. Blood and dark hair and bone, a spray on the pine walls, Benny's body limp in the chair, gun fallen on the carpet tiles between them.

He tried to scream. Nothing came out of his throat. No noise, no breath. Explosion roaring in his ears as if it were still happening, bullet leaving gun.

Thuds on the stairs and Lou, turning, saw Allie standing at the bottom, her hands over her mouth. She stared at Benny's body, then she stared at Lou, and that was when she started to scream.

Lou scrambled to his feet and ran to her. 'Call an ambulance, we've got to call 911,' he said, but he threw his arms around her and held her tight to him so she couldn't go, so she'd stop screaming. She breathed hard and then she pushed him away from her.

'What happened?' she asked, her voice on the thin edge of hysteria.

He looked down at himself. He wiped his bloody hands on his bloody sweatshirt.

'He had one bullet in the gun, and I thought he was putting it down, I thought he was finished, and then he pointed it at himself.'

'He shot himself? Benny?'

'Where are your parents?'

'They're out. He's . . .' She stumbled closer. 'Oh my God, Lou. He's dead!'

Lou couldn't look. 'We have to call 911.' He headed for the stairs, but Allie caught his hand. 'No.'

'What?'

'No. Not yet.'

'But we can't leave him like ...' He gestured. Not looking. Looking at the picture of Jesus' footprints on the beach instead.

'Lou, did you shoot him?'

Force of guilt so strong that he could barely stand. But he made himself meet Allie's eyes. 'No. He did it.'

'OK. I believe you.'

'But I ... I was holding the gun before he did. I tried to get it away from him. Oh God, what if I—'

'Stop. Lou, stop for a minute.'

She was pale, but upright. Her sneakers only inches from bloody carpet, blood on her shirt from him. She looked straight into his eyes. She was breathing hard, eyes so wide he could see the whites all round her irises.

'Lou, if people find out that you were here with him when it happened, you might get the blame.'

'But I didn't—' But had he? It kept running through his mind. Click, empty. Benny grabbing the gun. Benny pointing the gun, Lou trying to take it away. Explosion.

'Nobody's going to care what actually happened. You're an Alder. You're management. You can't be here. They fired shots at the picket line last week. If people know you were here when ...'

Her voice faltered and she looked down at Benny and sobbed once, loud, her hand over her mouth.

'OK,' he said. Knowing she was right. Knowing it made him a coward anyway.

'Then go! Someone might have heard the shot.'

He went up one step. 'Allie—'

'Go! We can't talk about this again, ever. Go, Lou!'

He saw her kneel beside her brother. Put her hand over his. And then he was running up the stairs, through the kitchen and out of the house, pulling his bloodstained sweatshirt over his head and stuffing it under his arm to hide his guilt as he ran away.

Louis

While Lou speaks, Allie sits still and perfectly quiet in a cream-coloured chair, her hands folded on her lap. Irving, on the sofa beside Lou, takes his glasses off and polishes them and puts them on and takes them off again. He doesn't know he's doing it, and when Lou finishes, he does it again, even though the lenses are perfectly clean.

Finally he says, 'Why are you telling me this now?'

'Because you feel responsible for what happened,' Lou says. 'And you're not.'

Irving says, 'We profited off that boy's death.'

'All of us,' Lou agrees. 'Our whole family. If he hadn't died, the mill would have gone out of business. That house Mom lives in, your travels, that book I wrote: all of it came out of Benny dying. But it wasn't your fault, Dad. It was mine.'

'It wasn't your fault, Lou,' says Allie.

Lou shakes his head.

'I've never believed that it was your fault,' she says. 'Never for a minute.'

'You've carried that for thirteen years,' says Irving. 'Oh, son.' He puts his arm awkwardly around Lou's shoulders.

As a child, Lou rode his father's knee like a horse. He sat on his father's shoulders and tried to touch the sky. He was picked up by his father when he fell and scraped his knee bloody; he was tucked in at night, a kiss on his forehead. But then he grew and his father's touches changed. A hand on the shoulder, a clap on the back. A handshake. When his grandfather Alder died, Lou lifted the coffin along with Irving. They walked in step, pallbearers and parallel. Space between them.

Today is the most physical contact Lou has had with his father since he was about ten years old.

'But why are you telling me this now?' Irving asks. Lou draws back, so he can see his dad's face.

'Because we have something else to tell you,' he says. 'We need you to come home to Casablanca.'

The next flight isn't until the following morning and Irving's condo only has one bedroom, so Lou and Allie book into a hotel. The receptionist gives them rooms on the same floor and they ride the elevator up in weary silence. Lou feels emptied out; his shoulders slump and his ears ring. Allie stands straight, her eyes on the elevator floor. She's hardly spoken since they got here to Cape Canaveral.

The elevator doors open and they step out into a long corridor with patterned carpets and plain walls. Doors after doors after doors, somewhere that could be anywhere in the country.

She's in room 305 and he's in room 307. He stops with her in front of her door.

'Thank you,' he says to her. 'I know that was really hard for you.'

She's still looking down at the patterned carpet. 'That was the first time I heard the whole story.'

'I'm sorry.'

She shakes her head. 'I've always thought that if I hadn't been drunk and passed out in front of the TV, if I'd heard you guys coming home, I could have stopped it. Until I heard your side of the story today, I didn't know how angry he was or how determined. I'm not sure I could have stopped him that night. Maybe that afternoon, if I'd talked to him, if I hadn't been so upset that my big moment was ruined. That might have made a difference

Or if I'd done something before. But that night ... he grabbed the gun from you. He was going to do something. If it hadn't been that, it would have been something else.'

'Sometimes I wish that I'd got the bullet.'

'No, Lou. Never wish that.'

'I left you to deal with it.'

'That's what I told you to do. It was the best thing. I still believe it was.'

She looks up at him then and she's so sad that all he wants to do is hold her like he used to. Head to heart.

'I still miss him,' Lou says. 'I miss you too.'

Allie shakes her head again, but this time she has a ghost of a smile on her face. 'You don't miss me,' she says. 'I read your book. You miss Maine. You miss belonging somewhere.'

She touches his arm briefly and then turns, opens her hotel room door, and disappears.

The next afternoon he drops off Allie at her house and then he and Irving drive home. Before they go into the house, Irving takes a walk around it. Lou wonders if his dad is walking down memory lane, or if he's delaying going inside and seeing Peggy. Finally he nods, and says, 'Good,' and they go in.

There's a casserole dish on the doorstep; when Lou picks it up it's still warm. 'Is it from Odette Baker?' asks Irving, and when Lou checks the note on top of it, it is.

'How'd you know?'

'I recognise the dish. And the smell of her Swedish meatballs. She's made that for every pot-luck dinner for the past twenty years. They're pretty good.' Irving opens the door into the kitchen. Mulder barrels into them, fluffy tail wagging. Jeanne, one of the hospice nurses, is loading the dishwasher.

'Oh, hi, Irving,' she says as if he's just walked in from a trip to the store.

'Hi, Jeanne. Are you here looking after Peggy?'

'I certainly am. Hi, Lou. She's awake, she's watching TV. I brought her some Jell-O but she didn't want it.'

'Thanks for your help, we really appreciate it,' Irving says, and though Lou expects him to look around like he did outside, he goes straight for the stairs. Lou deposits the meatballs on the counter, picks up the dog and follows.

His father fits in this house like he didn't in Florida. Even though he hasn't been in it for several years, as far as Lou knows, he takes the stairs two at a time like he always has done, moves through the rooms as if he never left. The door to Peggy's bedroom is open but he knocks softly on the frame.

'Hi, Peggy,' he says, standing in the doorway. Lou, behind him, can see his mother turn her head on the pillow. He told his mother he had to go to New York to see his publisher, because he didn't want her to know if Irving refused to come. For a moment he's frightened that she's going to get upset, that he's made a mistake.

But when she says, 'Irving,' she doesn't sound surprised at all.

Irving clears his throat. 'Looks like Ed's doing a pretty good job of taking care of the house for you.'

'He's been great.'

'Looks like those gutters held out over the winter.'

'They were good.'

He takes off his glasses and polishes them on his shirt. 'It sure is good to see you, Peggy.'

'Irving,' she says again, and this time Lou knows he hasn't made a mistake. Irving puts his glasses on and goes to her. He sits on the bed, takes her hand, and bows his head over it. Peggy raises her other hand and she strokes his cheek.

'I'm so sorry,' he says.

'There's no need to be,' Peggy answers, and Lou decides this would be a good time to take the dog for a walk.

Louise

Dana has never had lobster, and Lou hasn't had it since she was a teenager, so Irving drives twenty miles to the seafood truck in Norway and he buys three pound-and-a-half soft shells. He comes home with them in a cooler, as proud as if he trapped them himself. Dana lifts the lid.

'What the hell!' she says. 'They're still *alive*?'

'You have to cook them from live,' Irving explains. 'That's how you know that they're fresh.'

'Ugh. What do you do, cut their heads off or something?'

'You drop them into boiling water.'

'*Ugh.*'

'But they're delicious,' says Irving. 'Real Maine lobster. These were caught yesterday.'

Lou reaches into the cooler and takes out a lobster, holding it carefully by the thorax. Eight spidery legs flail, tail uncurls, claws wave. It's a giant insect with antennae and beady eyes on stalks.

'That is gross,' says Dana. 'Why are there rubber bands on its claws?'

'So it won't snap your nose off,' says Irving. He makes his hands into mitten-shaped claws and pretends to snap at Dana's nose. She giggles, but then looks at the lobsters again and grimaces.

'They're brown. They look like dirt bugs.'

'They'll turn red when they're cooked,' says Irving. 'You will love them.'

'How do you even eat them?'

'You crack the shells and pull out the meat.'

'You are seriously telling me you're going to take living creatures and boil them and rip them apart with your bare hands?'

'Yup.'

Dana considers. 'That's sort of badass.' She takes a picture of the lobster that Lou is holding on her phone and then wanders off to post it online somewhere. As Dana hasn't actually picked an argument with her, Lou takes this as a win.

'You always had a tuna sandwich,' Irving says to Lou.

'Don't tell Dana that. I want her to be more adventurous than I was.'

'You went and lived in New York. That's pretty adventurous.' Irving considers the lobster in Lou's hand, almost with pity. Carefully he takes it from her and puts it back into the cooler. 'You know, I heard there was an opening for a sixth grade English teacher at the middle school here…'

'I've got a job, Dad.'

'Of course you do. But these kids don't have a lot. There aren't many prospects here in the valley any more. It's valuable for them to have the perspective of someone who's like them, but who has seen more of the world.'

'I've seen Brooklyn. That's pretty much it.'

'Just saying.' Irving holds up his hands. 'You'd have more time to write your book.'

Lou gets out the big pot and fills it with water to boil. 'Who told you I'm writing a book?'

'Nobody. I just know it's what you always wanted to do.'

'Brooklyn's my home now.'

'But Casablanca will always be your home, too.' He starts rummaging around cupboards. 'Should I make Dana a tuna sandwich, in case?'

'That's a good idea.'

'I'm glad she's talking to you again.'

'She's not talking to me. She's talking to the room while I'm in it. But it's a start.' Lou washes the lobster smell off her hands and sighs. 'Parenting is hard.'

'I think... I've always thought that you have to let them sort it out themselves, and if they come back, then it's all right.'

She looks at her dad. He hasn't asked her why Dana is angry at her. In all these years, he never asked her why she and Peggy fought. In her angrier moments, when she was alone and pregnant in New Jersey, she thought it was because he was too cowardly to ask, too afraid of conflict. But that's hypocritical. After all, she never told him either.

'I never wanted you to have to choose sides,' she says.

'I'd never choose sides. Peggy's my wife, you're my daughter, Dana's my granddaughter. I'm on all of your sides.'

'Can you be on every side at once?'

Irving shrugs, and pushes up his glasses. 'That's sort of what love is. Listen. Your mother was angry when you moved away from home and got pregnant. I guess she wanted something else for you. But she loves you, and she loves Dana, and that's all that matters now, right?'

'I don't know, Dad. It's complicated.'

He takes off his glasses and polishes them and puts them back on. Then he takes out a can opener and addresses his next words to the can of tuna. 'Is it because you're gay?'

Before this summer, Lou would have said that her father was as predictable as clockwork. She lets out a surprised bark of a laugh. 'For a man with Coke-bottle glasses, you see a lot.'

'Casablanca used to be an old-fashioned place. But we've moved with the times, even up here.'

'Still boiling lobsters alive and ripping them apart with your bare hands, though.'

'It's "badass", my granddaughter tells me.'

She goes to her dad and hugs him. 'I'm bisexual. That's not the reason I left Casablanca, though. And I know that you're going to be lonely up here without Mom, but I have to think about Dana too.'

'I won't be lonely. I've got a lot of friends.'

He pats her back. He *is* going to be lonely, and that complicates everything for Lou.

'I'll let you sort it out yourself,' he says. 'Between you and Dana, and between you and your mother. I trust you to get it right.'

Louis

Allie lives outside Casablanca. Lou drives down the road that curves along the river and turns left up a hill. It's a couple miles before the turnoff to her house: a narrow road with trees looming up either side of it. Her house is set back from this road. He would've missed it if not for her mailbox with PHELPS written on it.

Her car is out front so he knows she's home. The house itself is a small neat Cape covered with cedar shingles that have been painted forest green. White shutters frame the windows, and the front porch holds a rocking chair and a big pot of geraniums. It would be a good spot for kids, out here; there's plenty of space to play and the forest is close, pine and maple trees and silver birches. You could hang a swing from a tree, make a slide to put on the lawn.

Allie always wanted kids. She was going to be a doctor and have two, at least. Twins, she always said. *They run in my family.* She'd never said outright that she wanted to have kids with him; probably just as well, because as a teenager that might have freaked him out. But he'd known that was in her future. Maybe in theirs, if they had stayed together.

She hasn't told him why she doesn't have kids. He hasn't told her why he doesn't, either, how it never felt like the right time. Carrie was busy with her career, he was busy with his writing. Carrie'd had a pregnancy scare once and Lou had been just that

– scared – but he'd talked himself into the idea by the time that she found out she wasn't expecting. He hasn't really sat down and thought about whether he was scared because he wasn't ready for kids, or because he knew, even then, that their marriage wasn't going to make it.

Allie must've bought this house thinking about kids, though. She never did anything without thinking through all the permutations, and if Lou can see the tyre swing, the slide and the sandbox, the snowmen in winter, she will have seen them, too.

He parks behind her car. Probably he should've called first, but in Casablanca people do pop by for a visit, and he felt like going for a drive anyway. Revisiting what happened thirteen years ago has made him restless, like he needs to do something, fix something, but since they got back from Florida he doesn't know what to do or how. He picks up the foil-wrapped banana bread from the passenger seat – it's roughly the size and weight of a brick – and heads for the porch.

Before he gets there, he hears a gunshot.

Lou drops the banana bread. It thuds to the grass and he stands, uncertain of whether he should run towards the sound, or away from it, and he's thinking, *Hunters, it's just hunters*, but this isn't hunting season, this is July, and then there's another shot. It's close. Coming from the back of Allie's house.

'Allie!' he yells and runs around the side of the house. As he runs, he's seeing Benny. What was left of Benny's head. Then he rounds the corner and there's Allie, dressed in jeans and a striped blouse, holding a shotgun and pointing it towards the woods.

'Lou?' she says, lowering the gun.

'What's the matter, why are you shooting?' he gasps.

She points at a row of tin cans set up on a sawhorse.

'Oh. Oh, target practice.' He lets out a long breath of relief. 'I didn't know you shot.'

'I don't. I've never even fired this gun before. I got rid of all my dad's other ones and I only kept this one because people kept telling me I should have something if I lived out here. This is the first time I've ever loaded it.'

'Why are you—'

'Because I'm angry, Lou.' She brings the gun up again, settles the stock on her shoulder. Points the barrel at the cans. 'I've had to be the good girl. The strong one. I've never been allowed to be angry. Not at my dad, who was an utter shit, and who told us that he was doing what a man had to do.' She fires the gun, and Lou jumps. The bullet goes into the woods without touching a can.

'Not at my mom, who was too scared to stand up to him and too scared to leave. I can't be angry at her for needing me so I couldn't have the career I wanted or the family I wanted.' Another shot. This time he's expecting it, so he only flinches.

'Not at Benny, because Benny is a goddamn hero. Benny saved the fucking town by sticking a gun in your mouth and then putting a bullet in his brain.'

This shot hits a tree. He sees splinters fly, leaves shake.

'I wasn't allowed to be angry at you because you let him do it, even though you didn't want to. I couldn't be angry at myself because I didn't wake up until I heard the shot. Not at the whole. Fucking. Town. Who had to wait until my brother died to see that they were wrong, that people mattered more than money, or the whole fucking world that took my twin away and took you away and left me all alone.'

She squeezes off a volley of shots, each one kicking at her shoulder, pushing her back but she squares herself again and again and pulls the trigger.

A single can pings off the sawhorse.

Allie is breathing hard. Lou's ears are ringing. He stares at her as she bends and puts the gun on the ground. Her nose wrinkles as if she's disgusted.

'I never want to fire another gun again in my life,' she says. 'Get rid of this one for me, please, Lou. Thanks.'

And she turns and walks away. The back door closes behind her.

Lou picks up the gun. It's warm. For the first time he notices there's an open box of ammunition on the ground, too.

He hasn't touched a gun since that night. He has no idea how to get rid of one. Bring it to the police station, he supposes. They can figure out how to dismantle it or sell it or something. He can already picture the look on the officers' faces when he brings in a perfectly good firearm and tells them to dispose of it for him. *He's really turned into a New Yorker.*

Lou tucks the box under his arm and carries the gun awkwardly, pointed at the ground well away from his feet. On his way to the car, he sees the foil brick of banana bread on the lawn. Allie is probably not in the mood for banana bread, but Candice Farmer put it on Peggy's doorstep this morning and though he's not entirely sure of the etiquette of regifting it in the first place, it seems downright ungrateful to leave it on the grass. He stows the gun and bullets in the car and puts the banana bread on Allie's porch, near her front door. Out here in the woods, there's a chance an animal will come for it before Allie sees it, but knocking on her door with baked goods is too much of an anticlimax. It would be diminishing her anger and its explosive, scattering force.

Louise

Before they get in the car, Lou stops Dana. 'I know you're still mad at me, but I need you to be cheerful today. For Nana's sake. This is her last trip to the beach.'

Dana grunts, so Lou knows she's unforgiven.

'Just be nice to Nana,' she says.

'I'm always nice to Nana.'

She is. Lou lets it go.

Peggy is always cold, so for their trip to Morocco Pond on a sunny day in the middle of July, she is wearing leggings, a shirt, a cardigan, thick socks, boot-style slippers, a chiffon scarf, and a hat. Dana chose the hat: it's straw, wide-brimmed, and has a silk flower tucked into the band. It was a good choice; the other clothes are not exactly stylish, because they have to be things that Irving can put on and take off her easily, and they have to be loose enough to conceal her catheter bag and her morphine pump. But the scarf and hat make Peggy look like a film star, especially when she puts on a pair of sunglasses.

Lou is reminding Dana to be cheerful because she's reminding herself. She, Allie and Irving have done a lot of planning of logistics, figuring out how to get Peggy into the car, out of the car, onto the beach, and while Lou is glad to be doing something for her mother that will give her a good day – maybe one of her last good days – she's aware that she finds it easier to plan nice things for Peggy than to actually be nice to her. Her mother, in the abstract, is easier to forgive than her mother in the flesh. Maybe if she could have it out with Peggy, explain how betrayed she's felt and how that one deep cut paved the way for a thousand little cuts to happen, then they could let things heal over for good. But her mother's weak and in pain, and it would be evil to bring up her past mistakes.

But without that, how can she forgive?

Lou tries to, anyway. She's cheerful, perched in the back seat of the car while her father drives and her mother's bundled into the passenger seat. 'I feel about five years old again,' she jokes. They used to drive up here every weekend in the summer to come to her grandparents' camp on the privately-owned part of the lake. The camp got sold to out-of-staters when the mill closed down – unlike in Casablanca, property prices here on the Pond haven't gone down at all. Today they're going to the public beach, the beach Lou used to cycle to with Allie and Benny when they were teenagers, to spend the summer afternoons swimming and lazing on the sand. It's the beach where Lou had her first kiss with a boy, the beach where she stepped on broken glass and cut her foot open so badly she needed seven stitches, the beach where she tried her first sip of beer, the beach where her parents first spoke with each other.

It's only five miles away, past the falls, around a mountain and into another valley. The river that feeds Morocco Pond also feeds Pennacook river that passes through town. The lake itself is deep and cold, cupped by mountains. It's a small lake compared with Sebago or Rangeley or Mooselookmeguntic, about half a mile in diameter, with only one beach that runs along the south side. The rest of it has a rocky shore, with marshes near the inlet and outlet of the river. In winter the lake freezes over and is studded with ice-fishing shacks; in summer it's busy with jet skis and canoes and swimmers bobbing in the waves.

'She won't make it up there again,' Lou said to Allie when they were planning this in the rocking chairs on the front porch, when

Irving had gone inside to check on Peggy. 'She might not make it out of the house again.'

'She's declined quickly in the month since you got home,' Allie agreed, and reached over to rub Lou's knee in sympathy. 'I think she's felt that now you were here, she could let go.'

'I can't let go.'

Allie rocked back and looked at the porch ceiling. 'When my mother was dying, I told her how mad I used to be about how she didn't protect us. She never once stood up to my father, you know. But as soon as I said it to her, I knew she felt she didn't have a choice. He'd never have changed, and she would never have had the strength to leave him.'

'My mom had a choice. She chose the town over me.'

'Would you have pressed charges?'

'I don't know.'

'You still could now, maybe.' Allie glanced at her. Lou understood the permission being granted here.

'I don't think I can, though. I don't want Dana knowing.'

'I—' Allie stopped herself, seemed to be considering her words carefully. 'If it helps, I don't think he's done anything else like that since.'

'You can't know that, though.'

'No. I can't. I thought I knew everything about him, but... I don't.'

'You know everything about me, now.'

They rocked together for a few moments, quiet. It was a hot day; the small breeze from the movement of the chair cooled the sweat on Lou's upper lip. On a close day, the absence of the smell from the mill was almost a presence in itself. A yellow ghost on the clear air. Lou breathed in deep. This was OK. Casablanca, nestled between the mountains, was OK. She felt safer with Allie knowing.

'It felt good to tell my mother how I felt,' said Allie at last. 'That's all I'm saying. It felt good to tell her I forgave her.'

Lou shook her head. 'Let's talk about Morocco Pond.'

Allie looked like she was going to say something else, but then Irving came back outside with some iced tea and that was that.

Now, Irving pulls into the beach parking lot. 'There's a disabled spot near the front,' Lou tells him.

'We haven't got a sticker.'

'I think we can bend the rules, Dad.'

'I don't want anyone thinking we're taking a space we're not entitled to,' says Peggy, and Irving parks in a regular space, several cars' length away. Lou attempts to exchange an exasperated look with her daughter, but her daughter is pointedly gazing out the window away from her. One thing about Dana Alder: she can hold a grudge. Maybe she's come by it naturally.

Irving gets the foldable wheelchair out of the car trunk while Lou fetches blankets, the umbrella, cooler. Dana takes the bag with sun cream and towels and sticks close to Peggy as Irving helps her out of the car into the wheelchair. The packed-dirt parking lot is fine, but when they get to the beach they realise they have a bit of a problem when the wheels sink several inches into the sand and the chair refuses to budge. Dana drops the bag, bends down and grabs the two small front wheels of the chair. 'Lift it, Grandad,' she says.

Lou drops her own stuff and helps Irving by taking the other handle. Together, the three of them hoist the chair a few inches into the air and carry Peggy, Miss Western Maine 1976, down the beach towards the water like the queen of an ancient land.

Dana helps set up the umbrella to shade Peggy; they have to dig a hole in the sand and then prop the umbrella up on the back of the wheelchair, which means the umbrella lists at an angle, but it performs its purpose of shading Peggy from the sun. Irving spreads a blanket on the sand while Dana fusses with Peggy's hat and scarf.

'Whoo,' says Irving, fanning himself. His face is pink. 'I'm ready for a swim, how about anyone else?'

'I'll stay here and work on my tan,' says Peggy, smiling. The pink umbrella has lent colour to her cheeks. 'Maybe I'll build a sand castle.'

Lou sits on the blanket next to the wheelchair. 'You go ahead, Dad. I'll sit here with Mom for a while and take in the view. I haven't been up here since I was a teenager.'

Irving unbuttons his shirt, takes off his glasses, and goes down to the water in his blue swimming trunks. As far as Lou can tell, they're the same ones he used to wear when she was a kid: baggy, cinched at the waist with a drawstring, with a fraying hem.

'Who's going to make sure he wears decent clothes?' says Peggy.

'I will, Nana,' says Dana.

'From Brooklyn?'

'I'll make him send me a selfie every day before he goes out.' Dana kisses Peggy on the forehead. 'I'm going to go look around.'

Lou shoots her a look, but Dana isn't paying attention. 'I think you should stay with your grandmother and me,' she says.

'I'm not a little kid. I can be trusted around water.'

'That's not what I'm saying. I just think—'

'You think that I shouldn't do anything but hang around where you can watch me 24/7,' snaps Dana. 'I'll be back before it's time to go.'

She walks off down the beach, so quickly that sand sprays behind her heels. Lou gets up to follow her.

'Let her go,' says Peggy. 'She needs some space.'

'Today isn't about space. It's about family.'

'It's OK.' Peggy pauses. 'Your dad says that you haven't been letting her play soccer.'

Lou doesn't know how to explain herself without bringing up Benny, which she does not want to do today, so she merely says, 'Yes.'

'She can't see your point of view. She can only see that she's hurting.'

'She should trust me to know what's best for her. I'm her mother.'

'Mothers don't always know what's best,' says Peggy.

Lou frowns. She says: 'Mom, I don't need—'

'Lou, honey, I need to say something. Can I say something?'

The 'honey' brings Lou up short. 'OK.'

'I've had a lot of time to think, especially lately, and I was wrong. All those years ago, I was wrong. I should have put you first. There is nothing more precious than my child. Not the business, not the town; nothing. At the time I didn't know what to do. I'd lost my parents because of that strike and I thought I was going to lose my best friend. I didn't know I was going to lose you, too.' Peggy takes a deep breath. 'I thought we were doing the right thing by keeping quiet. But I should have put you first. I spent my whole life being afraid to rock the boat, and you suffered for it. I'm sorry.'

She's thought about her mother saying this, many times over the years. Thought about how she would feel if she did.

Allie said that she'd told her mother how angry she'd been with her, and that had helped. But now that Lou has the chance to say that, finally, she finds she doesn't need to.

'Thank you, Mom,' she says. 'That means a lot to me.'

'I lost two babies after I had you,' says Peggy. 'I always pretended it was OK. But I thought about them every day. I thought I couldn't bear to lose anything else. But then I made the wrong choice and I lost you. I was angry that you stayed away after Dana was born, but it was my fault.'

'You didn't lose me, Mom.'

She kisses her mom and puts her arms around her. Chanel N°5, the same perfume her mother used to squirt onto her wrists as a treat when she was a little girl and she thought her mother was the most flawless creature in the entire world, the person who could do anything, who wore an invisible tiara.

Lou doesn't think her own daughter has ever seen her as

invincible or omniscient. And she's always thought that was a good thing, because that means that Dana has less scope to be disappointed; but maybe it isn't. Maybe Dana missed out by not having a mother she could look at with awe, who would squirt her with perfume and let her try on high heels and her satin sash.

Peggy hugs Lou back. She kisses Lou's cheek, and wipes off the lipstick mark. 'Though I think… maybe you should let her play soccer.'

Lou pulls back. 'Mom, you know why I can't.'

'Is he actually her father? And if so, doesn't she deserve the chance to know him, in whatever way?'

'No,' says Lou.

'All right,' says Peggy. 'I trust your judgement. I love you, Louise.'

'I love you too, Mom.'

She hasn't said this in thirteen years. It feels much better than she thought it would. It feels better, even, than hearing her mother say, 'I'm sorry.'

Louis

As soon as they get to the beach, Mulder is out of the car and running like an overexcited puppy to the water. He barrels over several beach towels, leaps over a sunbathing teenager like he's a hurdle, and flings himself into the waves.

Peggy, watching through the windscreen from the passenger seat of the car, laughs. 'That dog is in heaven.'

'He's never been to the beach before,' says Lou. 'I'm surprised he knows what to do.'

Irving is in the back seat with Allie. He helps her get the wheelchair out of the trunk and she shows him how to unfold it, put the footrests down. They wheel it round so Lou can help Peggy out of the car and into it.

Peggy is so very thin; much thinner than she was when he arrived in Casablanca a month ago. Since Irving has arrived from Florida, Peggy has been trying to eat a little. Last night she had a dish of ice cream – only a small dish, but she ate it all – and Lou allowed himself to think, for like half a second, that she might be feeling better, that she might rally a bit before the end. Even, maybe, that the doctors were somehow wrong. That all of this was a big mistake and all Peggy really needed was her family together and she'd be OK.

Wishful thinking. When Peggy couldn't manage the stairs and Lou carried her down them and into the car, she was like a wisp of dandelion fluff in his arms. A few extra calories aren't going to halt the march of this disease in her body. Even the drive has exhausted her; she leans on him as he half lifts her into the chair.

When they carry the chair across the sand, Allie and Irving in front and Lou taking the back, Mulder runs back to them and barks, not sure about this strange flying contraption. 'Be a good dog,' says Peggy, and he whines and stops barking for the time it takes to set Peggy up. It's a nice day, sunny but not too hot, with a little breeze. They put up an umbrella to make some shade for Peggy and Allie tucks a blanket around her lap. She's got a scarf tied around her hair and she's wearing sunglasses and the lipstick that Carrie gave her and she looks a tiny bit like Ingrid Bergman, all cheekbones.

She tilts back her head and takes in a long, deep breath. 'Oh, I love the smell of the air here. It's so clean.'

'It's always been my favourite place,' says Allie. 'Except when we had to take swimming lessons here at eight o'clock during the summer vacation. I didn't like it then. It was freezing.'

'It's not freezing now,' says Lou, looking at how his father is hovering over Peggy, as if he's not quite sure what to do. 'Want a swim?' he asks Allie. His parents could maybe use a few minutes by themselves.

'Will you be all right, Peggy?' Allie asks. It's actually her day off, but she wanted to come along after helping to plan it.

'I'm more than fine,' says Peggy 'I feel like the queen of the beach.'

Lou's wearing his trunks; he pulls off his shirt and tries not to obviously look when Allie takes off her shorts and T-shirt. He's been thinking about Allie almost constantly: her beside him on the plane, sitting in Irving's featureless apartment, that afternoon shooting her father's gun. They've spoken, but not about any of these things. She hasn't even asked him if he managed to dispose of the gun – which he did, though he's sure the police started laughing about it the minute he left the station, and they're probably still laughing about it now. She trusted him to do it and that makes him reluctant to mention it, because that will seem as if he doesn't feel trusted.

They've been concentrating not on sadness and anger, but on giving this bright day to Peggy.

'C'mon,' he says to Mulder, and the dog prances behind them as they run to the water. Lou's conscious that he's putting on a show of having a good time for his mother's benefit, but then Mulder barks and snaps at a wave and he laughs for real.

The lake is sandy underfoot and, even though the day is warm, the water is cold. He remembers those swimming lessons too. The teenage swimming instructor would stand warm and dry on the beach, wearing swimming trunks and a sweatshirt, and yell to the shivering kids in his care, 'Get in! It's fine when you get used to it!' And they always grumbled and whined and crossed skinny arms over chests rough with gooseflesh, but when they got in and braved the shock of the cold, it was fine. You can get used to anything.

Allie plays with Mulder near the shore, but Lou pushes off into the water. He swims in New York – it's his preferred exercise because it's hard to run fast in the city – but it's always in a pool. It's almost strange to be swimming in a lake, even the lake he learned to swim in. There's no temperature control, no chlorine, no one swimming laps around him. The water smells fresh, like minerals and ice, and there's a breeze that whips up small waves around him. He ducks his head underwater, opens his eyes, and sees the world around him turned to greenish murk.

It's not the same water he swam in as a child: the lake has renewed itself, frozen and melted, the water only pausing here before constantly flowing downstream to the Penacook river, to the falls and Casablanca. But it feels the same. It holds him up, makes him weightless, ageless, a floating body in something bigger than himself. It makes him feel as if he doesn't matter, as if all of this would still exist if he wasn't here.

Then Allie splashes out to join him and, as they're swimming, her hand brushes his and he remembers, not the times they came here for swimming lessons, but another afternoon years later in high school, when they rode their bicycles up to the Pond with a group of other kids, and while they all played volleyball on the beach, the two of them came out to swim alone. And instead of swimming they bobbed in the water, heads apart, but hands under the water touching each other's skin. He learned her secretly, this first girl he had kissed, this first girl he loved, all the ways she was different from him, and she did the same while they were in plain sight and no one could see what they were doing, both held up by the water that concealed their eager hands. He'd come in her hand and it had dissolved, flowed away, and later, years later, when he wrote a book about Maine, its shape and history, snow in forests, dying trees, the river's flow, he was writing about her. He was writing about Gill Lafayette and Pierre Dubois and their forbidden love in the logging camp, their difference and sameness, but he was also writing about Allie. Allie, who knew him and knew this place formed by glaciers and water. Because water freezes, flows and changes – rivers divert, lakes flood, streams wear away the soil – but it stays the same.

'Race you to the rock,' he says, and she laughs and starts swimming and Lou swims in her wake.

Louis & Louise

Sun sparkles on the surface of Morocco Pond. Irving sits on the blanket at Peggy's feet like a suitor and takes her hand. In town it was a hot day, nearly stifling; they had to put on all the fans and open the windows in the house. But up here at the Pond, there's a fresh breeze off the water and in the shade, it's comfortable. Peggy's hand is cold but it nestles inside his.

'Pretty Peggy Sue,' he says, and he's rewarded by her smile. It's the same smile she gave him when they were both young, that day when they first met. She was lying on a beach towel in a pink bikini beside her best friend and he knew who she was. Everyone knew Peggy Grenier, the beauty queen. He had no idea that she knew who he was too. If he had, he might not have said anything. For a dizzy few seconds after he stopped awkwardly next to them and said, 'Hi,' he thought that they would laugh at him.

But then she'd smiled instead. His pretty Peggy Sue.

She's still beautiful enough to knock him out, especially here with the breeze lending her cheeks a small flush.

'Thirty-three years since that day,' he says to her. 'It's a lifetime, isn't it? I still remember what it felt like the minute I saw you, and I still don't know why you smiled back at me.'

Peggy takes off her sunglasses. She squints a bit in the sun but her eyes sparkle, too. They're the same colour as the Pond.

'You were different,' she says. 'None of the other boys were like you. You were the first boy I ever met who made me think I might not be good enough.'

'You were always good enough for me. Too good.'

'I was a failed model. I didn't know what to do with my life. And then you came over, and you knew everything.'

'I didn't know anything. Not then. I'm not sure I know much now, but then I was scared to even talk with you.'

She squeezes his hand. There's not much strength in that squeeze now: not like their honeymoon where they stopped off at Old Orchard Beach and rode the rollercoaster and she held onto him for dear life. He'd never felt so strong.

'I've been thinking a lot,' she says. 'You and I have been married for thirty-two years, but I never showed you who I really was. I always put on a face. I always tried to make everything perfect and I always said that everything was OK. I never showed you how afraid I was of failing everyone.'

He brings her hand to his lips and kisses it.

'I knew,' he says. 'You haven't failed.'

'I should have done more. There were things I could have done. But it's too late now.'

They watch the water. The way the sun dances. The silhouette of Lou's head as their child, now an adult, swims. The shadow of the pine trees on the other side of the lake. On a summer's afternoon like this, it's hard to believe that the sun will ever set.

Once, he'd wanted more children. He'd wanted them all to live a life somewhere else. He'd maybe wanted, in his secret self, a wife who was better educated, who had more ambitions, who loved travel, who he could talk with about books, about films, about the poetry of mathematics.

In this moment, though, it's hard to believe that he could ever have done better than this woman who holds his hand, who has suffered loss and come through it whole, who is beautiful and brave and loving.

'Are you afraid now?' he asks her.

And she says, 'No. I'm not any more.'

Louise

Dana follows the path around to the road. She brushes the sand off her feet and slips on her sandals. It literally makes no sense that her mother should get all protective now, when they're out in the middle of nowhere. She's been walking home by herself from school with all her friends since she was nine. She's been riding the subway by herself since she was ten. She's seen drug deals going down and looked the other way, she's crossed the street to avoid drunks, she can cross a busy road against the light (she wouldn't tell her mom that). She knows the difference between a macchiato and a flat white, she's been on overnight trips with school, she's played soccer all over New York state.

But God forbid she should wander around a little bit in a place that has more moose than people. Or play a non-contact game with a bunch of kids her age.

She's not great at school. She's OK, but she gets some Cs along with her Bs and the occasional A. She likes to read, but she can't imagine being a teacher like her mom or a computer programmer like her grandfather; she thinks, sometimes, that she probably got her truck driver father's brains, but then she thinks that's probably being unfair to truck drivers. She can't do anything musical or artistic, and she's not particularly pretty. Soccer is her one thing. She likes basketball, too, and baseball (she's not keen on softball, even though that's supposed to be the girls' version). But nothing as much as soccer. That's when people look at her like she's something, when her body and her brain come together and work exactly like they're supposed to, when she's not Dana, or even a twelve-year-old girl, but the simple essence of herself.

She walks along the road. It's a narrow one, with enough room for a single car. Houses line the left-hand side of the road, the lake side. Most of them are pretty modest wooden houses; a couple are actual shacks. Her grandfather told her that her great-grandparents used to own a house up here, back when their family used to be sort of rich. She'd like to go back and get Grandad and ask him which one it was. Maybe this one, the big old-looking one painted blue with a Range Rover parked outside it. The car has New Jersey plates. Maybe if Grandad asked, the owners would let them go inside and have a look, and she could see where Grandad spent every summer when he was growing up.

Dana keeps walking, scuffing her feet, till the road stops. The houses have lawns open to the road so you can see straight down to the lake – but the house at the end of the road has a high wall made of piled-up stones, with a metal gate. There's a keypad by the gate and everything. The gate's open, though, and there's rock music playing: Aerosmith, she thinks. She probably shouldn't, but she peeks her head inside the gate and there's Coach, washing a red sports car.

He looks up and recognises her, and something flits across his face. He sort of looks angry, which makes Dana step back and say, 'Sorry, Coach, I didn't mean to be nosy.'

He puts down his bucket and sponge. 'No problem, Dana. How are you doing?'

Her mom always tells her not to go into strangers' yards or houses or cars but this is Coach and he's also Mom's friend's brother. So she steps past the gate. 'I'm OK. I'm sorry my mom won't let me be on the team any more.'

'That's your mom's decision.'

'It's a stupid decision,' she says, not bothering to conceal her annoyance.

'Did she … tell you why?'

Dana snorts. 'That would require her to consider that I'm a human being.'

'Oh.'

'I know that she's best friends with your sister,' Dana dares. 'Did you do something to piss her off?'

'I … it's a long time ago, we were kids, I don't really remember.'

'It's ridiculous that she wants to control me because of something that happened in, like, high school or whatever.'

She hoped Coach would take the hint and tell her something, but he doesn't. 'I didn't even know you were Lou's kid when you started playing,' he says. 'I didn't even know she had a kid. You don't look much like her. I guess you look like Peggy's side of the family.'

'Yeah, maybe I look like my dad too.' She takes another step in and stands by the sports car. 'This place is really nice.'

It is. She can see the house, now: it's made out of logs, like a log cabin, but it's much bigger than any cabin, and it looks pretty new. It has shutters with pine trees cut into them and a wraparound porch that faces the lake. The place looks professionally landscaped, with flowers and trimmed bushes. The garage, which is made out of logs too, is open and she can see another car in there, a white truck with lots of chrome on it. She can also see a couple of ATVs and what look like snowmobiles.

'Did you really used to play for the Red Sox?' she asks.

'Yeah.'

'What's that like? Playing for a pro team?'

'Pretty good, I'm not gonna lie. There's pressures too, though. You're only as good as your last game. If you make a mistake, nobody's gonna let you forget it.' His face twitches, in the way that it did earlier, but maybe that's normal for him. Like a tic. 'Baseball's the only thing I was ever good at.'

'Why do you coach soccer then?'

'I coach anything they'll let me. I do soccer on my non-baseball days.' He smiles at her, picks up the sponge again, and starts rubbing suds on his car. 'Are you thinking of being a pro someday?'

'I'd love it.'

'Lots of opportunities for girls now. Didn't used to be that way.'

'Nobody ever takes me seriously.'

'Well, don't listen to them. If you know what you want, you go for it. Biggest things we regret are the things we never do.' A tic again. It must be a normal thing for him, that she never noticed when she was on the team because she was playing ball.

She comes around to the front of the car, where he is, and watches him work. She's set her phone to silent, but it vibrates in her shorts pocket. It's her mom again. She ignores it.

'You want some help?' she asks.

'If you want to, sure.' He tosses her the sponge and goes into the garage for another one while she rubs at a headlight. The car's a Corvette. She's not much into cars. Farah's dad has a sports car and according to Farah, her mom was furious about it when he bought it. She said he was having a midlife crisis and he was trying to make up for the inadequate size of his dick. That was before they split up. It might even have been the reason why they split up.

Maybe this car is a midlife crisis – she's not 100 per cent sure when 'midlife' is, but Benny seems old enough to her, as old as her mom, at least. Anyway, maybe you have midlife crises early when all the kids in town call you 'Piss-Pants'.

He comes back and dips his sponge in the soapy water. She works on the front, while he works on the side. Her phone buzzes again.

'You going to answer that?' he asks.

'No.'

He shrugs.

'Are there baseball cards of you?' she asks him.

'Yeah.'

'Do you have any?'

'Yeah, they sent me them. They're in Lucite blocks.'

'How much are they worth?'

'I have no idea.'

'Do you have any kids?'

'Nope.'

'Are you married?'

'You always ask this many questions?'

'I'm just making conversation.'

He straightens up and rubs his forehead with the back of the hand holding the sponge. 'It's hot out here. Giving me a headache. You thirsty?'

'Sort of.'

'I'm going to get a cold beer. You want a Coke?'

'OK.' She puts down her sponge and makes to follow him to the house, but he shakes his head.

'I'll bring it out. Be right back.'

She sees it happen. She's reaching for her sponge again, about to say thanks in advance for the Coke, when she sees his face go slack and his eyes roll up into his head. He starts twitching, not only the side of his face but his whole body, twitching and jerking, and then he crumples. She hears the back of his head hit the driveway.

'Coach?'

She drops the sponge and runs to him. He's jerking, it's some kind of seizure, and his mouth is opening and closing and he's making some kind of guttural choking noise, like he's dying. *Please don't be dying, not in front of me.* As she watches, the front of his jeans goes dark as he wets himself. And there's blood on the driveway, more blood every second.

'Oh my God oh my God,' she says, and she pulls her phone from her pocket and dials 911 while she drops to her knees beside him.

*

When Louise comes back to the blanket from swimming, Irving has spread out the picnic. She wraps a towel around herself and takes a peanut butter sandwich. 'Dana's not back yet?'

'I thought she was swimming with you?' says Irving.

'No, she went off to explore.' Lou finds her phone in the beach bag and calls Dana's number. It rings and rings, but she doesn't pick up. 'Honey, we're having lunch,' she says to the voicemail. 'I'll save you a sandwich but come back soon, OK? Nana can't stay here all afternoon.'

But the sandwiches are eaten and the sun gets lower in the sky and Peggy dozes in her wheelchair and Dana isn't back yet.

Lou calls again, with no luck. She borrows Irving's phone and sends a text message in case Dana is purposely ignoring her number. 'I'll walk along the beach and look for her,' she tells Peggy and Irving. 'Maybe she's run into some of her friends.'

Lou walks to the end of the beach in one direction, checking the people for anyone familiar, gazing out at the water in case she can spot Dana swimming. 'Have you seen a girl,' she asks a family in a circle of chairs near the end of the beach, 'twelve years old, dark hair, wearing shorts and a red T-shirt? She might have tucked her hair up under her hat and looked more like a boy.'

The woman, picking up toddler toys, shakes her head.

The beach ends here, with the boat ramp, and beyond that there's no beach, just rocks. Lou climbs up on the ramp and looks in that direction. Dana could have thought it would be fun to climb on the rocks. She could have fallen, hit her head, landed in the water.

Stop being silly. She isn't five.

She trudges back to where her parents are waiting. Peggy is dozing; Irving is looking a little anxious, as if he'd feel better if they were in the house. 'No answer?' she asks her dad, and he shakes his head.

She walks more quickly down to the other end of the beach.

This isn't the way she saw Dana going, but she could have looped back via the road. The beach here ends at a fence marking the boundaries of the public part; from here on in it's all private houses and lakefront. Lou follows it up via a path to the main road. It's not a busy road, especially here; it's mostly for access to the summer houses, and as she remembers, it goes to a dead end where the houses stop and the forest begins. Maybe Dana wanted to look at the houses. Maybe Dana met someone she knew and went to their house.

Maybe she went into the house of someone she didn't know.

Lou calls her again, and again Dana's phone goes to voicemail without even ringing. She hangs up and checks to see if she's missed a call from Dana, but she hasn't. Dana's either turned off her phone or she's talking to someone else.

She'll walk up the road to the end, she decides, and then if she hasn't seen Dana she'll start knocking on doors.

She's only taken three steps on the road when the ambulance roars past her, lights flashing, towards the dead end.

'Dana!' she yells, and starts to run.

The ambulance is parked at the end of the road, in front of a set of metal gates. The lights are still flashing. Lou runs up, out of breath, and squeezes her way between the front of the ambulance and the stone wall.

Lou doesn't see the sports car or the sponges or the paramedics working at the front of the car. All she sees is Dana. She rushes to her daughter and grabs her by the shoulders, and that's when she sees that her hands are covered in blood.

'Dana! What happened?'

'Mom,' says Dana, and she falls forward into Lou's arms and starts to cry.

Lou holds her tight. 'Are you hurt?' Why isn't anyone helping Dana? Why is there an ambulance here if they're not here for her little girl? She looks around and sees the paramedics – a man and a woman, the man looks vaguely familiar – stand up. There's an unconscious person on the gurney. It's Benny Phelps.

'Oh my God,' whispers Lou, and she holds her daughter tight, so tight that Dana squeaks. 'What did he do to you?'

'You can be proud of your girl,' says the female paramedic, as they wheel Benny past. 'She might have saved his life.'

'What?' She still holds Dana, but leans back a little so she can look at her face. 'What did you do?'

'He had a fit,' Dana says. 'He had a fit and he fell and hit his head and he started bleeding, and I called 911 and they stayed on the phone with me while I held a rag to his head to try to stop the bleeding.' She wipes her eyes with her hand and smears blood on her face.

Not her blood. Benny's blood.

'I was scared,' she says to Lou. 'But they kept talking to me and the ambulance got here really fast.'

Lou wipes Dana's face with the palm of her hand, trying to get rid of the blood.

'You did the right thing,' she says to her daughter. 'Are you all right? Are you hurt too?'

Dana shakes her head.

The paramedics have loaded Benny into the ambulance and the male one comes back. 'Will he be OK?' Dana asks him.

'Hope so. We're going to get him to the hospital as quick as. You all right?'

'Yeah.'

'This your mom?'

'Yeah.'

'She's had a shock,' the paramedic says to Lou. 'Keep her warm. Sit for a while before you go anywhere. If she feels faint, get her head lower than her heart. Some sugar might help.' He snaps off his glove, then reaches over and ruffles Dana's hair. 'You did good, kid. Maybe look into a future in medicine.'

Then he goes back to the ambulance, climbs in, and it drives off, lights flashing. They hear the siren as the vehicle reaches the main road.

Lou helps Dana sit on the ground. She sits next to her, her arm around her shoulders.

'This is Benny's house?' she says. It's all so strange. The house is like an overblown log cabin, and Lou has a flash of those toys that Benny and she used to play with, Lincoln Logs, with the notches either end so you could build absolutely anything as long as it was made out of right angles. 'What were you doing here? Did he invite you?'

'No, I went for a walk and I saw him washing his car and we got talking.'

'That's all?'

'I helped him wash his car. He was going in his house to get some drinks and he started going …' She twitches her arms and legs violently. 'Then he fell down. I thought he was going to die.'

'I'll call Allie and let her know that he's on his way to the hospital.' But she doesn't reach for her phone. Instead, she holds Dana close and kisses the top of her head.

'Am I … am I in trouble for taking off like that?'

Lou shakes her head. 'I'm proud of you, sweetheart. You were very level-headed and brave.'

Dana clings to her, like she used to when she was a very little girl and she'd had a nightmare. 'It's going to be OK, right?'

Lou strokes her hair. 'Everything's fine, now. Nothing else is going to happen.'

Louis & Louise

That night, Peggy dies.

Lou has gone to sleep and is woken sometime after midnight by Irving. 'She needs you,' Irving whispers, and Lou gets up and goes to Peggy.

The bedside light is on. It casts a circle of golden light on Peggy's face. She has her eyes closed and she is breathing so slowly that at first, Lou can't see her breathing at all.

Lou lies down beside Peggy, head on her chest. Irving lies down on the other side of the bed and puts his arms around her. Peggy's breath is shallow, her heartbeat no stronger than a wren's. Lou lies with her and listens and waits.

This is both Louis and Louise, now, lying here feeling the last shadow of life leave their mother's body.

Right now there is no past, there is no gender, no he or she. There is no betrayal or pain. There are no secrets or withered hopes. There is only a mother and a child, the child who grew in her body, the child who fed at her breast, the child whose small hurts she kissed, whose fat cheeks she patted, who curled up and slept in her arms. None of the lessons learned, none of the toys bought and discarded, the clothes of pink or blue or yellow or red, none of those things that shape a life in one direction or the other mean anything right now. Only this.

Peggy slips from this world the same way that Lou slipped

from Peggy's womb: with love. Lou came to life noisily, but Peggy leaves it quietly. Lou on one side of her, Irving on the other. A final flutter. A full stop.

Louise

Lou goes into Dana's bedroom soon after sunrise and sits on the side of her bed. She strokes her hair back from her face, and Dana opens her eyes. She must see something in Lou's face, because she whispers, 'Did Nana die?'

Lou nods. She pulls back the blanket and crawls into bed beside Dana. It's a soft, warm space, and it smells of child sweat and vanilla sugar. Lou cuddles Dana into her, listens to her strong breathing and her steady heartbeat, feels her warmth, her youth. So alive and precious.

'Is Grandad OK?'

Lou nods again. She feels calm now, peaceful, but she knows that if she says anything she will probably cry, and she doesn't want to cry in front of Dana.

They lie there together for a while, both staring at the white ceiling. Lou's not sure if she came in here to comfort Dana or to get comfort from her.

'After someone dies, it's not scary,' says Dana. 'I was scared when Coach was bleeding, but I'm not scared of seeing Nana. It's just her body. It's not really her. Bodies aren't important. What's important is in here.'

She taps her own chest, over her beating heart.

'How did you get to be so smart?' Lou whispers. She doesn't cry after all. Not now.

Dana shrugs. 'Born that way, I guess. Also Jim gave me a tour of his mother's funeral home and I got to see the room where they treat the dead people.'

Lou exhales, nearly a chuckle.

'Mom,' Dana says after a moment of quiet.

'Yeah?'

'Can you whistle?'

Lou props her head up. 'Where'd this come from?'

'Allie said something. Can you? I've never heard you.'

'I'm not sure if I can still do it.' Lou thinks. She purses her lips and whistles, clear and loud, the first two bars of Beethoven's 'Ode to Joy'. It surprises her as much as it does Dana.

'Nice,' says Dana with respect.

'I argued with Nana,' Lou tells her. 'When I was a teenager we had a fight and we didn't talk, really, for years. I don't want that to happen between you and me.'

'Me neither.' Dana pauses. 'If you really don't want me to play on Coach's team, I'm OK with that. I'm going to be jumpy every time I see him anyway, remembering what happened.'

'Let's … leave that for another day, all right?'

Dana nods. She kisses her mother's cheek, something she hasn't done for months, and they lie there together as the world brightens around them.

Louis

The morning after his mother dies Louis goes swimming in the river. Not in Casablanca – you can't swim in the Pennacook in Casablanca; quite aside from the pollution that is probably still there even after all the clean-up in the nineties, the current is too strong and you'd get swept away. But about a mile upstream from Casablanca there's a bridge and under that bridge there are great slabs of granite where the water is shallow.

This is where the loggers hauled the logs out of the Pennacook a century and a half ago and where, in his book, Pierre is trapped under a jam and drowns. The river has carved hollows in the rock: round-edged caverns and chutes and pools, steps for a giant and teardrops the size of your hand. When the water is shallow you can see how the rock is layered into stripes of grey and white and pink, how glaciers have bent it and water has shaped it. In sunlight, the granite sparkles with chips of mica and quartz as if stars are twinkling beneath the surface.

Lou parks the car by the side of the road near the bridge and goes down the bank to the river. He strips off to his trunks, walks across the sparkling granite, and slides into a pool so deep he can't see its bottom. Around him the river rushes and foams but here it's still – and so cold it takes his breath away.

As soon as he gets into the water, he knows this was a mistake. He's come here to be alone, following the same habits he's followed since he left Casablanca: to be alone, to be strong, to show his feelings but only under a layer of fiction and prose, to surround himself with water so no one will notice if he cries.

But where have those habits got him? Why is he here, in a swimming hole by himself, while his mother's body lies in Bigelow's Funeral Home and his father sits in the house they all three once shared? When did he decide that it was safer to feel things from a distance?

He climbs out of the pool, dripping water onto the rock, muting its shine. He dries himself off and goes home.

'You are not wearing that,' Carrie says to Lou less than twenty minutes after she's arrived. It's the day before the funeral. She's marched him upstairs to his room and pointed an accusing finger at the clothes he showed her: grey slacks and a white shirt.

'What's wrong with it?'

'This is your only mother, and she has passed away. You need to wear a suit.'

He looks at her, helpless. She always makes him feel this way about fashion. This is part of the reason why he rarely wears anything but casual clothes. 'You didn't bring my suit up with you.'

'That's because your only suit is the one we got married in.'

'So?'

'Number one, it is blue, which is fine for weddings but no good for funerals, and number two, it is seven years old and you should not disrespect your mother by wearing a suit that is older than your dog, and number three, it is the suit that you married me in, and you should not disrespect *me* by wearing your wedding suit to a funeral.'

'How is that disrespect?'

'Trust me,' says Carrie. 'You don't double-up with suits and the important women in your life. Weddings or funerals: one suit per woman per event. That's the rule.'

'I wore my wedding suit to other weddings.'

'Doesn't count. You weren't part of the wedding.'

'Can I wear our wedding suit to your funeral, if you die before me?'

'No. Now let's go see what your father is planning to wear. I bet it's even worse.'

Even Lou can see that Irving's suit is worse. He found it in the back of Peggy's closet, an old suit that he neglected to pack and she neglected to give away. It looks about as old as Lou is.

'You two,' declares Carrie, 'must go shopping. I'll stay here and look after the dog and make the rest of the calls on your list.'

'Is there even anywhere to buy a suit in Casablanca?' Lou asks his father.

'Not since Taylors' shut down in the eighties,' says Irving. 'My father bought some of his clothes there, though my mother always wanted him to go to Portland. There's Carlisles on Main Street but they're mostly casual wear. Let me call Fred and ask him where he'd get a suit.'

'Is Fred well-dressed?' Carrie asks him, and Irving looks at her as if she'd asked if Fred was a purple flying unicorn.

'Well, I don't know, but he's the hospital administrator, so he's at least decent.'

'You call Fred,' says Carrie. 'I'll Google.'

It turns out that Fred and Google say the same thing, which is Bruno Brothers in Lisbon Falls, about forty-five minutes' drive away, so Lou and Irving allow themselves to be hustled into Lou's car. They're pulling out of the driveway when Allie pulls in beside them, and they stop.

'Where are you going?' she calls through the open window of her car.

'Suit shopping,' Irving tells her.

'Bruno Brothers?'

'Er... yes.'

'Good call. I'm dropping by to see if you need anything for tomorrow?'

'Ask the boss,' says Irving, nodding at Carrie, who's standing in the doorway as if making sure that they actually go to buy new clothes.

'She's a good woman,' says Irving, after they've driven off.

'Yes, she is. She's always thinking about other people, though, and not enough about herself.'

'I can see why you married her.'

Lou realises that his father's talking about Carrie, not Allie. He backtracks. 'I'm sorry I didn't tell you that Carrie and I were splitting up when it happened.'

'Marriage is hard,' says Irving. 'You never know how hard it is until you're actually doing it. Like most things, I suppose. But marriage seems like it should be easier. For something that so many people do.'

'It's something that a lot of people fail at.'

'Yes. That too.'

Lou drives and they don't say much else. Though their conversation for the past few days has been limited to practicalities – funeral arrangements, warming up meals, writing the obituary, making lists of people to contact – he feels closer to his dad than he has in years. Maybe closer than he ever has. Growing up, his father was always a kind man, gentle and fair. He read Lou stories at bedtime and carried him on his shoulders until Lou got too heavy. He came to track meets, ate dinner with them every night, helped Lou pick out his first car; but he never invited confidences, never confided anything himself. At first Lou thought that was just what Irving was like; then he thought that was just what men were like. When Irving left Peggy, Lou began to think his father had never shared his inner life because he'd always secretly wanted to escape.

But then again Lou has never told Irving or Peggy that he has been attracted to men; he's never told them the details of the failure of his relationship with Carrie, never discussed his writing, or how his novel feels to him like a stunted and beautiful child, an imperfect love. He hasn't mentioned his fear that he'll never be able to write a second book. Until that night in Florida, he always hid the truth about how Benny had died.

Maybe this is what men are like, or maybe this is how the two of them have chosen to be. Maybe they can choose to be different.

Bruno Brothers is in an imposing building on a street of gift shops, hair salons, bottle depots and pizza places. The red letters on the sign are straight out of the seventies and the gold lettering on the window, though fresh and clean, looks like it was first done in the fifties. Headless mannequins in suits and tuxedoes fill the front window. Someone has made a concession to summertime by putting a straw hat at a jaunty angle on one of the mannequins' necks. A silk daisy sticks out of a jacket pocket.

When Irving opens the door, the bell on it jingles and a roundish man in shirtsleeves, waistcoat and tie greets them immediately. 'Mr Alder and Mr Alder? Come in, I've been expecting you.'

Lou, feeling a little as if he's walked into a British sit com, asks, 'How?'

'Your wife called to warn me. She said you both needed suits for a funeral and she didn't quite trust you to choose them on your own, so she left you in my hands.'

'Ex-wife,' says Lou, to clarify that he's not being entirely bossed around by Carrie. Though as soon as the words are out of his mouth they sound like it's much worse.

'Best kind,' says the man cheerfully. He points at Irving. 'So: black for you, charcoal grey for Junior. She said you needed shirts and ties, too. Any preference for tie colour?'

'Green?' says Lou, not because he cares for green particularly, just to see what will happen.

'No,' says the man. 'You've got auburn hair and you don't want to look like a leprechaun. Why don't you both go into the changing rooms and I'll bring some things over for you to try on?'

Lou thinks that this man should probably meet Carrie. He and Irving go meekly through a blue curtain to the changing rooms, which are a series of cubicles shielded by swinging half-doors like you see on taverns in Western movies. There's a full-length mirror at the end of the row of cubicles, where Lou can see exactly how scruffy he and his father currently look.

'We didn't tell him our sizes,' Irving says.

'I have a feeling that if we did, he might have taken that as an insult.' Lou goes into a cubicle and starts getting undressed. He's hanging his shirt on the peg when the man, he assumes one of the Bruno brothers, comes in and drapes a suit, shirt and tie over the top of the door. The tie is a very muted purple. 'Start with these,' he says. 'Yell if you need anything.'

The suit, in a soft lightweight charcoal, fits Lou perfectly, even down to the length of the trousers. He tightens the tie and steps out of the cubicle at the same time that Irving, in black, steps out of his. His father is holding his glasses. He gazes at Lou, blue eyes looking strangely bare, and blinks.

'Your mother would have been very proud,' Irving says, and his eyes suddenly flood over with tears.

'Oh,' says Lou. His own eyes prickle. 'Oh, hey, Dad.' He steps forward at the same time that his dad steps forward. They meet in the middle of this small space and wrap their arms around each other. The familiar scent of Gillette shaving foam and Head & Shoulders shampoo, the slightly awkward way that Lou is taller than his dad so Lou's chin ends up against Irving's ear.

'I loved her so much,' says Irving, face pushing into Lou's shoulder, wetting the fabric of this new suit.

'Me too.'

'I never stopped loving her.'

'I know.'

Then they cry, without words, and although it hurts, this is what Lou was looking for and couldn't find in that cold pool in the river. This is the powerful current that he needs.

When they emerge from the changing room, they are wrinkled and tousled. They have done the best job they can with Irving's handkerchief, but the front of Lou's jacket is wet and Irving's hair is plastered to his forehead. The Bruno brother is hovering near the cash register, a discreet distance away from the changing room.

'How… are the suits?' he asks, with considerably more hesitation than he had before they went into the changing rooms.

'They're perfect,' says Irving. 'We'll take them.'

Louise

The funeral is at Bigelow's. Louise wears one of Allie's dresses. It's a little short on her and it's more of a dark grey than a black, but she feels comfortable in it and it's also comforting. Even though Allie is there with them, staying near her and Irving and Dana, wearing her dress feels like an extra hug, a supportive hand on the small of Lou's back.

She'd thought the funeral would be hard but there are so many people here to talk to that she hardly has time to think. Everyone offers her something: a memory of Peggy, a promise to pray, a compliment on the flowers, maybe a handshake. That's the point of funerals, she supposes, much like the point of all the casseroles that have been turning up. They're excuses for the offering of kindness. They're meant to make the living feel less alone.

The three of them, Irving and Dana and Lou, have gone through the photographs of Peggy and put together a slideshow that's playing continuously in the viewing room. Irving delivers the eulogy, handkerchief in one hand and notes in the other, and though he cries a little and dabs his eyes under his glasses he still manages fine. Dana sits next to a boy who is the son of Georgia Bigelow the funeral director. The kids whisper to each other during the service which isn't respectful at a funeral but Lou doesn't stop them. Peggy would probably be glad that Dana has a friend. The calm structure of the service is reassuring, as is the weight of the pamphlet with Peggy's picture on the front in her tiara and sash. Miss Western Maine 1976.

She'll feel the sadness of it later, she knows. She'll feel the empty space inside her, the impulse to reach out to someone who's not there. The past thirteen years have given her practice in not talking to her mother but she has still had a mother all that time. There has always been the possibility of forgiveness. And now she's had the forgiveness and her mother has gone and Lou feels a strange peace knowing that the grieving is to come.

Lou has insisted on being one of the pallbearers though she's not a man, so after the service she takes her place at the front of the coffin beside her father. She lifts the coffin by the handle. It should be heavy but it's not. It's shared.

On the way to the hearse that will take her mother's body to the graveyard, she glimpses a dark-suited figure at the edge of the gathering of people. She can't see his face but she has seen this way of walking, this compact stance, since she was a little girl. Benny doesn't approach, though, and if he did, she thinks that she could bear it. These people around her, Allie's dress, the shared weight of the coffin, her mother's apology, her own forgiveness, even Dana having a friend, make her invulnerable. She hasn't felt invulnerable like this for a very long time.

Then they slide the coffin onto the rollers, into the hearse, and she looks around and he's gone.

Louis

The wake is at the house. The catering is what Lou remembers from every wedding he happened to attend as a kid in Maine, nearly every funeral he's been to in Casablanca: white finger rolls of chicken salad, egg salad, tuna mashed to a paste; pasta salad shining with mayonnaise, bowls of pickles, a bowl of olives next to a shot glass of toothpicks. Devilled eggs with a sprinkling of paprika, a platter of cold salami and ham rolled into cylinders. A frosted white sheet cake which has already been cut into slices and put on paper plates. Coffee in urns, regular or decaf. It's the same menu from church basements and American Legion halls, school gymnasiums and garden parties. When the caterers turned up this morning with their cling-film covered platters, Carrie was astonished. 'I didn't think these foods existed any more.'

'They do in Casablanca,' said Lou, who had insisted they use someone local instead of a fancier caterer from Auburn or Portland.

In any case, Lou hasn't time or appetite to eat any of it. He's never mastered the art of eating standing up and talking at the same time, anyway. He manages a cup of coffee and when the crowd thins out a little bit, someone puts a plate of cake in his hand and he takes it as an excuse to sit down. The sofa is occupied and so are all the dining room chairs that have been lined up along the walls, but miraculously the green armchair is free.

However, before he can have so much as a bite of cake, Mulder jumps up into his lap and licks his face.

Allie perches on the arm of the chair. She's got a styrofoam cup of coffee in her hand and is wearing a simple dark grey short-sleeved dress, with her hair pulled up into a bun. 'How are you holding up?' she asks.

He's been aware of her the whole day, but she's kept a bit of a distance. Several times he's caught the scent of her perfume. It occurred to him fairly early in the day that the last time the two of them were at a funeral together, it was for Benny. He doesn't remember much about that funeral; he left town for good a few days later. He wonders how often she thinks about it.

'I'm all right,' he says. 'How are you?'

She shrugs. She reaches down to fondle Mulder's ears. 'Not as good as this guy. He jumped on the table and managed to snaffle three devilled eggs before I caught him.'

'Sorry.'

'Can't be mad at that face.' She leans down and Mulder licks her, too. 'Egg breath.' But she's smiling.

'You always wanted a dog,' he says.

'I'm not home enough. It's been good spending time with this guy, though. I'll miss him.'

Mulder's fluffy tail thumps. Lou strokes his back as Allie scratches his ears. He thinks about how much he's wanted to touch Allie all day, how he's wanted to touch her for weeks, now. Quite possibly for years. It's so easy with this dog between them. He glances up and she's not looking at the dog, she's looking at him.

'Louis?'

It's Carrie, calling him from the doorway to the kitchen. She's got her rental car keys in her hand.

'Excuse me,' he says to Allie and puts Mulder on the floor so he can go to Carrie. 'Are you going already?'

'Flight's at five. I've got a meeting tomorrow. Walk me to the car?'

Outside it's started to drizzle, but it's a warm rain. Carrie kisses him on the cheek and wipes her lipstick off his skin. It's a gesture she's made thousands of times.

'You two make a cute couple,' she says.

'Me and Mulder?'

She elbows him. 'Does she know you? The inside you?'

'Better than anyone, I think. But it's not like that. It was a long time ago.'

'It'd almost make me feel better if I knew I'd never had a chance because you've been pining for your high-school sweetheart all along.' She stands on tiptoes and kisses him again, but this time on the lips. It's both familiar and strange, as if a thin layer of tissue has settled between the people they used to be and the people they are now.

'You've been great,' he tells her honestly. 'Thanks for coming up.'

'You're welcome. I lied, by the way. I don't have a meeting tomorrow. I have a date tonight. I'm going straight from JFK.'

That hurts a little. But maybe that's a good thing – that they still care enough to cause and feel these small hurts. He nods. 'Have fun.'

'You too. Wear a condom.'

He ignores that. 'I guess I'll see you when I get the rest of my stuff. I'll call you when I'm back in town. We can have lunch.'

'No hurry. You should maybe stay here a while. You've put on a little weight, you've even caught the sun. This place might be good for you.'

She kisses him again, lightly on the lips, and gets into the car and drives away. He stands there watching her go. From the driveway, he can see the cars of his neighbours all parked on the sides of the roads, the house across the street that used to give out caramel apples at Halloween. In the sky, the white of the church steeple, the grey of the sky, and the greyer plume of smoke from the mill flowing downstream. Sunny weather.

This place might be good for you.

Despite everything she's said, Carrie does know him. Maybe he's become more open since coming here. Or the truth has been so simple and so obvious that he hasn't been able to see it.

When he goes back inside he looks for Allie, but she's not where he left her and he can't see her in the dining room or kitchen either. Mulder is sitting in front of the buffet, eyes fixed on the finger sandwiches, waiting for another chance. Lou nudges the plate back from the edge of the table. 'Be good,' he says to the dog without much hope, and goes upstairs to wash his face.

The bathroom door is shut. He's raising his hand to knock on it, to see if it's occupied or if someone just closed the door, when it opens and Allie is standing there. 'Oh,' she says. 'Has … has Carrie left?'

'I just came up to wash my face.'

'Good idea. You've got some …' She rubs her own lips in pantomime, and he wipes his with the back of his hand. Red lipstick.

'She likes to leave a mark,' Lou says.

'I thought … she said you'd separated.'

'We have.'

'Oh. OK. So that was a …'

'A kiss goodbye,' he says.

Allie hasn't moved out of the doorway. He hasn't moved out of the way to let her. The conversation buzzes on, downstairs, and probably Mulder is up on the table again, but here they're alone.

'Allie,' he says, and she takes the step forward and it's natural to put his hand on her waist, draw her in and kiss her. She's the way he remembered her, the person he missed, except different. Grown up, tasting of coffee, warm and new.

'I've missed you so much,' she whispers. Then she looks stricken and steps back. 'I'm sorry. Your mother just died.'

'I don't think she'd mind.' He kisses her again, this time for longer.

She links her fingers with his and pulls him down the hallway to his bedroom.

When they come back downstairs – Lou having changed into shorts and his holey Sufjan Stevens T-shirt, Allie with her hair hanging loose – all of the guests have gone and Irving is sitting at the kitchen table feeding Mulder a tuna finger roll. It feels like it's been half a lifetime, but when Lou passes the coffee urn, it's still hot.

'Oh, that's where you two are,' Irving says, as if they're still in high school, and pretends not to notice when both of them blush.

Louis

The day after his mother's funeral Lou writes and writes. Whatever dam that was stopping him before has been broken and he sits on his single childhood bed, the same bed that he and Allie shared as teenagers and yesterday again as adults, and types into his laptop words that are more truthful than anything he's ever written.

He types about how he fell in love with Allie when he was thirteen and he types about how he's fallen in love with her again. About how he's never been so happy as he was yesterday, lying here in this bed whispering with her. He types about the river, not the old dangerous ice flow of a river that he wrote about in *Light In Winter* but the one that really exists now, the one that's been polluted and cleaned up and polluted again, the one that gives Casablanca its water and life. He writes about the strike and how his name and his family's money protected him from it until the night of his graduation. And he writes about that night. What he did, and what he didn't do. What he wishes he could have done. The gun in his mouth, the gun against Benny's head.

He writes about how it was his fault that Benny died and how he's carried the guilt from this every day since. About how he loved Benny, a frustrated baffled love, and how Benny hated himself. He writes about how he's not sure, to this day, if he was meant to die that night instead of Benny and how if he had, maybe everything would have been different. He writes a vision of how it might have been different if he had stayed behind and told the truth. Maybe the strike wouldn't have ended. Maybe it would have got worse. Families turned against each other, management against workers, the mill gradually failing and falling into ruin along with the town.

Maybe it would have all stayed exactly the same. Maybe Benny's death didn't save Casablanca; maybe it was a combination of less dramatic things, the simple ability to compromise. He doesn't understand the forces of labour and economics, but he does understand the weight of guilt that brought a town together and forced his parents apart. Because he's felt it himself all his adult life.

He writes about Allie, starts and finishes with her, because she's the one who's stayed here and has had to bear the responsibility of keeping the myths about her brother alive. Lou's been able to escape and never speak of the past, but Allie has had to lie a little bit every day. She put her own dreams aside to help her mother cope, and then to help her mother die. She came back to a town that never appreciated her for herself, who always saw her as the twin of the tragic dead boy. He writes about the twins' anger, how Benny used his rage to frighten and destroy and Allie shot her rage out harmlessly into the summer air, the only casualty a tin can. About how the real hero of the story isn't Benny, who wanted to die, or Lou who tried, helplessly, to stop him. It was Allie who saved Lou from blame, maybe prison. Allie who called the ambulance for her dead brother, who consoled their mother and never threw words of reproach at their father, who let her silence heal Casablanca, who adjusted her dreams and has stayed here ever since and tended to the dying. Allie, the saviour of lost causes. Allie, who has given Lou back himself.

He writes it in a frenzy, clothing raw emotion in details and story not to hide it, but to reveal. He only leaves his bedroom to use the bathroom, devour a plate of leftover finger sandwiches and take Mulder for a walk.

He walks through the wilderness behind his parents' house and lets Mulder off the leash to sniff and lift his leg on the rocks. This is the first time he's felt able to come to the place where the three of them used to play. It's not as wide or wild as he remembers. You can see the backs of the houses easily, even during the summer with leaves on the trees. Castle Rock is only about as tall as he is. Curious, he goes down the hill and stands at the edge of the lawn that used to be the Phelps's house. There's no one there, but the house has been painted blue and there are children's toys scattered across the backyard.

When he looks for Mulder, he can't see him. The dog isn't used to being off the leash. 'Mulder!' he yells, thinking he can't have gone far. 'C'mere boy!' But the dog doesn't appear. Lou goes back into the wilderness and looks in The Hollow, up around Face Rock.

'Mulder!' he yells again, and when there's still no dog, he purses his lips and gives a shrill, powerful whistle. He's surprised at how easily he can do it, how loud it is after all this time. It echoes off the backs of houses.

The dog appears instantly. Lou picks him up and carries him back to the house so he can keep writing.

He finishes the piece at 11.43 p.m. and he connects his laptop to his mother's old inkjet printer and prints out the pages in a stack, then he sits down with a glass of wine and reads it back. He can see, almost right away, that it's the best thing he's ever written. Much better than his novel, infinitely better than the stunted, untruthful stories that he's tried writing since. He might be wrong; he might reread it later, with the benefit of a good night's sleep and some distance, and think it's not so good. But he doesn't think he will.

He could send it to his agent, try to get it into *The New Yorker* or a literary magazine. Even as he considers that, he knows it's wrong. The people who should read this story are the ones right here in Casablanca: if it's printed, it should be printed in the

Casablanca Herald, in between the photos of church dinners and anniversaries and Little League teams, in between the recipes and letters to the editor about the PTA, the same paper that published Lou's first poem age eleven and ran Benny's obituary seven years later.

But that's not right either. He didn't write this for Casablanca.

Lou finds his phone and starts to call Allie, but then he realises that it's after midnight, so he writes a text and then deletes it. Writes another one – and deletes that too. He's been writing all day with a fluency he's never had before but when it comes to texts, everything sounds too cavalier, too cliché, too day-after-the-night-before. He realises belatedly that although he's been thinking about Allie all day, writing about her and how he feels about her, he hasn't actually contacted her and that makes him a dick.

'Shit,' he mutters, and Mulder who has been snoozing under his feet looks up at him, not alarmed at all.

He did this to Carrie, too. He wrote instead of talking to her. Shut himself away in his own head and thought that he was justified in doing it because he was creating something, and maybe that's what being a writer is all about, giving your words to paper instead of to the people who should hear them, but that's not what he wants to be to Allie. That's not how he wants to live his life any more.

Lou finds a manila envelope in his mother's desk and stuffs the pages inside it. Then he shoves on some sneakers and drives through midnight streets along the river and up the hill and through the woods to Allie's house. It's dark and quiet and he parks in the road at the end of her driveway so he won't wake her if she's sleeping, though she could be at work. He doesn't know because he hasn't contacted her because he's a dick and maybe he's ruined this fragile thing they're rekindling between them before it's even started.

By the dome light in his car, he writes on the outside of the envelope:

> Allie
> I'm sorry I didn't call you today because I was writing this. It's for you, all of it, and everything I've written before, too. Do what you want with it. I'll call you tomorrow, at a decent hour.

He wants to sign it with 'love' but although his feelings are clear in what he's written in these pages, this note is different. It's more like the texts he was trying to send, which all read as if they were written by an oaf. So he puts his initial instead and, after a debate, adds a single kiss.

He walks as quietly as he can to the front of the house and then stops, remembering leaving the banana bread on her porch. She never mentioned that; maybe an animal got it after all. In Maine, front doors are for company, for salesmen and out-of-town guests. They have doorbells and knockers for strangers to announce their presence. The back door is for everyday coming and going, for family. So Lou walks around the side of the house, carefully placing his feet in the near pitch-dark, and slips the envelope between the screen door and the back door. She will see it in the morning as she goes out to work, or as she comes back in to sleep.

Louise

Before the funeral they got an avalanche of mail every day, but then it slows down to a trickle. Still, when a handwritten envelope arrives along with an LL Bean catalogue and a fundraising request from MIT, Lou thinks it's a late sympathy card. It's addressed to her.

She takes it to the kitchen. Irving is out at the bank and Dana is upstairs watching television. They're planning to go to the state park later and hike up Baldpate. The days since Peggy's funeral have had a similar feeling to the day after Christmas or Thanksgiving, where everyone is slightly stunned and unsure what to do with themselves. An aftermath. Lou's instinct is to draw her remaining family close. She checks on Dana during the night. The paraphernalia of dying has been removed from the dining room, and Irving is sleeping upstairs again; she listens at his door too at night. Sometimes she hears him snoring. Sometimes she hears him crying.

There's a hole in the house which seems concentrated around the dining room. After she helps Irving to put the room back to normal, with table, tablecloth, chairs neatly tucked in, she avoids it. But now that her mother's gone Lou sees her in other places, too: at the kitchen sink, at the top of the stairs, weeding the garden. It isn't a ghost – Lou doesn't believe in ghosts, despite all that playing around with Ouija boards that she and Allie did when they were pre-teens. It's more like a memory, a visible absence.

In these quiet days, Lou has started writing again. She doesn't sit down to write anything in particular; she opens her notebook and starts, like she used to when she was a girl. Sometimes she writes about the river or the mountains or the fantasy Casablanca she inhabited as a child. Sometimes she writes about Dana. Sometimes she writes about her mother. About how she couldn't cook, how she was always so careful about her accent, about the way she used to laugh at the *Peanuts* comic in the newspaper every morning. Nothing profound, but then again, who's to say which details are the important ones, the ones that can change everything?

She writes some tentative fiction, too. She tries to write a scene or two about Gill Lafayette in the winter logging camp. Snow, wood, straw; beans, salt pork, the long bunk along the side of the cabin shared by all the lumberjacks. She writes a scene about a dark winter night and Gill, dressed in breeches and shirt, watching a man called Pierre playing a fiddle and suddenly she realises the way into this story about a person born as a girl, living as a man, surrounded by men. What has to happen, the shape of it.

It's a love story. It's about light in winter.

And with that realisation, a dozen scenes open up to her and her pencil can hardly keep up. The words take off, her mind escapes. The fiction becomes truthful and the truth becomes sharper than it ever was when she lived it. She blinks and turns a page and realises that hours have passed.

Now, she pours a cup of coffee and rips open the envelope, already thinking about the lunch she'll pack for their hike. There's another envelope inside along with a folded sheet of paper. The envelope has a single word on it: *Dana*. She puts it aside and opens the paper. It's written in blue ballpoint pen on lined paper, and the handwriting is a little shaky.

Dear Lou,
This is a thank-you card to Dana, for saving my life. I don't know if you want her to have it or not. So you can give it to her if you want. She's a good kid. You must be very proud of her.
I'm giving up coaching so you can let her join the team again if she wants to. Joan McDonald who coaches the high school team is going to do it.
I'm not very good at writing things but I wanted to say I'm sorry. I guess I paid for some of what I did but I guess maybe not enough.
Benny.
PS I'm sorry about your mom too.

Her heart is hammering, her hands slick. The coffee she's already drunk rises acid in her throat.

Sorry? *Sorry?* He thinks he can write her a note, fold it up and stick it in the mail, and that will make up for it?

She crumples up the note. Then she thinks twice and rips it up instead, into tiny little pieces so none of the words are whole. Then she rips up the card in its envelope addressed to Dana without opening it. This is harder, because the card is pretty thick, but she does it anyway. She can see the edge of something blue on the card, but she doesn't look at what it is, a flower or a bear or a rabbit or whatever. She sweeps all the scraps into her hand and then puts them into the trash and then she empties the bag from the trash and takes it outside to the bin in the garage.

I guess I paid for some of what I did.

How? By becoming successful and rich and donating money for a hospital, like a saviour of cancer patients and the town's economy? Because he took a baseball to the head and now has epileptic fits? How is any of that supposed to make up for her nightmares, her shame, the secret she has to keep from her own daughter? For losing her best friend for thirteen years? All the time stolen from her and her mother that she will never, ever get back?

She had less than one day of forgiveness with her mother. Not even a whole day, only an afternoon in the sunshine, and then Peggy was gone.

Lou hasn't cried much for her mother's death. But here in the garage now, with the lid of the bin in her hand, she sobs and can't stop sobbing. Loud wails that echo off the ceiling of the garage, bounce off the side of the car. Knowing no one can see her, she cries until her legs are weak and her head is full and her heart is aching. She wipes her nose on the hem of her favourite T-shirt and keeps crying. For the years she lost and for her mother.

She hardly notices the garage door opening but she does see, through her tears, her father's car driving in. As she tries to hiccup back her sobs the car stops, engine ticking. Irving gets out and the car beeps its pleasant alarm to tell him he's left his keys in the ignition. He goes to Lou and takes her in his arms. She ducks her head and presses her wet face against his shoulder. So many memories of scraped knees, bad dreams. She'd wanted to do this the night Benny raped her: nestle against her father's chest and cry. But instead she'd left.

'Shh, Lou-Lou,' he murmurs to her, as he did when she was a little girl. 'Shh, I know. It will be all right.'

'Did you talk with him about it?' Lou asks.

Lou is on the phone with Allie. It's after the hike up Baldpate, when Dana climbed on ahead up the steep and rocky path and yelled back, 'Oh wow!' when she got to the heights where the trees parted and she could see the view, miles and miles over the green and blue mountains and all the way to New Hampshire. At the top, on the bare rock that gives Baldpate its name, Lou sat down beside Dana and watched an eagle soar, a speck in the distance. It rode the thermals in great swoops. From here, you couldn't see a single road or house, only the rounded mountains that the glaciers left behind thousands of years ago. When Lou was a kid and hiked up here, you would be able to see harsh squares where the woods had been clearcut for paper, but with the death of the paper mill those have healed over into patches of lighter, shorter trees.

Lou feels calmer after the hike. The eagle and the mountain and her daughter and her dad: they've removed her fear and some of her anger, though not all of it. Not by a long shot.

Lou's sitting on the carpet in the living room with her back against the wall. It's the same place she used to sit as a teenager when she talked to Allie on the phone, because it was as far as the coiled cord stretched from the kitchen where the phone was mounted on the wall. She's using her cell phone but she's sitting there now out of habit, or maybe as a comfort reaction.

'I did talk with him about it,' says Allie on the end of the phone. 'He's my brother, Lou. He's my twin. I saw him on our birthday and I had it out with him.'

'That must have spoiled the cake.'

'Are you mad at me for talking with him?' Allie asks.

'I don't blame you, I just thought . . .' What did she think? That if Allie believed her she wouldn't ask for corroboration from Benny too? 'What did he say?'

'Not much. He didn't deny it, if that's what you're asking. But I didn't need his version of it.'

'Did he . . . ?'

She doesn't have to finish, because she knows Allie will know. 'I don't think he suspects Dana is his. He mentioned her and I said that her father was out of the picture.'

She lets out a long breath. 'OK. Thanks.'

'I can't lie to him, but I don't think he'll ask. He's not a big one for revisiting the past.'

'He sent me a note. To apologise.'

Allie doesn't answer right away, but Lou can hear her thinking. She can imagine the look Allie gets on her face when she's trying to figure out whether she should say the kindest thing, or the truest thing. She loves Allie for that.

'How do you feel about that?' Allie says at last.

'Are you sure you're an oncologist? You sound like a psychiatrist.'

'Shut up. How do you feel?'

'I was really angry. As if a note is going to make up for anything. A note written in ballpoint on a sheet of notebook paper.'

'He's never written me a note, ever.'

'That's supposed to make me like it more?'

'No. It's supposed to make you think... maybe he means it.'

'I don't care if he means it! Why should I give a shit if he's sorry? That is not my problem.'

'I'm angry at him too,' says Allie quietly. 'All these years I thought I could trust him and I couldn't. He's changed from when we were kids, though, Lou. His disability has made things hard for him. The one thing he was always good at was taken away. The kids laugh at him sometimes. They have horrible names for him. He owns these cars he's not allowed to drive. His life is pretty small.'

'Poor Benny.'

'That's not what I'm saying. I don't expect you to forgive him.'

'Good.'

'I'm just saying... please don't hate me if I understand him.'

Lou doesn't know what to say to that.

'I'm on your side,' continues Allie, 'but he's my brother. He's my *twin*. I love him. He's all the family I've got left.'

'Except me.'

'Yes. But to be blunt, you're going back to Brooklyn.'

'Allie, I can't stay here. I've got a job, Dana's got a life, and how can I stay in a place where I might run into him any time? There's too much to say. I think I'd explode.'

'You could say those things to him now.'

'I don't think I can.'

'Maybe you can write it.'

'Maybe.'

'You don't have to figure out how to live with him,' says Allie. 'I do.'

Quietly, Lou asks, 'Do you wish I hadn't told you?'

'It's selfish to say yes.'

'But you do wish I hadn't told you.'

'My life was easier before you told me. It's harder to know what happened. But I'd never choose not to know.'

This is always how Allie has been. She's always wanted to know everything, to learn about everything. She's the one who's needed to know the facts, while Lou was the one who needed to invent them. But this is more than that mere impulse towards truth; this is Allie deliberately choosing the knowledge that will hurt her. For Lou's sake.

'Thank you,' says Lou, swallowing hard.

'You don't need to thank me. It's what it's about, Lou.'

Lou pauses. 'I'm sorry that it's hard for you to figure out what to do. And I'm not angry at you for loving your brother. My anger is, specifically and generally, focused on him. Not you.'

'Same. Except …'

'Except what?' She remembers Allie's fury in the supermarket car park. Allie angry is quite a terrifying thing. And beautiful, too.

'Once you're gone,' Allie says, 'who am I going to watch old movies with? I'm pretty pissed off with you about that.'

Lou laughs. 'I love you,' she says, and for some reason her voice chokes on the last word and her mind catches up a second later as she realises why. Because she does love Allie. Allie is the missing part of her. She always has been. That's the shape of their story too: a love story. Lou has never really understood it until now.

She goes for a drive in her crappy Subaru like she used to when she was a teenager and owned her first crappy car of a line of crappy cars. It seemed, those days, that all there was to do around here was to drive. The boys often drove up and down Main Street and parked their cars at the falls to blare their radios and drink beer out of paper bags, but Lou didn't do that. Lou drove the state. Sometimes with Allie beside her, blasting out music and singing along, sometimes alone. Down Route 27 to Lisbon to buy a Moxie that she could have found at the Food Trend half a mile from her house; up Route 5 to the Height of Land to sit on the fender of her car and look at the scenery, lakes spread out beneath her like jewels in a setting of trees. With a car she was free, the state was hers. She could go anywhere as long as she was back for dinner.

Today, she doesn't let herself think of a destination. She leaves Casablanca, past the town sign, and drives, turning where she wants to. Once upon a time she knew all these roads. She might have forgotten them now, she might get lost twisting through woods or strange towns, but if she does she can find her way home. When she was younger she thought all roads led away from Casablanca, but now that she's older, she knows that all roads lead, eventually, back.

Driving is a way to think. Movement untethers her mind, but maybe the space does too. Maine is full of forests, lonely stretches of road, towns with only a few houses. In Brooklyn there's always something to see and it's easy to be constantly distracted. Maybe she chose to live there for that very reason. She keeps the radio on: music she's heard so many times she doesn't have to listen to it, even when she's singing along. She drives and lets her mind wander, and it isn't really a surprise when after forty minutes of driving any which way as the sun gets lower in the sky, she finds herself turning onto the road to Morocco Pond.

She loves Allie, so she has to figure out how to live with that. Which means she has to figure out how to live with Benny, too.

But more than that, it's time. She's spent thirteen years running away from what happened that night, and as long as she keeps running away from it she's letting that one event define her.

She's often wondered who she would be if she'd never gone down to the basement that night. If she'd let Benny sleep it off. Maybe she'd have gone to college and got her degree in creative writing like she wanted to. Maybe she'd never have become a teacher; maybe she'd have finished that novel by now, maybe even had it published. She would have stayed friends with Allie. She might have realised a long time ago how she felt about Allie. Maybe she would have said something. Maybe she would have been too frightened of destroying their friendship, and never said a thing.

Without a secret to hide, without the fear of trusting someone, she might have been married by now, or at least had a relationship that lasted for more than a year or two. She might have a child who wasn't Dana. She might be someone completely different.

The only way she can stop and define herself, be the person she was meant to be – or be the person that she is – is to turn around and face what happened head on.

So she drives past the public beach and along the private road to the end. She expects the gate to be closed and locked – she expects to have to buzz to be let in and to say her name into the intercom, and maybe be turned away – but when she reaches the end of the road the gate is open. Even though Allie told her that Benny couldn't drive any of his cars, she parks considerately on the side of the driveway. On the edge of the property she takes a deep breath before she steps in.

The garage is closed, the car is put away, there are no paramedics and, most importantly, no Dana with blood on her hands, so it looks different. The lawn is well-groomed and edged with shrubs and flowers. Beyond the big log cabin of a house, the sun is setting over the lake; light glimmers off the water in aggressive pink.

Lou walks up to the door and raises her hand to knock, but her courage falters. What if Benny actually invites her in? She hasn't been alone with him since that night.

Instead she goes around the side of the house. If she lived here, she'd be sitting out on the lakefront porch watching the sunset, so it's reasonable that he might be, too.

As soon as she rounds the corner of the house she sees him. The porch is screened in, but it's easy to see inside. Benny's sitting in a wicker chair looking out onto the lake. She can see him in profile: his short spiky hair, his rounded nose that's the same as Allie's, his slightly stocky shoulders. It's quite clear that he has a gun in his hand and he is raising the gun, slowly, to point at his head.

He pointed the gun at her, thirteen years ago, and then pointed it at his own head. *'Bang. Bang. All done.'*

'Benny!' she yells, even though as soon as she does she thinks *He's going to shoot me instead.*

He doesn't point the gun at her, but he doesn't lower it, either. He merely glances over.

'Oh,' he says. 'It's you.'

'What the hell are you doing?'

'Beautiful sunset, huh? Red sky at night, sailors' delight. Going to be a nice day tomorrow.'

'Benny,' she says again. 'What the fuck are you doing with that gun?'

Her heart is thumping and everything in her tells her to run away, to save herself from this person who's hurt her before. But she makes herself step forward. She walks to the front of the house and stands by the steps up to the porch. Technically, he's inside and she's outside, but all that separates them is thin wire mesh.

'I should have shot myself a long time ago,' he says. 'It would've saved everyone a lot of trouble.'

'I think you should put down that gun.'

'I wanted to kill myself. Instead I hurt you. I got hit by a baseball, you know. Ruined my career. I get fits now. Can't drive. Can't play ball, and that was the only thing I was ever good at.'

'Benny, stop it, OK?'

'Right here. That's where it hit me.' He points the gun at his temple again. 'Line drive. Cracked the skull. I heard it. Sometimes I still hear it. Over and over. *Crack*.'

'I'm calling the police,' she says, and she reaches for her phone.

'Not much point. A bullet's faster than a police car. They call me "Piss-Pants" now. Did Dana tell you that?'

'Yes.'

'Why are you here?'

'I came here to yell at you.'

'Go ahead.'

'Somehow that's the last thing on my mind right now.'

She glances around to see if there's anyone else nearby. The fence around the house extends to the water's edge. She can't see over it to the neighbours' house. There aren't any boats on the water: no canoes or swimmers she could hail.

'Allie has already yelled at me,' Benny says. 'Not that she actually yells, but you know how she gets when she's disappointed. That's the only thing she got from our dad. That power to wither you with a look. While me, I got everything from Dad. I got his temper and his drinking and his ability to turn everything I touch into fucking shit.'

'Is this what you do up here all day?' Lou asks him, trying to match his tone, hoping maybe the challenge will do something when plain old pleading hasn't worked. 'Sit up here feeling sorry for yourself? Because there are other people to feel sorry for.'

'Yeah,' says Benny. 'Like you.' He lowers the gun a little and reaches for something on the floor. Lou takes a step back before she realises that he's picked up a bottle. Jack Daniel's from the squared shape of it. He rests the gun in his lap and takes a swig from the bottle. 'You want some?'

'No.'

'You should have some.'

'Will you promise not to shoot anyone if I do?'

'Maybe.'

Cautiously, thinking she is making a mistake, she climbs the two steps up to the porch screen door and pulls it open. The porch floorboards creak as she steps across them to where Benny sits. As soon as she gets close to him she can smell the liquor.

'You're drunk,' she says.

'Yup. Here.' He hands her the bottle. 'Sit down, make yourself at home.'

'I think I'll stand.' She lifts the bottle to her mouth but she allows the Jack Daniel's to barely touch her lips before she gives it back to him.

He takes another drink and puts the bottle down. Lou takes encouragement from the fact that the gun is still in his lap, although for all she knows it's cocked and ready to fire. 'Do you drink a lot?' she asks him.

'Sometimes. I'm not supposed to drink at all. Head.' He gestures towards his head with the gun and she draws in a sharp breath. 'It interferes with the drugs they give me to stop the seizures. But the drugs make me feel drunk without any of the good parts of drinking; so, damned if I do, damned if I don't. You got my letter?'

'Yes.'

'That why you're here?'

'Because I thought it was the lamest apology in the history of apologies? Yes.'

He heaves a sigh. Lou's anger is beginning to come back now.

'Do you expect me to feel *bad* for you?' she says. 'After what you did to me?'

'I didn't even think about you afterwards,' he said. 'I guess I tried not to. If I let myself think about you I told myself that you probably wanted it. Or that you deserved it.'

'You raped me,' she says, and the moment she says it she's not scared any more. He's still got the gun, but she's named what he did, to his face. And that gives her more power than she's had in a very long time. 'I didn't want it, and I didn't deserve it.'

'I wanted to take you down a peg,' he says. 'I wanted to make you feel what I felt. To hate yourself as much as I hated myself. That's the only way I can understand it now. What I did. I hated myself and I've made everyone who matters hate me too.'

'So you think it's going to help if you blow out your brains on your porch.'

'I want to make it end! Look at you, you got out of here, you have a kid, you have a job. I'm thirty-two years old. I don't have a wife, I don't have any kids, I'll never play ball again, I'll take drugs for the rest of my life. I'm worthless. Fucking worthless. I sit here every night alone and I drink and it's no life. I'm done with it, fuck it, it's over!'

He lifts the gun again and there is actually a part of her, as he presses it against his temple again, finger on the trigger, which wants to shout *It's not my responsibility to make you feel better, to help you live, to stop you from doing this!*

But most of her reacts by instinct, most of her shouts 'No!' and lunges forward to grab his wrist, pull his hand back, the gun back, knocks over the bottle of Jack Daniel's and the gun explodes and kicks like a live thing and falls to the floor between them and she lets go of Benny's wrist and staggers, ringing in her ears, wondering who has been shot, Benny or her?

He's still there. She's not hurt. He's staring at her as if he can't quite understand what's happened.

'Fuck sake, Benny!' she yells. 'You were really going to do it!'

She stoops and picks up the gun before he can. It's landed in the puddle of Jack Daniel's and sweet liquid drips down her arm. She looks up and there's a hole in the porch roof.

'You shoot me,' he says. 'You do it. Go ahead. I want you to.'

'If you really think that killing you is going to make me feel any better, you're even more of an asshole than I thought.' She has no idea what to do about the gun, so she holds it tight, pointing it at the floor. 'You need help, Benny. You need proper help. But I'm not the person to give it to you. I'm going to take this ...' she wiggles the gun the slightest bit '... and I'm going to call Allie and tell her to get over here so you don't try anything stupid again.'

'You ... don't want me dead?'

His voice is incredibly small. This person who she's allowed to shape her life, who she's allowed to make her feel ashamed.

'I don't forgive you,' she tells him. 'But I don't want you dead, either. I used to love you – and your sister loves you now.'

He shrinks even further into his chair. In the pink light from the sunset, she can see that he's crying.

She stays outside the porch until Allie arrives, wide-eyed and frantic. Ironically Lou, who's still holding the gun that Benny tried to use to kill himself, is much calmer. She locks the gun in her own car and then she puts her arms around Allie and hugs her. 'He'll be all right now that you're here,' she whispers to Allie, though she's not sure if he will.

'I don't know how to make it better,' Allie whispers.

'Maybe you can't,' Lou says. 'But I can be here for you. Always for you.'

It's only when Lou gets into the car and starts driving home, the gun on the passenger seat beside her, that she realises that her arms are shaking, her teeth are chattering together, and she has to pull over to the side of the road for a few minutes to breathe deeply and centre herself.

On her way home she stops off at the falls. It's dark by now and the place is deserted. She stands on Big Water Rock where she told Allie about what Benny had done, the place that used to be the limit of her world, and she flings the gun as hard as she can into the falls. She doesn't know if it has any more bullets in it; she doesn't care. She wants this thing, this symbol of power and violence that's been passed from father to son, to be battered by water, drowned and made harmless, forgotten out of the world.

Then she goes home to where Dana is lying on the couch reading a book, and she doesn't say anything. She sits beside her, this girl who she loves, this girl who happened that night when everything else happened, and Lou knows that being raped by Benny hasn't defined her. It never has. She has been defined by this person, her daughter, who took pain and fear and transformed it into a miracle.

Lou reaches over and strokes Dana's hair and Dana looks up from her book and says, 'What?'

'Nothing,' says Lou. 'I was thinking that I wouldn't change a thing.'

Louis

'Meet me at the cemetery,' she said when she called him a few days later, and nothing else. She didn't say anything about him not calling her, or what he'd written, or the fact that he'd crept round the side of her house in the dark to deliver it.

So he drives to the cemetery.

This morning he's been going through Peggy's papers and her computer. When he opened her email account he saw an inbox full of messages from his father. He didn't read them, but the dates and the subject headings told him all he needed to know: for the past six years his parents emailed each other at least once a month, sometimes several times a week, seemingly to talk about the house and the car and the bank accounts. He suspects that if he read the emails, he would find much more between the lines, unspoken.

He's talked to his dad about what to do with the house. It's Lou's, if he wants it, to sell or rent or live in. 'Do you think you might want to stay?' he asked Irving, and Irving shook his head and said, 'No, I'd rather go somewhere without so many memories.' And it strikes Lou that he himself might want the opposite. After all these years in Manhattan, where he didn't know the names of the people who lived next door, he might want to stay in a place that is full of memories, with people who remember him.

The cemetery is full of familiar names. French and Irish mostly, but also English and Scottish and Italian and Polish, the names of the people who came to Casablanca all those years ago to work in the mill and stayed so their children and grandchildren and great-grandchildren could do the same.

The Alders have their own plot, with a large square granite memorial block carved with ALDER presiding over the smaller graves. Before she died and before Irving came back, Peggy said she'd arranged to be buried in it, which Lou thought was a little strange given that she and Irving were separated and that she'd never particularly got along with that side of the family, but then she'd said, simply, 'You're an Alder', and that explained it. It means that she expected Lou to be buried there too, one day. He doesn't believe in life after death, at least not beyond the memories and the consequences that you've left behind you, but the thought of all of those generations buried in the same soil together is weirdly comforting.

Peggy's grave has been filled in with soil and is covered with turf. Her headstone's not up yet. Lou's got a little bit of sand from the beach at Morocco Pond, and he scatters it over her grave. Then he straightens up, puts the empty bag back in his pocket, and goes to the other side of the cemetery where Allie is waiting, slender and still in a blue dress and sunglasses.

He's never been to Benny's grave before but he's not surprised to see it's a large granite block, nearly as large as the Alder family memorial. BENEDICT KENNETH PHELPS it says, and underneath, 'BENNY' above a carving of a baseball bat and glove. *Forever In Our Hearts*, it says. The smaller grave to the side belongs to Allie's mother and father: united under the earth in a way they never were in life.

She looks up when he approaches and she smiles at him, which gives him considerable relief. 'Hi,' she says, and leans up to give him a kiss on the cheek. 'You checked in on your mom?'

'I gave her a bit of the beach.' He'd like to kiss her lips, but he follows suit and kisses her cheek. 'Why did you want to meet here?'

She pulls the manila envelope out of her handbag. 'I read this,' she says.

'OK.'

'It's good. It's really good. You should publish it.'

'Do you want me to publish it?'

She pushes her sunglasses onto the top of her head so she can look at him. There's a little breeze, and it blows strands of her hair into her face, and she brushes them away. 'This is hard for me.' She gestures to Benny's grave: the size of it, its heft, its promise of forever. 'I won't lie. Everything's been hard since he died. I miss him, but sometimes I resent Benny for being the one who always got all the attention. Even when my dad was hitting him, at least he knew he existed. Is that fucked up?'

'I don't know,' says Lou honestly. 'I have no basis for comparison. I don't think it's fucked up.'

'*He* was fucked up. He was unhappy. But now, the way people around here remember him – his life means something to them. His death means something and I don't know if I want to take that away from him, Lou.'

'OK,' says Lou. 'Then this is only paper.'

He takes the envelope out of her hand and takes out the first few pages of what he's written. He tears them in half, and then in half again, and again and again until all that's left is shreds, falling to the ground in front of Benny's grave. Then the same with the other pages, into thin strips and then tiny pieces, like the confetti that you throw at a wedding, or big white flakes of snow on the summer grass. An offering of words and paper. When it's done he hands her the empty envelope.

'Thanks,' she says. 'That was a little radical. You could have just not sent it to a publisher.'

'Occasionally I like a grand gesture.'

She takes his hand and leans against him. She fits perfectly under his arm, her head on his shoulder. 'Do you know what I'd really like?' she says.

'What?' He leans down a little and inhales the scent of her hair in the sunshine.

'I'd like to move away from here for a while. Not forever, maybe. But for a little while, to be myself.'

'To be yourself, or to be by yourself?'

She tilts her face up to look at him. 'Maybe both. It depends. I never got the choice to leave. From what you wrote, it felt like you were considering staying here.'

'From what I wrote, it also felt like I was falling in love with you.'

She smiles gently at that. 'I'm not the person you wrote about. You might love that person but she's much better than I am. You haven't spent enough time with me to know what I'm really like.'

'Maybe I can find out?'

'If you want. If you want to come with me somewhere else. Maybe we can both find out.'

'I thought I was coming back to Casablanca,' he says, 'but I was coming back to you. If you're with me, I don't really care where we go.'

'OK,' she says. She squeezes his hand. 'Let's go, then. It doesn't matter where.'

Louise

On the screen, Humphrey Bogart is in the train station in Paris. He looks down at the note that Sam's given him. Ilsa's words blur and drip in the rain like inky tears.

Lou and Allie are on the sofa, sharing the knitted Afghan, a half-empty bowl of popcorn between them. Irving's gone up to bed so Dana's curled in his La-Z-Boy, her phone up near her face. She keeps on texting someone, and giggling, and texting again.

'You can see it right there,' says Allie. 'That's the moment, the exact moment where he becomes the bitter, cynical Rick we meet in the first part of the film. When Ilsa leaves him without any explanation at all.'

'Oh I don't know,' says Lou. 'You weren't *that* bitter when I came back. Were you?'

Allie punches her. 'Shut up, Ingrid.'

'I wish.' She watches the train leave the Paris station with Rick and Sam on it, and watches the steam transform into Rick drinking bourbon, the train's whistle meld into piano music … 'As Time Goes By'. Then she looks at Allie, who is watching. Black-and-white images reflected in her eyes.

'I've applied for a job at Casablanca Middle School,' Lou says. 'Don't know if I'll get it. Though I'm the only applicant, so it's likely I will.'

Allie pauses the movie. 'You what?'

'I applied. I don't have to take it. I can't take it till after

Christmas anyway, if I get it. It's just . . . Dad's going to be lonely. And Dana likes it here, don't you, Dana?'

Dana shrugs. 'Brooklyn's gross in the snow,' she says. 'And I sort of want to learn how to ski.'

'I thought Casablanca was a hick town?' Allie asks Dana. 'What changed your mind?' Dana shrugs again. Her phone buzzes and she giggles at the text that's come in.

'Jim,' explains Lou. 'Jim changed her mind.'

'Not *just* Jim,' says Dana and she starts typing furiously, to Jim.

'Good, because you're too young to settle down,' says Lou. She nudges Allie with her foot. 'Don't you want to watch the movie?' Allie picks up the remote again and restarts the movie.

Allie watches *Casablanca*. Lou watches her.

Lou hasn't seen this film in years. Not since she left Maine, because this film has always been Allie's. Allie says she hasn't watched it since then either. Lou doesn't have to watch it now to know what's happening, because every single emotion on the screen is echoed in Allie's face.

Her foot is curled comfortably around Allie's calf, Allie's knee tucked up behind hers. They're both wearing sweats and their favourite T-shirts, Lou's with the hole in the shoulder. She could be here for Allie, too, if she stays. She can't deal with Benny, but she could help Allie deal with him. They could both be less lonely. Because Lou hasn't been alone for the last thirteen years, but she has been lonely. Like Rick and Ilsa in *Casablanca*, except without the good tailoring.

As Rick sends Ilsa away and the plane takes off, the most bittersweet happy ending surely in existence, Lou glances at the La-Z-Boy. Dana is curled up asleep with the phone underneath her cheek. So much for introducing her to classic movies.

The music swells and Allie sighs with contentment and wipes her eyes with the back of her hand. 'The thing is,' she says, as if they've been having a conversation all through the movie, 'that I never understood as a kid that Renault was blackmailing women into sleeping with him, which is totally disgusting. And Ilsa is utterly controlled by the two men in her life. She never speaks to another woman through the whole film. She doesn't even have a friend to talk to.'

'What would you have told her if you'd been her friend? Should she have stayed with Rick or gone with Lazlo?'

'I'd have told her to send them both off to America together, swear off romance, and stay behind herself with Sam to run an underground resistance ring from Rick's Café.'

'A kiss is just a kiss,' agrees Lou, and it might be a bad move for every single reason, but she leans over and kisses Allie on the mouth. Not sexy: tender. Hand on the back of her neck. But in no doubt about what she wants this kiss to mean.

Because if there's a point to this movie it's that the lyrics are wrong: a kiss isn't just a kiss. Not between the right two people, and Allie has always been the right one for her.

Allie's eyes widen. Lou finishes the kiss but she doesn't pull away and nor does Allie. They look at each other in the flickering light of the television, rolling credits.

'Oh,' says Allie. 'I didn't … know.'

'You knew,' says Lou. 'As soon as I said I liked men and women, you thought about it.'

'OK. I did. But …'

'You don't know how you feel.' Lou chews the inside of her lip because she doesn't know how Allie feels, either.

'I've never kissed a woman before.'

'It's just lips. You've kissed me before.'

'I didn't know what I was doing then.'

'I don't know what I'm doing now.'

This time, Allie leans forward and Lou meets her halfway. It's more conscious, this kiss. Of softness, of similarities, of all the years and breath they've shared.

Allie breaks it off but she doesn't move; presses her forehead against Lou's. Lou can feel her breath on her cheek. 'I don't know,' says Allie. 'I'm going to need to think about this. I love you more than I love anyone but... maybe that's why I have to think about it.'

'If I come back after Christmas, maybe.'

'If I come to visit you in the autumn. It might be... easier in New York.'

'Wait and see,' agrees Lou, and Allie curls up against her, closer, and Lou puts her arm around her. 'You've always been there,' Lou murmurs into her hair.

'So have you.' Allie leans her head against Lou's shoulder. She tucks the blanket around both of them.

'What do you want to do now?' Lou asks. Warm, comfortable. This person she loves is in her arms, maybe forever. Wait and see.

Allie tilts her head to look up at her, and smiles. She points the remote at the TV. 'Play it again?'

Louis

April 2011

Allie is eating pineapple. She's got the can balanced on her swollen belly and she's eating from it with a fork, spearing the chunks and bringing them to her mouth one by one as if she's following orders. Mulder is watching every forkful on its passage from can to mouth. He hasn't quite understood the idea that something other than dog food can come in cans.

The baby is two weeks overdue. Irving has been calling them three times a day. If Allie's not in labour by tomorrow, Lou has to drive her to the hospital and she'll be induced. 'We don't want the baby to be overcooked,' said the kind Ob/Gyn when they saw her last week, and Allie had muttered, 'I feel like *I'm* overcooked.'

It's all an act. Allie is the happiest that Lou has ever seen anyone. Pregnancy makes her blossom – eyes bright, cheeks pink, skin clear, hair glossy. She's delighted with her newly large breasts (so is Lou) and the growing curve of her belly, the unapologetic pregnancy smocks. She has filled their apartment with books about pregnancy and newborns, found a new joy in shopping, suffered swollen ankles and stretch marks with cheerful resolve.

For Lou it's a revelation. Allie is growing their child inside her and he feels all of the clichés of wonder and protectiveness and love – and none of them are clichés at all. He writes every day, but he isn't locked inside his own head. Every word has an extra significance. He's part of this miracle which is the exact same miracle that his parents experienced when he was born, the exact same miracle that happens with every single human being, and he feels connected with them all. He thought he'd have to stay in Casablanca to feel part of a community; but he hasn't. Allie talks to other pregnant women on the street, women with babies. In the dog park, he isn't isolated in his story and he strikes up conversations with the regulars there, recognising them by their dogs and then, eventually, by their faces.

The baby wasn't planned, of course. Allie got a job in a hospice on the Upper East Side and it was a month later that she did a pregnancy test. Lou was terrified at first – they'd hardly been together a few months, and now they were going to have a baby. Of course they knew each other from their whole lives beforehand, but what if they'd changed too much?

Now, Lou brings Allie another can of pineapple and sits down next to her on the sofa. She's different, yes. She said to him all those months ago in Casablanca that he only knew the good parts of her but everything he has seen since, he has also loved. Including the way she's spent the last twenty-four hours eating pineapple and drinking raspberry leaf tea in an attempt to go into labour naturally so she won't have to be induced tomorrow. It isn't what he expected of her: he'd have thought she would be more laid back. After all, this baby is going to be born no matter what. Their new life is going to begin, and Lou is happy enough with this life to be in no hurry to begin a new one a day earlier. But then again, he's not the one who's the size of a house and can't tie her own shoes.

'Ready for this one?' he asks her, holding up the can of Dole.

'Not yet. I feel like I'm half made of pineapple.'

He settles next to her. 'Mary Margaret,' he says.

'I still think it sounds like a nun. Peggy Sue, if it's a girl.'

'Everyone will sing Buddy Holly to her.'

'There are worse things. What's today's boy's choice?'

This is trickier. There are so many names to avoid. It's one reason why Lou voted that they should find out the baby's sex at the scan, but Allie is vehement that she wants to be surprised, that she wants to have no preconceptions about her child before she even meets them.

'Edward,' Lou suggests.

She makes a face.

'What's wrong with Edward?'

'"Eddie" is wrong with Edward. What about a nice non-gender-specific name? Leslie? Alex? Chris?'

'Irving?'

'I love your dad but "Irving" is a lot to saddle on a poor unsuspecting infant.' She sighs and leans back against him. 'We'll have to see what the baby looks like when they come out.'

'At this rate, the baby's going to be going off to college and we'll still be arguing about what to name it.'

'We'll know,' she says.

'My mom always said I was two weeks late and she thought I'd never come out.'

'Your poor mother. Hit me with some more pineapple, will you?'

'I'm beginning to think it's an old wives' tale that it helps start contractions.'

'If there's one thing I've learned from my years as a nurse, it's never to underestimate the old wives.' She puts the empty can to the side, where Mulder sniffs it. She ruffles the dog's ears and puts her other hand on Lou's leg. A family of three, soon to become a family of four. He wonders, sometimes, if all that happened hadn't happened, if Allie and he had never had to separate, if they'd be in this same place right now, or if they'd already have two kids and a house in the suburbs, or if they wouldn't be together at all. Whether they were meant to be together no matter what, or if their shared secret is what brought them together.

As Lou pops the ring on the new can, a memory comes to him. Roy Pelletier marrying them in the playground. *Spiritus sancti domine*. A ring wrapped in silver foil to fit a small finger. And he realises that all this wondering is beside the point. He doesn't believe in meant to be. He only believes in what is. We can know a river, but we can't know all the drops in it, every journey they could have taken instead of this one.

He hands Allie the can of pineapple and when she's not looking he twists the ring pull off the lid and slips it into his pocket. To give to her later.

Louis & Louise

For generations, the portrait of Louis Alder hung in the Alder house outside the study where all of the decisions about Casablanca Paper Company were made. It was framed in gold, wide as a pair of outstretched arms, tall enough to let you know that here was an important man, here was a man to be reckoned with. The founder of a dynasty that would never die, the father of an American town named after one of the most important cities in Africa. Lou Alder the first wore a black suit and a white shirt and a black tie and the expression of the master of all he surveyed. His hand rested on a book made of paper from his mill.

If the first Louis Alder had been born Louise, there would be no such portrait. In 1862 the dynasty created by Louise Alder would have been quite different. A debutante, an Alder daughter of the Pennsylvania Alders, Louise would have married an eligible man and had children, generations of children, with other last names. She may have had visions and plans, dreams of a city on a river, but no one painted imposing portraits of housewives. Her likeness, dressed in white, would have been in exquisite miniature, painted with a small brush and kept with a lock of her hair. The memories she left behind would be made up of love, not dead trees and paper. There would be no Alder plot in the cemetery, no dam on the Pennacook river, no mill belching smoke.

Or maybe the story would have been the same, with different players. The mill, the dam, the paper, the chemicals and the cancer and the river in ice and sun: everything done by someone else. Or perhaps Louise Alder, the first Lou Alder, might have had the uncommon strength to stride out into her dreams, stake out a valley, harness the river, build her legacy.

Male and female, large brushstrokes and small. Neither of these stories are true, or both of them are. We can't depend on absolutes or definitions. Destiny isn't written indelibly on our bodies, or at least not every part of every destiny is. All we have is people, people with their messy indefinites, their changes and inconsistencies, their desires and fears, their acts that echo down the years and change the world.

But if any stories are true, the next story is true for both Louis and Louise.

After David Alder's death the portrait of Louis Alder, the first Lou Alder, lay in the attic of Peggy and Irving's house until Lou and Allie found it when they were going through the house with Irving to sell it. They brought it home, to their home in New York or in Casablanca, and they put it on the wall in their dining room where it watched them when they ate their meals with first one child, and then two. It watched them when Lou set up their laptop on the dining room table and wrote book after book in the heart of their house, pushing their glasses up in the same way their father always did. It saw kisses and champagne and tears, birthdays and a wedding, messy fingers and burned dinners and laughter and homework.

When they moved to a bigger house, to Casablanca or to New York, the portrait came with them and went up on the wall of their new dining room. It became such a fact of life that no one saw it any more except in glances: the sombre ancestor, the weight of the past that was no longer a weight.

It stayed up on the wall of Lou and Allie's house until they were both very old, and their children were grown and had children of their own, every one with their own story too.

Acknowledgements

Once again I owe enormous gratitude to my agent, Teresa Chris, and my editor, Harriet Bourton. These two professionals have utter faith in me and they both push me to produce the best work I'm able to. It's humbling and a privilege to work with them both.

Thank you to Lauren 'The Gin Fairy' Woosey, Jen 'The Whole Cheese' Breslin, Olivia Barber, Jo Carpenter, Rebecca Gray, Kati Nicholls, Paul Stark, Clare Hey, Katie Espiner and all of the team at Orion and also Hachette Eire and Hachette Australia who are all-around wonderful in every way. What a pleasure it is to write for you.

While writing this book, I had fascinating conversations about gender expectations with many people, but particularly with Leon James Harris and with Lucy Dyer. I was inspired and educated by hearing CN Lester speak and by their book *Trans Like Me*. Lizzie Huxley-Jones did a sensitivity read on this manuscript for nonbinary representation. My protagonist Lou is a cisgender binary person, but Lizzie advised me on how to make my language and ideas more inclusive of people who are trans, nonbinary, genderqueer and/or intersex. Any errors are my own, not Lizzie's.

Although this book is set in 2010, it was written during a very particular political mood, the rising of the #MeToo movement, and it has been informed by that movement as well as by my own experiences. My sisters and brothers and siblings: I believe you. Thank you for being brave. Me too.

Thank you to Naomi Alderman and David Higham Associates for permission to use a quotation from *The Power* as an epigraph. Novels speak to novels and the novels that spoke to me as I was writing this one were *The Left Hand of Darkness* by Ursula K Le Guin and *Orlando* by Virginia Woolf.

Thanks to GRAMPA Food Pantry in Mexico, Maine, and to Arthur Meader of Meader & Son Funeral Home in Rumford, Maine. Although I didn't end up using the food pantry or funeral home scenes in the finished book, my time with these people taught me a great deal about life, death and compassion in a Maine paper mill town. Thanks to my childhood friend Stewart Smith and several others who talked with me about the 1986 strike at the Boise Cascade mill.

Thanks to my mom and dad, Jennifer and Jerrold Cohen, who are not Peggy and Irving but who did meet on the shores of Roxbury Pond one summer and have been together ever since.

Thanks to Anne Wood, Monica Wood, Rich Kent and Barry Longyear, all teachers and writers from my own personal Casablanca, who went before me and showed me it could be done.

Parts of this novel were written while being nurtured and inspired by Janie Milman and Mickey Wilson at Chez Castillon, France, and by Debbie Flint at Retreats for You, Devon. Thank you to The Romantic Novelists' Association for the support they give to me and to other writers of relationship-driven fiction.

Writing a book takes a lot of courage but this one took a peculiar amount of it, which I borrowed from others. As always and ever, thank you to my dear writing friends: Rowan Coleman my evil twin, Miranda Dickinson, Kate Harrison, Tamsyn Murray, Cally Taylor, Claire Dyer, Brigid Coady my Pride partner. Thank you to Harriet Greaves who keeps me sane and running and Ruth Ng who keeps me sane and reading, and to Andrea, Cherish and all my friends who have helped me with child care and gin. Thank you to my gloriously weird Fannibal family, particularly Muffy, AK, Mura, Lotus, Bentley, Mischa, Jimmy, Brian, Wilson, Jack, TE and Bev.

And to Dave, Nate and Meg: I love you.

Credits

Julie Cohen and Orion Fiction would like to thank everyone at Orion who worked on the publication of *The Two Lives of Louis & Louise* in the UK.

Editorial
Harriet Bourton
Clare Hey
Olivia Barber

Copy editor
Kati Nicholl

Proof reader
Linda Joyce

Audio
Paul Stark
Amber Bates

Contracts
Anne Goddard
Paul Bulos
Jake Alderson

Design
Charlotte Abrams-Simpson
Rabab Adams
Joanna Ridley
Nick May
Helen Ewing

Editorial Management
Charlie Panayiotou
Jane Hughes
Alice Davis

Finance
Jasdip Nandra
Afeera Ahmed
Elizabeth Beaumont
Sue Baker

Marketing
Cait Davies
Jen Breslin

Production
Ruth Sharvell

Publicity
Leanne Oliver
Rebecca Gray

Sales
Jen Wilson
Esther Waters
Victoria Laws
Rachael Hum
Ellie Kyrke-Smith
Frances Doyle
Georgina Cutler

Operations
Jo Jacobs
Sharon Willis
Lisa Pryde
Lucy Brem

The two lives of Louis & Louise

Readers' Notes

Afterword

Thank you so much for picking up and reading *The Two Lives of Louis & Louise.*

I wrote this novel almost as a game. What would happen if I took one single protagonist, a character with dreams and talents and best friends and family, with red hair and myopia and a really good whistle, and only changed one thing about them: their gender? What if I wrote those two stories separately, with the same setting and characters but in two different realities? How would that one difference – male or female – change the entire world around them?

From the day we're born, the people around us treat us according to the gender they think we are. We're categorised according to the shape of our genitals instead of the contents of our minds. Pink or blue, we're handed different sets of expectations and limitations. But we're all more than the sum of our gender. This book is about how gender changes everything . . . and nothing.

This is probably the most personal novel I've ever written, and it made me think about my own beliefs about sexuality, parenthood, masculinity, femininity, and forgiveness. It made me clarify my own understanding about how biological sex is more complex than a binary, and how sex is not the same as the social construction of gender. It made me think about the ways that I relate to the world because of my gender, and the gender preconceptions I may have unconsciously imposed upon my son.

It was written during the growing tide of the #MeToo movement and all the discussions we've been having all over the world about gender and power and violence and inequality. I knew when I began writing it that *The Two Lives of Louis & Louise* would be a feminist book about the social restrictions and violence imposed on girls and women, and it is about that. But I didn't quite anticipate how much it would be about how patriarchal structures hurt everyone, no matter their gender. How the expectation to 'be a man' hurts boys and men who aren't allowed to express their feelings. How sexual assault is one human being hurting another, and is also the bodied, terrifyingly specific expression of the inequality that humans experience every single day.

Casablanca is based on my own home town in Maine and although all the characters and most of the events are fictional, the strike really happened in 1987. It lasted sixteen months and every single person I spoke to about the strike says that it still affects the community to this day. I've portrayed Casablanca as quite a homophobic society, which was my experience back in the 80s in my real home town, but things change: last year, when local pastors protested a display of LGBTQ+ books at the public library, the community turned out in force to defend freedom of speech and the rights of LGBTQ+ people. The books stayed.

We've called this book *The Two Lives of Louis & Louise* but to me, it's one book about one person: Lou. And it's about all these complex things like gender and class and sexuality and family, but in the end, it's a book about a simple thing: love.

I hope you've enjoyed it.

Questions for Readers

- The early chapters of the novel trace the ways that Louis and Louise are treated differently as children because of their gender. How does this reflect your own experience? Do you think that our society has become more or less split along gender lines?

- The novel says that there are some things that are universal, regardless of our gender: death, loss, love, fear, parenthood. Do you think that formative life events are experienced differently by people of different genders?

- How do you feel about the character of Benny, in both realities? Did you feel there is a difference between Louis's Benny and Louise's Benny?

- Did one reality (Louis's, or Louise's) appeal more to you? Why or why not?

- Chapter One is called 'Daddy's Girl' and Chapter Two is called 'Mummy's Boy' – how was Lou's relationship with their parents different as Louis and as Louise?

- Gender is not the only binary in the book – what are some of the ways that the town of Casablanca is split into two?

- *'Destiny isn't written on our bodies, or at least not every part of every destiny is. . . But if any stories are true, the next story is true for both Louis and Louise'.* Some things remain true for Lou in either world – most notably, their love for Allie. How does the novel investigate the concept of fate?

Books you might also enjoy

Fiction

Orlando by Virginia Woolf
The Left Hand of Darkness by Ursula K LeGuin
The Power by Naomi Alderman
Whisky When We're Dry by John Larison
The House on Half Moon Street by Alex Reeve
Empire Falls by Richard Russo

Nonfiction

When We Were the Kennedys by Monica Wood
Queer, a Graphic History by Meg John Barker and Julia Scheele
Testosterone Rex by Cordelia Fine
The Trauma Cleaner by Sarah Krasnostein
Trans Like Me by CN Lester

If you loved Julie Cohen's tender and thought-provoking storytelling in *The Two Lives of Louis & Louise*, you'll adore

together

A love story told backwards . . .

Robbie and Emily have been together for years, but their love is still fresh and fierce. They have shared a bed, a home, a bond so deep it can't be broken. But there are things they don't share, things best left unsaid.

On a morning like any other, Robbie wakes, dresses, writes Emily a letter – and leaves their home for good. There is a secret they've been keeping since the day they met. The sacrifices and choices that have sealed their fates could be exposed, and this is the only way to keep it all hidden...

Is this a great love story or a story about great love?

Whatever you decide, theirs is a story that will never leave you.

Available in paperback and ebook now

Help us make the next generation of readers

We – both author and publisher – hope you enjoyed this book. We believe that you can become a reader at any time in your life, but we'd love your help to give the next generation a head start.

Did you know that 9% of children don't have a book of their own in their home, rising to 13% in disadvantaged families*? We'd like to try to change that by asking you to consider the role you could play in helping to build readers of the future.

We'd love you to think of sharing, borrowing, reading, buying or talking about a book with a child in your life and spreading the love of reading. We want to make sure the next generation continue to have access to books, wherever they come from.

And if you would like to consider donating to charities that help fund literacy projects, find out more at www.literacytrust.org.uk and www.booktrust.org.uk.

Thank you.

hachette
CHILDREN'S GROUP

*As reported by the National Literacy Trust